UNCERTAIN LUCK

By the same author:

The Unexpected, Book Guild Publishing 2010

UNCERTAIN LUCK

Nicholas V Taylor

Book Guild Publishing

Sussex, England

First published in Great Britain in 2012 by
The Book Guild Ltd
19 New Road
Brighton, BN1 1UF

Typeset in Baskerville by Ellipsis Digital Limited, Glasgow

Printed in Great Britain by
CPI Group (UK) Ltd, Croydon, CR0 4YY

A catalogue record for this book is available from The British Library.

ISBN 978 1 84624 743 9

1

The teenage boy moved carefully to ease the cramp in his legs. He had been in the highest branches of a sturdy oak tree for several hours and was beginning to wonder how much longer he could remain relatively motionless and not attract attention. The whinny of horses, the occasional clank of steel and muted voices of men to his left and right were constant companions, but after the camp fires had burned out the ghostly definition of figures disappeared as the light cloud coating blocked out the stars of the moonless night.

As night had fallen he had crawled silently to the tree at the bottom of a very shallow valley. Its gentle grassy sides formed two low hills, and from atop these came the intermittent sounds he could hear. He had climbed the tree slowly and carefully in order to see the anticipated drama unfold.

Just as the pain in his numbing legs started to scream into his brain, hesitant birdsong and the lightening of the easterly sky immediately ahead of him signalled the dawning of the day. The sun rose, chasing away the cloud covering and giving light which glinted on the polished metal arrayed on each hill. As the daylight strengthened, so the noise from the hilltops increased as the men there prepared to do battle. All thought of cramp and discomfort was forgotten. The boy was transfixed as horses, already saddled, were brought into line and knights attended by squires stood by to mount, with foot soldiers and archers deploying on each side. Neither army appeared to be in any hurry, letting the sun rise higher above the horizon to allow sharp vision for the task ahead. Almost simultaneously the knights on both sides slowly put on their helmets, adjusted surcoats over hauberks of chain mail, clambered into saddles and took shield and lance from their squires.

The armies were small: two local barons unable to reconcile their differences choosing the time-honoured arbiter of combat. With the barons there were but six knights on each side, their squires mounted behind them, and no more than fifty archers and foot soldiers – the latter armed with pikes, the familiar round shields and axes, the former with shields slung over their shoulders along with knives and axes to use in close combat when arrows could no longer be effective. Except for the pawing of the ground by the horses and the occasional shuffling of soldiers' feet, all was now still as the armies awaited the command to engage. One squire on each side was holding their baron's standard, fluttering listlessly in the gentle morning breeze.

A full thirty minutes passed. Each side waited for the other to advance. Very slowly, a squire on the hill to the left of the boy lowered his standard and raised it again. The army started moving steadily at walking pace down the hill towards the valley. The army on the right hill also advanced, equally slowly. From his vantage point at the top of the tree the boy could see that, while the army to his right was walking directly down towards the valley where they anticipated battle would take place, those on his left had angled their approach diagonally down the hill and were taking small steps. This meant that the army on his right would be in the valley first, with the troops on his left keeping the advantage of the downward slope to give greater momentum to their charge. Almost too late, the baron on the right realised this and just before his army reached the valley he ordered his archers to let loose. After two waves of arrows had sped towards the opposing men, he called the charge and horses and foot soldiers raced into and across the narrow valley towards their still walking opponents.

The arrows fell on the army to the boy's left, causing some injury but not deflecting the slow, purposeful movement diagonally down the hill. On seeing the charge, the baron on the left hill did not respond immediately with a charge of his own, but called his troops to a halt, allowing his archers time to aim at the advancing army. Their arrows were far more effective. None of the knights or horses appeared to be affected, but foot soldiers fell with shafts penetrating their lightly armoured bodies. As the army from the right-hand hill reached the opposite side of the valley and started to ascend the hill to the boy's left, so the baron signalled his stationary troops to charge. The knights and squires on horses quickly closed with the knights and squires charging up the hill and the added momentum gained by descending the slope gave greater force to the clash, with two knights from the right-hand hill tumbling to the ground as lances struck their shields. Both sets of riders wheeled their horses to face each other once again. Broken lances were abandoned and swords wielded as the knights and squires clashed once more, seemingly hacking unmercifully at each other.

By this time the foot soldiers too were engaged in the fight, but the depleted numbers caused by the more accurate arrows gave the men from the left hill the advantage and, it soon became clear, the potential victory. The unhorsed knights could not support their comrades, who were soon overwhelmed, and the standard was struck.

The battle was over in less than an hour. Bloodied bodies of foot soldiers, dead, dying and injured littered the ground. The defeated army had dropped their weapons and were standing at the mercy of the victors, who were stripping bodies of weapons and valuables. The boy noticed that, while two of the squires on each side had been killed, none of the knights had suffered that fate and, although bloodied, the defeated and disarmed knights were now quietly talking to their opponents. The obvious animosity which had led to the clash seemed to have gone and after a while all the knights went to the victor's camp to sit around the dead embers of a camp fire drinking wine. The foot soldiers on both sides were tending to their injured comrades as the boy forced his stiffened limbs to clamber slowly down the tree to the ground, where he paused for a while to allow feeling to return to his lower body. The soldiers on the battlefield were too occupied or too tired to notice the boy as he walked carefully away from the tree. Once out of sight, he started to run steadily to the north, adopting an easy, relaxed gait which ate up the miles and caused him no loss of breath or discomfort.

As the sun reached its zenith, the boy stopped by a sparkling, fast-flowing stream, took a drink of the crystal-clear water and sat down on the grassy bank to eat a hunk of bread and cheese retrieved from a small bag slung over his shoulder. After eating, he remained seated in the midday sun, resting and reflecting on what he had just seen.

2

It was the year 1146. Stephen, King of England, had been on the throne for eleven years, during which time he had failed to unite the country. Although he was frank, generous, courageous and robust, he possessed little statesmanship. He offered a sympathetic ear to all, but did not have the diplomacy to please everyone: he was inclined to follow the recommendations and advice of the last person who had spoken to him, even if those expressed views were diametrically opposed to the good counsel he had previously entertained. His financial resources were limited, as the treasury of his uncle Henry I had become rapidly depleted and the church was reluctant to provide more funds, so he created a mercenary army and a royalist party under his direct command and not affiliated to any baron. This offended the barons and in 1138 Robert of Gloucester felt particularly slighted and renounced his allegiance to Stephen in favour of Henry I's daughter Matilda, whose earlier bid for the crown was outwitted by Stephen when he was informally elected king, confirmed as such by the pope and crowned.

There followed years of unrest, with barons frequently changing sides or manoeuvring to try to remain neutral, while Robert of Gloucester championed Matilda's cause and Stephen and his army chased around the country trying to win back land and loyalty. Without the strength of a dominant king in the centre, barons and knights felt free to enhance their own fortunes – and as such fortune depended on land ownership, there were constant battles and sieges designed to seize estates by force, laying waste to much of the countryside and driving the peasants into greater and greater poverty.

Although the barons fought almost continually against Robert of Gloucester, Stephen or themselves, pitched face-to-face battles were not usual. From 1139 the manor houses or castles of the barons, built primarily as administrative centres in timber on top of an earth embankment and offering some protection from lawlessness but not military threat, were rapidly rebuilt in stone, behind which a baron and his men could sit out a siege.

The county of Devonshire was not immune to the ravages of these wars, but suffered less than Middle England. Many of the peasants in that county were poorer because of the fights between barons, but some there applied ingenuity and cooperation to the task of maintaining their centuries-old way of life and, in some cases, quietly and gently prospered. The village in which the boy Peter Bart lived was one of those which offered a comfortable, although far from luxurious living for its inhabitants. Many years earlier, some determined and forward-thinking peasants, both villeins and freemen, had pooled their resources and shared equally the grains, meats and other produce so no one man's misfortune or a poor harvest would send him and his family into abject poverty, leaving him unable to pay the baron or the church rents or tithe and so suffering the loss of his only means of livelihood, his strip of gifted or rented land. Peter's village worked as one. The strips of each family's land, still delineated by posts or markers, were treated as the village land and everyone tilled the soil, sowed the seed and harvested the crops together, setting aside a portion of the land each year to remain fallow so that productivity was kept at its highest. The animals were treated in the same way. The oxen and the single horse were shared out, the cattle corralled and looked after together, the sheep tended by a single shepherd. That single shepherd being Peter.

When he was only twelve summers old, Peter was selected by the village as the next shepherd and he was taken into the fields with the sheep to be taught the skills required to maintain the flock. He was lucky in being a quick learner and he found he had an instant rapport with the sheep, which seemed to trust him from the outset. Instead of spending many months with the shepherd he was going to replace, after two months he could be taught nothing more and so he took control of the large flock, spending weeks away from his village in the hills, staying in a small hut by himself, living off the land and the food his mother had prepared for him. At first, Peter's family were concerned that one so young should be away from the village for so long, but Peter was happy and the sheep thrived. Indeed, if a sheep was sick or injured it would make its way to Peter and with plaintive bleats offer itself up for inspection, treatment and cure. Peter's life was tranquil and contented.

Peter's flock grew with very low mortality and the wool from the sheep was traded to the local town, fetching a good price even in the turmoil of Stephen's England. The quiet prospering of the village meant that the local overseeing baron could be paid his rent and dues in full and on time, and when that baron called for extra meat or produce for a festival or celebration at his castle, the village could provide for these demands without injuring its own livelihood.

The local baron, Robert de Cours, was a directly descended Norman upholding the traditions of his ancestors. Like all the barons and knights, he spoke Norman French with a little Latin, but he had also learned the Anglo-Saxon tongue in order to understand and control his peasants and freemen. In this time of unrest and uncertainty, Robert de Cours was a relatively kindly man who appreciated the efficiency of Peter's village – and so the abundance of his own table – and therefore spared the village men from conscription into his army and kept all hostilities away from the village and its land. It was therefore a surprise to Peter that two neighbouring barons had chosen to fight the battle he had just witnessed barely three days' ride away from his own village. The reports which filtered slowly through to Peter's village of King Stephen's successes in recovering his territories could mean the disaffected barons were pushing further west to gain a stronghold. Peter frowned thoughtfully at the dazzle of sunshine on the water flowing before him. Were things about to change?

He knew he would get no answers by gazing at the sparkling stream. After a while he stood up and resumed his steady run back towards his hut and his flock.

3

By the middle of the afternoon Peter's unwavering pace brought him in sight of his hut. He slowed as an old man appeared in the doorway.

'Before you ask,' said the old man, 'all the sheep are fine. Even the ewe with the damaged hoof is springing around like a lamb. You need not have hurried back, because you leave them for two days each month when you return to your village. But I'm pleased to see you.' He handed Peter a bowl of cool water, which Peter gratefully accepted. 'Now tell me, what did you see?'

Peter put down the empty bowl, sat on the ground and smiled. The old man also sat down in an easy fluid motion belying his apparent age. Carefully, Peter related all he had seen, leaving out nothing but making no comment of his own.

When he had finished, the old man thought for a minute and then said, 'What are your reflections on what you have seen? Do you have any observations?'

Peter smiled again. 'Well, first of all you were completely right: the knights killed any soldier within their reach, but whilst they fought fiercely with the opposing knights, they were far more intent on disarming than killing. Injuries were sustained, but the wounds were relatively minor. As you said, the object was to capture to seek a ransom for release. When the fighting was over, the knights and barons sat around and seemed to be exchanging friendly conversation. It was the poor foot soldiers who took the brunt of the killing and maiming, and they were left to fend for themselves after the battle had finished.' Peter paused for a few moments, then continued. 'The battle was really won by thinking rather than fighting. The baron on my left fooled the other baron into believing both forces were going to meet in the valley, and by walking his men slowly and diagonally down the hill he kept the advantage of the higher ground.' Peter paused again. 'In fact, there was no great high ground advantage, but the other baron perceived there was and so started his attack too soon. In his haste he used his archers badly – they were effectively shooting and moving forward at the same time – and his rapid charge meant his foot soldiers had to run much quicker in support and so had expended energy before engaging in the battle. There may well have been great skill in the knights' fighting, but it seemed from my vantage point those on the left hill were more composed.'

The old man smiled. 'You have learned very well and I hope seeing that battle, small though it was, emphasises the importance of thought and preparation. Even overwhelming force and power do not necessarily guarantee victory. What else?'

'I was surprised at the limited use of the archers. It may well be that they were not trained very well, or did not have the best bows, but an accurate and sustained wave of arrows should have had a high hit rate, or at the very least should have slowed down the advance, for it would take a very brave or foolhardy man to run closer to arrows whose accuracy and penetrating power increases as the distance shortens. Also, I was very surprised how unmanoeuvrable the knights' battle horses were. They charged at a great pace and with great force, but when the knights had clashed it seemed difficult to slow down the horses and turn them back to re-engage. It might be a lighter, more agile horse could be an advantage.'

The old man grunted. 'The heavy destrier is needed to get the weight behind the lance so the force on impact will knock a man out of the saddle. A lighter horse would not do that.'

'But if a lighter, more agile horse is faster, then surely the extra speed would compensate for the lack of weight. Also a lighter horse reaches a gallop quicker than a heavy horse.'

'A very interesting thought. You may be right. I had not considered this before.' The old man gave a wry smile. 'Perhaps I've taught you too much! Go and look at your sheep and I'll skin this hare and prepare it for our meal tonight.'

Peter stood up and started walking towards the sheep at the top of the hill. Seeing him approach, the sheep raised their heads but did not flee or even move, continuing to chew contentedly at the grass. As he cast his experienced eye over the flock, for the second time that day Peter allowed himself time to reflect – this time on what the old man had said. Had Peter been taught too much by this old man? He had appeared from nowhere during Peter's first year as shepherd and refused to identify himself, yet was all too ready and eager to pass on knowledge, skills and information to the boy, alone in his hut up in the hills. Now Peter was nearing his fifteen summers and would start to train another youth to take over from him as shepherd. He wondered how he could fit in with village farming life now, full as he was of the knowledge and skill the old man had passed on to him. The old man . . . what would become of him?

4

Peter had completed his training as a shepherd when he was just twelve summers old and was then left to tend the sheep by himself. He had been doing this for a little over two months, slowly gaining confidence and continuing to win the trust of the sheep. Then, one bright, crisp morning, just as autumn was slowly morphing into winter, Peter walked from his hut down the hill towards the stream to get water and saw, on the bank of the stream, half in the water, a rag-bag of clothing. Puzzled, Peter approached with caution and soon realised the clothing concealed a human being, lying on its stomach, forehead in the icy water.

Peter stopped and watched, but there was no movement, so he called out, 'Hallo!' There was no sound or acknowledgement from the prone figure. Peter approached and put his hand on the body. Again no movement. He pulled and tugged to turn the body over, using the whole of his twelve summers' strength. The body seemed to be that of an old man and in touching his face, Peter felt the cold of death. Death was no stranger to the boy. Peasant life, even in his relatively prosperous village, was short and from the look of the man lying on the bank of the river, he had seen more than his fair share of summers. Death was dealt with by the older women in Peter's village, however, he was at a loss what to do next. He was not strong enough to carry the old man back to the village and he felt the village would not welcome the task of preparing and burying a stranger. Somehow, though, it felt wrong just to leave the old man there, so Peter caught hold of his ankles and started to drag him away from the stream towards a small copse of trees where he thought he could dig a grave.

Although the old man looked like a bag of skin and bones, he was surprisingly heavy and it was all Peter could do to move him a few feet. He stopped for breath and dropped the old man's ankles. The body gave a groan as the legs hit the ground. Peter jumped back, startled. Was this the sound some people make long after death, or had life not fully escaped? Cautiously, Peter ran his hands over the old man's face. The eyes briefly flickered open and Peter, putting his ear to the old man's nose, could just detect the faintest sound of breathing. He might not be dead yet, but he would not live long if Peter left him outside as winter began to gain its grasp on the earth. In this state, it was unlikely he would see tomorrow's dawning. Peter shook the old man's shoulders and gently slapped his face, but he was not to be roused.

Without more thought, Peter left the man and went to the copse. Selecting a number of suitable saplings and cutting them off with his sturdy dagger, he fashioned a triangular stretcher and took it to where the old man was lying. Rather unceremoniously, Peter rolled the old man onto the makeshift stretcher with his head at the top of the triangle. Grasping the two handles, Peter lifted and pulled. With just the pointed head of the stretcher dragging on the ground, it was easier to move the man, but Peter could not get sufficient leverage to drag him more than a few yards at a time. He went back into the copse and found a very young, thin sapling. Cutting it lengthways, he made a strap which he tied to the handles of the stretcher. With the sapling strap braced across his chest, he found it easier to lift the stretcher and move the old man. The gentle slope of the hill still felt like climbing a mountain, and by the time Peter had reached his hut, he was exhausted. Resting to regain his strength, he rekindled the fire outside the hut and put a pan of water to heat. When he felt strong enough, he pulled the old man right into the hut and rolled him off the stretcher onto his own bed of clean, soft rushes, covering him with his blanket. When the water in the pot had heated sufficiently, Peter washed the old man's face, hands, arms and legs, hoping the warmth of the water would put some heat back into the icy body. Replacing the blanket, he could think of no more to do, so he left the hut to tend the sheep.

Mid-afternoon, Peter returned to his hut. The old man was still alive and his breathing seemed stronger, if still unnaturally shallow. Once again Peter heated some water and with difficulty undressed the old man to bathe him from head to toe. When the old man was naked, Peter was surprised to find that his body was clean (bathing was not a priority with most peasants) and well muscled. Somehow it did not match the ageing visible in the man's face. There were also a number of vivid and sizeable scars. This one is not a stranger to battle, Peter thought. When the bathing was over, Peter did not replace the man's clothing, but covered him with the blanket and piled rushes and straw on top to try to give the body some heat.

Peter's evening meal was a thin stew made from dried meat, which his mother had given him, with roots and herbs he had gathered himself. He cooked it for longer than normal to infuse the liquid with as much goodness as possible from the meat, roots and herbs, and after he had eaten he took some warm liquid to the old man. Lifting his head, Peter slowly and carefully spooned some of the liquid into the old man's mouth, massaging his throat to get him to swallow. Peter was far from sure he actually accomplished anything useful.

With no blanket and no rushes beneath him, Peter's sleep

was fitful and he was glad winter had not yet taken full hold. He resolved to find some dried grasses and leaves the next day to make himself a bed and a covering of some sort.

Rising with the sun, Peter heated the remainder of the stew liquid and once again tried to spoon-feed the old man. Was it just hope, or did he detect stronger breathing and less chill in the old man's body?

Each day for a week Peter bathed the old man in warm water and spoon-fed him, morning and night, feeling sure strength was returning to that silent form. Still there was no movement. The old man lay in precisely the same position as Peter had left him. On the seventh day Peter was beginning to despair. He was due to return to his village the next week for a couple of days and wondered if the old man would survive so long without being tended. There was no other option: Peter should go back to the village the very next day and get help. The old women there would know what to do and likely the old man could be taken to the village to be properly cared for. So resolved, Peter returned to his hut late that afternoon to cook food for both of them once again.

As he entered his hut, two bright blue eyes stared at him. Peter was so surprised, he was speechless.

'I must thank you for my life,' croaked a voice from beneath the blanket, rushes and straw. 'How long have I been here?'

'A week.'

The old man grunted.

'Who are you?' Peter demanded. 'Where did you come from? What are you doing here?'

The old man was silent for a long time, his eyes closed as if it was more than his body could do to keep them open. With his eyes still shut, the old man said, 'Later. I must sleep.'

'Sleep if you will, but I'm going to make some food. Do you think you will be able to eat?'

Another grunt and another long silence. 'I'll try. I certainly need food.' Peter thought he detected a wry smile cross the old man's face.

Peter left the hut and busied himself preparing another stew. When it was ready, he put small pieces of meat and roots into a bowl with some liquid and took it into the hut. The old man was sleeping again, his breathing still shallow but regular. Peter gently shook him awake and held the bowl out. The old man tried to lift his head, but the effort required was too great. He raised a feeble arm from beneath the blanket as if to wave Peter away. Peter pulled him into a reclining position, supporting him with his left arm, and slowly spoon-fed the old man. At first, swallowing seemed to be an effort and chewing impossible, but gradually the jaws started to function and the old man ate half the bowl of food before waving the rest away. Peter laid him gently back down onto the rushes and before the old man's head touched them, he was deeply asleep.

The following morning the remainder of the stew was rewarmed and Peter once again spoon-fed the old man. When he had finished, the man looked at Peter with his bright blue eyes conveying gratitude.

'You are not strong or well, and I do not know what more I can do for you,' said Peter. 'I am going to go back to my village today to get some help. The women there will know what to do.'

The old man's hand shot from beneath the blanket and grasped Peter's arm with surprising strength. 'No. Do not do that,' he said. 'Do not tell anyone I am here. I will be all right. If you could just help me for a few more days, I will be on my way. I am really much stronger than I look.'

Peter was somewhat sceptical of the old man's ability to be able to do anything in the near future, let alone in just a few more days, but from the grip on his arm Peter realised that indeed the old man was not without strength.

After thinking for a moment, Peter replied, 'I have to return to the village anyway at the end of next week, but I am willing to do what I can for you until then. Luckily, you don't eat too much so my food will last and I have some snares laid, so I might be able to catch a hare or two, maybe even a pheasant, which will swell the larder.'

'Thank you. I promise, I will be a burden to you for as short a time as possible.' With that, the old man let go of Peter's arm, sighed and lapsed back into a deep sleep. Peter tucked the man's arm back under the blanket and left the hut to go to his sheep.

Peter's snaring was successful and he roasted a hare over the fire for the old man that evening. Still the man could not feed himself, but as Peter lifted his shoulders, he could feel the life and strength returning. Indeed, three days of feeding was enough, for on the fourth day, when Peter returned to the hut, the old man was sitting up and managed to feed himself, though somewhat slowly. By the end of the week he had dressed himself, was on his feet and walking unsteadily. Two weeks earlier he had been all but a corpse. Now he was a living human being gathering strength almost by the hour.

'I must return to the village tomorrow,' Peter told him. 'And no matter what you said, you are not strong enough to go anywhere. There is sufficient food for you, so why don't you stay here until I return? A few more days in the shelter of the hut with some good food will give you time to recover properly. If you try to leave now, with the winter nights getting colder, you will not last more than a few days.'

The old man smiled. It lightened the whole of his face and Peter detected the strength and charm he must have had when he was younger. 'I will stay here if you promise to tell no one about me,' the old man said. 'I know it will be difficult for you and I will explain all when you return. Can you promise?'

'Yes of course,' said Peter, quietly intrigued by this mysterious old man. 'I will say nothing to anyone.'

'Good. First, though, close to the stream where I was trying to drink, before I remember no more, is a small copse. In the middle of the copse close to a big oak tree you will find a pile of leaves. Underneath the leaves is my bag. Could you please get it and bring it to me?'

Peter ran off to the copse and easily found a long bag which proved to be rather heavier than it looked. He returned to his hut and handed the bag to the old man.

'Thank you. Did you look to see what was inside?'

Peter flushed angrily. 'Of course not! It is your bag and nothing to do with me.'

The old man grunted in appreciation and stowed the bag inside the hut.

When Peter returned from the village after his two-day absence, the old man was nowhere to be seen. Peter was surprised, but went off to check on the sheep. Later in the day he was close to the copse and saw the old man walking out, heading towards the hut with his bag slung over his shoulder. The old man walked with determined step and, if not fully recovered, showed every sign of returning health and strength. Peter waited for him.

'So you did not trust me and hid away in case I brought someone back with me,' Peter said, a little miffed.

'I did trust you, but I cannot take chances in this uncertain time. It would have done you harm if I had been found sheltering in your hut.'

'Why? Tell me why you are so secretive. What have you done wrong?'

'It is a very long story and I do not wish to burden you with it for now. I promise, before I leave I will tell you what you want to know, but for the moment, can you please trust me? I will do you no harm.' The old man smiled his charming smile again. 'In fact, I owe you so much I do not know how to repay you.'

'Well,' said Peter. 'You are not from these parts, I guess, so you could repay me by telling me about the ways of the world you have seen. In our village we get any news very late and even then much of what is happening is not explained.'

'I will gladly do that, but first let's eat. I have a very fine pheasant in my bag which we can roast with herbs I have gathered. Make the fire, and I will pluck it and rub in the herbs.'

They walked back to the hut. The old man kept pace with Peter and although his movements were not flowing, his steps seemed sure and light. Peter lit the fire while the old man plucked and gutted the pheasant, scored cuts across the body and rubbed in herbs pulled from his bag. Skewering the pheasant, the old man put it over the fire on the spit supports and gently rotated it so that it cooked slowly and thoroughly.

'I have some fresh-baked bread,' said Peter. 'It will only last a couple of days so we may as well eat a good portion of it with the pheasant now while it is still soft.' The old man smiled once again and they busied themselves getting the meal ready.

'I don't suppose you have any wine, or ale?'

'No. None at all. I've never tasted wine, though I do have thin ale in the village, but my mother will not allow me to bring any here as the water from the stream is clean and clear.'

'A pity. It would make this meal memorable. I haven't tasted either for months now.'

When the food was ready, they both sat close to the warmth of the fire to ward off the chilling of the evening and ate the succulent pheasant with the fresh bread. When they had finished, the old man said, 'Tell me about yourself. You seem very young to be a shepherd by yourself. Does anyone ever come here to check on you?'

Peter detected a note of personal concern rather than a direct enquiry about Peter's own abilities, but it did not bother him. If the old man was in fear of detection, then it would be natural to want to find out if anyone would come to the area.

'I am over twelve summers and it is the right age to begin as a shepherd,' he replied. 'I seem to have a natural talent for it, so I do not need any help from my village and the villagers would not think of coming out here to check on me. It would be an insult and would show they have no faith in my abilities. In the spring, when the sheep are lambing, some of the older men will be here to help, because it will be my first lambing and such a large flock needs more than one person to help if things go wrong.'

'And what of you? Did you choose to become a shepherd?'

'No. I am the eldest with two brothers and a sister. My father is a farmer and, as the eldest, I will take over from him in time. Our village is organised so we all help each other. All the village sheep are looked after together and our tradition is that shepherds are trained from the age of twelve summers and if they are good and like it they remain shepherds until they are fifteen. Then they stop, for they are strong enough to contribute to the labour on the farmland. When the last shepherd was fifteen, I was chosen by the village to take over because I am good with animals. I don't know why, but animals seem to trust me and I like them. I also like it here. I'm not afraid to be alone and the quietness seems to suit me.'

The old man's eyes did not leave Peter's face as the boy was speaking. When he had finished, the old man said, 'You are a very resourceful boy. Not many would do as you have done. You saved my life. From the way you speak, you seem to me to be intelligent as well. I wonder . . .' He stopped speaking as his eyes remained looking at Peter. There was a long pause.

'You wonder what?'

The old man smiled. 'Tell me, can you read and write?'

Peter shook his head. His father could, unusually, read a few words, but no one in the village could write. This was something for the priests and monks. The common people had no need for such things.

'I cannot give you anything to reward you for saving my life – except for knowledge. If you let me remain here until the lambing, I'll teach you to read and write. I can also help in finding food to eat, cook and even, if you need it, assist with the sheep. I confess I am no expert so far as sheep are concerned, but I can do anything you want. I may not look very strong at the moment, but I have a lot of life still in me and resting here for a few months with good food will make me a new man.'

Peter did not have to think about his answer. He certainly liked his solitary life, but he was strangely drawn to this old man and the chance of being able to learn how to read a few words, even write his name, could not be thrown away. He had no idea how it might be of any use to him, but who was to know what the future might bring?

'Yes. You can certainly stay here with me and I'll try my best to learn to read and write.'

'Good. Then we start tomorrow.'

The old man said no more, but got up and went into the hut to his bed. It was not quite sleeping time yet for Peter, but he guessed the old man's strength was not as great as he tried to portray, so Peter sat watching the embers of the fire die until the coolness of the night drove him inside to his makeshift bed of reeds, leaves and straw.

True to his word, the old man explained both reading and writing to Peter and, producing a slate and marker chalk from his bag, showed Peter how to form letters. The days were spent with divided labour, the old man snaring hare or pheasant, cooking and keeping the hut clean and tidy, while Peter tended the sheep. When all tasks were done they sat together, teacher and pupil.

Peter was a very able student. He learned easily and avidly. The more the old man taught him, the more he wanted to learn. Quietly, without even knowing it, Peter began to speak to the old man in Norman French. At first, the old man introduced the odd Norman French word into the Anglo-Saxon conversation and gradually more and more. Surprisingly, it took Peter several weeks to realise he was beginning to use unfamiliar words and phrases, but then he challenged the old man.

'Why are we speaking this way?'

'I am amazed it has taken you so long to realise!' the old man replied. 'If you are to read and write, and if it is to do you any good, you must do so in Latin and French. French is the language of the nobility. The most important things are written in Latin, for in that language the spelling of words is constant, but French is being written down more and more for communication between members of the nobility. I will teach you Latin for reading and writing because all the Good Books are written in Latin. It is the language of the church. If you can master a little French as well, then apart from being a great asset in your life, it could give you many opportunities.

'I cannot possibly think how French will do me any good, let alone Latin,' retorted Peter. 'But I do enjoy learning . . . so why not?' The old man smiled in contented amusement.

Save for the depths of winter, in late January, when – unusually for Devonshire – the snow was particularly deep and the days, as well as some of the nights, were spent digging sheep from snow drifts and clearing snow so the sheep could forage the wilted grass, teacher and pupil continued with the instruction and learning. By spring, just before lambing, Peter and the old man were speaking entirely in French, barely uttering a word of Anglo-Saxon. It felt completely natural to Peter and the old man, who had grown in strength and now walked about like a youngster, glowing with pride for his pupil. As lambing approached, however, the mood between the two became slightly strained – until the old man broke the spell.

'In less than two weeks,' he said, 'you will be fully involved in lambing and will have men from the village here to help you. I will be of no use and in any case I do not want to be seen here, so, as promised, I have to go. To be on the safe side for both of us, I think I ought to go tomorrow.'

Peter nodded slowly, knowing this time had to come, though he wished it had not. 'Are you sure you cannot stay? My village is good and friendly and I am sure they will take you at face value, not ask too many questions and be happy to have you as part of the community.'

'No. I would not fit into village life and I have nothing to offer your villagers. I am very pleased, though, you want me to stay.'

'Yes I do! I have enjoyed the last few months and I will miss you and your teachings.'

'Very well then. I propose that I leave tomorrow – there is somewhere I need to go anyway – and I return after the lambing. In two months. Would you like that?'

'Oh yes! That would be splendid.' Peter's face lit up and the strained mood lifted immediately.

The following morning the old man took up his bag, bade Peter farewell and walked off to the east, leaving the boy with an odd sensation of loneliness.

Although the old man never really left Peter's mind, the weeks of lambing which followed occupied every minute of his days and most of his nights. He learned quickly from the men in the village and insisted on doing more than his fair share. His natural empathy with the sheep seemed to be a help, for a ewe in difficult labour calmed at his touch and the birth became easier. Snatching moments of sleep when he could, he felt exhausted but exhilarated. They lost few lambs at birth and the only difficulty Peter had was explaining away why, at a moment of crisis, he called out for help in Norman French. Luckily those hearing him did not understand that it was a different language and accepted Peter's explanation excitement had garbled his speech.

When the lambing was over and the men returned to the village, Peter was surprised the old man did not appear instantly. For two weeks he waited. Just as he was starting to believe that the old man would not come back, he arrived after all, his bag over his back alongside another, much longer bag.

'I was a little delayed, but I wanted something which took longer to find than I expected. But now I'm here. How was the lambing?'

Peter told him, not leaving out the Norman French exclamation, at which the old man smiled.

'Once you become fluent, that is something you must guard against. In time you will automatically only speak in the language being spoken to you, but in these early days you will mix both when you are not thinking. Do not worry.'

Over the next three months they resumed their earlier routine. In the first month there was less time for teaching, for the lambs, cute and appealing to look at, exhibited extraordinary stupidity. Peter spent a great deal of time pulling them out of ditches and bramble bushes, at the same time placating the bleating mothers who appeared incapable of teaching their young the basics of safety and survival.

One afternoon at the end of the third month, Peter arrived back at the hut to see the old man preparing a meal as usual, but beside him were his two bags. Although full of curiosity, Peter did not enquire why these bags, which had remained virtually out of sight in the hut until now, had suddenly appeared, but the old man saw him looking at them. He stopped his preparations, wiped his hands, opened the smaller bag, put a hand inside and pulled out a sword. He carefully withdrew the sword from its sheath and laid it on the ground.

'Would you like to learn how to use a sword?'

With no hesitation Peter replied, 'Oh yes!'

'Pick it up and try it.'

Peter leaned down and grasped the handle. It took a surprising effort to lift the sword off the ground. 'It is so heavy!'

The old man laughed. 'Indeed it is. I do not expect you to wield this for a long time, but if you are good enough, then some day you may be able to manage it. Next week we will start with some basic lessons in swordplay and also exercises to strengthen you. You are as thin as a beanpole and need much more meat on your bones if you are going to be any good.'

He leaned over to the second, longer bag and pulled out a bow and six arrows. 'What about this? Would you like to learn how to use this as well?'

Peter nodded enthusiastically. Like all villagers, he could use a bow and was, for his age, reasonably proficient, but the bow the old man had produced was much larger and appeared sturdier than the kind Peter was used to.

'This is a Welsh bow. Few people in England use these yet, but I predict they will take over from the much inferior English bow. The crossbow is too slow to arm and the English bow does not have the penetrating power of the Welsh bow. The one I have here is lower-powered than the full Welsh bow which has been giving the barons on the Welsh border so much trouble. It is no good trying to teach you anything with the full bow, because you would not be strong enough to pull it back and unless the bowstring is brought right up to the cheek, it is useless as a weapon.'

During the following week, when he was not engaged in other tasks, the old man fashioned two swords out of sturdy wood cut down from the copse. When these were finished, he combined his teaching with swordplay lessons. Peter lacked strength to strike blows with sufficient force, but was agile and again quick to learn.

For nearly three years the old man stayed with Peter in the hut, leaving at lambing time to return when it had finished. On each return he brought with him new scrolls, manuscripts, parchment, pen and ink. He taught Peter to read and write in French and Latin, explained the convoluted politics of the times and passed on every skill with the sword he knew, attaching weights to Peter's sword as the boy grew stronger and eventually allowing him to wield his own real sword.

He also taught Peter how to use the Welsh bow, the axe and the pike, building up his strength with exercises aided by increasingly weighty stones and then rocks from the stream. Peter was a naturally gifted runner and so the old man encouraged him to run everywhere to improve his stamina.

As for the old man, Peter never learned his name and soon realised he was not nearly as old as his face appeared to indicate. He remained 'the old man' in Peter's mind, however. Every time Peter tried to find out more about him, he would skilfully turn the conversation onto another topic. Nonetheless, in his own time he did slowly tell Peter something of his history and explain why he was so keen to remain out of everyone's sight.

The old man was born the second son of an influential baron. The first son of a baron or knight always inherited and the remaining sons – while at first an insurance against the eldest dying before inheriting or begetting a son of his own – were something of a burden. From a young age, sometimes as young as eight summers, they were sent off to learn to become squires to other knights and then, hopefully, to qualify themselves as knights by achievement on the battlefield or at tourneys, so that they could win spoils sufficient to support themselves or, better still, marry an heiress. The alternative was for the younger sons to go into the church. Not all younger sons managed to achieve a noble independence and they were a drain on the father, often taking to banditry or becoming mercenaries to supplement their income.

The old man's elder brother was sickly as a youth and the baron was not at all confident that his firstborn would survive to inherit. Consequently the old man was not sent off to another knight for training, but was kept at home to learn the skills of battle and the concepts of knightly honour. He became adept at both and acquitted himself well in the minor skirmishes which occurred from time to time between barons. His mother had, unusually, been classically educated by priests and somewhat favoured him over the other sons, perhaps because he was willing to learn to read and write Latin. Surprisingly, even the most senior barons had but a rudimentary ability to read and write in French and virtually none in Latin, leaving these un-knightly chores to the scribes and clergy – so mother and son spent hours together going over old manuscripts and discussing the teachings of the church.

The eldest son shook off his sickliness as he approached his teens and the old man was happy to joust and train with his elder brother, teaching and encouraging the skills of combat. The baron, seeing that his eldest son would indeed survive to adulthood and, perhaps, become a passable if not glorious fighter, contracted his younger son to go into the church. He reasoned that no knight would take on a squire he had not trained himself and the boy's learning would suit him admirably for the clergy. His mother, though, cautioned against a hasty decision in this respect and convinced the baron that the younger son should stay at home until the eldest son reached his majority age and won favour as a knight – for, she argued, the sickliness could return. So the old man remained at home, training in fighting, pitting his skills against others in tourneys and reading with his mother. This very contented life came to an end when his eldest brother, against all expectations, won a tourney in grand style and the king was so pleased he was granted a knighthood on the spot. The old man did not point out to Peter that he never entered a tourney himself if his elder brother was down to participate.

While it was not the life he would have chosen, the old man was content to go off to the local monastery, to receive instruction from the church. He was much older than the usual novice, but the learning from his mother and his natural abilities soon shone through and he was accepted as a worthy potential candidate. The old man, however, was far more interested in the manuscripts than in any advancement and he taught himself some Greek, spending far more time amongst the scrolls than at prayer. This did not go unnoticed and to avoid continual chastisement, a bargain was struck. The church was obliged to provide the king with a number of knights, squires and fighting men when called upon to do so and, while the old man had not qualified as a knight, he agreed to continue his knightly training and go, when ordered, into battle for the king with other knights supplied by the church. In return, the church would allow him to continue his studies and not require more than the usual knightly church service attendance. This suited the old man, for Peter came to understand that he was not particularly pious.

At this time Henry was on the throne and ruled his

kingdom with a rod of iron, knowing how to frighten, encourage and reward barons and knights in the right measure to maintain an uneasy peace. The power of the throne was no more than an ability to satisfy the greed of the barons and placate the ever-strengthening church. Henry was without a natural male heir and chose as a successor his daughter Matilda, forcing the barons by sheer willpower to swear allegiance to her. On Henry's death, Stephen, usurping power, was reluctantly rather than readily accepted as king by the barons who were not keen to be governed by a woman. However, the barons who had sworn fealty to Matilda were uneasy, for honour and oaths were the cornerstone of the ruling society. Some of them, while content to have Stephen as king, avoided pledging their oath to him. Thus it was a tussle between honour and greed. As long as Stephen could satisfy the greed of the barons through grants of land or handouts from the treasure chest inherited from Henry, so the honour of the barons who had abandoned their fealty to Matilda could be placated. Once the barons realised Stephen's fickle nature and the treasure chest became empty, however, the hidden unrest boiled to the surface. Some barons became reluctant to send their knights and men to aid Stephen in his quest to bring all England under his direct control.

The church was initially loyal. The ever-increasing power and influence of the church depended on support from kings who believed they were chosen and appointed directly by God and so were the final arbiters in matters of religion, seeking support from the pope in Rome only in extremis. So the church readily sent knights to Stephen to aid his battles, and the old man soon had his first taste of major conflict. He found to his surprise that he relished battle as much as he enjoyed pouring over dusty parchments, and his fighting abilities soon won him the coveted position of knight. As fewer barons appeared on the battlefield to aid Stephen, so the knights of the church were called upon to do more and the old man was constantly chasing around the countryside going from skirmish to skirmish, siege to siege.

The shortage of willing fighting men eventually became too acute and so Stephen raised a mercenary army. This infuriated the barons, who felt the honour of battle could not be maintained by those who had not won their knighthood by valour. So it was that Robert, Earl of Gloucester, renounced his allegiance to Stephen, aligning himself with Matilda. Stephen became more and more suspicious of all those around him and, short of funds, sought to exert pressure on the church to provide more money for his campaigns under the not-too-veiled threat of seizing church property. The church resisted hotly, declared against Stephen, and, in 1139, Stephen arrested three prominent bishops. Such a move could not be tolerated by the English church and so its knights were withdrawn from Stephen's army. It would not have been wise for the church openly to support Matilda against the king, but it 'allowed' some of its knights to assist Robert of Gloucester. The old man was one so chosen.

Stephen continued to rail around the countryside bringing barons to heel and, when not able to gain voluntary allegiance, replaced some barons with his own chosen men, often after fierce fighting. The old man was involved in minor skirmishes against Stephen's support troops, but as yet Robert had not fully organised his army for a serious revolt, simply standing aside in defiance of Stephen until Matilda arrived from France to place herself at the head of her own army. Once Matilda was in England, Robert made his move. Everything came to a head in Lincoln in 1141, when Stephen was caught between two opposing armies and, despite fighting gallantly, was taken prisoner.

The old man was at the battle of Lincoln, and this proved to be his downfall. It was widely believed that Stephen was knocked out by a rock during the battle and taken prisoner by William de Cahaignes. The truth was that Stephen, with two loyal knights, became isolated and found himself face to face with the old man. In dispatching the knights, the old man's helmet was knocked off and the king instantly recognised him as the second son of one of his keenest supporters. Screaming 'Traitor!', Stephen lunged uncharacteristically wildly at the old man, leaving himself wide open for the killing blow. The old man could not dispatch a king against whom he had no personal quarrel, so he feinted and brought the flat of his sword blade against the head of the king, knocking him senseless. The old man, being associated with the church, could not officially take the king prisoner, so it was left to William de Cahaignes to have the honour.

Stephen was taken to Bristol and Matilda chose the title Lady of England in anticipation of her coronation. Before that could happen, however, Stephen's wife raised reinforcements in Kent, marched them to Winchester and besieged Robert and Matilda in Wolvsey Castle. Matilda escaped, but Robert was captured, to be exchanged with Stephen later that year.

King Stephen became even more resentful and blamed his capture upon the treachery of the old man. He vowed to have revenge and instructed all his knights and barons that the old man was to be hounded throughout the land. The church could not shield the old man from such an edict and he became something of a liability to Robert of Gloucester, so the old man left both the field of war and the cloisters to wander around the countryside, living off the land and waiting for Stephen to recant or be overthrown by Matilda. The rough life out in all weathers and the need for constant alertness to avoid being recognised and captured aged his face prematurely with deep worry lines. He was not without friends, but in deference to their safety did not stay with anyone, merely visiting from time to time – hence his ability to get hold of writing materials and scrolls.

Stephen neither forgot nor forgave and, far from being overthrown, slowly became more successful in defeating the recalcitrant barons. Few of the barons were fervent supporters of one side or the other, simply taking whatever side was convenient or more profitable at the time. This led to many petty quarrels between barons and there was constant fighting, requiring even the most peaceful barons to maintain large fighting forces in order to defend their property from regular attacks. The whole countryside seemed to be at war. Thus it was that Peter could witness a small battle even in his own rural backwater, as the unrest of the local barons spread into Devonshire.

5

Peter's fifteenth summer meant he was no longer to be a shepherd and would have no more time with the old man.

'What will become of you?' Peter asked him.

'Do not fear for me. I have survived and Stephen is far too intent now on holding onto the throne than putting too much effort into chasing me. All I have to do is avoid any baron who is thinking of ingratiating himself with Stephen, as I would be a good prize to exchange for a pardon or treasure and acceptance at Stephen's court.'

'Will I ever see you again?'

'Who knows what the fates might bring. I have taught you as much as I possibly could, and if you use your skills and knowledge wisely and sparingly, you will prosper.'

'As a farmer?'

'Maybe, but I feel you will not be a farmer for very long. These are troubled times and your village cannot remain immune for ever.'

During their final days together Peter and the old man talked more about life than about instruction, war or battles. The old man seemed to be concentrating Peter's mind on the application of knowledge to everyday things, rather than painting a picture of the possible glory and riches which might be in the world somewhere ready to grasp.

They parted quietly but with sadness. Peter ran back to his village and the old man walked away to who knew where.

When he arrived in the village Peter was greeted by his waiting father. Unlike the old man, his father looked much younger than his years. He was beaming and clearly delighted at Peter's return.

'At last! I thought you would never come. Your mother has prepared a feast for us tonight to celebrate your return to the village and the start of your farming life. We have chosen a replacement shepherd boy. You can spend a few days with him in the hills, then a few days back on the farm, until he's ready to take over – both of you learning new skills.'

They walked together back to the family house, to be greeted with equal enthusiasm by Peter's mother, two brothers and sister. Such a welcome seemed so strange. The family were clearly pleased to mark the end of an era, but Peter was less certain. He knew he would miss the old man and the opportunity for conversation about the wider world rather than the state of the harvest and the all-important weather.

That evening was a great celebration, with many of the villagers calling in to welcome Peter back. Although going to bed very late, Peter was up with the sun and went with his father out into the fields to inspect the crops and animals. At midday they were quietly weeding around the vegetable patch – usually tended by the women in the village, but occasionally aided by the men – when Peter's father stopped and looked into the distance. Peter followed his father's eyes and saw a band of men, some on horses and some on foot, approaching. Riders meant trouble, so Peter immediately rushed around the village warning the women and some of the wives ran to the fields to tell the men. Pikes and axes were made ready but hidden from view. Although all men and women of whatever class carried a dagger, swords, being expensive, were largely confined to the nobles. As the band of men came closer it could be seen there were six on horseback and about a dozen on foot – not a formidable fighting force, but sufficient to defeat the inexperienced villagers. The men on foot were not armed, however, and seemed to be following the horses reluctantly. The man at the head of the troop was Robert de Cours, the local baron. Everyone heaved a sigh of relief. No bloodletting today then. But why was he here? If he had wanted extra food or even an additional call on the rents, he would have sent a squire, or at most a knight. The baron would not come himself. Tension appeared again in the villagers' faces.

The baron brought his troop to a halt in the middle of the village and surveyed the crowd. Small children hid behind their mothers' skirts and the men stood still, frightened but not intimidated. The baron heaved a deep sigh and spoke to them all in Anglo-Saxon.

'I am afraid that our good king . . .' (Peter detected a note of irony in the baron's voice) '. . . has been unable to maintain peace in our land and we barons are forced to increase our armies to defend ourselves from attack by other barons. I therefore have to take two men from each of my villages into service to strengthen my fighting force. I know that up to now you have been spared from this because of your contribution to my treasure chest and table, but I am afraid times are desperate. I have no choice. Two men will be selected to serve for two years, or until the troubles end.'

There was a slight release of tension among the listeners. The men on foot had been selected from other villages, hence the reluctant walking. Things were not as bad as they could have been, but the loss of two able-bodied men would be a blow. Who would be chosen?

One of the knights walked his horse around the centre of the village looking at the men, each of whom shrivelled up and tried to look weak and unsuitable. The knight was experienced and took no notice. Completing his circle, he started again, pausing at a big strong man of twenty summers and pointing to him. The Master of Arms detached himself from behind the baron and went up to the man, directing him to join the others on foot. There was a loud wailing from the man's wife.

'With my man gone, who is to look after us? We have two children!'

The baron smiled. 'I am not moved, particularly in this village where I know you all look after each other.' He spoke to the knight in Norman French. 'Carry on.'

The knight urged his horse forward and stopped at Peter and his father. He pointed to Peter's father.

Peter immediately leaped forward. 'No, take me! He is my father and is much older than he looks and not nearly as fit as he appears. He ails in the winter. I would be much better for you.'

The knight looked puzzled and turned to the baron, who translated what Peter had said. The knight gave a hoarse laugh. In Norman French he said to Peter, 'You are just a child. We want strong men, not babes in arms!'

Just in time, Peter remembered not to give away the fact that he could understand French and ignored the knight, simply walking towards the other men on foot. His mother was stunned, pleased his father was being protected but frightened her firstborn was getting himself into trouble.

'Sir John says you are too young and weak to be of any use to us,' the baron said to Peter.

'I am nearly fifteen summers and much stronger than I look. I will serve you better than my old father. Try me, and if I cannot come up to your standards, you can send me back.'

The baron translated what Peter had said to Sir John, who laughed cruelly. 'We cannot waste time trying out children and sending back those who are not up to it. The

Master at Arms will make sure everyone we pick can fight bravely and it is our duty to supply him with real men.'

The baron turned to Peter and translated what Sir John had said. It was a mark of the baron's good governance that he was wasting time with such a trivial matter. He needed only to indicate that Peter's father was to be taken, and that would be the end of it.

Peter bristled. 'If Sir John does not wish to spend time finding the best, perhaps he could settle it now. Do you have a man I can fight? If so, I will show you here and now that I am worthy of selection.'

The baron laughed at this boy's assertiveness. Usually the peasants could hardly raise their eyes to the baron, would speak only in monosyllables and never dream of questioning an order. Perhaps there was more to this lad than met the eye – perhaps too much, and he would have to be watched. No, he was far too young. The baron turned to Sir John.

'The boy is challenging you to a fight.' This was not actually true, but it had been a difficult few days for the baron and he was enjoying the light relief.

Sir John sputtered. 'You surely cannot be serious!'

'Well, if you do not want to fight him . . . Anyway, we are wasting time and you are right. We need a man.' Robert de Cours was not a baron for nothing. He knew the right words would produce the right result, and by giving Sir John the option to leave things he was essentially suggesting that Sir John was a coward, or at least frightened to put his honour to the challenge of a mere boy.

'Give him a pike,' growled Sir John to the Master at Arms.

All those on horseback were by that time amused at the situation. Sir John, who was not the most popular man, had landed himself in a difficult position and the Master at Arms gladly dismounted and gave Peter a pike. In heavily accented Anglo-Saxon he said to Peter, 'Sir John has accepted your challenge. Here is your weapon, unless you prefer a sword!'

Indeed, Peter would have preferred a sword, but mindful of the fact that a peasant would not know how to use one, he simply shrugged and held the pike loosely in his hand.

Sir John dismounted, took off his helmet and unsheathed his sword, holding it in his right hand, down by his side, with its tip resting on the ground. He stood straight in front of Peter with his legs apart, waiting.

'Go on then, attack me,' he said.

Peter pretended not to understand and looked at the baron.

'He is giving you the opportunity of striking first. I would accept it if I were you.'

Peter nodded and advanced slowly. The village was completely still. Even the horses seem mesmerised by the sight of a callow youth having the temerity to challenge an experienced knight.

When he was a pike length from Sir John, Peter made as if to jab his weapon into the knight's left side. With lightning speed, Sir John's sword came in an upward arc to the left of his body to sweep the pike away. So confident was Sir John that he did not move his feet. Even more quickly, Peter did not go through with his jab but rocked backwards, pulling the pike away from Sir John's body, and when the sword had passed on its upward arc, he pushed the pike into Sir John's stomach, just enough to make and hold contact.

There was an intake of breath from the horsemen. The villagers knew enough to remain completely silent. The baron looked at Peter.

'Clever. Where did you learn that?'

'My lord, I feel I was just lucky. Sir John was not completely ready for me and I took advantage of him. It was not an honourable thing to do.'

The baron grunted and translated to Sir John what Peter had said. Sir John did not reply. True, he had been too casual, but a knight should be able to squash a mere boy without a thought.

'I think we should try this lad,' said the baron. 'As we gave him the opportunity to show his prowess, we have no real option even though he is possessed with the most incredible luck.' He laughed. 'Well, we could all do with a bit of luck at the moment and perhaps he will be our lucky mascot.'

With that, the baron indicated to the Master at Arms Peter should join the foot band and he wheeled his horse away, moving out of the village, followed by the rest of the men.

Peter walked next to the other man chosen from his village, but did not speak. He was shaking inwardly at what he had done and hoped Sir John would not seek retribution. The old man was right. Peter was not going to be a farmer – not yet at least.

The band of men trudged wearily behind the mounted knights for the remainder of the day, reaching the next village at nightfall. The newly recruited but untrained foot soldiers were left to fend for themselves whilst the baron and his knights commanded food and shelter from the villagers. This was the beginning of a pattern Peter would learn to accept. Nobility made sure it was looked after, whereas everyone else had to look after themselves. The village was poor, but gave the new recruits a small amount of food, washed down with weak ale. Peter introduced himself to all his conscripted fellows and in return was given names and backgrounds. All were farmers who, although resenting the recruitment, accepted it as a fact of life. None had been under arms before and whilst Peter felt a shiver of excitement at the idea that he was going to a new place to experience new things, the remainder were apprehensive to the point of fear. Peter felt that although all the recruits were friendly, banding together for comfort and consolation, they were just a little reserved with him. Peasants do not disobey their masters and certainly do not challenge nobility to fight. It was unheard of, so Peter must be a madman.

The Master at Arms, William Decar, was also unsure of Peter. Decar was the bastard son of a very minor knight and had been given no favours or succour, being thrown into the army at the first opportunity to fend for himself. He had risen through the common ranks by skill, endeavour and loyalty, gaining sufficient respect to command the ear of his superiors and freedom to train soldiers any way he liked, but he was not allowed the privileges of the nobility, nor was he permitted to compete at tourneys to qualify as a knight. He was not bitter. This was the way of life and he accepted his lot, grateful that his position was secure and taking pride in his ability to train and hold together the common soldiers for his master, the baron. He had in the back of his mind the notion that there was still the possibility of glory on the field of battle, marking him out for merit, as a knight perhaps, or even the dream of capturing a wealthy knight or baron and sharing in the ransom. William Decar was fiercely loyal to Robert de Cours, however, and would suffer no lack of effort from his soldiers. Every man had to do better than his best at all times, or punishment would be swift and harsh.

Discipline was strict, but William Decar was not mindless or even completely single-minded. Being of common stock, he understood the fears and problems of men not brought up with the tradition of knight's honour and appreciated even the most lowly had knowledge and skill of some sort, so he always had a listening ear. By and large, his men liked and trusted him completely. In the castle, William kept himself apart, as his position required, but would not hesitate from joining the men in an ale house on a rest day to carouse as an equal. Surprisingly, his broken Anglo-Saxon was not ridiculed by the men who, out of his hearing, often made fun of his mispronunciation or wrong use of words. William was aware of this and did not mind. He had been brought up speaking French with only a few words of Anglo-

Saxon, but when he was sent to the army he had to leave his French behind. He had no gift at learning languages, however, and could not lose his heavy accent. As he rose through the ranks, he realised this was no handicap and so, while his language knowledge increased, he maintained the broken way of speech which seemed to those around him to be an endearing vulnerability.

When the knights were ready to leave the following morning and the conscripted men, with the two newly selected from this village, were on their feet preparing to follow, William had a good look at Peter. He wanted to find out more about this lad, but was wise enough not to do that now. To single Peter out for comment or enquiry would likely make the other men feel that he was getting special attention, and what William needed was for all his soldiers to feel bound together as one. Animosity, jealousy or resentment in the ranks was stamped out ruthlessly, for in battle each would rely on the other and the slightest chink in this could, indeed often did, lead to a gaping crack that weakened the whole fighting force.

The group moved at a steady pace to the next village, where their ranks were swelled by two more reluctant villagers, and then they travelled on to Robert de Cours' castle. Peter had seen this castle some years earlier, but was surprised at the change. The wooden walls atop earth embankments surrounding the castle had disappeared, replaced by thick stone, and the castle itself was no longer stone and wood but fully stone-built. There was no moat, although the gate into the courtyard was narrow, just wide enough to allow a cart through, and closed by the thickest wooden doors Peter had ever seen. He wondered how many men would be needed just to heave at the doors to close them.

The troop went through the gateway into the courtyard. The knights dismounted as their squires took the horses, and prepared to go into the castle with the baron. William directed the men to a wooden structure away from the castle, nestling under the great stone wall, where food was waiting for them. The common soldier was not quite at the bottom of the food chain in a castle, but William made sure his men were fed as well as possible, arguing with his superiors that a well-fed man is not only a fit man, but also a loyal one. Once fed, they were taken outside the walls to huts where the soldiers were billeted, and where they remained unless they were required inside the castle to defend it.

The new men were distributed between the huts, cramming hastily given bedding into spaces grudgingly ceded by the old hands. There was no animosity from the trained soldiers, most of whom were farmhands taken into the baron's service to train and remain for the usual two years. However, until the new recruits had shown their merit and mettle, there was an unspoken barrier which kept them apart.

Training started at once: no time for resting under William Decar. The new men were summoned to the training ground outside the walls of the castle, each given a blunt pike and a blunt axe and made to run in circles around the training ground while William watched. All the men were fit from the fields, the weight of a pike and axe was nothing to them, and after half an hour or so they all looked fresh. William grunted and was pleased. A man with a shortage of breath was not going to make a fighting machine. William then demonstrated the basics of fighting with a pike. For the common foot soldier the pike was the first weapon of attack and defence. Being longer than a sword, if used correctly it could defeat a sword or an axe, but its disadvantage was at close quarters, where there was not enough room to use a pike efficiently so the axe was brought into play. The new recruits practised the moves shown by William and then against each other, again while William watched.

Peter was in a dilemma. Was he to show his skills or not?

He remembered the words of the old man, who had told him that knowledge should come first in everything. Peter decided to pretend he was inexperienced until such time as he could learn what advantage, if any, there was in showing what he could really do. He found no difficulty in warding off exercise attacks from those pitted against him in practice and also made fumbled attempts to spear his opponent. The following day the new recruits were paired with the more experienced soldiers, receiving more instruction, overseen and occasionally corrected by William.

Each day developed into a pattern. Up at first light. No breakfast – peasants did not normally eat breakfast unless they were setting out on a journey. On to the training ground to practise and learn more skills and moves with the pike and axe. A short rest and a light meal at noon, followed by a long run. Every man was given a pack on his back loaded with stones, and with his axe and pike ran through the countryside for a minimum of an hour at a steady pace. As each recruit became more honed to the military life, so William extended their run and increased its pace. William did not shirk from these exercises, for he too ran with his men, urging them on and occasionally cajoling when some began to flag. Immediately after the run, there was more training, which on one day a week was turned into a free-for-all with every soldier fighting every other soldier with blunt pikes and axes in a melee. These melees became more and more competitive, with each man trying to outdo the other, and although the weapons were deliberately blunt, there was much bruising, the odd wound and an occasional broken bone. William was unhappy when bones were broken, for this meant a man would be out of training for weeks – but pain was encouraged, for if nothing else, war brought a lot of that, so the quicker the body became used to it the better.

Peter could have shone in the melee, but he was careful, ensuring he received the odd blow or two and did not hurt his many opponents too much. He was quietly confident that he had hidden his skills successfully and at the same time had demonstrated a willingness to pull his weight and be a part of the fighting force. While he was the youngest by far, he was accepted by all and treated as an equal.

'You do not fool me,' said William one day after a melee as Peter was walking away to store his pike and axe. Peter stopped and looked bemused. William stared hard at Peter. 'I have been a fighting man all my life and I can recognise talent and experience. You may play the buffoon with these men, but I can see this is not the first time you have handled weapons.'

'You are mistaken. I am a quick learner and it seems I have good reactions, so perhaps that is why I appear to be able to stay out of trouble.'

William grunted. 'Not so. If you don't want to tell me, that is your choice, but be careful. Not all of the men are fooled. You could make enemies and in playing around you will lose your skills.' With that warning, he walked away.

Training continued every day except for Sundays. This was a day of rest and a time to go to the local church attached to the nearby monastery. Churchgoing was not compulsory, though most men went most of the time. The service took place just before midday and afterwards the men often went to the nearest small town, about three hours' brisk walk away, returning well after midnight. There they went into one of the three ale houses to spend what little money they had received from the baron. Although it was called a town, in fact the place was little more than a big village that attracted a local market each month. The number of ale houses was unusual, but the town was situated conveniently between three castles and so attracted soldiers and, of course, wenches ready to satisfy a man's needs. At first, Peter went to the town with the rest of the baron's men, but he took little enjoyment in sitting and drinking. Tales of battles from the experienced soldiers were interesting and sometimes entertaining, but those stories grew in imagination and quickly became repetitive.

One bright, warm Sunday, after the church service, when Peter had no desire to go to the town, he walked around the church and monastery grounds enjoying the day. Suddenly he became aware of a monk sitting under a tree gazing into space with a manuscript on his lap. It was not the first time Peter had seen this monk sitting under a tree, and while the sight of monks was familiar, they were usually busying themselves with various tasks, not sitting in the open air with manuscripts. Peter watched the monk, who did not move, not even to blink. Peter wondered if the monk was sightless, but realised this could not be because of the manuscript on his lap.

'Are you just going to look at me, or do you intend to speak?' The monk's voice was soft and warm.

'I did not want to disturb you, but I was curious as to why you have a manuscript, but you are not reading it.'

The monk's face turned and he looked Peter square in the eyes, smiling slightly. 'It is good to think about what you read. Is this not so?'

'Yes,' said Peter. 'I agree.'

'So you think you can read?'

Peter was annoyed with himself that he had so easily fallen into the trap of admitting he could read. 'Oh, a few words,' he said hastily, trying to cover his mistake.

'Well, if you have to think about it, then it is more than a few words, I would say.' The monk beckoned to Peter to come closer. 'Come, sit here with me. Let us both enjoy this lovely day.' The monk patted the ground beside him. Peter slowly complied and sat down next to the monk. They remained silent for a while, then the monk placed the manuscript in Peter's lap. 'Tell me what you can read. Do not hold back. If you want to keep it a secret, it is safe with me.'

Peter looked at the dark brown eyes affectionately holding his gaze and opened the manuscript. Looking down, he saw it was not one of the reverent texts he assumed the monk would be reading, but a story in poem form – a story about an ancient warrior who had angered the gods and was being tested. He read the first two pages slowly, enchanted by the music of the words. 'What is this?' he asked.

'It is a Greek poem translated into Latin which explains all the powers of the mythical gods. It reads better in Greek, but we do not have the Greek manuscript here. Do you like it?'

'Oh yes,' said Peter.

The monk smiled broadly. 'It is a great pleasure to meet someone who can appreciate fine words. My fellow brethren read only the holy texts and I have no opportunity to discuss more temporal matters. Perhaps you can be my saviour! Why don't you take this manuscript and read it and then we can compare thoughts, next Sunday or the Sunday after. Whenever you can get back.'

'But surely the manuscript will be missed and you would get into trouble if it was known you gave such a valuable item to a mere soldier?'

'I can deal with that, and you do not strike me as a mere soldier. Mere soldiers do not read at all, let alone Latin. You are doing me a favour. Go, take it and you can spend the rest of the day reading if you like.'

Peter needed no urging, but was still reluctant to take the manuscript away. The monk got up and, bidding Peter farewell, walked slowly into the monastery, leaving Peter with the manuscript still on his lap. Peter left the grounds of the monastery and walked into the countryside to find a comfortable place to sit, and there he read until he could not make out the words on the page in the failing light. He had not eaten or drunk. He did not notice the passing of time. He was enchanted by the unfolding story written so beautifully.

On returning to the castle, he stowed the manuscript carefully away in his belongings, well out of sight. Privacy in
the soldiers' quarters was fairly non-existent and it was an
unwritten rule, fiercely held, that a man's belongings were
his alone and no one would touch them, not even to move
them when the hut was cleaned. Each man cleaned and
tidied his own space where he kept his spare clothes and
trinkets.

There was little time during the week of training to escape
the eyes of his comrades in order to finish reading the manuscript, so the next Sunday when he sought out the monk,
he had read only half of it. Nonetheless, he had read enough
to be able to discuss his thoughts and exchange views with
the monk, learning how to interpret the text to bring out
hidden or suggested meanings in the words. Both he and
the monk missed the church service, seemingly more interested in the words of the ancients than the Word of God,
and it was not until mid-afternoon that the monk left Peter
to go back to the monastery, while Peter continued reading.

6

For the next six months Peter trained with the others during the week and spent most Sundays with the monk, reading and discussing various manuscripts or texts he gave Peter to read. One saint's feast day – of which there were many – fell on a Saturday and unusually the men at arms were given that day as well as the Sunday off. Peter took the opportunity to run back to his village and spend a night with his parents. They were delighted to see him and explained everything which had happened in the village, mapping out Peter's future when his stint with the baron was over. After tearful farewells, the following day he ran back to the castle and with every step he became more and more certain village farming life was not for him. But what was? He equally knew that he would find no comfort in being a soldier, even if he were to rise through the ranks as William had done. The church, perhaps? No. Far too restrictive, and the old man had sown sufficient seeds of knowledge for Peter not to be overawed by the church. He mentally shrugged. Something would come up.

Training continued and moved on to the use of the bow. While the crossbow was extensively used by men at arms, William did not favour it. Although its range was greater than the ordinary bow, it took much longer to load. Every villager could use an ordinary bow to some extent and Peter did not have to pretend too much that he had no expertise. The bow used was the English bow, far inferior to the Welsh bow with which the old man had trained him. The English bow's range and penetration was less than the Welsh bow and, it seemed to Peter, its accuracy was also wanting. Peter was not the best shot among the new recruits, but when he tried hard he was very close. Approximately a third of the baron's forces were bowmen and although under normal circumstances Peter's accuracy would have marked him out to join this band, William did not permit it, maintaining that Peter was too young and did not have the physical strength. To some extent this was true, as bowmen developed a very high upper-body strength which would have taken some years for Peter to achieve.

During this time the new recruits were fitted out with their fighting clothing: conical metal helmets with nose protection fashioned by the blacksmith, but needing to be padded inside by the men to fit comfortably; thick leather jerkins onto which were sewn metal plates to act as some protection; leather breeches held tightly to the lower leg by cloth strapping and boots. Each man had his own dagger and was given an axe and pike, both of which required sharpening. Shields were small and round, made of wood and hardened leather. Bowmen had their bows and arrows, supplemented by a shield and axe to use at close quarters. Although only the nobles owned good swords, William had a number of rough metal swords for the men to train with. He said that on the battlefield a fighting man had to be able to use whatever was to hand and also, if they could learn the fundamentals of sword fighting, then this would help when they were using an axe or pike against a swordsman.

The routine of this life, into which Peter fitted quite happily, was broken one rainy morning with the arrival at the castle of a courier on horseback. He went straight to the baron, but his speed of approach was such that everyone in the castle knew that whatever news he was bringing was of an urgent nature. Sure enough, within a very short time William was summoned to the baron and when he came back he sized up his men with a grim face. 'I have taught you well,' he said. 'I hope you have also learned well, for today training is over and we are going to fight for real.'

A murmur passed through the soldiers' ranks. Some were eager, the experienced were cautious, and most felt apprehensive.

'Go and get your equipment and some food from the feeding hut; we will assemble here within the hour.'

As they moved off to gather their things, squires were racing about getting their masters' horses ready and knights were appearing from the castle. The knights at least were keen to do battle. Well before the hour was up, all had assembled. The baron on his horse was in the lead, the knights and squires behind him, followed by the fighting men at arms with servants scrabbling at the rear with equipment, food and essentials for the baron and knights. They headed out through the rain, leaving only half a dozen old soldiers to guard the castle, and marched steadily all day. They paused only briefly at noon for a handful of food and by nightfall reached a large plain where, in the distance, Peter could see an army camping. So this was the battlefield. Too late for any fighting that day, they made camp, lit fires and warmed through the food they were carrying. The baron and knights had tents pitched for them to sleep in, but everyone else had to stay in the open air. At least it had stopped raining. Conversation that night was muted and restrained. Each man had his own thoughts, knowing that after the morrow some of them might never see another dawn.

William walked around his men giving words of comfort and encouragement, telling them that they were far better trained than those clods who would be facing them the next day, and victory would be swift though the battle might be hard.

When he reached Peter's group, Peter asked, 'Why are we fighting? What is it all about?'

'We are fighting because our master commands us to fight. That is all you need to know,' replied William.

'But surely, if we were told the reason, that would give us greater strength of purpose. Not knowing the reason for doing something will not bring out the best in us.'

The men around Peter nodded. William scowled. 'You are too clever by half, young man. Too much imagination causes a man to lose his purpose and tomorrow we have only one purpose, and that is to fight and win – which we will do.'

Peter continued to look at William, expecting him to say more. William scowled again. 'If you really must know, Baron Fortiscue has decided he wants our lands and villages, so he is raiding small manors to chip away at our holdings. Luckily a loyal man sent a messenger to us, so we can stop this usurper in his tracks before he can gain more support and more fighting men. If we do not do this, then you will be under the less benign rule of another baron. Is that purpose enough?'

All the men nodded and stiffened their backs in resolve. Everyone knew Roger de Cours was basically a kindly man and, while he suffered no backsliding from his men and peasants, he was understanding. Most barons were not and many were simply cruel. This indeed was a good reason to fight.

The reason for the battle swept around the camp and by morning, each man was ready to fight for Roger de Cours with every last grain of strength in his body. The mood was buoyant and positive.

The troops assembled in the usual pattern. The baron was in the centre with his knights on horseback and the squires on their own horses behind. The foot soldiers were divided into two equal groups, deployed on each side of the mounted nobility. Archers were behind the foot soldiers, ready to shower their opponents with arrows until the two sides became too close to distinguish accurately between friend and foe, and at that moment the archers would join the battle with their axes.

Peter was stationed on the right, his colleagues a mixture of new recruits and experienced fighters. William was assigned to Peter's side of the battle and this gave Peter much comfort. William walked slowly up and down, speaking quietly to the men to take their minds off the impending slaughter. Roger de Cours was in no hurry and everyone waited and waited. It seemed that Roger did not want to take the first steps.

William eventually stopped in front of Peter. 'Well, young fellow, you can see the battlefield and the men we are going to be pitted against. What would you do?'

Peter was taken aback. He frowned and shook his head as if not understanding.

'Come on. You seem to be able to size things up. Do you have any suggestions, thoughts?'

Peter cleared his dry throat. William waited expectantly. 'Well,' Peter said. 'If you look towards where we are going to do battle, on our side, in the middle there, the grass is rather spiky and looks a little longer than the grass around it.' William looked and nodded. Peter continued. 'That sort of grass only grows where there is a lot of water.' William looked at Peter with narrowed eyes. 'We have had fairly continual rain for the past week, though it has stopped now, and if I am right, then the area with the spiked grass will be waterlogged, perhaps a little marshy. If I was able to suggest anything, I would make sure our opponents cross that ground and we do not, for if it is waterlogged, it will be difficult to walk through and could slow a man down and make it almost impossible to manoeuvre. So if we are in position on the dry ground, then we have the advantage.'

William's eyes narrowed even more while he considered what Peter had said. 'But if the ground is not marsh, then we will be behind the baron and out of position.'

'True, but not far behind. I can say with some certainty that the ground will at the very least be soggy and so will slow down anyone crossing it. I was a shepherd and I know grass. If the baron advances more slowly than the other side, then our being behind him can be kept to a minimum.'

William grunted, looked long and hard at the terrain ahead and walked slowly away towards the baron. The men around Peter were silent, but being mostly farmers could understand what Peter had observed and were inwardly seeing sense in what Peter had said. Peter watched William approach and speak to Roger de Cours. The baron looked at the area Peter had pointed out and turned to speak to the knights around him. The conversation did not last long and William came back to his men.

'The baron has agreed. When we move off, we will do so slowly and try to entice the fighters on the other side into that wet area. I hope you are right, lad. I've taken a big chance on you.'

Still they waited. The horses seemed to be eager to get into the fight, stamping their hooves and shaking their heads, but the knights held them back. Peter was beginning to think Baron Fortiscue was not at all eager to pitch his men into a battle. Both sides seemed fairly evenly matched. Baron Fortiscue had the same number of horsed riders but, if anything, a few more foot soldiers.

Then, as the sun appeared behind clouds which had been threatening more rain, so there was movement from Baron Fortiscue. Peter could detect no signal to advance, but the opposing army started forward at a steady walking pace. Baron de Cours remained still. When less than a hundred yards separated the two armies, Baron de Cours gave the signal to advance and everyone moved off, at a slow walking pace. There was no dip or slope in the ground ahead to give advantage, so the two forces converged slowly and Peter could see that they would most likely both reach the spiked grass area at the same time. How, then, to get the other side there first? Baron de Cours was not a baron for nothing. He gave an order and all the knights lowered their lances and raised their shields in the fighting position, but did not increase their pace of advance. This lowering of the lances ready to charge was detected by Baron Fortiscue, who gave the same order and immediately spurred his horse forward, believing that Baron de Cours' actions would be accompanied by the start of a similar charge. Baron Fortiscue's foot soldiers also broke into a run. Only when it was clear that the enemy soldiers would reach the marshy area first did Baron de Cours and his knights also charge, with the foot soldiers following.

Peter did not watch the clash of the nobles, but concentrated on the fighting force ahead of him. He was right. The spiky grass was marshy and Baron Fortiscue's foot soldiers ran headlong into the soggy ground, which slowed their advance and made it difficult for the men to keep a fighting formation. With William in the lead, Peter's force hit their opponents just before they reached the drier ground. Far too hampered, out of breath with the effort of crossing the marshy land and unable to step forward, back or to the side with any degree of haste, they were easy prey for the de Cours fighters, who impaled man after man on pikes, hardly needing to resort to close-quarter axes. In no time at all, the men in Baron Fortiscue's left flank were dead or seriously injured. William summoned his men to the left, over firm ground, towards the centre of the battle where the knights and squires were fighting it out.

The surprise arrival of William's force meant that Baron

Fortiscue's knights and squires who were still on horseback were vulnerable to the pikes of the foot soldiers, a complication they certainly had not expected so early in the battle. However, once the knights realised Baron de Cours' foot soldiers were amongst them, they quickly changed tactics and grouped together, fighting both the de Cours knights and the foot soldiers. The knights were battle-hardened and Peter soon realised the wisdom of William's words that to suppress skills was to blunt them. For the first few minutes, Peter had difficulty parrying and avoiding the cuts and thrusts of the knights' swords. After one particularly fierce blow on his shield that almost knocked him to the ground, Peter took a step back and concentrated. He was glad to find that very quickly his skills did return, and the combined weight of Baron de Cours' knights, squires and foot soldiers took its toll. In short order, Baron Fortiscue's knights were unhorsed, surrounded, outnumbered and ready to surrender.

Robert de Cours' left flank did not fare so well as the men under William on the right. They were holding their own, but suffered many casualties. However, once Baron Fortiscue's knights had surrendered, the cry went out and battle ceased. Each side stood still, looking at the other, as the men drew breath into aching lungs and lowered shields, swords, pikes and axes to rest weary arms. Baron Fortiscue, bloodied and defeated, formally gave up his sword to Baron de Cours and the knights and squires trudged slowly back to the de Cours camp, leaving the foot soldiers to follow. Before moving off, the de Cours foot soldiers relieved their opponents of their arms and valuables, then searched through the bodies lying on the battlefield, taking anything of value. Spoils for the victors. The badly injured were dispatched into the next world and those with wounds which would likely heal were treated and helped away. Any wound, even the smallest cut, could well fester and cause death, but there was always optimism for healing. Although moments before both sides had been attacking each other with the greatest ferocity, now the battle was over they helped one another, everyone knowing that come the next battle they might be in need of care and treatment themselves.

Peter, although splattered with blood, was unscathed apart from bruises, largely on his shield arm and shoulder. He helped bind his comrades' wounds – every man carried bindings into battle in case of need – but did not join in the plunder of the defeated. His first experience of battle was not enough to harden him to the point of searching the dead and wounded for things of value.

When all that could be done had been done on the battlefield, the foot soldiers wandered back to the camp, made fires and huddled around them, numb from the fighting. The initial euphoria of victory had worn off and each was contemplating his own experiences, mourning the loss of fellow fighters and realising how close death or serious injury had been. William, knowing well the after-battle effect, went around his foot soldiers, quietly praising and encouraging them, joking with them at some transgression or mistake in fighting technique he had noticed and sympathising with the loss of comrades. Peter was no different from the others and although he quietly admired William's abilities to raise the spirits of the men, he wondered if it was all really necessary. So much death and injury simply because of one man's greed. While the nobles might enjoy battles – indeed, their whole life seemed to be geared towards fighting – it was the foot soldiers who took the brunt of the carnage. He began to realise the wisdom of what the old man had said: England needed a strong king, even if that meant a tyrant, for this would keep the barons in line and stop such petty quarrelling which took men from their farms and villages to become the fodder of battle.

7

After the battle with Baron Fortiscue, spirits lifted quickly and Peter's comrades regaled each other with tales of courage and expertise, told mainly to keep their own confidence high rather than to impress the listener. Come the following Sunday, while Peter ached to go to the monastery and immerse himself in the world of words, he could not avoid going with his comrades to the town to celebrate the victory. They went to the usual hostelry, which they dubbed the de Cours ale house, ordered their drinks and expanded, to anyone who would listen, on the vigorous fighting and eventual triumph. By the end of the evening Peter wondered if he had been at the same battle, for the stories told did not relate in any way to his experiences and observations. William was with them and encouraged the story-telling, but gave no account of his own feats. From time to time Peter caught William's eye and they exchanged understanding looks. Both, it seemed, were not overly willing participants in the revelry, but understood their presence was necessary.

Buoyed with the fighting success and money to spend from the spoils, the men availed themselves of the whores who realised that this was a short time of plenty and congregated in the ale house from all around the town. Peter, not having robbed the dead, did not have very much money, but this was no disadvantage: all the men agreed that the cost of the ale, and later some bread and cheese, should be shared and if one of them was unfortunate enough not to have the money, then others would pay his share. This also went so far as the whores were concerned. Peter, by far the youngest and fairest of face, attracted the women who wanted either to mother him – for a price, of course – or simply to be with such an agreeable person. Peter had no desire at all to go with any of the women and although urged by his comrades and encouraged by the women, steadfastly refused. This did not save him from the embarrassment of having his hand seized by one of the women and shoved under her ample bodice – to the delight of his fellows.

By the time the ale house closed, all were drunk, and some very drunk. Helping each other, they staggered unsteadily and slowly back to the castle, singing loudly at first. As the castle approached and the effect of the ale wore off, so the merriment withered, and they all went gratefully into their respective huts to collapse on their beds.

Some two weeks after the battle, William took Peter to see the baron. Peter was not afraid or cowed, but wondered why he had been singled out and was a little apprehensive. They entered the great hall, where the baron sat on one side of the great fireplace, the baroness on the other, and various knights and squires were scattered around the hall on chairs or benches. The hall was clean, with new rushes spread on the floor, and smelled fresh. William walked Peter up to the baron, whose eyes had been on them both as they entered.

'So this is the young man,' said the baron. 'You seem to have a very keen eye for things.'

Not wishing to put himself in any difficulty, Peter replied, questioningly, 'My lord?'

'It was you, was it not, who suggested we hang back and lure Fortiscue's left flank into the marshy ground.' This was a statement, rather than a question, so Peter merely nodded.

'So then, we have to thank you for a somewhat earlier reso-
lution of the battle than we anticipated.' Peter said nothing
and looked at his feet. 'Do not try to be modest. You should
be proud. What made you so sure?'

Peter looked up at the baron and held his eyes. 'Before
joining your forces I was a shepherd, and it is important for
a shepherd to know about grass and ground if the flock is
to be tended properly.' The baron grunted, knowing that
Peter's village produced more sheep meat and wool than any
other village. Peter went on. 'Sheep might look appealing,
but in reality they are very stupid creatures. Even though
they ought to know marshy grass isn't very good to eat, they
still wander into it and the wet ground can cause foot rot,
so shepherds quickly get to know the different types of grasses
and soils which are best for the sheep or can harm them.
The ground on our side of the battlefield was typical light
marsh. In the height of summer it is completely dry, but after
prolonged rain it is yielding, perhaps very sticky. It seemed
to me better to have others treading in it rather than us.'

The baron grunted again and was silent for a while.

'What do you think, then?' said the baroness to the baron
in Norman French. 'Is this boy your lucky mascot, or is he
possessed with a spirit?'

The baron laughed and replied in French, 'He is certainly
no spirit and seems lucky. From accounts of his fighting abilities, he will make a fine soldier and if he has as much sense
as it appears, perhaps a leader of men.' The baron laughed
again, this time ironically. 'Mayhap I should be afeared he
will take over my position!'

The baroness blustered. 'Impossible. Do not say such
things. He is only a peasant, though I have to say, a very
pleasing-looking peasant. What will you do with him?'

The baron shrugged and turned to Peter, not answering
the baroness. Peter all the while kept his eyes on the ground,
pretending he did not understand what had been said.

'Young man, my Master at Arms is the best in the whole of England and I am grateful to have him in my service.' William stiffened slightly in pleasure at this unusual praise. 'He tells me you have fighting skills and I have seen that you can also think.' The baron looked around the hall at the knights. 'Too many men have much brawn and very little brain, so if you turn out to be any good, you have a future. Decar here has no real deputy. His sergeant is a good fighter, loyal to a fault, but lacking in imagination – so if you train well and use your talents, there is a possibility that I may in time be asking you to become Decar's deputy. It will take a long while, for even at your young age you are late to come to arms and you have much to learn. It is up to you.'

With that, not waiting for a reply from Peter, he waved a dismissive hand. William and Peter backed out of the hall, a manoeuvre required as a customary courtesy for a noble baron.

'What do you think, young Peter?' asked William when they were outside the castle.

'I am honoured,' replied Peter cautiously, 'but I do not know if I can come anywhere near the baron's expectations. It is much too early to make any decision.'

'I do not know how you came to learn how to use weapons.' William raised his hand to silence anything Peter was going to say. 'But I know you were not inexperienced when you came here and you show a natural talent with quick and good reactions. The baron is right: you can think, and I have seen you looking at everything, as if to question and understand.' He gave Peter a knowing sidelong glance. 'I suspect you do not spend your Sundays in the monastery on your knees, but that is for you alone. I'll say nothing and the rest of the men do not care. What I would urge is that you use your skills and talents to the full. Do not pretend any longer that you cannot fight better than most of the other men. You can. If they say anything, then I will tell them that some men suddenly develop extra talent and determination after their first battle and that is the reason for your rapid improvement. Can we agree that from now on you will do your best?'

Peter was quietly pleased. It had been hard holding back and pretending to be inexperienced. It gave him no pleasure and absolutely no sense of the achievement he had become used to when he was learning from the old man. 'I will do my best,' he promised.

'Good. I am not going to show any favouritism or give you any privileges. You are still one of my men. I would, though, deem it a favour if you would tell me any thoughts or ideas you have. I might not agree, but I would like to know.'

'Agreed.'

'So then, any ideas?'

Peter laughed. 'So soon! I have only just said I will do my best.' He paused as they continued to walk towards the training area. 'Perhaps one. Have you ever thought of using the Welsh bow?'

'I have come across it fighting on the Welsh borders, but I have never actually tried one. Is it good?'

Peter replied cautiously. 'I have been told it is more accurate and powerful than the English bow, but it does need special training and great strength in the arms and shoulders to pull the string back to the ear so as to get the best from it.'

William grunted and thought. 'I can vouch for the power. Those renegades could pick us off at a distance far outside our own range. Even crossbows, which I dislike, could not reach them with any real effect.'

They reached the training ground and William went off to his quarters. The men had been training together under the supervision of the sergeant, but when Peter arrived, they stopped and crowded around him.

'So, what did the baron want?'

Thinking quickly, Peter replied with a not wholly inaccurate paraphrase of the baron's words. 'He said I was a lucky bastard that the ground was soggy, otherwise he would have had my head, and I should practise my fighting skills, not try to take over his position.' They all laughed and slapped Peter on the back, knowing that Peter had been right about that grass and that, deep down, they had a growing admiration for this youngster.

Training continued as before and an uninhibited Peter used all his skills in fighting to become the best with every weapon, lacking only the brute strength which was required to wear down an opponent receiving blows on the shield. The men accepted his prowess and, far from showing any jealousy or curiosity, redoubled their own efforts to try to beat Peter, or at least get him to make a mistake. The only resentment he received for a while was from the sergeant, who seemed to sense that his position was at risk. Peter spoke to William about this, and between them they convinced the sergeant Peter had no desires to remain at arms past his two-year conscription.

Soon after the start of Peter's second year with the baron's forces it was rumoured there was to be a tourney where the knights, and some squires, would fight each other to gain favour and reward. King Stephen was nowhere near Devonshire and as the best tourneys were those commissioned by, or at least attended by, royalty, no one really believed in the rumour. Furthermore, tourneys were usually held to celebrate an event – a betrothal, wedding or a major feast day – and none of those was imminent. However, the rumour was not false: a tourney was to be held in Somersetshire, hosted by Baron Gelling, who had invited all knights from surrounding counties to take part and the barons to contribute to the prize money. There was suppressed excitement among Baron de Cours' knights, but no enthusiasm from the baron himself. Although Peter was totally inexperienced in tourneys, he knew the events were spectacular and eagerly anticipated by the nobility, so de Cours' apparent reluctance was strange. Peter was sure it had nothing to do with the request to provide prize money, as de Cours was not a skinflint, so he approached William.

'Why is the baron not pleased his knights have been invited to a tourney? I thought all the nobility loved those events.'

William looked uncomfortable. 'It is not something we talk about.' Peter continued looking at William expectantly. Heaving a great sigh, William continued. 'The fact of the matter is that Baron Gelling does not get on with Baron de Cours. In both their fathers' time it was suggested that during a battle the old Baron de Cours wrongly took a prisoner who had been beaten and subdued by Baron Gelling's father and so got the ransom. The prisoner was particularly wealthy and the ransom was large, enabling Baron de Cours' father to purchase more land from the king and, effectively, have a greater empire than Baron Gelling. Baron Gelling's father appealed at once to King Henry. Baron Gelling was not popular, known to be cunning, cruel and manipulative, with a fierce temper, so few believed the accusation and when the king said it was not proven, Baron Gelling immediately swore revenge. Sadly, the current Baron Gelling has not only inherited all the bad traits of his father, but has also taken to heart the necessity for vengeance. So far, apart from the poison he spreads about Baron de Cours to anyone who will listen, including King Stephen, he has done nothing, but an invitation to his tourney would give ample opportunity for something underhand. Baron de Cours has a dilemma. If he attends, he is exposing himself and his knights to risk. If he does not attend, then he will be branded – by Baron Gelling with force – as a renegade, preferring his own wealth and comforts to sharing with other knights.'

'What will be done then?'

'We will go, there is no doubt. The knights are bursting to show off their expertise and although they know the difficult situation, they will hold a grudge if they do not go. Those sort of men just cannot understand anything beyond their own little worlds.'

Sure enough, a few days later Baron de Cours announced his attendance at the tourney and pledged a large sum in cash prizes for the winners of events. The knights were ecstatic and the following two weeks were spent in frenzied preparation of horses, weapons and equipment, all cleaned and burnished to make the right impression. In order to sharpen their skills, the knights not only jousted with each other, but also involved the foot soldiers in swordplay. As in the battle some months earlier, Peter was impressed with the stamina and strength of the knights. It seemed nothing for them to hack away with their swords at their opponents for hours. Peter had the opportunity of sword fighting with several of the knights. His skill and agility kept him out of harm's way, but the sheer force and power of the knights made it almost impossible to mount an attack, far less a successful one. Peter learned the value of the larger, kite-shaped shield of the knights, which gave far more opportunity to use the shield in attack to push the opponent away, not just in defence. He also discovered that the knights' chain mail hauberk deflected all but the most precise of sword thrusts. If he was ever to overcome a knight in a straight sword fight, he would need to improve his guile and hone his skills to ensure a wounding thrust actually reached its mark cleanly.

It was usual for the baron and knights to attend tourneys with a dozen or so of their foot soldiers, more for pageantry and to show off their strength than for any other reason, but on this occasion William not only picked his best men but also increased the number to twenty – sufficient to protect de Cours but not so many as to arouse resentment or suspicion in Baron Gelling. Peter was one of those chosen and all the men made sure that their helmets were burnished and tunics and breeches were clean. They were each given a shift emblazoned with the de Cours crest to put over their tunics.

The journey to Baron Gelling's estate in Somersetshire was undertaken with an air of excitement and anticipation. The knights, usually aloof from the common men, often slowed their horses to allow the foot soldiers to come alongside and engaged them in light-hearted banter. Even the servants bringing up the rear, guiding horses, oxen and carts with the tents and equipment needed, joined in with the anticipation of excitements to come. Peter was surprised that Sir John, whom he had bested in the village before he was recruited, was friendly to him and joked about Peter's fighting skills, showing no sign of malice or resentment. When Peter questioned William about this, William laughed.

'That man has the attention span of a gnat. Oh, he can fight like a demon and is the best jouster we have, but unless it's about his winning glory he is not interested. He barely notices anything going on around him and has probably forgotten all about what happened in your village, particularly because we all told him you played unfairly by attacking before he was ready! You and I know differently though, don't we?'

Baron de Cours' band was the last to arrive at the tourney, but a place was reserved outside Baron Gelling's castle for their tents. All the barons and knights mixed freely, with much laughter, slapping of backs and boasting of prowess. William encouraged his men to mix with the others too, but first gave them a very stiff lecture on their primary duty to Baron de Cours. He did not mention potential danger to the baron, but all knew of the bad blood between Gelling and de Cours and needed no urging to be on their guard at all times.

The tourney marquees were set up and the tournament area marked off. Tradition was that the jousting would be first and the Master in charge of the tourney was taking names and drawing lots for the pairing of the knights. It was a knock-out competition, with the winners of every joust pitted against each other until one knight was left. Not all put their names forward, some preferring to save themselves for single combat, which rarely resulted in death, but often led to injury, with the winner being declared either by judges or by the vanquished yielding. At the end there was to be the melee, where knights, squires and some chosen foot soldiers would fight as in battle, not as teams but as individuals. Knights and foot soldiers from one baron would not fight each other, but nor would they defend their comrades. Only at the very end would comrade fight comrade if there were no other baron's men left. Again, it was not a fight until death, as any man disarmed or forced to the ground would yield. The melee could last for hours, but to limit the time it was scheduled for the end of the day, so that the Master could legitimately call a halt when dusk approached. Those left standing and still armed were declared winners and given cash prizes. Because of the potential cash prizes, foot soldiers were keen to participate, although they knew that being less skilled and more lightly armed than the knights or squires, their chances of still standing at the end were slim.

There was a further day of preparation before the tourney began, with everyone helping to get the horses and arms ready. Surprisingly, William was not to be seen until late in the afternoon. He appeared at Peter's side while Peter was helping a man called Paul from another baron's force to stack the knights' lances in random order. Knights could not joust using their own lances, but had to accept the lance given to them to ensure there was no unfair advantage.

'When you are ready, come and speak to me,' said William.

Peter finished the stacking and wandered over to William, who was sitting under a small tree away from everyone else, sharpening his dagger. Peter sat down next to him.

'It has taken me all day, but I've pieced together what is going to happen,' said William. 'I thank God I was raised speaking French, for I could listen in on conversations which the Gelling nobles thought I could not understand.' He paused and thought. 'Gelling has a new champion, Sir David. A big brute of a man who has never been bested in the joust or in single combat. Where this Sir David came from, I could not find out, but he is firmly behind Gelling. The plan is to arrange the jousting so that Sir John and Sir David are the winners of their jousts and will face each other in the final. There is always a risk that either of them might not make it through, but it is unlikely as both are really good and even without these arrangements I would be surprised if Sir John was not in the final joust.

'The lances are blunted for jousting to avoid serious injury, but Sir John's will be sharpened – not completely, but enough to give an advantage if Sir John makes a clean strike. Sir David is confident that he can avoid a clean strike and best Sir John. If he does, then not only will he be the winner, but Sir John's sharpened lance will be "discovered", he will be branded as a cheat and this will reflect on de Cours. If Sir David loses, then it will be worse, for a winning cheat is more hated than a losing one. I do not think, though, that Sir David would go so far as to lose his reputation by being willingly beaten.'

William paused for thought again. 'The problem is, I cannot tell Sir John, for there is no way he will enter the jousting knowing that his opponents have been picked so he can likely win. It would be against his honour and he would make a big fuss before the jousting. As nothing could be proved, it would look as if Sir John was trying to avoid jousting and cast a slur on Gelling who at this moment, being the organiser of the tourney, is a very popular man.' William stopped speaking and looked at Peter expectantly.

'If it is going to be arranged that the lesser-skilled jousters are to be matched against Sir John,' said Peter, 'then it is possible that with Sir David facing the more skilled, he might not make it through. So if, as you say, it would be a disaster to tell Sir John before the joust, I suggest we do nothing and wait and see. We must assume, though, that Sir David will be in the final joust, so the key is the sharpened lance. Somehow, we must substitute this lance for a blunt one. I've been stacking the lances and have got on well with the Master of the tourney, so while I would probably not be allowed to actually help in handing out the lances, I could easily be in the area with no suspicion and make as though I am there to assist if needed. I can identify the sharpened lance and if we can cause a diversion just before it is being handed out, there is a good chance I can switch lances. If all else fails, I can "notice" the sharpened lance and point out this unfortunate mistake before it is given to Sir John.'

William grunted. 'Not foolproof, is it!'

'No, but it is the best I can think of at the moment. What I would urge is that you tell Baron de Cours now and explain to him what you have planned. He might come up with a better solution, but at least he will be forewarned and will not say anything to Sir John for the reasons you have already given.'

Another grunt from William. 'You are right. I will seek him out now.'

William got up and walked slowly towards de Cours' tent and Peter went back to the stacks of jousting lances to renew his friendship with the men there.

Later in the evening, William spoke to Peter.

'I have told him. He was livid but not at all surprised at anything underhand from Gelling. His first inclination was to leave the tourney, but he realised there was no way he could make allegations without proof, so his leaving would be viewed as a weakness and his knights branded as not courageous enough to face other knights. He approved of the plan and said that he would arrange the diversion.'

With nothing more to be done, they both went to their beds.

The following morning was bright and sunny with a clear blue sky. Nothing could be better for a tourney. The foot soldiers donned their shifts emblazoned with the de Cours crest and squires and knights busied themselves preparing for the first event. Peter made his way to the lances and continued to ingratiate himself with those around, laughing and joking. Bets were being placed on the jousting knights and Peter wagered a small coin on Paul's knight, for it seemed that Paul would be assisting in the handing out of the lances, even if he was not in charge. Peter had no idea who this knight was, or whether he was any good, but pretended to be swayed in his decision by Paul's powerful boasting of the knight's prowess.

Soon the nobility appeared. Barons and their ladies, with attendant ladies-in-waiting, seated themselves in the covered marquee directly opposite the centre of the jousting area where the jousters would clash. All were in their finery and made a dazzling sight with many bright colours. Last of all to arrive was Baron Gelling with his wife and daughters. Peter was immediately taken aback. He expected the evil man to look evil, but it was not so. Gelling was tall, taller than average, with a well-proportioned body, a shock of thick fair hair, blue eyes and a very appealing face. As he smiled to all around him he looked far from an ogre and Peter wondered whether in fact William's account of the baron was true. He could not dwell further on this thought, however, for once Gelling was seated, trumpets sounded and the knights paraded before the nobles, giving the usual homage.

Leaving the jousting area, the knights went to their horses. The first pair mounted, were given a lance by their squires and made ready fifty yards from each other. At the signal of the Master of the tourney, both horses were urged into a gallop and with lances levelled the knights charged. At the first pass, lances struck shields but neither rider was unseated. Wheeling their horses around without a pause, they charged again and this time one of the knights was unhorsed. Loud cheers came from the squires, foot soldiers and spectators standing around the arena. With little ceremony, the second pair arrived in the arena. Peter, although fascinated by the joust, was more intent on looking around to understand the pattern of the lance allocation. It was certainly random. Paul took the next lance and handed it to the waiting squire, who gave the lance to his knight once he was mounted on his horse. Unless Paul was in on the sharpened lance switch, there seemed to be no opportunity to change the random selection. Paul was quite happy for Peter to help and Peter could not see any lance which looked other than blunted. The only way a lance could be switched was by a squire, and no Baron de Cours squire would be party to such deception.

Soon it was Sir John's turn and his squire dutifully took the randomly selected lance from Paul. But it was not Sir John's own squire. This was a man Peter had never seen before. Where had he come from? Where was Sir John's squire? The squire carried the lance to Sir John, who took it from him without a glance. Peter did not wait to see the joust, but walked swiftly away to find William.

'Sir John's squire is not his squire. He is a man I have never seen before. Do you know what has happened?'

William looked startled. 'No idea. It is news to me. Go back to the lances and I will find out.' William hastened away and Peter returned to Paul who, enthralled by the joust, had not noticed Peter's absence.

'Your Sir John dispatched his man with a cunning shoulder blow. Perhaps I should change my wager to Sir John?' said Paul.

'Probably a lucky strike. Stick to who you know,' replied Peter.

The jousting continued all morning, with some of the jousts lasting for several passes before one rider was unhorsed or yielded. Sir David was indeed a brute of a man, large in every sense, with a huge chest and shoulders supporting a bull of a neck and an enormous head. His mere appearance seemed to overawe his opponents, who did not last long against him. Peter noticed that Sir David did not sit still in his saddle, but just as his lance was about to strike, he threw himself forward with all the force of his enormous upper body, adding weight to the strike which was rarely parried by his opponents. Sir John was equally clinical in wining his jousts, but with more grace and style which endeared him to the cheering and knowledgeable crowd.

It was a long time before William appeared and Peter was becoming worried.

'In short, Sir John's squire has been racked with stomach pain all night and could not get out of his bed this morning, so Sir John took a substitute squire offered by – you've guessed it – Baron Gelling. I have, with some difficulty, managed to tell Baron de Cours. I told him not to bother with a diversion. I will sort out the squire. You stay here.' Peter raised an enquiring eyebrow. 'Leave it to me,' retorted William, striding off.

As Gelling had planned, both Sir David and Sir John won through to the final round. Before that took place, however, the midday meal was served, with nobles moving to another marquee where meats of all kinds were laid out. Knights, squires and the men also broke away from the jousting arena to have something to eat. Peter made his way towards Baron de Cours' camp to seek out Sir John. He had no intention of telling Sir John of the plot against him, but thought he could pass on some information which might be of use. Sir John's substitute squire was nowhere to be seen and Sir John was sitting on a stool eating a large hunk of meat without a care in the world.

'May I speak to you?' asked Peter.

'Why not?' Sir John continued eating with his eyes on Peter.

'Your final joust is against Sir David, Baron Gelling's champion.'

'Why do you bother me with things I know already?'

'Well, I am sure you have noticed this, but I think he has a weakness.' Sir John said nothing, but stopped eating and his eyes bored into Peter. 'You will have seen that he increases the force of his lance's blow by lunging forward in his saddle just before the lance strikes. As well as getting extra weight into the strike, his moving body upsets the aim of his opponent, and in most of his jousts the opponent's lance has gone over his shoulder. His shield covers most of his upper body and as he leans forward into the blow, more of his body is behind his shield, making it very difficult to hit him in the body.'

'I have noticed this,' said Sir John, going back to his meat. 'But so what? I just have to be more accurate.'

'I have no knowledge of jousting and hesitate to suggest that it might be better if you did not aim for his body at all.' Sir John spluttered, trying to shout something with a mouthful of food at this upstart boy, even though it was extremely bad manners to speak with food in the mouth. Peter went on regardless. 'If you were to hit Sir David's shield at the top, slightly to the right of centre – his right, that is – then the force of the blow would be greater because he is thrusting himself forward and if the lance glances off the shield, it will go upwards and left, because of the angle you are striking, towards his head. He will not be expecting that and may not get his head out of the way in time.'

Sir John stopped spluttering and looked at Peter long and hard. Peter could see Sir John's mind working, slowly evaluating what Peter had said. William was right, Sir John was not the sharpest of men.

'Hmm. I'll see.' Sir John went back to his food, ignoring Peter, who took this cue to walk away.

After a hasty mouthful of food for himself, Peter went back to the lances and was soon joined by Paul.

'I should have changed my bet for Sir John,' said Paul. 'Although from what I have seen of Sir David, it seems he is the better. He needed far fewer second passes to defeat his man than Sir John.' Peter smiled, but said nothing.

When the nobles had eaten, they returned to their seats and after much blowing of trumpets, Sir David and Sir John strode out into the arena to bow to the nobles and the eagerly waiting crowd. They walked towards their horses and, once mounted, trotted to their allotted end of the joust run. As they were doing this, their squires appeared to fetch the lances. Peter watched Paul give out two blunt lances and barely suppressed a smile when he saw that Sir John's squire was not the man who had been there before. William had already taken care of things and there was going to be no lance substitution.

The first clash between Sir David and Sir John was uneventful. Sir John's lance swept harmlessly over Sir David's shoulder and Sir David's blow was skilfully deflected by Sir John's shield. The second pass was the same. It seemed to Peter that Sir John was not really trying to hit Sir David at all, but was concentrating all his efforts on deflecting Sir David's lance. Others in the crowd, more knowledgeable than Peter, also sensed a lack of endeavour by Sir John and there were quiet murmurings.

The horses wheeled for the third pass. Sir John's lance, steady as a rock, was again angled for a shoulder strike – a strike doomed to failure as Sir David lunged forward. However, at the last minute, with effortless grace, Sir John changed the angle of his lance towards Sir David's shield and also thrust his body forward into the blow. Sir David noticed the change of angle, but thrust too late and in trying to move his shield position his lance wavered and struck Sir John's shield only a glancing blow. Sir John's lance hit the top of Sir David's shield, deflecting off and upwards, striking Sir David with full force in the centre of his helmet. Had the lance been sharp, the blow would have pierced the metal and killed Sir David outright. The blunt lance merely dented the helmet, but it did knock Sir David unconscious. Amazingly, although unconscious, Sir David remained seated, slumped on his horse, which continued charging past the jousting run and towards the crowd of watching people. They scattered hastily in all directions. Sir John wheeled his horse for the fourth pass, but Sir David was being carried away by his still running horse. By not appearing for the fourth pass, Sir David had forfeited the match.

The crowd, at first stunned by the turn of events and not least by the fact that Sir David's unconscious body was still on his horse, set up a mighty cheer. Those who understood jousting realised that Sir John had deliberately led Sir David into a trap – and Baron Gelling's face was a mask of fury. He was well aware that his sharpened lance plan had not worked, and he had seen his champion bested. However well Sir David might recover from the blow to the head, there was no way he was going to take any further part in the tourney that day. In the fury of that face, Peter saw Gelling's true character and no longer doubted what William had told him.

The afternoon's single combats went off without major incident. As usual there were a few wounds, but Baron de

Cours' knights acquitted themselves well and received their cash prizes amid the cheers of the de Cours men. Baron Gelling, without his champion, was in an ill temper, which was not improved by Baron de Cours' knights achieving more success than those of any of the other barons.

Before the melee there was a break for a light meal. William took Peter aside. 'De Cours has told Sir John of the plot and has given me specific orders for the melee. I know it is not usual, but all our knights, squires and men are to stick together, defending each other as far as possible but not making it obvious. This will reduce any chance of last-minute skulduggery by Gelling. Now his champion is out of it, I would not put it past Gelling to try something underhand in the melee, so we have to be prepared. I will be in the melee with four foot soldiers. You will not.' Peter grunted disappointment. He was sure he would have been chosen and would have welcomed the chance to do battle when, unless there was a very ill turn of luck, no one would be killed. 'No, you are to stay out of it and hold the rest of the men as close to us in the fight as you can get without becoming a part of the melee. If there is anything underhand, you will be able to judge whether these extra men will be needed. It will be regarded as a very poor show if you and the men are involved, but better that than one or more of our knights being killed.'

Peter gathered the non-combat men together and told them to have their shields, lances and axes ready in case of need. He did not want to say in so many words that Baron Gelling might try something underhand, so he told the men that Sir David had recovered consciousness and was spitting venom because he was not fit enough to take part in the melee, and had therefore encouraged his knights and men to harm Sir John. Whether indeed Sir David had regained consciousness Peter did not know, but then nor did anyone else.

The melee was just that. Upwards of a hundred knights, squires and men fought each other and it was difficult to see if there was any pattern or movement which could indicate the de Cours men were being targeted. They kept fairly close together, but not so close as to raise suspicions that they were watching out for each other. Peter got his men to move slowly around the arena to be as close to the de Cours fighters as possible, but he was at a loss as to what to look out for and wished that William had stayed out of the melee. Having seen many melees before, he would have spotted anything untoward more easily than Peter. Others too were moving about to get the best view of their own champions and encourage them to greater effort.

Peter looked around in desperation and his eyes alighted on Baron Gelling, who was only half watching the melee. His attention seemed to be on something behind Peter. Peter turned around and saw a number of foot soldiers in Gelling's livery standing idly next to the food marquee. Unusual, Peter thought. Everyone else was crowded around the melee shouting encouragement to their men. Peter looked back at Baron Gelling, who at that moment nodded towards his men. Trying not to draw attention to himself, Peter turned again and saw Gelling's men walk slowly from the marquee towards him and towards the Baron de Cours fighters. No one noticed and anyway, as so many people were moving freely about, it did not look at all suspicious.

What was their intention? Gelling's men could not do anything outside the melee and if they were to join in, it would be a severe breach of the code of honour and would not escape attention. The sun, although sinking in the west, was still bright and it provided the clue. As Peter watched the Gelling men walk slowly towards him, he saw the sun glint off chain mail worn under a livery shift. Foot soldiers do not have chain mail, only knights. Peter looked carefully and saw that at least two of the men wore chain mail. It became clear. These knights were going to join the melee behind Sir John's knights and attack from the rear. All that was needed was a small diversion and the knights could strip off their shifts and join the melee unnoticed.

The diversion was quick in coming. Two horses bolted into the crowds immediately opposite where Peter was standing, scattering men hither and thither as grooms chased after the animals. The horses, bred for battle, were not diverted by the melee and charged into a number of the fighting men who were knocked to the ground. All eyes were on this and the spectators were in uproar at the unwarranted interruption to the spectacle. As soon as Peter spotted the horses, he shouted to his men and moved towards Gelling's men, who were by that time gently forcing their way through the crowd to the front. Peter and his men had no such compunction and thrust people aside to get to Gelling's band. One knight was stripping off his shift and another, already disrobed, was being handed a shield by someone obviously planted in the crowd.

Screaming at the top of his voice, Peter lunged forward and hit the disrobing knight on the back of the head with the flat of his axe, knocking him to the ground. The other knight wheeled around, drawing his sword. Peter made as if to swing his axe at the knight, but held back the blow so that he could avoid the countering sword lunge as the knight's shield parried the axe. Peter attacked again, with the same result. By this time Peter's men had caught up with him. Although they were armed, Gelling's band were not expecting to be challenged and suddenly found themselves outnumbered, surrounded and at the mercy of the pikes and axes of Peter's men. Discretion dictated that they should stand still and not seek to draw their weapons.

The attention of the crowd around Peter was drawn from the bolting horses to the fight of foot soldier against knight. Whatever happened next, there was no way any Gelling knight could join the melee without being seen, so Peter had achieved his objective. He stepped away from the knight, offering no challenge, and the knight, looking over his shoulder and realising he could not now join the melee unobserved, lowered his sword and slunk away, together with the felled knight who had struggled to his feet. Peter told his men to let the Gelling group go, and they too walked away.

Peter was not sure if the crowd around him knew what the Gelling knights had intended, but the fact that they had approached the melee disguised as foot soldiers was enough to start a murmur. Capitalising on this, Peter shouted 'Cheats!' to the backs of those retreating. The refrain was picked up by his men and then by the crowd. People not in the immediate vicinity were startled by the chant and moved around to find out what the fuss was about. Soon the word spread that knights without honour were trying to take advantage by joining the melee late, when others were tiring, and although no one was brave enough to accuse Baron Gelling, many suspected that his knights had been involved.

Attention had been well and truly distracted from the ongoing melee and the Master of the tourney grasped the fact that things could get out of hand, so immediately called on the trumpeters to sound the end of the melee. The Master strode into the middle of the fighters, saying that as this melee was one of the best ever, it was appropriate to award prizes to as many men as possible, so the judges had decided to stop it now. Those in the melee had no idea what had been occurring outside their immediate fighting zone and so cheered this generous decision. The cheers were taken up by the spectators, who although a little disappointed the melee had been stopped early, realised that additional prize cash would be welcomed by the fighters, who themselves would be generous to supporters.

While this was happening, Peter drew his men away from

the area and told them to scatter into the crowd but to keep an eye on him in case they were needed again. Peter hoped that by not staying where he had fought the knights, he would not be picked out when calm descended. He took off his emblazoned shift to make himself less conspicuous and when he saw the melee breaking up and the fighters moving away, he walked quickly back to the de Cours camp, where he was met by Sir John's squire looking pale and weak.

'What was all the fuss about down there?' asked the squire.

'Some horses bolted into the melee and following the confusion the Master of the tourney called a halt to it and said prizes would be given to all the men left standing.'

'Oh, and I was not there! What ill luck. I could have made it, but I was told I was too ill.' The squire staggered away back to his tent.

Before long, all the de Cours knights, squires and men returned to the camp. Those who had been fighting still did not know about Peter's intervention and many, far too engaged in fighting, did not even realise that any horses had bolted. William did not know either, but immediately drew Peter aside and asked what had happened. After Peter had explained, William was silent, thinking.

'What is going to happen next? I think we can assume neither the knights nor Gelling's men are going to say anything, for if they do, they will have to explain what they were doing. Your surrounding the soldiers could be brought up and you could be accused of being hostile, but having two disguised knights in the group is unheard of and I do not believe Gelling would take the chance. Assuming that no nobles saw you, any reports from the crowd would be unsubstantiated and could be dismissed as fantasy brought on by the excitement of the melee. I think we will be all right. What do you think?'

'Well,' said Peter, 'Baron Gelling's plans have twice been thwarted and from what I have seen of him, I cannot believe he will let things lie. He is bound to find ways of turning it against us. For example, if he says we attacked his men without provocation and denies that any knights were with those men, it is only my word to the contrary. I doubt we could now find anyone in the crowd who saw what happened and even then, there is no real evidence the knights were going to join the melee. I am afraid we may have to force things a bit, but by doing so we will make a bigger enemy of Gelling. Will you take me to Baron de Cours so I can explain to him what happened? If everything does go wrong it would not be fair for you, as Master at Arms in charge of us, to take the blame.'

William considered this for a while. It went against the grain not to take responsibility and he was slightly uncomfortable a junior – indeed, *the* most junior – soldier was outthinking him, but then again, without Peter's abilities and actions William could well be mourning the death of some of his knights. Even his own death could have resulted.

'Wait here. I'll go and see the baron.'

After a tourney it was the custom for a big feast to be held at the castle with all the nobility, knights and squires attending, so Baron de Cours was preparing himself by dressing in his best clothes. He was not pleased to be interrupted by William and if William had not insisted, almost to the point of rudeness, he would not have listened. William outlined what had happened and suggested Peter ought to be seen so that the baron should know precisely how events had evolved. Then, if anything came up during the evening's feast, de Cours would be ready with an answer. The baron needed no further persuasion, so Peter was called for and he explained everything he had seen and exactly what had happened.

'As I said to the Master at Arms, there is no real proof of all this except for my word and that of our men, so if you are accused of ordering, or allowing, your men to threaten

Baron Gelling's men and he denies any knights were with them, you are bound to appear at fault – for no one can deny that we did surround his men and hold them.'

'And you have a solution to this?'

'No. I have a suggestion you might consider.' De Cours looked at Peter expectantly with a slightly lopsided smile, as if to humour him. 'From Baron Gelling's position he could see there was a large crowd around where I was fighting his knight. He also heard the crowd shouting "Cheats!" when his soldiers left the area. It seems to me, then, it would not take a great deal to convince Baron Gelling that your men and the crowd saw the disguised knights, and you have the names of some in the crowd who could identify one of the knights. If this was said to Baron Gelling in such a way as not to implicate him, but merely to "pass on" the information so that he could make his own enquiries into who infiltrated his troops and sought to disrupt his tourney, he would not accuse you of anything, because he would know that if enquiries were made, you might come up with information to condemn him. The downside is that he will know you know it was he who hatched the plot, but I'm afraid I can't think of anything which will stop that.'

Baron de Cours' lopsided grin broke into a full smile. 'Nice. But what happens if he asks for the names of the people in the crowd who can identify the knight?'

'He will not. If he does, we will have to make up some names. By the time he finds out the names are wrong, we will be long gone.'

The baron dismissed William and Peter and made haste to complete his dressing for the feast. He left his tent and got a servant to summon the knights and squires to go off to the castle. This was unusual, for all the barons tended to time their arrival to make the most impact. The first to arrive would be unseen by the rest and the last would likely find the feast already started and no one would take any notice of their arrival. So it was that the barons usually arrived at about the same time, trying to be the latest, but not too late. When the knights and squires were assembled, the baron addressed them. He did not tell them anything about his intention to tell Gelling he had information which could uncover the miscreant knights, but reminded all of them of their unpopularity with Gelling and advised that they should eat well, drink little and constantly be on their guard for any trouble. It was far from unusual that these feasts became brawls as the effects of the wine led to boasting and rivalry.

So warned, they mounted and rode in a stately way to the castle, where grooms were waiting to take the horses as they dismounted to enter the castle's great hall. Baron de Cours was greeted warmly by Baron Gelling, who was all smiles and affability, though his eyes were cold. He joked with the knights and congratulated them on their success at the tourney, even laughingly referring to his 'oaf of a champion who couldn't get his big head out of the way of Sir John's lance'. Baron de Cours noticed this 'oaf' was not in the hall for the feast and concluded he was still suffering from the blow he had received. This gave de Cours a certain amount of satisfaction.

Before any other baron arrived, de Cours drew Baron Gelling to one side. 'Can I have a private word before the others arrive?'

Baron Gelling grunted assent and they both walked away from the knights, de Cours slipping his arm through Gelling's in a comradely way. Gelling stiffened, but de Cours pretended not to notice.

'When I arrived for the tourney,' began de Cours, 'I heard a rumour that someone was planning to cause trouble and upset proceedings. I thought little of it as there are always rumours, often rumours of rumours.' He laughed. Gelling stopped walking and turned to de Cours. His face was expressionless, but his eyes looked like dagger points. 'I was a little concerned when Sir John's squire took ill. He is usually most robust, with a stomach like iron, and I could not believe this was a coincidence, but then you very generously gave one of your own squires to Sir John, so I dismissed it from my mind. However, my men reported to me that during the melee two knights, if indeed they were knights, tried to disrupt it by sneaking in late and, of course, fresh.' Baron de Cours paused and shuddered at the disgrace of it all. 'We do not know who could possibly plan to ruin your tourney and I can not but think that the unusual escape of those horses might have been a part of the plot. Luckily my men spotted the two knights before they could enter the melee and managed to stop them. It was unfortunate your men were in the area at the same time and I must wholeheartedly apologise that my men drew weapons and held your men at bay. I have spoken to the man in charge and he said that he thought your men would believe there was a private fight going on and join in to restore the peace, so letting these impostors escape. Sadly they escaped anyway. You probably heard the crowds jeering as they ran away.'

Gelling grunted. 'I do not know what happened. I was going to ask you about it this evening.'

De Cours smiled. I bet you were, he thought. Aloud, he continued, 'Although they got away, my men had the presence of mind to take the names of some in the crowd who saw the incident and one of them said they recognised one knight. I was furious that anyone could be so underhand and dishonourable as to try to enter a melee halfway through and I was going to investigate, but I thought that as it was obviously you whom someone was trying to upset, for it was your fine tourney, you should be the person to do the investigating. If you send someone to my Master at Arms tomorrow, he will provide the names of the witnesses.' The baron said nothing about the knights wearing the Gelling crest on their shifts.

Above his smile, Gelling's eyes flamed with hatred and loathing. He had not only been caught out with his scheme to provide Sir John with a dishonest squire, but also de Cours knew full well that the knights were his men.

'I thank you for this information,' he said stiffly. 'I will make the fullest of investigations and personally cut out the heart of the man who planned this atrocity, bringing disgrace on our honour.'

At that moment – it could not have been better timed – a baron and his entourage entered the great hall and Gelling excused himself to greet the new arrivals.

Satisfied that enough had been said to ensure there would likely be no more treachery that evening, de Cours made light conversation with Gelling's wife while the hall filled up with barons, knights and squires.

The evening passed off well, with the usual merriment and the inevitable brawl at the end, which the de Cours knights and squires avoided. Gelling was an impeccable host and in his perambulations around the table to speak to the various barons, he did not avoid de Cours as he glowed in the congratulations and gratitude of his guests for such a fine tourney.

Although all were late to bed, de Cours and his men were up early, striking camp to go back to Devonshire even as others were just emerging from sleep. There was much waving and banter as the group moved off.

8

The de Cours band arrived back at the castle with no difficulty, making good time. All were pleased at having attended
the tourney, particularly as the de Cours knights had distin-
guished themselves. Nothing was said about Baron Gelling's
attempted treachery. If the knights and squires were offended
that honour, so important to them all, was broken, then they
shrugged it off. The common men were not concerned with
a knight's honour.

The days and weeks once again fell into the usual pattern
of training and leisure. The only difference was that William
had obtained some Welsh bows and the bowmen in the
group started to practise with them. Indeed, anyone who
wanted could have a go and Peter was not slow to try. At
first they all had difficulty drawing the bowstring steadily
back far enough to gain the fullest power and holding it
there to sight for accuracy, but once the technique was
mastered, the Welsh bow became a favourite and William
was able to convince the baron to get more. In time, three
quarters of the bowmen were armed with the Welsh bow
and, because of the bow's abilities, took particular pride in
using it accurately.

Most Sundays, Peter went to the monastery to read scripts
and discuss their meaning with the monk. Many of those
scripts were religious, but some set out the rules of nobility

and the laws of land ownership, tenancies and possession. A strong friendship developed between the two, but the monk would tell Peter nothing of his background or why he seemed to be exempt from the usual rigours of attending prayers and masses. Peter also continued to go to the ale house from time to time, largely to be a part of the fighting group rather than for personal pleasure.

After some months, rumour began to spread that Baron Gelling was up to no good. There were always rumours of one sort or another – men seemed to feed on them and find some comfort. Real news was slow to come and infrequent, so rumours filled the gap.

Six months were left of Peter's conscription in Baron de Cours' army and he was beginning to wonder what he might do next. He discussed this with his monk friend, who failed to advise him, simply saying that when the time was right, Peter would know what to do.

The pattern of daily life changed when rumour turned into news. Baron Gelling was, it was said, on the move to challenge Baron de Cours in battle for the 'slights' on Gelling's honour perpetrated by de Cours. Peter assumed that those slights were perceived as a result of the tourney, but knowing precisely what had happened and being convinced of de Cours' total innocence, he could not understand why Gelling was pursuing the matter. He sought out William for an explanation.

'It is Gelling being Gelling,' said William. 'As I understand it, and so far as I can glean and so far as anyone here can understand it, Gelling is maintaining that de Cours orchestrated an attack on his men to bring dishonour to the Gelling name and that he later made up the tale about disguised knights to try to cover up the unsuccessful attack.' Peter raised his eyebrows in disbelief, but before he could say anything William continued, 'It is said that our leaving the tourney early in the morning after the feast meant that we had no intention of giving the names of witnesses to the attack and that could only mean those witnesses would identify de Cours' actions as being totally unwarranted. Furthermore, the horses which caused the diversion belonged to the de Cours knights and that proves the intention to dishonour. That bit *is* right: they were our horses. The grooms were intent on watching the melee and left the horses, which they say – and I believe them – someone else let loose and drove into the melee. Very clever of Gelling to think that far ahead. Whether or not Gelling is actually on his way, I do not know, but we must prepare for the worst.'

Training was intensified, arms and equipment double-checked and made ready. Knights and squires also prepared themselves. All waited, with no hard news, until a Gelling messenger arrived one evening. His approach was steady and unhurried and he took the letter he was carrying straight to de Cours. The letter blatantly accused de Cours of trying to dishonour the Gelling name and challenged him to battle, as such dishonour could not be quenched simply by personal combat. In truth, it was not a challenge but a declaration of war. Baron de Cours quietly read the letter and slowly dictated a reply for his scribe to write. He denied any act of dishonour and said that following such a successful and popular tourney it was a shame Gelling had been so misinformed, but with reluctance de Cours was bound by his honour to accept the challenge. The messenger was given the usual courtesy of a bed in the castle for the night and, with his horse fresh, he returned to Gelling the following morning.

While the messenger was still in the castle, nothing was done in the de Cours household. Everything was calm and orderly. As soon as the messenger was out of sight, however, de Cours sprang into action.

'That miserable, underhand Gelling is already on his way to us! His messenger's approach was too slow, timed to be in the evening so that we would have little time to prepare. We cannot simply defend the castle, as Gelling will lay all our lands to waste, so we must meet him in the field. At least it will be in our territory and, mayhap, we can choose the place.'

With that he sent out fast riders with two horses apiece to find out where Gelling was and, with the second fresh mount, to ride back quickly with the information. Knights, squires and soldiers were called to get ready to leave the castle as soon as the scouts returned. Baron de Cours did not want to leave the castle undefended until he was sure Gelling had not split his troops – one section to goad de Cours into a fight and the other to attack the undefended castle. He did not believe Gelling would be so imaginative, but thought he was sufficiently underhand to try something.

Two days passed before one of the scouts reappeared. He reported that Gelling's army was large and two or three days' march from the castle. The other scout was checking other routes to see if there was a second force on its way. After some thought, de Cours calculated that if the Gelling force was large, it was unlikely he had split it, so he instructed the Sergeant to select six men to remain at the castle to defend it if necessary, and to redirect the second scout to meet up with de Cours once he returned. The order was given and the de Cours battle force set out towards the approaching Gelling.

Everyone soon knew Gelling's force was sizeable, although William played it down. As the de Cours knights had already demonstrated at the tourney they were better than Gelling's knights, he said, it was logical that Gelling would enlist more knights to even up the odds – but the de Cours forces were superior in every way, so there would be no problem defeating this mad army. Although buoyed by William's words, the men were apprehensive nonetheless, knowing that the forthcoming battle would be hard and lives lost. They had all had at least one experience of battle, so they knew what to expect and how to stick together when fighting.

Peter did not view the impending battle with any enthusiasm. He was not frightened, and certainly did not show his feelings to others. Once again he thought how stupid it was that a perceived honour, whether validly motivated or not, should cast men into injury and death, particularly when those whose honour was being offended or defended were unlikely to be killed themselves, but at worst perhaps injured, or merely captured and held for ransom. Deep in his own thoughts as he marched behind the knights and squires on their horses, he was interrupted by William.

Speaking quietly, William said, 'I reckon you have as much enthusiasm for this as I do. Bloody stupid men. If there is a real grievance or real danger, then we fight, that is the way of things, but not for this stupidity.' He heaved a sigh. 'No matter. We have to do our utmost and if the report of the size of the Gelling army is right, more than our utmost. Any fine ideas this time?'

Peter laughed, drawing the attention of the men around them. William scowled at them and they backed off. After a short silence, Peter replied quietly, 'We are going to be outnumbered. The form of the battle will likely be the same as it always is – knights and squires in the centre, troops on each flank with archers split behind.' William said nothing. 'The knights and squires will fight each other and we will fight the foot soldiers, only helping the knights and squires if we manage to vanquish those in front of us.'

William let out a deep breath. 'So you tell me what I already know?'

Peter was silent for a while. 'I tell you what everybody knows. This being so, can't we rewrite the rules a bit?' William said nothing, but looked at Peter, waiting for him to go on. 'You know our strengths. First, we are likely to be better trained than Gelling's men, so unless we are extremely unlucky, we ought to best them, even if we are outnumbered. Second, and I believe this is the most important, we have a weapon they do not have: the Welsh bow, with greater range, penetrating power and accuracy. So why don't we use it in a different way from what is going to be expected?'

'How?'

'Normally, the archers shoot their arrows mainly at the other foot soldiers, because at the distance they let fly, an arrow would likely not penetrate a knight's chain mail. Also, an arrow from an English bow that hits a horse does not do great damage, and certainly does not kill the horse. But, as we have the Welsh bow, why don't we change our formation a bit and have some of the bowmen concentrate on the knights, or rather the knights' horses? The horses are big targets and with the penetration and range of the Welsh bow, I reckon we could kill a fair number of horses, and Gelling's knights on foot would be fairly easy meat for our own knights. At the very least, it will even up the odds.'

William thought for a moment and smiled. 'I like it. I don't know if Baron de Cours would like it, though, as it might smack of dishonour . . .'

'Well then, do not tell him. He knows the bowmen will eventually be shooting at the knights and horses anyway, and if horses are suddenly killed we can explain later that we did not realise the power of the Welsh bow. I doubt he will actually believe us – he is far too clever for that – but it will be an acceptable answer. Also, I would suggest the remaining Welsh bowmen are used differently. Instead of being behind the foot soldiers, when we start moving forward why not send them out on a run on each flank, a little forward of our lines? As the Welsh bow has greater range, the arrows will hit the foot soldiers earlier and the extra accuracy with the bowmen on the flank, rather than behind us, will mean that when the foot soldiers clash, the rear lines of Gelling's foot soldiers will not be masked and so our bowmen can hit them.'

William grunted as he was thinking this through. 'There is still a chance of our own men being hit.'

'Yes, well, that raises the last thought I have. There is a limited supply of arrows, so the Welsh bowmen should be instructed not to shoot unless they are absolutely sure of a hit. Any doubts, wait and look for another target. This will give us greater advantage, for normally arrows are shot at the enemy haphazardly in the hope that the mass of men means there will be hits. Take out this uncertainty. Better to have half the number of arrows if every shot hits a target.'

William broke into a broad smile. 'I like it. Let me think it through a little more.' With that, he resumed his position in the marching ranks.

They camped that night and were up early the following morning. The scouts sent off during the night reported back. Gelling's men were directly ahead, a day's march away. The number of Gelling's men had not depleted and it appeared there was to be no trickery: Gelling expected his superior numbers to win the day. Baron de Cours set off with his men behind him, moving briskly towards Gelling. By mid-morning they were close to a very large flat field and de Cours directed his men off the road to set up camp ready for Gelling to arrive. Scouts continued to come and go, reporting Gelling's movements. The scout who had been sent out to go around the countryside to discover whether Gelling had split his forces also returned and reported that there were no soldiers anywhere else. So a straight battle it was to be.

No sooner had camp been set up, than Gelling's forces appeared with Baron Gelling riding in the front with his knights around him. There was a slight intake of breath from the de Cours men when they saw the size of the Gelling force. It was almost two to one. Even William looked a little taken aback.

The usual couriers were sent out to meet each other halfway between the two forces to carry the barons' messages, one to the other. Baron de Cours asked if the perceived slight was sufficient to sacrifice so many men on both sides. Baron Gelling was adamant that battle should take place. By the time these formalities and forced courtesies were over, it was well into the afternoon, so there would be no battle that day. The forces would be thrown at each other the following morning.

The place de Cours had chosen, and in effect forced upon Gelling, was good. The ground offered no advantage to either side and de Cours had camped in such a way as to allow Gelling to marshal his troops so that the rising sun the following day would not blind either of them. It was a perfectly honourable position which none could criticise.

That evening's meal was eaten with forced jollity, each man encouraging his fellows, and indeed himself, to be buoyant for the impending battle. All thoughts of death or injury were banished, but would return as the night wore on and each man tried to sleep. William, as before, was constantly moving among his men, encouraging them and playing down the size of the Gelling force. 'Three quarters of them are obviously untrained peasants. You can see this yourself from the way they carry themselves. They are going to be more of a hindrance to Gelling than a help. Just remember, lads, do not take pity on them because they are such a shambles.' They were fine words, believed by some, but said with such conviction that all spirits were lifted.

After they had eaten, William came over to Peter. 'I've asked all the bowmen to move quietly away from the camp and go towards that wood behind us, so that you and I can instruct them on what to do. I have said nothing to de Cours and if he notices we are absent he will just assume I am giving extra encouragement to some. It's not unusual. Make your way to the wood, and I will follow.

Peter did as he was bid and in less than an hour all the bowmen had assembled, with the Sergeant also present. The Sergeant would be in charge of the left flank foot soldiers. William outlined the plan and gave specific instructions to each man. When the de Cours forces moved off, a quarter of the Welsh bowmen would move towards the knights and as soon as Gelling's knights were in range, they would shoot the horses. The remaining Welsh bowmen would be split into two and run out to each flank to take up positions to shoot. He repeated his instructions so that everyone had it clear in their mind. At the end he turned to Peter. 'Do you have anything to add?'

'No, just to emphasise: Do not shoot unless you know you are going to hit. This is the most important thing. We are outnumbered, but if every one of your arrows hits a man, not only will you drastically reduce the fighting force against us, but also they will see comrades hit and falling each time an arrow is loosed and this is very demoralising. In fact, if you are lucky and can reduce the front rank significantly, those following behind, who are bound to be the less trained peasant fighters, will not have too much heart for a fight.'

With nothing more to say, they slipped back into the camp. There they told their comrades that William, as usual, had a plan which would make things easier for all of them.

The following day dawned bright and sunny with barely a cloud in the sky. Neither army hurried to prepare. They were waiting for the sun to rise so its rays would not affect either side in the battle: honour to the fore. By mid-morning the knights and squires were mounted and the troops deployed in the usual formation on each side. No one noticed that de Cours' Welsh bowmen were split, with the greater number of them on the edge of the flanks rather than behind. Both armies moved forward, stopped and waited two hundred yards from each other. Horses kicked the ground expectantly, knights and squires sat still and rigid in their saddles.

'At this distance, our Welsh bowmen could pick off their front line without any trouble at all and kill a horse or two,' William said to Peter. They were both together again on the right flank.

'Certainly, but all that would do would be to make Gelling retire and charge from a greater distance and we would lose the advantage of picking them off at close range while they were still at walking pace,' replied Peter. William grunted.

Then, at the same time, both armies moved slowly forward, reducing the gap to less than a hundred and fifty yards. There they stopped once more. Gelling's standard bearer lowered his standard to show they were ready for battle, and de Cours' standard bearer did the same. Yet another honourable and traditional move.

'Ready, lads?' said William.

The signal came and de Cours started moving slowly forward, gradually increasing the pace ready to change into a gallop. Gelling did the same. All was set for the traditional battle. As soon as de Cours started moving, however, his Welsh bowmen ran at full speed forward and further away to the left and right flanks. Peter saw that de Cours himself had noticed this, but it was too late to do anything about it: the advancing pace was increasing. Just before the horses on both sides broke into a gallop, the de Cours bowmen started shooting. Immediately, three horses on Gelling's side went down, pitching their riders onto the grass. Gelling's first line of foot soldiers were also hit and before the foot soldiers reached a run, Gelling's front line was decimated.

Baron de Cours, his knights and squires charged at full gallop, signalling to the foot soldiers to break into a run. 'Run slowly, lads!' screamed William, wanting to allow more time for the bowmen to have an uninterrupted line of sight to the Gelling men. The inevitable clash between foot soldiers came and to a large extent William and Peter were proved right. Gelling's rear lines were indeed less well trained and, having seen their comrades felled by long-distance, accurate bowmanship, they were unnerved and uncertain. Fight they did, but they were not a match for the onslaught of William's trained men and many turned and ran. Seeing this, Peter moved to his left towards the knights and squires. The bowmen had done their job: many dead or dying Gelling horses lay on the ground. Swiping aside with his axe any foot soldier in his way, Peter moved to the centre of the knights' action. Few were now on horses, and just about every knight and squire was on foot battling it out man to man with swords clashing on shields. Peter came upon a Gelling squire apparently besting a de Cours squire and hit him a mighty blow on the back of the head with the flat of his axe. Then he moved on to the next pair.

Before he could get involved, the de Cours knight knocked the Gelling knight to the ground and it seemed to Peter that he was in complete control. However, the fall of this man meant that Peter could see ahead, and what he saw chilled his blood. Baron de Cours was on the ground and above him stood Baron Gelling, raising his sword above his head for a fatal blow. Gelling was clearly not intent on taking de Cours as prisoner for ransom. He was going to kill him. Without a thought, Peter sprinted the short distance and threw himself at Gelling, knocking them both to the ground. Peter rolled away and got to his feet, expecting de Cours to be on his feet as well, but it was clear that de Cours had been dazed, and his movements were slow and sluggish.

Peter immediately moved towards Gelling to engage him in fight. Gelling, on his feet as quickly as Peter, was snarling with rage. Revenge had been snatched from him by a mere foot soldier! He rushed at Peter, swinging his sword at Peter's head to dispatch him without ceremony. Peter, seeing the intention, did not retreat as Gelling expected, but moved forward into the blow, which he took on his shield before the full momentum of the swinging sword arm could reach its full force. Nonetheless, the weight of the strike was sufficient to knock the unbalanced Peter to the ground. He rolled away from Gelling and spotted de Cours' sword lying very close. He dropped his axe and took up the sword as he leaped to his feet.

This changed the odds a little and gave Peter a chance – but not too much of a chance, as Gelling was bigger, stronger, more experienced and propelled by the overwhelming rage which still showed in his face. Peter's puny shield had been largely shattered by Gelling's first blow and was now useless. He shrugged it off. Perhaps the odds had not changed after all. Gelling came at Peter again, this time with less rage and more determination. Peter deflected the sword thrust relatively easily, but was knocked to the ground once more by Gelling's shield. Peter was right in his earlier observation: the knight's shield was as much for attack as it was for defence. Rolling quickly to his feet, Peter did not wait, but advanced on Gelling, knowing that his thrust would be parried by the shield and that Gelling would then use his sword. Peter was ready for this: his thrust was weak and, keeping his balance trim, he stepped outside Gelling's swing and managed to bring his own sword back to hit Gelling's sword arm. No blood was drawn, but Gelling was shocked by the move and stood still, eyeing Peter.

'Being your usual cowardly self again, I see, and attacking an inferior?' The voice came from de Cours, who was by this time on his feet but swaying about, still under the influence of the blow which had felled him. 'Leave him and come and fight a real man,' he said. 'Give me my sword.' It was a command that Peter should not ignore, but he did.

'No, my lord, you are in no fit state. You give me your shield. I'm sure Baron Gelling's honour would demand that I was armed as equally as he.' Peter almost held his breath, expecting a tirade from de Cours, but surprisingly, Gelling burst in first.

'Yes, give him your shield. When I have finished with this upstart, I will finish my business with you.'

For a while there appeared to be an impasse. All around, the fighting was at its height, but there seemed to be a little oasis of calm around these three men. Baron de Cours loosened the straps holding his shield and gave it to Peter, who put it on his arm. He tightened the straps as best he could, but the shield was not made for him and the fitting was far from ideal. It was better than nothing, though. When he was ready he advanced slowly towards Gelling. De Cours sank to his knees, too weak to stand, but keeping his eyes glued on the two combatants. Peter hoped he could hold out long enough for de Cours to gather his strength.

Peter, always the thinking man with a plan, had no plan now. He knew he was outmatched in every way. Simply retreating and defending could not save him against one so experienced. If I cannot retreat indefinitely, thought Peter, all that is left is attack. So he attacked, carefully giving full force to his blows, but not with all his weight behind them. He remembered his observations of months ago that the only possible way to overcome both the skill and the chain mail of a knight was to deliver a single accurate thrust. He had one chance. If he failed, Gelling would not fall for it again.

So they battled. Peter's natural agility helped him to move outside or around the Gelling blows he could not take successfully on his unfamiliar shield. He attempted a couple of times to use the shield in attack, but he had neither the power nor the experience to trouble Gelling. A plan formed in his mind. Peter defended or avoided two Gelling blows, then attacked with his shield and sword together. Gelling easily withdrew his sword arm from Peter's attacking shield and parried Peter's sword blow with his shield. Again and again he followed the same pattern, but each time Peter's attack was less strong. Gelling sensed Peter weakening and bided his time. Why waste skill and effort on someone who was likely to collapse with exhaustion anyway?

Peter made another move, barely forceful enough to be called an attack, and Gelling's face broke into an evil smile. Then Peter started panting as Gelling attacked in return, and made as if to fall over. Gelling attacked again, and Peter only narrowly avoided the flashing sword. He then made a visible effort to gather himself for another attack and launched himself once again at Gelling, shield first, followed by his sword. This time, however, he withdrew his shield at the last moment and held back his thrust, allowing Gelling to start to move his own shield across his body to knock Peter's sword aside, so exposing his own right shoulder. With lightning speed and maximum power, Peter thrust his sword into Gelling's right shoulder, cutting deep through the chain mail and disabling his sword arm. Withdrawing the sword, he swiped the flat of the blade against the side of Gelling's head, knocking him to the ground.

'Yield!' demanded Peter, pointing his sword into Gelling's throat. Gelling choked with anger and disbelief, hatred streaming from his eyes. 'Yield!' repeated Peter, putting more pressure on Gelling's throat.

'I yield!' spat the knight, knowing that Peter was not bound by any code of honour and would almost certainly kill him. Peter withdrew his sword and allowed Gelling to get to his feet, taking hold of Gelling's sword so that he could not rearm himself.

Baron de Cours was on his feet now, still a little unsteady. Peter gave him back his sword, but held on to Gelling's weapon, which he kept pointing at the defeated knight. 'You know what to do with him now – I do not,' said Peter. Baron de Cours nodded and Peter unstrapped the shield and handed it back to the baron, turning away to find another adversary.

The battle was virtually over. The knights and squires saw that Gelling was captured and they too surrendered, realising they could not retreat without losing honour. The Gelling foot soldiers immediately stopped fighting too. It was a victory for Baron de Cours – and, as Peter saw from the battlefield, a fairly conclusive one. He was amazed at the efficiency of the bowmen, for bodies with arrows sticking out were littered everywhere. As in the previous battle, once it was over each man helped the others to bind wounds or to dispatch men to their Maker if the wounds were too bad to heal. Then came the stripping of the bodies of all valuables.

Peter walked away tired but uninjured. He got back to camp and sat down next to the burned-out camp fire, too weary to do anything. Others slowly drifted back, each with stories of their deeds and experiences. Peter smiled and encouraged them, but said nothing of his own adventure. William was the last to return, having made sure that all his wounded men were taken care of.

'How did it go, young fellow?' he asked.

'The usual,' Peter replied. 'Just glad to be alive and not injured.'

William nodded. 'We can all say that. I have to say, our bowmen were absolutely brilliant. There is no doubt they changed the course of the battle and they will be the toast of the troops at the tavern on Sunday.'

Peter laughed. 'I doubt we will hear the end of it!'

9

Peter was right. The bowmen described over and over again every detail, every arrow, every hit. They were elated. Often treated as the last-minute support contributing little to the battle, they were now the toast of every man. The Sunday ale house celebration was more raucous than it had ever been before and no expense was spared. They had the best of everything. The whores were delighted, helping the men to eat the meats and drink the ale as well as encouraging them into bed. Peter once again politely refused the services of the girls, and although they pouted in displeasure, the other men lavished enough money on them to keep them happy.

The only problem came at the end of the evening. One bowman, the best and acknowledged to be the senior, had drunk his way through jolly inebriation into a state of forceful command and control, a spit away from ugly hostility.

'We know it was your idea to put us on the flanks,' he slurred to Peter. 'It was like shooting at a target. We could not miss. These Welsh bows are absolutely fantastic. The greatest pleasure of my life. Me and the lads are determined you should be well rewarded. We have bought you the best girl in the town. You cannot refuse! It would be an insult to us.'

Peter laughed and tried to distract the man from his intent, but the drink was turning him nasty. The last thing Peter wanted was a fight, particularly with one of the heroes of the battle. William came to the rescue.

'Come on, Matthew, leave the lad alone. I'm sure he is grateful to you, but let us face it – the best whore in town? She is wasted on him! She needs a real man, one with experience, a hero even. Why don't you take her, then you can tell Peter what he has missed?'

William's authority and logic got through to the drunken Matthew and he grabbed the young girl and dragged her upstairs to one of the bedrooms. Truth to say, but for the girl helping him up the stairs, he would have collapsed in a drunken sprawl and never made it. Indeed, a few moments later the girl reappeared, indicating that sleep and the bed were a greater pull than her young body.

Back from a successful battle or not, the daily routine did not change. Men were training almost at once after William had grudgingly given them two days to rest – that is, two days staying around the castle and not going to the town. Towards the end of the second week after the battle, William called Peter to him.

'The baron wants to see you, by yourself. I suggest you go there now and do not lose any time.'

Peter walked into the castle, entering the great hall where, as before, the baron was sitting in a chair on one side of the empty fireplace and his wife on the other side. This time the baron did not look at Peter. Peter stopped in front of him and waited. Without looking up, the baron said, 'Well, you are a turn up, aren't you? Not only did you save my life, but you managed to defeat Gelling in straight combat. Then there's the business of my archers.' He looked straight at Peter then. 'I suppose you expect me to be grateful.' This was said as a statement rather than a question.

Peter remained silent, but eventually said, 'My lord, I was

merely doing what any of your servants would do: what is the best for you. I was lucky and luck doesn't need gratitude.'

The baron looked away and was silent.

'You have to tell him,' said the baroness in French. De Cours grunted.

'Of course, but what do you think he will do?'

The baroness shrugged.

De Cours turned to look at Peter again. 'Do you know what happens when a baron or knight, sometimes a squire, is captured in battle?' he asked.

'Yes. He is ransomed.'

'Yes, but do you know what our code of honour demands if the captured baron or knight has breached his honour and tried to kill an unarmed knight?'

'No. I did not know there was any difference.'

'There is, a big difference. If a knight's honour is breached by his wilfully trying to kill another knight in battle, the ransom is doubled, and if the killing is of a defenceless unarmed knight, the killer forfeits his horse, his weapons, his clothing, his chain mail, his tent and everything he brought to the battlefield.' Peter nodded, but did not understand why the baron was telling him all this. 'By rights, all ransoms should go to the baron, who distributes the greater portion to the knight or squire who took the knight prisoner, but if a killing is prevented, then that person gets the ransom and all the knight's battlefield possessions. The baron is entitled to nothing.' The baron looked once again at the floor. 'In addition, the king can be petitioned to withdraw the knighthood from any knight breaching our code of honour in such a way.' The baron paused and looked across at his wife.

'Do you think he has got it?' she asked in French.

Too right I've got it! thought Peter, but he said nothing, pretending not to understand and looking bemused and innocent.

The baron turned and looked once again at Peter. 'You are entitled to all Gelling's battlefield possessions, the whole of his ransom and, if you want, I can petition the king to have Gelling reduced to nothing. He is disliked anyway and unless Stephen feels particularly vulnerable at losing Gelling, it is impossible to think that he will not lose his knighthood. He will never be allowed to regain it and will be ostracised and driven from his lands. So, lad, you are a rich man and have Gelling in the palm of your hand. There is no way he can deny trying to kill me when I was down and unarmed.'

'Does everyone know of this bit of the code of honour?' asked Peter.

The baron thought. 'Well, the knights should know . . .'

He was interrupted by his wife. 'Pha! You give too much credence to those animals. Half of them know nothing at all beyond their own needs.'

The baron smiled and continued in Anglo-Saxon to Peter, ignoring his wife's outburst. 'Some of the squires might know and William knows far more than he ever lets on, so I would be surprised if it was a secret to him. As for ordinary men, no, they would not have the faintest idea.'

'Then it is very generous of you to tell me,' said Peter. 'You could have said nothing, perhaps rewarded me with a little, and I would have been more than grateful.'

'Did he say what I think he said?' asked the baroness. 'My Anglo-Saxon is nowhere near as good as yours and I understood him to say you could have kept your mouth shut.'

'Indeed,' replied de Cours. 'We seem to have a very unusual man here, and a polite one too.'

'Pfft!' puffed the baroness. 'No wonder Amelia spends half her time looking out of the window at this young man practising his fighting in the training area. We have to watch him.'

'Come on, my dear. Our daughter is only twelve and far too young for that.'

'Nonsense. Many girls of her age are betrothed and I want to make sure she is married to the right man. She is wilful enough as it is. Heaven only knows what she will do when this man becomes rich. I shudder to think. He is right – you should have kept your mouth shut.'

'No, my dear. You know that is not right. You would not have allowed me to profit in such a way.'

'It is true, but sometimes you really are too kind. Look what being nice to Gelling has led to. You were nearly killed!'

The baron smiled kindly at his wife and turned back to Peter. 'My wife thinks you are polite to have pointed out that I need not have said anything to you. What are you going to do?'

Peter's mind had been whirring from the moment he realised he could be rich. There was so much he could do, but then again, so much would be denied him. Not being of noble birth and unable to qualify as a knight, he would not be accepted by the nobility. He could make all his fellow villagers rich, but their life was farming, they knew nothing else, and if he took that away from them with wealth, what would they do?

'What I would like to do,' said Peter carefully, 'is to ask you to help me. That I trust you goes without saying. You have been kind to my village and during my time here at the castle I have never heard a bad word said of you.' It was unnecessary for Peter to have mentioned this, but he thought it would do no harm for the baroness to hear. Perhaps it might soften her towards him a little, although he had no desires towards Amelia, indeed could barely bring her face to mind. 'Therefore, I would very much like to finish my training with you here. I have only a few months left. I am learning every day and William is almost like a father to us all. When I finish my conscription period I would like to have six horses of my choice with saddles, provisions, weapons for up to six men and enough funds to sustain six people on the road for, say, a month. I would very much like you to give all your foot soldiers a special bonus of one month's pay in recognition of the tremendous job they did for us on the battlefield. As for Gelling's things, I would like his sword and chain mail, which I can get the blacksmith to alter to fit my somewhat slimmer body.'

'Is that all?'

'That is all I want. If I return to the castle here, then you may wish to consider giving me a piece of land on which to live and set up home, but that is not a request, far less a demand. Who knows what might happen between now and when I return – if I return.'

'Incredible!' said the baroness. 'Does he know how rich he could be?'

The baron was silent for a while, considering what Peter had said. 'So you wish me to keep the ransom, you receive only the requests you have made, and you are willing to trust that some time in the future I might give you some land. Is that right?'

Peter nodded. Again there was a silence.

'But what of Gelling?'

'My lord, indeed. What of Gelling?' Peter thought for a moment. 'If you were entitled to the ransom, would you consider, in the right circumstances, asking for the usual price rather than double?'

'In the right circumstances, I would consider anything. What might those circumstances be?'

'As yet, I do not know. Would it be possible for me to speak with Gelling?'

'Yes and no. I have no objection to your seeing him, but his arrogance is such that he may not speak to you, and anyway he cannot speak Anglo-Saxon.'

'If you were there and interpreted for me?' Peter did not want to admit his knowledge of French and although he was not too keen to have de Cours present, there seemed no other option.

'Let us go and try.'

The baron got up from his chair and started walking towards the staircase, beckoning Peter to follow. They went up to a small room in the turret where Gelling was lying on a bed gazing into space. His right shoulder was heavily bandaged and although he must have been in pain, his face was impassive.

'Gelling, you remember this man?' Gelling looked at Peter, but said nothing. 'He wishes to speak to you and I will translate what he says.' Still Gelling said nothing, although his eyes were fixed on Peter. Baron de Cours nodded at Peter for him to start.

'My lord, I have been told that I am entitled to your ransom, a double ransom, and your battlefield possessions, because I prevented you killing my lord de Cours. I can also arrange for a petition to the king to have you removed as a knight.' Peter paused while de Cours translated. No expression crossed Gelling's face and he stayed immobile on the bed.

Peter continued. 'This is a matter of your code of honour, and in the spirit of honour I am forced to say that in the press and excitement of battle I have no memory of your trying to kill my lord de Cours.' Another pause for translation. Peter saw a glint appear in Gelling's eyes – a glint of hope, or perhaps of an opportunity to take advantage.

'I am told as well that loss of memory from battle is merely temporary.' Translation. Gelling's eyes narrowed as he weighed up what was to come. 'It therefore seems to me only right that I should demand a single ransom for you and not petition the king. A slightly larger ransom than is normal, perhaps.' Translation. Still Gelling said nothing and his eyes narrowed even more as he waited to hear the conditions. 'As you will understand, there have to be promises on both sides. I will promise that if my memory returns, I will say nothing, but to safeguard myself I will dictate to my lord de Cours' scribe what I saw and will have two witnesses verify my mark on this document, which will be kept in a safe place – never, I hope, to see the light of day.'

De Cours translated word for word, without embellishment or expression. Peter let the ensuing silence run on until Gelling said, 'And what promise do you want from me?'

Peter waited until de Cours had translated. 'I want your promise to be more than that. I want you to swear on the cross of our Lord Jesus Christ, before witnesses, that you will never again take up arms against my lord de Cours, that you will never seek to do him any harm or evil, and that you will treat him as a brother and friend.' Translation. Peter could see the iron will that prevented Gelling from exploding. The knight was silent, but in that silence he was calculating all his options.

'What of my battlefield possessions? Can I have those back?' Again de Cours translated.

Peter smiled. 'My lord, no. While I am sure you would not break your sacred oath, it is always useful to have a reminder of it and my written account of your deeds would count for nothing if you returned with your battlefield possessions, for no baron or knight would allow this after the act you tried to commit. I understand that your horse was killed in the battle. It would not be unusual to lose a sword and shield when defeated, for who knows what person would pick them up and sell them? Your tent and possessions could easily be ravaged by a fire set by exuberant, unthinking peasant soldiers, and as for your chain mail, you could say it was damaged beyond reasonable repair, so you just left it behind. No one would question any explanation you want to give, unless it was being alleged those possessions were forfeit.'

De Cours translated slowly, making sure he did not miss

any word Peter had uttered. Gelling's expression conveyed that he fully understood that Peter had not lost his memory at all and would have no hesitation in telling the world what had happened if it was necessary. In truth, Gelling had no options.

'I must make it clear,' he said, 'I was not trying to kill de Cours. You are both mistaken, but I can see my situation has been made difficult by this conspiracy, so I will swear your oath and make sure the ransom is paid without delay.'

When this had been translated, Peter walked to the fireplace and took down the crucifix nailed to the wall. 'Can I suggest that Sir John is brought here as a witness?' he said. 'Not being a knight myself, I would not be counted as a valid witness for an oath.'

The last possible prop for Gelling had been knocked away from him. De Cours opened the door, shouted for a servant and instructed him to find Sir John and bring him there immediately.

While they were waiting for Sir John, nothing was said, but Gelling's eyes remained on Peter as he reflected on his ill luck in being kept from his revenge by someone he regarded as a mere boy.

Sir John arrived, was told that he was there to witness Gelling's oath, and Peter handed Gelling the cross. The oath was taken. Sir John and de Cours were satisfied and they left Gelling to his own thoughts.

When they returned to the great hall, the baroness was still in her chair and standing alongside her was Amelia. Peter looked casually at her and gave a polite smile. She did not acknowledge him. A noble's daughter! Amelia was very fair of face with a tall, graceful body hardly beginning to show womanly development yet.

'What happened?' asked the baroness.

'Later,' replied de Cours. He beckoned Peter to sit in his own chair at the side of the fireplace. Peter was reluctant, but de Cours insisted. The baron paced up and down for a while. He looked sharply towards his daughter, and she bowed her head and left them. Still the baron paced.

'For the first time in my life, I am at a loss. Apart from fighting skills and courage, you have shown a great insight into our way of life and handled what could have been a difficult situation with a diplomacy lacking even in most of the nobility. What am I to do with you!' This was not a question, so Peter remained silent. 'Tell me, why do you want the horses and arms?'

Peter broke into a broad grin. 'I really do not know yet. The request just sprang into my mind. Perhaps I have an idea there, but I do not know what it is yet. What I must say, though, is that I think my memory of the battle is returning and it would be a good idea if I saw your scribe and got him to write what I remember.'

The baron grunted. 'Yes, very wise. I will arrange it. As to your position now, why don't you reconsider taking all of the ransom? I will make you a squire. My own squire is soon to be a knight – although he was too busy getting honours on the battlefield to look after me, it appears.' De Cours laughed. 'And you can take his place. Although you would not receive the full training, in two years I will promise you I will get two of my baron friends to join me in recommending to the king that you be made a knight. Your wealth will help, for the king is always light in his coffers. I would suspect before that time you will be able to prove yourself in battle anyway, if not at a tourney.'

Peter was taken aback. This was an honour, so far as he was aware, totally unheard of. He did not know what to say. The baron sensed this. 'Say nothing now. Consider it for at least two weeks, longer if you like. Go now, see my scribe and come back to me when you have made your decision.'

Peter left the great hall to seek out de Cours' scribe, explained his purpose and then slowly recounted all he could remember of Gelling's attempt to kill de Cours. When he had finished, the scribe handed the parchment to Peter to read, but Peter shrugged and put it down as if he could not understand what was written.

'Can you please find two witnesses to verify my mark?' he asked. 'I suggest Sir John and William Decar. If I ask them, they'll turn me away, but they should listen to you.'

The scribe was not happy at being treated as a messenger, but Peter gave him his most charming smile and the scribe scurried away. When he had gone, Peter picked up the parchment and read what the scribe had written, in Norman French. The translation of what he had said was faithful, although Peter noticed more than one spelling mistake.

With the parchment witnessed, Peter took it and returned to the training ground. His fellows were curious and Peter made up a story about de Cours wanting to know how Peter had manage to tangle with Gelling during the battle. None appeared convinced, but Peter told them de Cours had indicated that they would all get a nice bonus in recognition of their bravery on the battlefield and this cheered everyone up – so much so they completely forgot all about Peter's interview with the baron.

10

The following Sunday, when Peter was with his friendly monk, the monk said, 'Next Sunday, go to the ale house with your friends.'

Peter was surprised and asked why, but the monk would say no more, other than emphasising that he would not be available on Sunday.

The next Sunday, Peter told his companions he would be going to the tavern. 'But,' he said, 'it is a long time since I have had a good run, so I will run there and you can walk at your usual slow pace.'

The men had long since accepted Peter's way of doing things and, apart from having a good laugh, said nothing. Peter started out first thing in the morning. At first, he had difficulty adopting the pace and relaxed gait he had always enjoyed. William's training had strengthened Peter, put muscle on his frame and taught him new skills, but long-distance running was not on the timetable. Soon, though, he found a rhythm and started to enjoy the run and the countryside around him, breathing in the smells and laughing at the small animals scurrying away from his path in surprise. Before he reached the town, he deviated to run around it and eventually arrived, slowing his pace to walking as he approached the ale house. He was pleased he was not out of breath, although his legs were feeling the strain. He walked into the tavern, ordered a jug of ale and sat down to await his comrades, who would still be at least an hour away.

Lost in his own thoughts, Peter did not notice an old man, hooded and walking with the aid of a strong staff, come into the tavern through the side door and sit down with a jug of ale. Peter's reverie was only broken by three women coming noisily into the tavern and sitting together at a table just inside the door. Peter immediately recognised them as whores and thought he remembered seeing two of them before, but not the older one. How old she was would be anyone's guess. That profession did not preserve youth. Nonetheless, she was good looking and carried herself well. The women looked towards Peter and waved, but did not approach him, for they knew there was no trade there.

Peter went back to his thoughts, but was again jarred back to the present by three men, obviously foot soldiers from another baron, banging through the door. While soldiers from different barons tended to use their 'own' ale houses, it was not unusual for them to change or try a different place. Peter would have taken no notice but for the first big brute of a man striding up to the whores' table, smacking the older woman across the face and knocking her to the floor, shouting, 'Bitch of a whore! You stole my purse! I want all my money back now. If you do not give it back, I will beat you to a pulp!' He leaned down, pulled the woman up from the floor by her bodice and smacked her across the face again.

Before he knew what he was doing, Peter jumped to his feet and dashed across the tavern, shouting, 'Just a minute. Leave her alone!'

The man snarled, let go of the woman and turned to face Peter. 'You are her guardian, are you? Well, you pay me, or I will beat her until she does.'

'If this woman has robbed you, as you say, go and make

a complaint to the constable of the town. He will do what is right.'

'Listen, sonny, you mind your own business, or you will be feeling this between your ribs.' The brute pulled his dagger from his belt and pointed it at Peter. The other two men did the same.

Peter looked around the tavern for support, but there was none. Just the old man sitting in the corner with his head down, trying not to become involved or even see what was happening, holding his staff planted firmly on the floor between his legs as if to support himself as he sat there. In two steps, Peter got to the old man, wrenched the staff from his hand – a hand which yielded easily to the dispossession – and in a single fluid motion struck the woman's attacker in the midriff, causing him to double over, swung the staff upwards to strike the second man firmly in the jaw, rendering him unconscious, then cracked the staff across the nose of the third man, bringing blinding tears to his eyes. Then Peter brought the staff swiftly back round to the two men still standing, striking each a paralysing blow on the wrist, causing their daggers to drop to the floor from senseless fingers. Then, just as the first man started to straighten up, Peter jabbed the staff into his throat.

'I suggest you and your cronies leave now before I get angry,' he said. 'If I ever see you again, you will be sorry, and if I hear you have attacked a defenceless woman again, you will not live long enough to be sorry. Go!'

The man gave a strangled whimper and moved backwards away from the staff. For a moment he considered whether to rush at Peter, but good sense prevailed and he grunted to his fellow to go. Between them they picked up the fallen daggers and dragged the third man, still unconscious, out of the tavern. When the door banged shut behind them, Peter lowered the staff.

'You must let me reward you,' said the older whore. 'If

you had not come along, he would have beaten me to death. I know what such men are like.'

'Did you steal his purse?'

'No, definitely not! Such a thing would be stupid for girls like us. We need the good grace and humour of men, and to steal something would mean we would, at the very least, be banned from the town and more than likely hanged. Such a thing is just not worth it in our line of work. He must have lost it somewhere. Probably spent all his money. When he was with me, he was raging drunk.'

Peter looked at the woman and realised she was talking sense. She did not appear to be lying. In any case, there was nothing he could do and he certainly did not want to become involved with such things. He grunted and started to move away.

'Please let me reward you.'

'Thank you, no. I was doing what any right-minded man would do.'

'No one bothers to protect a whore. You saved me. Let me reward you. I have no money, but if you come with me, I will show you how grateful I am.'

Peter smiled at her. 'Thank you. I really appreciate your offer, but I must say no.'

'Go with her,' came a quiet voice in his ear. A voice he knew. Peter whirled round, and there was the old man – his old man! Before Peter could speak, however, the old man retrieved his staff, repeated his instruction, 'Go with her', turned and walked out of the tavern, leaving Peter speechless and staring at the door.

The girls had seen the old man take back his staff, but had not heard his quiet voice, so they looked at Peter wondering why he was so shocked and motionless. The older one took Peter's arm and said, 'Come. Let us go upstairs and I can teach you much.'

Still shocked, Peter allowed himself to be taken up the

stairs and into a grubby bedroom furnished only with a double bed, on which an uninviting mattress lay, and a stool.

'Sit on the stool and listen. I will show you things. You do not have to touch or do anything. Just listen.'

Peter, finding himself sitting on the stool, had by now regained his senses. He made to get up off the stool, but the whore put out a hand to stop him. 'What is to be lost, just listening?'

Peter wanted to leave, but then the old man's voice came back to him. Why did he want Peter go to with this woman? There must be a reason. Peter stayed.

The woman undressed and showed Peter her body, explaining how a woman feels and likes being touched and caressed – gently at first and then more firmly as she warms to the embrace. She got Peter to caress her head and neck so he could judge the correct pressure, before moving slowly down her body. All the time the woman was talking and encouraging, explaining what was necessary and eventually demonstrating the secrets of rousing to a climax. 'Remember, slow and gentle will win your lady, no matter who she is, queen or whore.'

When it was over, they both returned to the bar. Peter's comrades were just arriving and were more intent on ordering ale than noticing Peter coming down the stairs with a whore, who in any case did not sit down with her girlfriends but walked out of the tavern, not looking back. Peter chuckled to himself. He had been set up: by the monk, the old man and the supposedly old whore. Perhaps by the three soldiers as well? Doubtful. That had been far too real and no one could guarantee Peter's intervention. Exchanging a few greetings with his comrades, Peter excused himself and went out of the ale house looking for the whore and his old man. He went into every ale house and the inn in the town, looked in every place he could think of, but there was no sign of them.

*   *   *

It was several Sundays before Peter returned to the monastery. The baron's groom had taken Peter aside to show him the baron's horses so that Peter could pick out those he wanted. None were suitable. All were knight's chargers, bred to thunder into battle, or heavy horses suited to drawing carts and carriages. Peter wanted a lighter horse, with a blend of stamina and agility. He explained his needs to the groom, who reported back to the baron. The baron ordered Peter, the groom and six men to go out into the countryside to find the horses Peter wanted.

The groom was well experienced in his trade and took the little troop to nearby manors where horses were bred and sold by minor knights to supplement their income. After two weeks of inspecting stock, the groom had picked out six horses for Peter – horses which were lighter than the knights' destriers, stronger than the coursers used for hunting, but still as agile. Peter's natural affinity with animals meant the horses were calm and yet eager to be close to him. Peter was pleased, as indeed was de Cours, for he was expecting to pay anything up to £40 for each horse, but those chosen by the groom for Peter were not much sought after and so cost less than £10 each.

The horses were stabled back at the castle and after 'talking' to each of them, Peter went to the blacksmith to see how the alterations to Gelling's chain mail was progressing. He was trying on the near-finished product when William arrived.

'Preparing to be a knight, I see.'

'Not at all. Simply taking precautions. Tell me, you have chain mail. Would it not be advantage for all soldiers to have it as well?'

'Yes and no. It would offer far greater protection than the metal plates on the leather jerkins, but the additional weight would sap energy, and as peasants do not train for combat from an early age they would find chain mail difficult to fight in. Until you get used to it, chain mail restricts your movement. Also there is the cost. No baron, no matter how wealthy, could afford to equip all his soldiers with chain mail and a lifetime's soldier pay would not be enough to pay for it either.'

Peter took off the part-finished product, recognised its weight was indeed formidable and urged the blacksmith to finish it soon, for he realised that he would need to train wearing the chain mail to ensure his fighting abilities were not impaired. Peter and William walked together towards the training ground.

'In a few months, your time here will be over,' said William. 'What are you going to do with your horses and chain mail?'

Peter stopped walking. 'I do not know. I have been thinking of several potential options, but I have not made up my mind. I think it is best if I do not stay here, but beyond that . . .' Peter trailed off.

William looked at him for a long time. 'Well, when you have made up your mind, come and speak to me. Perhaps I can assist, advise even. I will miss you.'

With that, William turned and walked away.

When Peter was at last able to return to the monastery, the monk was waiting for him. Before discussing texts and examining manuscripts, they had the usual talk about news of events taking place throughout the country. The monk seemed, as always, to have a source of information about the secular world and knew far more than Peter had imagined possible for someone in a cloistered environment. The main topic was that, following the death of Robert of Gloucester, all thought Matilda would return to France as Stephen was continuing to bring wavering barons gradually under his control. It was a slow process, but Stephen's actions were concentrated away from the West Country. The barons there were not hostile to Stephen, though many were not openly supportive of him, or, like de Cours, maintained a neutral stance, waiting to see what the tussle for the crown would yield. The monk felt the years of unrest were coming to an end and that local barons would no longer openly take advantage of a divided nation to seize land and power for themselves.

All this, heartening though it was for the nation, placed Peter in a greater dilemma. If the unrest was over, then staying with de Cours, something which he had dismissed anyway, would offer little opportunity. De Cours would honour his promised appointment of squire, but if all was at peace in the country, advancement to knight was far less assured. Not wanting land and a farmer's life immediately meant that Peter's options were limited. He could become a bandit and lead a troop of men to fight against harsh and cruel barons and knights, so freeing peasants from abject slavery and poverty. There were plenty of similar bands – made up of impoverished or disgraced knights and second sons of the nobility – roaming the country, whose aim was personal gain rather than freeing the peasants from servitude. Perhaps he could rid the country of these bands – but there again, where would the reward be? He was thinking about all this when he became aware that the monk was looking at him.

'What are you thinking?'

'Oh. About what I should do next. I do not want to stay a soldier, and neither do I want to be a farmer.' Peter shook his head as if to rid it of thought and turned to the monk. 'One thing I have been meaning to ask you. You urged me to go into town a few weeks ago and there I briefly met someone I had not seen for a few years. I cannot believe this was a coincidence.'

The monk replied immediately. 'The will of God takes many forms. You may believe what you wish, for I can have no comment on what God's will might be.' Peter scowled at this unsatisfactory answer. Up until then, the monk had been straightforward, honest and clear in everything he said, but Peter could not believe that he was being straightforward now. The monk continued, 'Perhaps your dilemma for the future can be resolved if you take a little more time for yourself. When you have finished your day's training, do not go back to your hut and play dice and chat with the men, but go for a walk in the countryside. With that peace around you, in an environment where you spent so many happy months as a shepherd, your thoughts might take wing and your future become clear.'

Peter nodded and they moved on to examine a new manuscript the monk had acquired.

Taking the monk's words to heart, over the following days Peter did indeed walk into the countryside and let his mind wander. It was, as the monk predicted, therapeutic as he allowed nature to get back into his body and envelop his mind. No startling revelation came to him, but he gathered an inner strength in the knowledge that at the right time he would do the right thing – whatever that might be.

On the fourth day, as he clambered out of a gully and faced the setting sun, Peter became aware of a shape huddled beneath a stout oak. He did not need to ask himself what this shape was.

'So, you have decided to reappear once again!'

The old man threw back his hood and laughed. 'Admit it, you cannot do without me.'

'I have done pretty well these last two years,' retorted Peter in a friendly way. Inwardly, he was so glad to see the old man again and be able to speak to him.

'Hmpf. If I hadn't given you my staff, you would have been in a right mess in the ale house.'

'Given! *Given*! I had to fairly wrench it out of your pathetically weak grip. You did nothing to help. It was three armed against one unarmed!'

They both laughed and Peter sat down beside the old man.

'What have you been doing these last two years? I will not bother to tell you what I have been up to, for I am sure your friend the monk has told you everything.'

'Indeed he has. We thought you would work out we were friends. He, like me, is a disgraced knight, but has found solace in manuscripts with an understanding abbot allowing him freedom to do very much as he wishes. As for me, I have continued to travel the country and done nothing of any note – except save your life in an ale house!'

Peter snorted, but did not rise to the bait. 'As I understand it, things are likely to get tougher for you with Stephen quelling the barons. Sooner or later there will be no conflict at all in this country and you may become a really hunted man. Perhaps you might have to join one of those bandit groups to keep your skin.'

'No. I will never do that, but like you, I suspect, I have no constructive plans for my future. I am beginning to tire of constantly travelling around.'

'Well then, join me.' Suddenly it all became clear. Peter knew what he wanted to do.

'Join you doing what?'

Peter paused long enough to marshal his thoughts, which developed detail as he began explaining to the old man. 'As you know, I had a stroke of luck in one battle and as a result have six horses of my choice, arms provisions and money for six men for a month.' The old man nodded slowly. 'Your friend the monk has given me many manuscripts to read, some of which have enlightened me about Normandy. The monk has told me as much about Normandy as he can and it seems to me it is very much like England, except that for the last twelve years or so Geoffrey of Anjou has been quietly and relentlessly attacking and taking towns and provinces from Le Sap through Caen and Touques to Cherbourg, adding Normandy to his Angevin territories before becoming Duke of Normandy a couple of years or so ago. While this has brought peace to Normandy, there are a large number of deposed knights, esquires and gentlemen roaming the Normandy country-side attacking travellers, towns and even occasionally manor houses for ill-gotten gains.' The old man nodded again. 'Now, Normandy is a very large area and Geoffrey has largely ignored these bands on the pretext that they will soon tire and succumb to his good governance, plus the fact that a large number of his knights and barons are in the East on the Second Crusade against the Turks. This gives us an opportunity. Why don't we go to Normandy and offer our services to some selected towns to protect them for a fee? If we can guarantee free passage between towns and villages and keep manor houses safe from attack, surely that is worth the French paying us for it. Think of the money they will be saving in not having their own guards and not losing goods to the bandits!'

The old man smiled. 'A good idea, but first, who are "we", and second, what makes you think a small band of six men can rid a country of large bands of outlaws?'

'To answer your second question first, we will not rid the country of those outlaws, but will simply convince them to move on to an area which we are not protecting. As to "we", there is you and me for a start, and that is worth six men. I have in mind a couple of others and we may well be able to pick up worthy fighters on the way.'

The old man grinned broadly. 'It is insane, but intriguing. If you can indeed get anyone else to commit to this mad idea, then I will go with you. There is nothing left here in England for me, so why should I not take my chances in Normandy?'

Dusk was falling and Peter had to return to the castle. Before bidding the old man farewell and arranging to meet at the same time the following week, Peter asked if the monk would be interested in joining the adventure. The old man said not. The monk loved the manuscripts too much to abandon them willingly.

11

During the week which followed, Peter took William to one side, confirmed he was leaving service at the end of the following month and outlined what he intended to do. He gave sufficient detail for William to understand his plans.

'While I know you have the best position here that you could ever have hoped for, I wonder if you might consider joining me in my adventure? I already have one potential recruit and the fact you can speak French would be an enormous asset.'

William did not hesitate. 'Quite honestly, I have had enough of instruction and training to last me for the rest of my life, and although I have been saving hard, I still do not have sufficient money to buy any land and build a house – well, not enough to buy a decent-sized piece of good land. I would welcome the opportunity for something fresh. It may not make my fortune, but then again, it might. Yes, I will gladly join you.'

Peter smiled warmly. 'But will you take orders from me?'

'Pfft! If I can take orders from those dolts of knights I've been pampering for years, I'll have no problem taking orders from a youngster who can at least think!'

'Good. That will be three of us. Do you know of anyone else you would trust and would fit in with our way of doing things? I have horses and arms for six, so I need three more.'

'Yes indeed. One of my comrades of some years' standing married a widow three years ago and retired from fighting to farm her lands. I have not seen him for a year, but I would bet my last farthing that he would welcome any opportunity to leave farming for an adventure. He is not suited to the land and I am sure the charms of the widow have waned by now, if not evaporated completely! If we turn up with a horse and arms for him, I reckon he would leap into the saddle before we have drawn to a halt.'

'What about Matthew? We need good archers, and he is the best. As long as we keep him away from drinking too much, he would be ideal. He can also wield an axe like a man possessed.'

'He was going to be my second suggestion. I am glad we are thinking along the same lines. He is certainly a possibility, and he has a wandering spirit. Let me talk to him and I will let you know.'

Sure enough, Matthew came on board with no persuading, glad to move on to new pastures. Apart from the final member of the team – Peter had no doubt the old man would live up to his word and join them – all that was left was to tell Baron de Cours that he would not be taking up the very generous offer of squire. Seeking an appointment later the following week, Peter entered the baronial hall with some trepidation. True, de Cours could not prevent Peter leaving his service at the end of the two-year conscription period, but in turning down the offer of becoming the baron's squire Peter would undoubtedly offend him.

The baron was in his usual chair, the baroness sitting on the other side of the fireplace, and their daughter Amelia was standing by her mother. Although Peter gave but a cursory glance and a respectful nod to both the baroness and Amelia, he could not help but notice how this young flower was blossoming. Perhaps he should take up the squire offer and his chances with the noble's daughter? But no, she was not for him. She was too great a prize, and the baron would marry her off to another noble's son to consolidate the position of both families.

'You are going to turn down my offer of squire,' said the baron as soon as Peter had stopped in front of him. Peter composed his face into an expression of regret. The baron held up his hand. 'Do not fear. I expected as much. You have to find your own future and I admire that. I will, though, repeat my offer to give you Gelling's ransom. Whatever you want to do, that money will secure you.'

'Thank you. You are far too kind. We already have an agreement, and to that end I think you should keep this.' Peter handed de Cours the sworn statement setting out Gelling's treachery. The baron took it and handed it to his wife.

'So what now? What are your plans?'

'I think I should keep my plans to myself. They do not affect you, nor will they impinge on you in any way except, unfortunately, that two of your men will be leaving with me.'

'Ah. Decar will be one, I wager. He is far too good to remain Master at Arms and yet I cannot do anything to advance him. He should be a knight, but fate has not bestowed this honour on him.'

'Yes, William will be one, and Matthew – the master archer – the other. I am sorry I will be depriving you of two good men.'

'Three, counting yourself, but I have every belief the future will be less bloody than the recent past. Stephen seems to be getting a grip on things at last. So you will need your horses soon. What else?'

'Swords, axes, pikes, knight's shields – not the round ones – and Welsh bows, please, my lord. I have my own, or rather Gelling's, sword. William has a sword too, so I would appreciate three more good swords.'

'Just three? We agreed six, and even though you and William have swords, you seem to be one short.'

'One recruit has his own sword, so if you could see your way to slightly better swords for three, rather than the original six, I would be grateful.'

'You will have the best I can muster. Go with William to the armoury and pick out exactly what you want. If something there is not of high enough standard, let me know and I will get better. In the meantime, I will give you enough money for three months' living for six people. I know we agreed one month, but take the extra as a gift from us all.' The baron looked around at his wife and daughter, the latter blushing faintly. 'Food: you take what you want before you leave.'

'I thank you, my lord. You have taught me so much, and I will be forever grateful, as is my village and those around, for your benevolence to everyone. I feel guilty at leaving you, but I believe I must.'

A long silence followed, and then Amelia said in French, 'Papa, can you not stop him going? I am sure he will be of greater use to you here than travelling around the countryside, as I am sure is his plan with six horses. Outside your protection, he could fall foul of any noble and simply be executed out of hand as an outlaw!'

De Cours grunted. 'My daughter feels you are at risk leaving this area without my protection.'

Peter smiled warmly at Amelia, whose blush deepened. 'Your daughter is wise and has thought ahead more than I have. There is every chance of my being accosted by nobles or knights as our little band rides through the country. Might I therefore ask you another favour? Would it be possible for you to write a letter for me to carry saying I am on your business and under your protection? In asking you this, I have to tell you that I plan to do nothing in England at all and will be leaving for Normandy within a month, so your letter could not be used to protect me or my fellows from any unlawfulness. In Normandy I will have to take my chances.'

The baron thought for a while. 'Very well. I am taking a risk, but you are obviously a man of your word. The letter will be ready by the time you leave. Good luck.'

Peter left the hall. Seeking out William and Matthew, he told them of the letter to protect their passage and asked them to go to the armoury and choose good weapons.

With evening approaching, Peter walked out of the castle into the countryside. He was a little too early for his prearranged meeting with the old man, so he started a gentle and relaxed run into the fields, letting the sound of the countryside envelop him. His peace was interrupted by the sound of hoofbeats. He turned round and saw Amelia riding towards him. She pulled the horse to a gentle stop and looked down at him.

'Why are you going?' she asked in her halting Anglo-Saxon.

'I have no real future here and I am restless to do something.'

Amelia frowned as though she did not follow. It was clear that while she had been learning Anglo-Saxon, she was not used to the indigenous accent and was having difficulty understanding him. Peter repeated his words slowly, continuing, 'A more important question is what you are doing out of the castle without a chaperone. If your father finds out, he will beat you, and if he finds out you have been with me, I am a dead man. How could you be so unthinking?'

Amelia screwed up her pretty little face as she tried to comprehend what Peter had said, and she started to dismount.

'No you do not!' said Peter in Norman French. 'We are in trouble enough without you getting off that horse. Turn around immediately and go back before you – or we – are seen. I do not want to finish my life so soon at the end of a rope.'

'I just wanted to find out why you are leaving us,' replied Amelia in French, too distraught to realise that Peter had spoken to her in her own tongue. 'Surely there is nothing wrong with that? My father is a kindly man and will understand.'

'Maybe. But what about your mother? She has you already earmarked for a noble husband and if you are seen cavorting with a mere peasant soldier, your reputation will be in tatters and you will never find a husband.'

'We are not "cavorting"! I am merely talking to you. There is no harm. And in any case, whatever my mother says, I will marry the man I want.' She stiffened her body and thrust her little chin forward in determination. Peter smiled inwardly. She was clearly vixen enough to cause her parents grief when she was older.

'No matter. This is not the time and certainly not the place for us to talk. Go back immediately. Perhaps we can have a conversation when you are properly chaperoned. This is to protect us both.' Amelia looked uncertain. 'If you have any regard for me at all, you will understand I am right.'

She did understand, and slowly wheeled her house around. Just before she galloped off, having calmed herself, she said, 'So you can speak French! My mother suspected as much as you were spending so much time at the monastery. That monk would admit nothing and merely said you were devout in your studies.' She smiled a broad smile. 'Tomorrow, then.' And she galloped off.

Peter watched her disappear towards the castle and heaved a great sigh of relief.

'Tricky one, that.' The old man appeared at his shoulder. 'I was behind the tree over there. I did not hear what you were saying, though it was clear you were giving her the big brush-off. Pity. I think she quite fancies you.'

'Hurrumph,' replied Peter, ungraciously. 'I have enough troubles getting men together for the next phase of my life without worrying about a slip of a girl who is too young to know anything.'

'Don't you be so sure. She's wise beyond her years, that one, and certainly wilful. A handful for her poor husband, whoever that might be.'

The old man gave Peter an appraising look. Peter ignored him, wondering where the old man got his information about Amelia's abilities. Then he focused on the task in hand and brought the old man up to date with events.

'So,' said the old man, 'on the assumption William's friend joins us, we just have to find one more. Someone will turn up. When do we move off?'

'I have lost track of time a bit. I think my term is up in two weeks, but let us say four weeks from today. We will bring the horses, with arms and provisions, here to meet you.'

'Perfect. This will give me enough time to find chain mail. I have long since abandoned mine, but I still have a couple of favours to call in so I will be ready in four weeks.'

With that they parted and Peter returned to the castle.

William and Matthew had chosen the arms and applied themselves to sharpening and making sure each item was in pristine condition. They had also found an old mail shirt which was rusty and broken but nearly fitted Matthew. This they took to the blacksmith and with a little bribing he promised to repair and make it as serviceable as possible before they left. The horses and saddles were inspected.

'The horses are a bit small,' said Matthew. 'I wonder if they will be strong enough.'

'To be truthful, I do not know myself,' replied Peter. 'My thinking is that we do not want destriers, as they are cumbersome and not too manoeuvrable, and we will have no need of such horses as we will not be charging about using lances on horseback. None of us is trained for that and in any case,

I believe it is a poor way of fighting. I think we will be better suited with horses which can change direction quickly and yet are strong enough to carry us and our equipment long distances. I am told by the groom that these are a cross with a courser, so they should fulfil our needs. Only time will tell.'

The shields which Peter had requested were also supplied and the three of them spent time making sure the straps were strong, fixed properly and fitted correctly for each of their left arms. It would not be possible to keep the baron's emblem on the shields, so they were all painted black. Nothing more could be done. They merely had to wait until the blacksmith had finished Matthew's chain mail and the time was right for them to leave.

Amelia did not see Peter the next day as she had promised. Indeed, she was not seen about for over a week. Peter suspected that her unchaperoned ride had been detected and she had been punished by her mother. It was on a Sunday, when Peter was with the monk, telling him in outline what he was going to do and making his grateful farewells, when Amelia and her lady-in-waiting walked into the room where the manuscripts were stored.

'I have brought my chaperone and you have yours,' she said, pointing to the monk. 'Perhaps now you will speak to me in a civilised way rather than shouting at me and making me cry.'

Peter could not remember any tears, and if there had been any voice-raising, it had not been from him. He simply bowed his head. 'My lady.'

Amelia walked across to him and looked up into his face. Her crystal-blue eyes were soft, and her fair locks tumbled freely over her shoulders rather than being held up in a bun as was the fashion. Young she might be, but she knew enough to make herself alluring. Peter remained motionless.

'Why don't we busy ourselves over at the other end of the room,' said the monk to the lady-in-waiting, 'and let these young people talk?' With that he took the lady-in-waiting's arm and gently ushered her to the furthest place away from Amelia and Peter.

'What is it you intend to do?' Amelia asked.

'Some friends and I are going to Normandy to see if we can use our combined talents to our advantage.'

'And what might that entail?'

Peter shrugged. 'Who knows until we get there.'

'Rubbish. You know full well what you are going to do. Tell me.'

Peter remained silent.

'All right then, if you are not prepared to take me into your confidence, I cannot see how you expect me to wait for your return.'

'My lady, I do not expect you to wait for me at all! The whole idea is impossible. I do not know what I will achieve, if anything, nor when I might get back. It may be never. This is not a crusade. I am going into the unknown to do the unknown. Besides which, as I said before, your mother, and I am sure your father as well, would not even contemplate your throwing yourself away on a peasant with no title, no future, no money and no home. I am deeply flattered and most grateful that you have looked upon me with a little favour, but I am not deluding myself it is anything other than that. You are young and in a few months I will be easily forgotten when you see the young nobles willing to offer you a hand in marriage.'

She looked at him hard. Everything he said was perfectly true, but while she was indeed young, she knew what her heart and mind told her.

'I firmly believe you will succeed in your quest, whatever that might be, and I really do know how I feel. You speak sense, but do not dismiss fate. I am convinced you did not come to my father's house by chance. It was fate. Look after yourself.'

She pulled Peter's head down and kissed him firmly but briefly full on the lips, then she turned around, walking swiftly out of the room with a stiff, straight back, her lady-in-waiting scurrying behind.

'Wilful little thing, that one,' said the monk. 'You are certainly best out of it. She could cause no end of trouble. While the manuscripts are full of romantic love and unrequited passion, real life is something else.'

Peter grunted, still feeling the warmth of her lips on his.

12

The time for Peter's leaving came. Carrying the promised letter from the baron, along with their money and arms, Peter, William and Matthew rode slowly away from the castle, waving farewell to all the friends they were leaving behind. Since the day in the monastery, Peter had not seen Amelia, but now she stood immobile on the castle wall watching them go. She did not raise a farewell arm. Peter nodded towards her and looked away.

They rode towards the appointed place where the old man was waiting, mail shirt on, sword at his waist and possessions in a bag over his shoulder. He got onto the proffered horse and Peter introduced everyone. 'This is William and Matthew. Perhaps you would like to tell us your name?' William and Matthew looked shocked that Peter did not actually know who the new recruit was.

'You have known me for many years as "the old man". Why don't we just leave it at that?'

Peter shrugged and saw the title appealed to the other two, so he did not pursue the matter.

Once the old man was settled – complaining a little that the saddle was uncomfortable, but in reality it was the years out of a saddle which were causing the discomfort – they moved off towards the hoped-for fifth member of the group, leading the two riderless horses and speaking in generalities while the old man got to know the others a little more.

The following day they arrived at a quaint, if small, farm hut showing every sign of being well looked after. A buxom woman bustled out of the door on their approach, showing no fear or apprehension. William smiled to himself. Married to Tom, his former fighting colleague, she need have no fear of anyone, he thought.

'What do you want?' she said, speaking directly to William. 'Why are you here? There's nothing for you here.'

Peter detected a charge of animosity, and saw a certain shrewishness in her pinched mouth. A wealthy widow catch she might have been, but in her full colours she was master of the house, taking nonsense from no one. From Peter's limited experience, even a poor peasant farmer would shudder at a life under her roof and if indeed Tom was any man at all, he would not be slow to shrug off this particular harness.

'I have come to see Tom,' William told her. 'He is an old friend and old friends have to keep in touch.'

The former widow scowled even more deeply. 'He does not want to see you. He is a farmer now and your sitting around filling him with ale and talking over old fights and battles unsettles him. Last time you were here, it took me weeks to get him to work properly again.'

I do not doubt it, thought Peter. You know full well that if Tom's given a chance to get away, he will be gone.

'Like it or not, we are going to talk to Tom. Come on, lads.' William wheeled his horse and drove it at a steady walk out into the fields. The rest followed, leaving the shrew to scream obscenities after them.

'My God,' said Matthew. 'How did Tom get fixed up with that one?'

'She was all sweetness and light before Tom married her. It was only after he had been there for some months she showed her true worth. Give Tom his credit, he has been trying to make a decent life out of it, but I see they have no children. Perhaps that speaks for itself.'

Soon they spotted Tom behind an ox and plough. He stopped his work the moment he saw the horses approaching, breaking into a beaming smile as soon as he recognised William.

'My good man! What are you doing here? I thought your days were taken up whipping young peasants into shape.'

William got off his horse and after much back-slapping told Tom the reason for their visit. At the mention of Peter being the leader, Tom looked quizzical, but did not interrupt William.

When William had finished, Tom said, 'So, you rate this boy then, do you?'

Peter bristled. He was now seventeen summers and well into manhood. He said nothing, however.

'He will be all right with us on board. Are you going to join us?'

'Like a shot! You have got arms for me?' William nodded. 'Then that is it. I am off. She can find another man.' Wasting no time, Tom hauled himself immediately into an empty saddle.

'What about the ox and plough?'

'She will sort that out. She is in charge of everything, so let her do what is necessary. I have had enough.'

They turned their horses in the direction of Peter's village. There he told his distraught parents he would not be returning to farming, but would see them soon. He gave them some money from his meagre savings and they left as soon as possible, heading east.

'So we are on our way, leader,' said William to Peter. 'What plans?'

'First we have to find our way to the east coast to cross the Channel to France. I believe Dover is the place to head for.' Peter turned to the old man. 'You are the wanderer in this group. Do you know your way to Dover?'

The old man smiled. 'So I've only been invited along as a guide, have I?' Receiving no response other than a withering look from Peter, he shrugged. 'Yes, I can get us to Dover.'

'Good,' said Peter. 'Whilst we are travelling, we have to form our strategy. First and foremost, everyone must learn Norman French. Three of us are fluent, but what about Matthew and Tom? Can you speak any French?'

'Only battle orders and military jargon,' replied Matthew.

'Same,' said Tom.

'Right then. From now on, we will speak simple French to try to get you two understanding the basics. Once we are in Normandy, you will improve.'

Surprisingly, none questioned the fact that Peter could speak French, so he continued, 'Before we start, though, I want to explain that we will no doubt be fighting from time to time and that means two things. First, I would like William to continue to be our Master at Arms and take us through training every day that is possible. I know, William, you said you have had your fill of training, but we are few in number and must be at the top of our skills, particularly Tom, who has been away from training for three years.' They all nodded.

'Second, we are not knights and therefore do not have to fight in the honourable way of knights. Therefore I propose we look to use our bows as a first line of attack or defence, leaving hand-to-hand fighting as the last resort. Many will not expect this, so we will have a big edge. This means extra practice and training using bows particularly from horseback, and we will be looking to Matthew to hone our skills.' Before the others could speak, Peter held up his hand. 'I know it is not possible to pull a Welsh bow fully when on horseback, but we must learn to be quick and accurate with a partial drawing of the bowstring. Again, no one will be expecting this.' Both the old man and William smiled quietly at the audacity of such an idea, whilst the other two simply looked bemused.

They travelled towards Dover at a steady rate, covering fifteen miles per day, all the time speaking French and pointing out features of the countryside to Matthew and Tom to get them familiar with the language. It was hard work, but by the time they were in Kent both could follow a conversation in French and string a few sentences together. They camped in the open, saving their money, and until daylight waned, practised bowmanship under the tutelage of Matthew.

One morning they saw a group of four men on horseback riding towards them. It became clear these were military men of some sort with full arms and chain mail.

'Loosen your shields discreetly and keep your hands in front of you at all times. Do not touch your arms unless I say so,' commanded Peter. They surreptitiously dropped their left arms behind their saddles to loosen the fastenings of the shields carried there, and then drew their mounts to a halt to wait for the advancing group. The soldiers pulled up ten yards from Peter and his men. Their shields were on their arms and each had a hand on his sword.

'So what have we here?' the leader spat out. 'Renegades, I don't doubt.'

'Indeed not,' replied Peter. 'We're Baron de Cours' men, from Devonshire, on the baron's business. I have a letter here, fixed with his seal, to verify our presence in your county.'

'Pah! A letter. What does that mean? Anyone can have a letter. If I say you are renegades, that is what you are.'

'But you can see,' replied Peter with his most disarming smile, 'that while we are armed, we have not made ready to defend ourselves. Indeed, we saw each other a good distance away and if we were indeed renegades, then we could have taken flight long before you arrived.'

'You are right,' said the leader after a pause. 'I have been hasty.' He took his hand off his sword and raised it so his men could see the action. They too lifted their hands away from their swords. Peter relaxed, but in a flash William dropped his right hand down to the side of his saddle and, swinging it back up in a speedy arc, let fly his axe. It sped towards the leader just as the leader's horse was spurred forward, striking him a mighty and fatal blow in the face. The leader's men were taken aback at this unexpected action and hesitated before drawing their swords. Peter and the old man did not hesitate, however. They had no idea why William had taken that action, but they both instantly realised a fight was on, so they spurred their horses forward, slipped their shields onto their left arms and drew their swords. The little horses responded immediately, gathering speed far faster than the opposing men on destriers expected. William and Tom were mere paces behind them. The opposing force was quickly overwhelmed. They managed to block the first thrusts of Peter and the old man with their shields, but then wheeled their horses around and galloped away. Peter did not follow.

'And what was that all about?' demanded Peter of William as the opposing force vanished into the distance.

'Sorry. I recognised the leader as soon as he started speaking. He is, or rather was, a knight who fell out of favour and worked as a mercenary for the highest bidder. I assume his men were the same. He was a particularly nasty piece of work, gaining advantage by dishonesty and guile with not the slightest trace of honour. His trademark was to loosen his sword, take his hand off the hilt to make his opponent believe there was no more risk, then drop his hand back, freeing the sword from a specially made scabbard which broke open to allow immediate use of the sword rather than having to draw its full length from the scabbard, and attack his opponent before that person could draw his own sword. When I loosened my shield, I took the opportunity of loosening my axe at the same time, so I was able to use it before he could perform his trademark trick. I don't know if his companions had similar scabbards, but they would have known the signal to attack, taking us completely by surprise.'

'Thanks from us all, I think,' replied Peter. 'Three things learned here. First of all, our individual knowledge has to be acted on, so no slavish following of orders. Second, it seems the choice of horses was correct, for they closed the gap far more quickly than our opponents believed possible and so gave us the edge in the end. Finally, one good thing. Tom, I believe you are about the same size as the fallen man, so you have yourself some chain mail and we have some extra weapons.'

Tom dismounted, stripped the chain mail from the dead soldier and struggled into it, while Peter examined the sword and scabbard. It was indeed a special design, holding the sword firmly when it was pushed deep into the scabbard, but springing open once the sword was pulled a quarter of the way out, freeing the sword for immediate use. The dead man's purse revealed a reasonable quantity of small silver coins, and this was taken by Peter to help with the group's expenses.

Once Tom was dressed in his newly acquired chain mail, they resumed their travels towards Dover, keeping a watchful eye out for any sign of armed men approaching.

On arrival in Dover, Peter soon found a boat and crew willing to take them across the Channel for a price. From the scowl on the old man's face, Peter assumed the price was too high, but he was willing to pay just to get them on a good boat with a competent crew.

The passage across the Channel was uneventful, with relatively calm weather and a good wind. In less than eighteen hours both men and horses were disembarking in fine fettle. They immediately made their way south-west.

During long discussions with the old man it was agreed that they should make their way to the town of Courcy, which was ideally placed some twenty-five miles south-east of Falaise, Chamblos and Caen and some thirty miles from Le Plessis-Grimouff. Peter reasoned that market traders would regularly travel between these towns and be open to attack from bandits, so giving the group the best chance to engage themselves as protectors of trade.

Once again they made steady progress, and every few days took a day out to train with their weapons. Tom, although rusty, was soon back in the swing of things, many years of combat ingrained in his being. The old man, his face weathered and crinkled, was as fit as any of them. Indeed, he proved to have the greater skill, often giving tips and correcting the use of the kite-shaped shields for attack and defence. William was grateful and soon an easy camaraderie sprang up between the two.

Armed men roaming the countryside would normally be treated with suspicion and some alarm by villagers, but in Normandy they found virtually every village deserted, as the inhabitants ran away into the countryside to escape even the sight of Peter and his men. While this caused some problems when they were hoping to get directions to the next place en route to Courcy, Peter said it was a sign that the bandits and renegades were holding the country to ransom and so potentially meant good business for them.

When they got to the town of Brionne some three or more days east of Courcy, they booked into an inn for two nights and Peter walked around the town seeking out merchants planning to go to Courcy. He soon realised that while in England merchants and travellers banded together for security when moving through the countryside, in Normandy problems with safe travel were even more acute. Numbers alone were not enough, for the ferocity of attack from bandits meant that extra men had to be found to defend the travellers. There were few such men willing to do this for the pittance traders and travellers were willing to pay, so trade between towns was being strangled. Peter found two merchants who were desperate to get to Courcy and brought them back to the inn to meet his little group.

'We are willing to escort you both to Courcy for no payment,' he told them. 'Our intention is to relieve the countryside of these bandits and to do this we must engage them in a fight and defeat them. I know we are small in number, but if you are willing to go to Courcy we have a plan which will guarantee all our interests. Are you willing?'

Both traders looked less than certain that just five men could protect them, but they really had no choice. If they could not continue trading, they were going out of business, so after some discussions between them, it was agreed.

'Good,' said Peter. 'Now we will not be riding with you, but will be close to protect you when necessary.'

This brought an immediate flurry of dissent from the traders, who expected their guardians to be with them at all times, frightening off potential attackers with their mere presence.

'Think about it,' said Peter. 'If we are seen with you, any attackers will be prepared and will undoubtedly strengthen their number before approaching. They will know precisely how many men they have to deal with and will fight accordingly. If, however, we are out of sight, they will see two unprotected ox wagons and will take few, if any, precautions. They will not actually attack you, for they will know you will not put up any resistance and they will be intent on just relieving you of your goods and wagons. When they are close, we will deal with them.'

This suggestion was far from welcomed, however, and it took the old man's intervention, confirming the excellence of Peter's plan, to convince them and get them to shake hands on the deal.

'So then, tomorrow you will both set out at first light. You will not see us, but we will be right behind and looking after you. Do not look back or try to find where we are. You might alert potential attackers to our presence.'

The traders left, speaking quietly to themselves, obviously not entirely happy and certainly not sharing Peter's confidence, but knowing that having agreed and shaken hands, they could do nothing but follow his wishes.

The following morning the two ox carts left the town and Peter's band followed, out of immediate sight, at a respectable distance. As soon as they were in the country the group split to each side of the road, keeping behind hedges and trees so as not to be seen. Peter reasoned that any attackers would be ahead of the traders and so would not look beyond their immediate target. This proved correct. Barely two hours into the day, a band of a dozen men sprang out from a ditch, surrounding the ox carts and bringing them to a halt. So intent were they on such easy prey they did not see Peter's band until it was too late. Well-placed arrows pierced their bodies and the three survivors took off and ran, only to be chased down by Tom and William and cleaved asunder. Matthew carefully cut the arrows out of the dead to be used again and the robbers' arms were collected and put into the back of an ox cart. They had no coins between them, and their clothes would have made better fire fodder than wearable garments. Then the procession wound off again, with Peter and his men dropping back out of sight.

In the middle of the afternoon there was an almost exact replica of the morning's attack, with precisely the same result: dead bandits. The traders' fear and discomfort were abandoned and they took on an air of festivity, warm in the knowledge of their protection.

That evening they all stayed together, with Peter's men taking turns on watch, but nothing happened.

So it continued for nearly four days. There were two more attacks, dealt with efficiently by Peter and his men. All of the attacks had been made by men on foot, and scouting around the area after each assault, Peter could find no horses. Obviously he was dealing with the dregs of society and this was not the area where the more organised disgraced knights, squires and gentlemen operated.

The traders rolled into Courcy without Peter's escort, with firm instructions to make it known to everyone that they had come from Brionne protected by Peter's band, which had fought off and annihilated four bands of outlaws. Peter reasoned that the merchants would embellish the story and, sure enough, when they all got into Courcy the town was abuzz with the news these protectors had slain dozens of bandits.

Peter and the men settled themselves at a respectable inn and made enquiries about the trade guilds and who was in charge of the town. Armed with this knowledge, Peter and the old man went out to see the leaders of the trade guilds to invite them to a meeting that evening at the inn. The proprietor of the inn was not at all happy at having in his establishment men who were not paying board and lodging, but Peter reminded him that his wine sales would soar. That evening all the guild masters, having heard of Peter's success in protecting the merchants from Brionne, attended the meeting with enthusiasm and Peter explained that he and his men would undertake to rid the area between Courcy, Falasie, Chambros and later Le Plessis-Grimouff and Caen from bandits to allow free trade.

'But you cannot kill them all,' said one of the guild masters.

Peter smiled. 'No, you are right. But we can and will kill many and create an atmosphere of uncertainty for any robber or bandit, which will encourage them to leave the area. If they are on someone else's turf, that will not worry us.'

The guild master nodded in agreement.

'But for what price?' asked another guild master. 'Nothing is for nothing.'

'Very true, there is a price, but you must remember, at the moment there is very little trade between towns and this is costing you money. If you venture out in convoys at present, you employ poor and ineffectual guards to protect you, so you lose your goods anyway. Think of the money you are losing and how much more you can make if you can trade and move about freely.'

'How much?'

'That is something I will discuss with the mayor of the town tomorrow. I suggest you all see him early and impress upon him that we are your saviours. Without us, the whole town will suffer.'

With that the meeting broke up, leaving the little group to discuss the attitude of the guild masters and lay their plans for the next day.

Just before mid-morning the following day, Peter sought out the mayor of the town and asked him if the guild masters had spoken to him. The mayor answered in the affirmative and Peter emphasised again the position the town was in and maintained that he and his men could free the countryside of bandits and allow trade to prosper once more. The mayor really needed no convincing, but was mindful of the fact that Peter was going to ask for money. 'Well,' he said, 'it is true things are bad now, but our lord baron has been informed and we are all confident he will send his men to restore order in the countryside.'

'Maybe,' countered Peter, 'but as I understand it, you asked him to do this nearly a year ago and nothing has happened. The knights he had depended on are now fewer because many went with Louis VII to the crusade, and although that crusade has ended in failure and the armies are returning, the loss of men and nobility was great, so it will take a long time before your lord baron will rebuild sufficient strength to tackle the unlawfulness around here.

How long can you hold out before the town is effectively ruined? We are here now, and can start immediately. I would suggest that if the problem with the bandits is not solved by winter, the town is going to have a very lean time indeed. It will not be long before the bandits realise greater spoils are in the towns themselves, and they may band together and attack you here, in your homes.'

This worry had not escaped the mayor, and he shrugged in acknowledgement. 'How much?'

'Ten marks per month.'

The mayor exploded. 'Ten marks? That is preposterous! It is a fortune. None of us have ten marks.'

'I'm afraid both you and I know that is not true. You are fully aware of how much money is being lost by being unable to trade. How many goods are now overpriced here because other traders cannot get into the town? Even work on your new church building has stopped because the carters cannot freely leave the town for the quarry to bring back stone, which means that skilled workers are idle. Ten marks is a pittance to pay for free trade and free movement of people between towns and into and out of this town. The trade guilds will contribute, travellers between towns will be willing to pay you a fee for safe passage, taxes for goods moving into the town will increase, tolls for bridges will increase, even the carters will pay you something. Ten marks a month will be recovered in the first two weeks. We both know that.'

The mayor appreciated the sense in all this and was weakening. Peter pressed home his advantage.

'As a gesture of good faith, we will not charge you for the first month if we fail to safely escort five goods trains of no more than five carts at a time between here and Falaise. If we succeed, then at the end of the month you will pay us twenty marks: ten marks for the first month and ten marks in advance for the next month, and thereafter ten marks a month in advance. If we fail to keep five goods trains safe in the first month, you will owe us nothing. There is one further condition. The drivers, merchants and travellers will obey our orders exactly. If they do not, then we will not be at fault.'

The mayor hesitated as he tried to think of a way around it, but he realised that if Peter did not succeed, then no one would be out of pocket.

'Agreed. But why Falaise and not Chambros, where we have greater trade?'

'Falaise is in the middle, between Chambros and Le Plessis-Grimouff. If we can clear this passage first, it will be easier to move on to the other two towns.'

The mayor grunted assent. Peter shook hands with him to seal the deal and returned to the inn.

'How did you get on?' asked William.

'Good. We are in business. Ten marks a month.'

'What?' shouted William. 'Ten marks! That is one hundred and twenty marks a year – over seventy pounds!'

'Seventy-two pounds one shilling, to be precise,' grinned Peter. 'But there is a catch. We are not paid until the end of the first month and during that month we have to escort five wagon trains of not more than five carts to or from Falaise.'

'Why Falaise, and why only five carts at a time?' asked the old man, knowing the answer full well.

Peter explained the choice of Falaise. 'As to the maximum of five carts, this is tactical. If there is a great wagon train, then all the local bandits will band together to attack and we are too few in number to succeed. With only five carts, the maximum number in any one attack will probably be twenty.'

Over the following month, Peter's band escorted the required five wagon trains, regularly engaging and defeating gangs of bandits. The most vulnerable places were river crossings, but soon a system of protection was developed to allow safe crossing. Most of the robbers were killed, but occasionally one or two escaped and Peter anticipated that their ploy of remaining out of sight would soon be known and he would have to adapt his plan.

When the last of the five wagon trains entered Courcy from Falaise – surprisingly but pleasingly having encountered no robbers at all – Peter went to the mayor for payment and the twenty marks were handed over with barely a protest.

13

Returning to the inn and paying the landlord for a further month's board and lodging, Peter gave the balance of the twenty marks to the old man, who was to act as purse keeper for them all.

'We have our first month's payment,' said Peter as they sat down to cups of well-deserved wine, 'and the advance for next month. So far we have been very lucky, not really exposing ourselves at all to any possibility of injury, but that is not going to last. Also, I have promised to open up the road between here and Chambros, which means that we cannot accompany every ox cart, so will have to rid the area of a lot more robbers before we can safely allow a wagon train to venture out without protection.' He paused to let this sink in. 'I would think that those robbers who escaped from our attack will be spreading the word and will also know there are only five of us. Also everyone in the town knows we are just five. Consequently I would reckon that in this month we will be accosted by a large band of robbers, probably reasonably well organised and certainly well aware of our number and abilities. In short, we'll be facing a major battle very soon.'

There were grunts all around. Each man knew that sooner or later their fighting as well as their bowmanship skills would be tested and consequently had made no complaints that days off between wagon escorts were spent training.

'On the assumption that we can survive this month and can keep the roads open to a reasonable extent, we must make preparations to get out of this inn. To reserve rooms here we are paying a high price for lodging for every day of the month, even though we are often away, and that is a waste of money. So we should find alternative accommodation. Perhaps we can take over a house, or you may wish to find separate lodgings.' Peter smiled at them. 'With a willing widow, for example.' This brought laughs from the others. 'Anyway, have a look around and see what would suit you.'

The first escort of the new month was to Chambros. They encountered gangs of robbers, but not as many as on their first trip to Falaise. Peter was not lulled into any sense of complacency, or into believing that word was spreading not to attack merchants coming from or going to Courcy. It was far too early for such an effect and the previous month had emphasised the high number of bandits in the countryside.

Sure enough, the second trip brought with it the anticipated face-off.

The five ox carts were trundling along in fairly open countryside, making it difficult for Peter and his men to stay close enough to protect them while remaining hidden from potential attackers. Off to the right, emerging from a wood, came a gaggle of men who made no attempt to approach the ox carts but started walking in the same direction about one hundred yards from the goods wagons. They were soon joined by more men, then men on horses, all making no attempt to approach the ox carts, but making it plain that this was eventually going to be their intention.

Peter signalled his men close. 'Go out wide both sides of the road and check to see if there are any robbers still hidden, or a second force assembling to catch us in a pincer movement.'

The old man, William, Matthew and Tom did as they were bid, with Peter remaining behind, watching the band of robbers swelling in number and arranging themselves in fighting order.

Peter's men returned shortly, reporting that there was no back-up force, just the men they could see in front of them.

'Yow,' said Tom. 'A small army.'

'Perhaps, but we can be sure they will not be very disciplined and, apart from those on horseback, they will not be particularly well trained or well armed. Let us move forward to greet them.'

Peter's party urged their horses forward and brought themselves into full sight of the bandit army, which stopped its march and turned to face Peter's group in the time-honoured way, with the mounted in the centre and those on foot evenly distributed on each side. Peter counted ten on horseback and a dozen or so on foot each side.

'I can only see a few bowmen, but to be safe, spread out, about fifteen yards apart to give them individual targets.'

As they advanced slowly towards the robber army, spreading out, so Peter's men strung their bows, using a stirrup to brace the bottom of the bow in order to bend it enough to get the string on the horn hook at the top, strapped shields on their left arms and, holding the bows in their left hands, eased out swords, axes and daggers and made arrows ready for use. The little party stopped a hundred yards from the robber army.

'The usual,' said Peter. 'Take out the horses first, then those on the horses. When the mob are thirty or so yards away, three of us go to the left, and you other two to the right, circling round and splitting them, then abandon the bows and fight with swords or axes – your choice.'

Peter's men grunted in answer and steeled themselves for the battle to come. They were not frightened or apprehensive. They had done all this before, some of them many times. Each man knew what to do.

Both bands stayed still, waiting for the other to make the first move. As Peter suspected, discipline was short on the robber side, for some of those on foot started to move, but were brought back by growls from the horsemen. In the meantime, the ox carts had quickened their pace and were trying to get away from the scene as fast as possible, fearing that their escort, greatly outnumbered, would soon be defeated.

Peter's band remained motionless. Even the horses seemed to realise the importance of the events to come, for they did not paw the ground or shake their heads and simply stayed still, waiting. The robber army lost patience first. With a shriek, the horsemen charged forward, followed by those on foot. Immediately Peter and his men started loosing arrows, carefully aimed at the horses. Even without being able to pull the bowstring back fully to the ear – because of the restriction caused by being on a horse – the power of the Welsh bow over one hundred yards was formidable and the practised aims of the bowmen devastating. All ten horses fell within a few strides of each other and most of the riders, picking themselves up off the ground, received an arrow in a vital part of the body.

When the robber army was thirty yards away, Peter's men spurred their horses away, left and right, causing the robber army to split as they tried to follow. The speed and agility of Peter's horses hurled them over the ground and they were soon behind the foot army, spinning around and charging into the robbers with swords and axes flailing, killing many before they could turn fully to defend themselves. Although the horses were not trained as destriers to kick and trample foot soldiers, they seemed to understand the essence of battle, for they adroitly outmanoeuvred attack with hardly any urging from the rider. Peter and his men continued to cut and slash, parrying only a few blows with their shields, and soon there was a rout. The few remaining robbers fled. Matthew, who had somehow kept his bow with him, drew his horse to a standstill and carefully picked off two fleeing robbers with well-aimed arrows.

Remaining on their horses, Peter and his men went around the bodies on the ground, instructing those still living to throw any arms they still had away from them so that Peter's men could not be surprised by a sneaky attack. Peter had no doubt that these men had no honour at all and a dagger in the back of one of Peter's men would mean nothing to them. This finished, they herded the injured together and while Peter and the old man watched over them, the other three went around the bodies left lying on the field, dispatching the mortally wounded and collecting arms, trinkets and purses. This done, they dismounted and relieved the injured of any possessions of value, then bound their wounds. One of the horsemen hit by an arrow cursed Peter roundly, promising vengeance. Peter ignored him and held him down while Matthew expertly cut the arrow out of his shoulder and applied a dressing to staunch the bleeding.

Of the thirty or so in the robber army, four had escaped and ten were wounded. The rest were dead. It was likely some of the robbers' wounds would eventually send them to the grave – even the best tended wounds could turn poisonous – and they were certainly likely to prevent any more carousing around the countryside. Save for a nasty gash on Tom's left leg, Peter's group were unhurt. Tom shrugged off this injury, but was chided by William that he was rusty and still in need of training.

When all wounds were bound, Peter addressed the remaining robbers. 'You have had a small taste of what we can do and if I ever see any of you again, you will certainly die a painful and lingering death. We will leave you your food and give you your daggers back, but I want you out of this area for good – and tell any of your bandit friends that if they do not leave the area and let travellers and merchants roam freely, they too will suffer the same fate as you. Understand?'

There were a number of begrudging grunts, although the man who had the arrow removed snarled openly.

Peter and his men picked up the spoils of the battle and moved off in the direction of the ox carts.

'I suppose it would be a cruel travesty if the wagon train has been attacked while we were dealing with this little band!' said Peter. There was muted laughter, but they soon saw the ox carts in the distance, speeding along as fast as an ox could go. Catching up with the carts, Peter assured the traders all was well, slowed the progress to the usual pace and then dropped back into the escort position.

'I have to say,' said the old man, 'I was mightily impressed by these horses. Their manoeuvrability and speed was worth two knights. Destriers are for the scrapheap, I feel.'

During the rest of the month Peter's band encountered a few robber attacks, but it was clear the word had now spread and travellers were being left alone. It was still far too early to be able to allow ox carts to travel unescorted, but the carters in the town were confident enough to visit the quarry and haul back stone for use in building the church. Stone masons, carpenters and workmen were happy and sought out Peter's men to buy them a cup of wine in celebration. Even the local priest was gracious enough to stand a round of drinks at the tavern.

In the meantime, Peter and his men found alternative accommodation. Tom actually did find a willing widow – although a disgusted William reckoned he ought to have learned his lesson with the viper he had left in Devonshire. The old man took up lodging with the priest, while William and Matthew bunked together in the back of a merchant's house. Peter discovered a small house for himself at a very reasonable rent. The lack of visitors to the town during the bandits' stranglehold on the countryside had depressed prices and Peter had no qualms about taking advantage. The house had two rooms: a large living room with a stone-built fireplace for cooking, two benches, a table, and a small bedroom containing a large double bed. At the back there was an area big enough for the group to train and so Peter's house became the place for them all to congregate.

'The shepherd isolation still continues,' said the old man when he had looked over Peter's new home. 'I am not surprised you have chosen to be by yourself. Heaven help any woman who tries to marry you.' Peter shrugged his shoulders and grunted.

At the end of the second month, Peter obtained advance payment from the mayor for the following month.

'You have opened up Falaise and now Chambros,' said the mayor, 'so shouldn't they be contributing to your fee and relieving Courcy of having to pay the full ten marks?'

'Indeed, in time they will contribute, and then you and I can discuss a possible reduction. However, it is far too early. The bandits may simply be regrouping and, more importantly, with just five men we cannot escort every wagon train wishing to go to these two towns, so it will be a while before there is really unmolested passage. My next target is the way between here and Le Plessis-Grimouff – a somewhat greater distance and so a more difficult challenge. Perhaps at the end of next month we can try a few wagons there.'

Just before the start of the fourth month, Peter was interrupted as he was preparing to welcome his fellows into his house before a training session. The front door burst open and standing in the doorway was the bandit who had received an arrow in his shoulder. Peter barely recognised him. His clothes were even more worn and tattered, he bore no arms, save for his dagger, and his face was haggard, his whole body giving off an air of exhaustion.

'What are you doing here?' demanded Peter. 'I told you to leave the area. Are you looking for death?'

The man gazed at Peter, staggered unsteadily to one of the benches and sat down. 'I am not here to harm you and I have walked for days without food to come and speak with you.' His head slumped into his chest as if he was fighting sleep. 'Please hear me out.'

Peter walked over to a small cupboard he had purchased and retrieved a piece of cheese and some bread. Pouring wine into a cup, he gave it to the man.

'Eat and drink first, otherwise you will collapse before you can say anything.'

The man looked grateful and slowly ate the bread and cheese, washed down with the cup of wine. When the wine was finished, Peter poured him another cup, which the man slowly drank as a little strength returned to his body.

In the meantime, the group started to arrive. 'What have we here?' said William. 'A man who has decided death is preferable to wandering the countryside, methinks.'

The man gave a weak smile. 'Not so. I've come here for a good reason, not to die. I want to join you.'

At this Tom exploded. 'A robber bandit in our midst? I do not think so! Scum like you have no honour and no place in decent society.'

'I agree, but please hear me out.' The man took a deep breath, straightened his slumped posture and looked at them all in turn, eye to eye. 'It is true I was a bandit and it is true I was without honour. It was not always so. However, the way you treated all us defeated men, with compassion and kindness, binding our wounds, returning our daggers, letting us keep food – it reminded me of what I had forsaken and how wretched I had become. If you wish, you can kill me now, as you promised.' He gave a wan smile. 'Or you can let me go and I will leave this area and never come back. But I would urge you to consider having me join you. I am willing to do so for no pay until I get my honour back, then you can decide whether I should be paid, or even told to move on. I put myself fully at your mercy.'

'Why do you think we might need you?' asked the old man.

'You are formidable fighters, but there are just five of you. One more at least will be needed shortly if you are to rid the area of robbers. I am an exceptional fighter. Your arrow prevented me showing how good I am. Then there is my knowledge of the bandits, robbers and outlaws in the area. I can tell you where they hide, how they select their targets and where they go to spend their money. With this information we can trap them in their lairs.'

Peter smiled inwardly at this man's use of 'we', exchanging looks with the old man, who had also noticed. The old man nodded almost imperceptibly.

'Frankly, I am far from convinced you are the sort of man we would wish to join us,' said Peter, 'but your courage is not wanting. Few would make the journey you have made to speak to those who have vowed to kill you the next time they met you. At the moment you are no good to anyone. I suggest you go to the inn and take a room, recover your strength and then come back so we can see what sort of man you really are.'

'But I have no money for an inn. You took what little coin I had.'

Peter laughed. 'True. The least we can do is to pay for your board and lodging. Matthew, can you help this man to the inn and tell the innkeeper I will pay?'

Matthew helped the man to his feet and they moved out of the house.

'By the way, what is your name?'

The man looked over his shoulder at Peter. 'Pierre,' he said.

Although Pierre was back on his feet within a few days, he was far from recovered from the arrow wound and Peter was impressed at the determination and stamina of the man who had walked so far, still injured and without food. He told Pierre that he did not wish to see him again for at least another week, so that he could regain his strength by resting. In fact, rest though he did, he also went for walks and started exercising surreptitiously, but not carefully enough to escape the attention of the group. Whether genuine or not, Pierre was no laggard and Peter started warming to him.

When Pierre was almost fully recovered, on a training day when the group was back in Courcy after an escort trip, he appeared at Peter's house and begged to be included in the training. They were all surprised at the change in him. He was no longer haggard. Bathed and dressed in clean clothes, he looked every inch a man of substance with a strong, handsome face beneath a neatly trimmed beard. William took him to one side, examined the arrow wound and noted it was healing well. Then he gave him a captured sword along with their spare shield and took Pierre through his paces while the others watched. Pierre was indeed good. Perhaps not as good as he made out, but it was clear he was no stranger to proper combat with sword and shield. The question was, could he be trusted? Peter turned to the old man for advice.

'We will not know for a while,' said the old man, 'but I have a good feeling about him. We should find out more about his past, though.'

So it was that Pierre came under cross-examination from the group. He was not in the slightest bit fazed or irritated, believing that the only way he could be accepted was to unburden himself of the truth. Pierre was a second son of a noble, sent out to be a squire at the usual age of eight years in the area of Cherbourg, training hard and supporting his master, the knight, and the knight's baron. Coming to the age of knighthood, he put himself forward in tourneys and fought fiercely in inter-baron skirmishes, eventually earning his knighthood. All went well until Geoffrey of Anjou swept down on Cherbourg. Pierre's baron was not willing to bow down to the will of Geoffrey, so Pierre found himself on the wrong side, defeated in the battle for Cherbourg. Pierre's baron seemed to hate Geoffrey and refused to surrender, even when given good and honourable terms, fighting to the death. This meant that all the baron's supporters were either killed or banished. Failing to surrender at the appropriate time was not viewed by an opposing army as worthy, and so retribution was swift and deep.

Pierre, wounded though mobile, managed to escape and for a while, even though he was regarded by Geoffrey as an enemy for not surrendering, he entered the service of other barons. However, when Geoffrey became Duke of Normandy and so brought peace – between the warring barons at least – Pierre was no longer needed and, in an ironic turn of fate, was wrongly accused of flirting with and holding the hand of the baron's young daughter. The girl in question unwittingly overstated the actual facts, but Pierre was hounded out, forfeiting his horse, sword and chain mail and being banished from ever finding service with a baron. Bitter, with no money, no chance of any employment as a soldier, with the slur of besmirching a baron's daughter hovering over him, and no land or other opportunity, he slipped into banditry simply to be able to live. He was not even allowed to join in the crusade to the East, whipped up by the eloquent Monk Bernard. It was not an unusual tale in these times.

The group accepted his story and so Pierre continued to train with them until he was fully recovered and was given the sixth horse, sword, axe and bow provided many months before by Baron de Cours. Pierre was surprisingly quick to pick up the rudiments of the Welsh bow, having a natural eye and good upper-body strength. He was not as good as the rest of them, perhaps, but soon approached an acceptable standard.

One evening after training, Peter addressed them all. 'We are now getting towards the end of the fifth month of our employment here and have not yet made any passage to Le Plessis-Grimouff. The mayor is getting restless and will not much longer accept my explanation that it is the volume of trade between Courcy, Falaise and Chambros needing our escort which prevents any expansion of the reasonably safe area. The number of robber attacks has dwindled to almost none and Pierre has said he can identify where bandits congregate so we can get rid of them before they try to attack a wagon train. However, before doing that, I believe we should all go to Le Plessis-Grimouff, see the mayor there and offer him the same deal as we have in Courcy. He will by now have heard of our successes and should be open to persuasion. Once we have his blessing, we can rout out the remaining robbers in the area. It would be unwise to do this first, for the mayor of Le Plessis-Grimouff would have no reason to pay us!' They all laughed. 'Therefore, I plan to go and see the mayor here tomorrow and tell him we will all be away for two weeks in Le Plessis-Grimouff, to convince the mayor there to contribute to our services. If merchants and travellers wish to leave here to go to the other towns, then they can chance their arms, hopefully successfully.'

The next day they all set out towards Le Plessis-Grimouff, planning to cover the thirty or so miles in just under two days. At the approach of sunset on the first day, Pierre said, 'While I appreciate that you normally camp out in the open at night, you may wish to spend this evening in an inn which is close by. It might be a useful experience.'

He explained no more, but William did not let the suggestion pass. 'Not strong enough to last a night in the open, then? You French don't have what it takes, needing a soft bed!'

'Not at all. At least I'm not a worn-out old English warhorse.'

'Worn out! I'll give you a run for your money any day . . .'

They continued to exchange light-hearted insults, with no animosity, until the old man broke in. 'Enough! You two are like a couple of children. If Pierre thinks it might be useful, let us accept his suggestion.'

They followed Pierre's directions and as the sun was setting came across a fairly substantial inn set a long way from any town or village. Handing their horses to a stable lad, they entered, secured a room for them all to share and sat in the corner of the main eating room with a jug of wine between them.

'So what is useful about staying here?' asked William.

'The fact it is here at all. In this location. That's quite interesting. It is not as though it is serving any nearby town. Then there is the fact it has not been robbed, and the landlord does not seem to take any particular precautions against attack, despite being so far from any help.'

They all grunted and looked around, confirming this was just like a usual inn, if a little larger than most.

'So what is the explanation?' asked William.

'I don't actually know. What I do know is the local bandits eat and drink here, but rarely take rooms, which is unusual. Then there is the fact that over the hill, about half a day or so away, there is a small castle inhabited by Baron de Villiers, a particularly noxious man called "The Toad". Not without reason either. He looks like a toad, squat and fat with a slobbering mouth and oily little eyes which dart about looking for the advantage. I spent a short time in his service, but it was not pleasant. He does not pay his men, believing that now there is no war between barons all he has to provide them with is food and shelter. He taxes his peasants to the hilt and spends absolutely nothing. He even levies a tariff on merchants and peasants wishing to sell their goods in the market which used to be held two or three times a week inside the castle walls. Needless to say, the market has all but disappeared.'

'That does not explain this inn, though,' said William.

'No, not really. I've never got to the bottom of it, but I would wager the local bandits pay him to keep this inn open for their own uses. He is such a toad, he will take money from anyone. He may even give them free passage around the countryside. I have been here with my group to meet others to share information, but no one has actually said de Villiers has anything to do with it.'

Before they could take the topic any further, there was a flurry of activity at the door of the inn as a band of riders pulled up noisily outside and a woman, dressed in finery far greater than any peasant, banged her way in, slapped the dust of the road from her riding clothes and screamed, 'Landlord! Landlord! Why were you not there to take my horse? Am I not going to get any service here? I want your best room – to myself, that is. I'm not going to share. And your best food and wine immediately!'

The landlord scurried up and bowed. 'My lady, I did not know you were coming and I will make arrangements immediately for your room and food.' Bowing again, he scurried away while the woman continued to brush dust off her clothing, then sat down on the nearest bench, her scowl marring a pleasant, if not beautiful, face. For the first time she noticed Peter and his men, who still had their hands on their swords in case the commotion harboured ill.

'You men,' she said, looking towards them, 'do not think for one moment you can mess with me! King Louis is my dearest cousin and if you try anything, his vengeance will be swift.'

Peter got slowly to his feet and walked across to her, bowing his head slightly. 'You can rest assured neither my men nor I would even think of messing with a lady.' He inclined his head again and returned to his table.

'That is not to say,' he said under his breath, just loud enough for his men to hear, 'I make any admissions that you are a lady.' They stifled laughter.

The landlord bustled up with a bowl of steaming food and a jug of wine, with his wife fussing behind to set out the table with a plate, cup, bread, knife and spoon. The woman waved them away and started eating.

'Your men, my lady,' said the landlord. 'A room for them?'

'Certainly not!' she snorted. 'They can stay in the barn with the horses.'

A few moments later, six well-armed men came quietly into the inn and sat down well away from the lady. Their leader ordered wine and food. Escorts they might be, but it was clear they had little, if any, affection for the woman.

'Pierre,' said Peter, 'if you have a chance, befriend those men and find out what you can about that woman. It is unusual for a woman of any quality to be riding about the countryside, even more so with such a small escort. I am curious.'

After they had eaten – a meal considerably delayed by the woman's demands for immediate service – they drifted out of the inn and eventually congregated in the bedroom assigned to them, ready to go to sleep. Pierre was the last to arrive.

'Interesting,' he said with a broad smile. 'The woman is called Elaine de Roche. It does appear that she is indeed the cousin of the king, although it might be a very distant cousin. She is somewhat reluctant to give any detail. Apparently, her elderly husband died the year before last, leaving her considerable but ill-tended lands and very little money. The husband was well liked but a terrible manager, and her manor is now run down and poorly served. She is a better manager and will eventually turn everything around, but her attitude and manner are such that everyone hates her and so they are slow to follow her orders or do anything other than the absolute minimum. However, the land-holding is large and the king has decreed that she should marry again, not something which has found favour with her. As you know, if she cannot find a husband herself, the king can impose one on her and last month he told her he was going to do that, so she has come here to stay the winter with another cousin in the hope that by the time she returns to her own manor, the king will simply leave her alone.'

'Will he?' asked Peter.

'Unlikely, but it will give her breathing space and time to find someone more suited to her needs than the man the king would surely impose on her. But . . .' Pierre paused for effect. 'The really interesting thing is that the cousin she is going to stay with is The Toad, de Villiers. Maybe that explains the small escort.'

They settled themselves to sleep soon after that, each with thoughts of his own about this possibility.

The following morning, bright and early, they were up and away before Elaine de Roche appeared. They made their way directly to Le Plessis-Grimouff where, as before, Peter and the old man sought out the guild masters and called a meeting to explain their proposals. The meeting with the mayor was less amiable than with the mayor of Courcy and he was very reluctant to agree to pay anything. He reasoned that as the general incidence of banditry to the south had diminished, Baron de Villiers, whose castle was relatively close to Le Plessis-Grimouff, would now willingly protect the merchants. However, the meeting was interrupted by the guild masters and after heated arguments it was agreed that Peter would be paid ten marks a month for three months, and after that there would be further discussions. While Peter was initially willing to offer the first month free unless five wagon trains had been successfully escorted, the mayor's belligerence stopped him doing so.

Reporting back to the others, he said, 'I fear our time in this area to make money is going to be limited. Once the countryside is free of bandits, memories will be short and we will be spending more time fighting mayors for money than fighting robbers. Still, we have at least three more months.'

William was struggling with the calculation of how much money they were going to make by the end of the three-month period. Peter brought his attention back to the important issue. 'Do not bother with the sums, William. It will be a good start for us and luck will allow something to turn up. First, though, we have to hit the robbers now, in their lairs, rather than wait for them to attack. We cannot be in three places at once, so we have to significantly reduce the chances of attacks.'

'Yes, that is true,' said the old man. 'We could try to recruit more to swell our number, but it would take time to find the right sort of men, time we do not have, and a band larger than us six will surely attract the attention of every noble in the area, probably the Duke of Normandy as well, fearing a revolution or uprising of some sort. I think we have to be very careful, so it is up to Pierre to let us know where we should concentrate our efforts.'

'Easy enough. Most of the robbers are on foot – small, straggling bands taking opportunity when it arises. They can be mopped up gradually and, more importantly, they are a cowardly ragbag, so if we make it known we are searching for them, most will leave the area. Those who don't can be prevented from attacking wagon trains by having, say, eight or ten wagons with a small escort of half a dozen well-armed men from the local towns who we could pay to travel with and guard the trains. The reality is that these small bands of robbers will only think of trying to steal from easy targets.'

'Good,' said Peter. 'I was hoping that we could fulfil our contract with the mayors to employ, at our expense, a token guard and if there is any trouble then we can deploy to sort it out. So, what of the hard core?'

'They are indeed a hard core. Tough old knights, squires and hangers-on who have long since passed the point of no return in their loss of decency, loyalty and honour. They are cruel, raping and killing for the delight in doing it. There are a dozen, perhaps twenty, their number is constantly changing. They fall out with each other as often as they attack houses, travellers or merchants and they do not have one permanent base. However, winter is coming and winter gives far less opportunity to rob as fewer people travel, so I would expect this hard core to make a concentrated effort on one lucrative target to get them enough money to last into, if not through, the winter.'

Pierre smiled broadly at this point. 'Before your intervention, pickings were becoming thin on the ground because anyone with money or goods was fearful of travelling. Last winter there was talk of attacking a small manor house, whose owner is modestly wealthy and which is guarded by three or four rather elderly former soldiers. In fact it never happened, because there was a big falling out over something. I never got to the bottom of it. However, with you cutting off their income from thieving more than before, I reckon they will be having a proper go at this manor house.'

'When?' asked Peter.

'Knowing the way their minds work, I would say fairly shortly, because if for some reason they are unsuccessful,

then there is still time before winter takes hold to try somewhere else.'

'How far is it to the manor house?'

'Two days if we ride swiftly.'

'Let us go, then.'

The band gathered their things together, paid the
innkeeper and retrieved their horses from the stables. They
struck out at good speed directly south towards the manor
house which Pierre believed was vulnerable, arriving in the
area within two days as predicted.

'We need some advice here,' said Peter. 'Old man, I
would favour scouting around until we find this hard-core
bunch, then we wait for them to attack and take them
from the rear. While I would be confident we will see them
easily – they will have no fear of being attacked and so
will be less than vigilant – I am worried that they might
gain rapid entry to the manor and so make our task difficult, if not impossible. The last thing we want is to mount
a siege. On the other hand, if we tell those in the manor
house of the likely attack, they may panic and leave. What
do you think?'

'You are right. If we accommodate ourselves in the manor
house, we will be able to defend it and, with our arrows,
reduce the attacking force number quite considerably, but
likely not eliminate them all, for men without grace or honour
are easily convinced to run away. On the other hand, if we
wait outside there is a high possibility the bandits will gain
entry and kill those in the house before we can really do
anything decisive. The compromise I suggest is that I go to
the manor house, inform them of the potential attack and
your presence out here to help them, and then organise a
defence. The guard may well be elderly soldiers well past
their prime, but with a bit of encouragement I should be
able to make them a respectable force.'

No one had any better idea, so the old man went to the

manor house while the remainder spread out, scouting the area for signs of the approaching band.

For two days there was nothing. Peter was beginning to get restless, not because he felt Pierre's assessment was wrong, but because he was concerned that the mayor of Courcy would be expecting him back after two weeks and there were only a few days left. He was quietly pleased with the old man's efforts, however. Nothing really showed on the outside except that the main gate leading to a small courtyard in front of the door to the house was left invitingly open – gates of manor houses were only normally opened when visitors had identified themselves – and all window shutters were fixed firmly in place. Also, outside the gates a few tents were erected with fires apparently showing that the inhabitants were busy readying themselves for a meal. It was a scene of peace.

The morning of the third day brought Tom riding at full gallop, indicating a large band of some fifteen mounted men not half a day away. Tom then went to collect the others and they waited, well out of sight opposite the inviting open main gate.

Inviting it was, for the band of robbers spotted it, with the tranquil scene of tents outside, and not believing their luck, immediately charged at full gallop towards the gate before it could be closed. Peter and his men followed behind at a slower pace, ready to loose arrows.

The robber band charged through the gates two abreast into the small courtyard, but before they got fully into the courtyard the first two horses fell to the ground, spilling their riders. The horses behind banged into them and also fell to the ground. As the others came to the gate, a steady rain of arrows came from the slots cut in the window shutters of the manor, and on this cue Peter and his men steadily picked off riders, sending deadly arrows into their backs. It was a long time before the robber band realised they were being attacked from the rear. With more than half their number down, by the time they managed to wheel their horses around Peter and his group were amongst them with swords and axes, lashing and slashing with no mercy. The old man and elderly manor house guards sprang out of the front door, dealt with those who had fallen from their horses, then attacked the rear of the surviving bandits who had turned their horses to meet the challenge of Peter and his men. It was all too much for the robber band. They tried to flee, but there was no chance. Every man was killed.

Peter wandered around the carnage, checking that all were dead, then walked into the courtyard, noting the old man had fixed long, thick staves into the ground with sharpened points at the height of a horse's chest. As the horses galloped in, they impaled themselves on the staves, throwing their riders to the ground and causing a bottleneck into which the riders behind crashed, many being unseated.

'Crafty. I could not see these from a distance,' said Peter.

'I thought you might like it. An old trick very rarely used these days and quite effective in small spaces.'

Although totally successful, this time Peter's little band were not without injury. Most had sustained gashes of some sort, particularly Pierre, who was complaining bitterly that his companions had an unfair advantage with chain mail. He started checking the dead bodies to see if any had chain mail which would fit him.

With the grateful assistance of the owner of the manor and his wife, they were all bandaged up with herbs and powders put in the wounds to prevent poisoning, and then they hauled the bodies away for the servants of the manor to dig makeshift graves.

That evening they had a fine meal in the manor house and slept well on good mattresses. The following morning they set out to make their way back to Courcy, with Pierre sporting his newly acquired chain mail, which was at least serviceable, if somewhat ill-kempt.

14

Once back in Courcy, Peter gathered together the merchants and travellers wanting to go to Falaise and Chambros over the next month or so, while the others in the group recruited suitable armed guards, equipping them with weapons collected from dead robbers. Specific instructions were given to all of them on how to travel and how to make sure any potential attackers would be aware of their number and their armed strength.

Then a small wagon train was prepared and set out towards Le Plessis-Grimouff, with Peter's band escorting in the usual way. The trip passed off without incident, potential thieves either having been banished from the area or now wary of making any attack.

Peter felt it safe enough to recruit more armed guards to cover the Le Plessis-Grimouff route, leaving his men to scout around the area to make sure any potential attackers knew they were being hunted down. Meanwhile, Peter went to Falaise and Chambros to see the guild masters and mayors to extract payment for the services being provided. There was no hesitation that payment was appropriate, but ten marks a month was felt to be far too much. Peter was right. Memories were very short. The recent peace and lack of bandits made everyone feel secure. In the end he agreed five marks per month from each town and, satisfied, he made his way slowly back towards Courcy on a roundabout route as the winter winds and gusty rain gave notice of what was to come.

One midday, as a short squall abated although the wind kept up its cold blast, he came across a small town which in truth was more like a large village making pretence at being a town. He walked his horse to the central square of beaten earth, to be confronted by a large crowd surrounding a dark, almost black, man who seemed to be conducting an auction. Peter drew his horse to a stop at the edge of the crowd and saw, to his disgust, the man was a slave trader. He was just taking the manacles off the legs of a man who was then led away by the successful bidder.

'Now we come to my last delight for you,' said the auctioneer, pulling a young woman into the centre of the square. At least, Peter assumed it was a woman or girl, for the pitiful cropped-haired figure, mere skin and bone, was wearing a makeshift dress. Pathetic as she looked, her demeanour was made to seem all the more downtrodden by heavy manacles on her ankles.

'Now look here,' continued the auctioneer, 'she is a little thin, but she is a great worker and most compliant – if you know what I mean. Come on, girl, show the men what you are made of!'

The girl looked at him with defiant eyes, pulled herself to her full height and did nothing. The auctioneer sneered and picked an evil-looking whip off the ground, swinging it back ready to strike. With reluctance, the girl leaned down, took hold of the hem of her dirty, tattered shift and raised it above her head, confirming her femininity but also displaying stick-like legs below an emaciated body with tiny breasts made all the smaller by the bitter wind.

'Boo!' shouted the women in the crowd. 'She is not worth anything. More of a liability, that one.'

It seemed most of the crowed agreed and, entertainment

for the day over, they drifted off, leaving just a few men to watch the outcome. The auctioneer was distraught, shouting after them that they were missing a bargain. Turning to the handful of men left, he smiled a crooked smile. 'Now, come on, lads. We have something here for you. What am I bid?'

There was a silence.

'One mark to start with, then.'

Still silence. Peter could see the auctioneer groaning inwardly.

'All right, half a mark to start me off.' Silence. 'A quarter mark.'

A filthy dirty, crumpled leech of a man directly in front spoke up. 'A quarter of a mark.'

The girl looked towards him and sheer horror crossed her face as she shrank away from the bidder.

'Now that is better! A quarter mark bid. Half a mark, anyone?'

No one replied. Peter edged his horse forward and saw the dirty leer on the bidder's twisted, pock-marked face.

'Come on, she is worth at least a mark in anyone's money!' urged the auctioneer. There was still no response from the few remaining. Looking around in desperation, the auctioneer shrugged his shoulders as if accepting that this was as much as he was going to get.

'Two marks,' said Peter. The auctioneer bucked up immediately and after smiling crookedly at Peter, he turned to the first bidder with raised eyebrows. Peter knew that two marks was more than this man could ever have. Indeed, he wondered where he had even a quarter mark. The bidder scowled and walked away. A brief glimpse of gratitude crossed the girl's face, to be immediately replaced by the blank look of the condemned.

The auctioneer secured his two marks from Peter and unshackled the girl. 'Be careful with this one. She may not look much, but she's a firebrand. Gave me no end of trouble

– and for two marks!' The auctioneer spat into the ground, turned and walked away, leaving the girl standing next to Peter's horse.

'Put your foot in the stirrup here,' said Peter, shaking his boot out, 'and swing yourself up behind me.' The girl hesitated. 'Would you rather walk?' She looked up at him and put her foot in the stirrup. Peter lifted her easily off the ground to sit behind him. She was no weight at all, just skin and bone.

Peter did not have any desire to stay in a town willing to buy slaves, so he turned his horse and walked it quickly out towards Courcy.

That evening they sheltered in a small wood. Peter gave the girl his coat to block out some of the cold wind and shared out a cold meal of bread and cheese. If she was grateful, she did not show it, but ate slowly and then lay down to sleep. Any attempt Peter made at light conversation was ignored by the girl or shrugged off. Mindful of the auctioneer's warning, Peter made sure his sword and dagger were well away from the girl as he too dropped off into a fitful sleep until the early signs of dawn.

Arising the next day, with the girl on the horse behind him, Peter made his way to Courcy as the clouds lightened and the cold early winter wind dropped. He took her into his house, telling her to sit on a bench, then took his horse to the stable at the inn, purchased some hot food and returned to give the girl a bowl of thin stew with bread. He poured a little wine for her and again went out, this time returning with a mattress and blanket, which he set down in the corner of the living room.

'So. You are not full of words, are you? At least you can tell me your name and where you come from.'

She looked at him hard for a long time. 'What difference does it make?' she said in French with a strange accent. 'Call me what you like.'

'Whether it makes a difference or not, it would be nice to know a little about you. What you can do, for instance.'

Her eyes fell to the table and her shoulders slumped forward. A long time passed and Peter thought he would get nothing from her. Then she spoke. 'I am called Simone.' Another long pause. 'I do not know if that is my real name, but that is what I am called.' She straightened up, looked at him and searched his face for some sign.

He smiled gently. 'Then Simone it is, unless you would like to change it to something else – a name you like, perhaps?'

She continued looking at him and slowly shook her head. 'I don't care. I come from the south, very far south, from Spain. When I was young the Moors came and took me.' She shrugged her skinny little shoulders. 'I do not know what happened to my mother and father. I was told they were killed.'

Peter knew words from him would not only be inadequate, but probably stop her hesitant talking, so he composed his face into a sad expression and tipped his head to one side, indicating he was still listening. Her eyes did not leave his face.

'I was sold to a wealthy French merchant and worked in the kitchen under the house cook for a few years. I was given all the dirty jobs and beaten – it seemed to me just for the sake of beating. Then the merchant decided to retire into the country and I was no longer needed, so I was taken for many miles and sold to a gentleman farmer.' Her pinched face screwed up into a scowl. 'Farmer he might have been, but certainly no gentleman. I thought my previous master was bad, but this man was an animal. He had no wife and was mean and employed no one in the household unless he was forced to, so I had to do everything. Washing, cooking, cleaning and attending to all his needs. The slightest imperfection, he beat me. I ran away a couple of times, but it was no good. I could not find anyone to take me in, so he found me and beat me more. Eventually he tired of me and sold me on to another farmer. At least this man had a wife and did not beat me unless something really bad happened, but I still had to do everything.'

She stopped talking, looked back down at the table, and her shoulders slumped again, as if the very act of saying so much had tired her out.

'So how did you get to become sold again?'

Simone continued looking at the table. 'I became sick. Perhaps it was all the work which wore me out, I don't know. I could not do a day's work. The farmer's wife screamed at me and beat me, but it was no good. Try as I might, I could not do anything for very long and I started collapsing, sometimes fainting. I was frightened more beatings might kill me, so I ran away. This time I was luckier and found an empty shepherd's hut which had some stale food in it. I ate and slept for days and days until I realised I needed more food. The sleep gave me back some of my strength, so I went begging in the nearest village. They gave me food, but knew I had escaped. They told the farmer, who came and took me back. His wife did not want me there any more, though. She thought I was going to be more trouble than help, so they sold me to the Moor you saw at the auction.' She shrugged her shoulders. 'That is my life.'

'How old are you?' asked Peter.

Her thin shoulders shrugged again. 'I do not know. The best I can guess is about fifteen summers, perhaps sixteen.'

'Well, Simone, that is a very sad life indeed. You look tired to me, so I suggest you go to bed.' He pointed to the mattress in the corner of the room. 'Make yourself comfortable and we can talk again tomorrow.'

Peter picked up her wine cup and bowl and placed them both in the small cupboard, straightened up the bench he was sitting on and went to his own room, undressed and got into bed. The rain clouds had passed over and the nearly full moon was shining in through his bedroom window, whose shutters were still open.

He was just drifting off into sleep when he became aware of a noise outside the bedroom door. Carefully, he eased his right hand under the pillow and caught hold of his dagger, which was always there to hand. The bedroom door opened and, through half-shut eyes, he saw Simone enter and walk to the bed, lifting her dirty shift over her head as she made to get into bed beside him.

'What are you doing?' asked Peter.

'What you have bought me for,' she replied.

He sat up and, taking hold of her thin shoulders, pushed her upright as the moonlight picked out her emaciated form. He smiled at her. 'Thank you for being so considerate, but I did not buy you for that. Go back to bed, and we can discuss it tomorrow.'

Simone looked at him long and hard, then picked up her shift and walked out of the bedroom. Peter sighed and lay down to sleep.

The following morning Peter was up with the first light and found Simone sitting on one of the benches. Her back and shoulders were straight, and the thin, pinched face seemed to have morphed from despair into a cautious expectancy.

Peter smiled. 'Sleep well?' She nodded. 'Right then, come with me. We have a busy day.'

Peter walked out of the house with Simone following half a step behind, and they went to the town market. Stall-holders were beginning to arrive and set out their wares. Peter waved and spoke to them as he strode past, eventually stopping at a clothing stall.

'This is my new housekeeper,' Peter said to the middle-aged woman who was arranging various items of clothing on pegs around her stall. 'Unfortunately, her clothing has been lost, so we need a couple of dresses, shoes and all the other things you women wear. Can you fix us up?'

The stall-holder was delighted at having so much potential trade so early in the day. She beamed and took Simone by the hand to gauge her size.

'Her name is Simone,' added Peter. 'You sort her out while I get something for myself. I'll be back in a few minutes.'

Peter returned after a while with a small parcel under his arm, to find Simone and the stall-holder deep in conversation as they were wrapping up the new garments. Peter paid without haggling and took Simone back to the house.

'I have to go out for a couple of hours to see my men,' he told her. 'I suggest you have a wash and put on your new clothes. There is enough wood to light a fire to heat up a pan of water, there is soap in the cupboard, and I've bought you this.' Peter opened his small bundle and took out some fresh bread and a small piece of cooked meat, along with a serviceable dagger. 'I think you need to eat more than anything else – and we cannot have you going about without a dagger, so take this.'

Before Simone could say anything, Peter handed her the dagger and walked out of the house.

It took very little time at all to find his men and get an update on how things were going. They had just come back from their scouting expeditions and reported the wagon trains had been unmolested and that general morale in the area was high. They discussed trying to open up the route to Caen, but agreed it was too soon, particularly as winter was but a few breaths away.

Peter told them he had acquired a housekeeper, but did not elaborate, merely suggesting they did not come to his house to train for a couple of days to let her organise things. No one was unhappy about having a few days' rest.

Returning to his house, Peter found Simone once again

sitting on a bench waiting for him. She was dressed in her new clothes and, while her skinny frame was still all too evident, she looked almost pretty.

'Come on then, let us go out again.' He held the door open and Simone obediently walked out. 'If you are to be my housekeeper, we will need pots and pans, cleaning materials for the house, extra plates, bowls, spoons and cups. I do not know what to buy, so you must choose for me.'

They went back to the market and at every stall Peter introduced Simone, telling everyone she was his housekeeper and asking them to help her if she needed anything. The men were happy enough, but one or two of the women did not appear so pleased – perhaps feeling some envy that Peter had not chosen them. Finally, their purchases made, the two returned to the house, laden down with household items.

'I will leave you to sort this lot out and prepare a meal for both of us tonight.' Peter opened his purse and shook some coins onto the table. 'For you, to buy food. I expect you will have to pay full price today, but you will get to know everyone soon and find the best bargains.'

Simone eyed the money on the table. It was far more than she had ever seen before, and was certainly more than was needed for a few meals. 'Aren't you frightened that I will run away? There is enough money there to keep me going for a long time and get far away from here.'

'If that is what you want. But I need a housekeeper and it is for you to decide whether it is what you want. I am going out again and will return later this afternoon.' Peter left Simone staring at the money on the table.

When he returned that evening, Peter was greeted by the smell of food cooking and, in the fading light, saw Simone standing at the fire tending a gently simmering pot. The table was laid with a bowl, spoon and wine cup. As soon as Peter entered, Simone left what she was doing, poured a cup of wine and put some hot water into a bowl by the fire for him to wash his hands. Gazing around, Peter could not but notice that the room was clean. He washed his hands and sat down.

'I am pleased you stayed,' said Peter, smiling, 'and I am famished!'

Simone returned his smile with a half smile of her own and brought the simmering pot to the table, ladling out a large portion of steaming vegetables into Peter's bowl.

'I see only one bowl, spoon and wine cup. Please, bring some for yourself and sit down opposite me to eat.'

Simone was reluctant, but brought a bowl and spoon from the top of the cupboard, filled it with food and slowly sat down. Peter got up, took a wine cup and filled it with wine for her.

'Come on, eat,' said Peter as he lifted his spoon ready to dip it into the bowl. Simone picked up her spoon and tentatively did the same. With a grunt, Peter started to eat, pausing after the first mouthful, chewing it slowly. 'This is really good, and most unusual. I detect herbs, but they seem to be spicy. Strange, but good.'

Peter carried on eating and when his bowl was empty Simone shot up to refill it. Peter gratefully accepted and when he had finished, he sat watching Simone finish her bowl slowly, as if not to offend. Peter took a draught of his wine and waited. When Simone's bowl was empty, Peter said, 'That was first class. I have not eaten anything so tasty for a very long time.' It was a slight exaggeration, but Peter felt a little praise would do Simone good. 'I will not ask what was in it. Let it be your secret. Did you have any trouble buying the food?'

'Not really. It seemed to me the prices were a little high, but I did not haggle too much as I did not want to make enemies of anyone. I had some trouble finding the spices – not least because this town knows them by different names

– and they are not particularly good. I did not get the blend quite right.'

'So you have no complaints so far?'

'Oh no. But can I make a suggestion?' Peter nodded and smiled. 'This fireplace is useless. It needs to be built up properly so I can cook things without the heat being all over the place. I am using far too much wood to do the job and not getting good results. Is there anyone who can change the fireplace?'

Peter nodded. 'I am sure there is someone. I'll find out tomorrow and get it fixed. Do you think you can cook for more than the two of us?'

'Yes, certainly, when the fireplace is fixed. How many?'

'As you have probably already found out, I have five colleagues who currently eat at whatever place in the town they choose. When we are not in the countryside, they all meet here each morning and train in fighting skills outside, at the back of the house. If you could prepare a meal for us all at noon, that would be good, and perhaps an evening meal as well. I will have to see what they want. I will wait until the fireplace is up to your standards, though.'

'I will do as you bid.' Simone got up, took the empty bowls and washed them in a pan of water by the fire.

After the first taste of Simone's cooking, save for some evenings when Tom went to eat with his widowed landlady, none of Peter's men needed any urging to take all their meals at his house.

As the mists, rain and cold of the winter took a grip on the countryside, a steady pattern emerged. They made occasional forays into the country to ensure potential robbers were aware that any hostile activity would be met with severe repercussions, and the now less frequent wagon trains with their attendant hired guards passed unmolested between the four major towns and other smaller towns and villages. When in Courcy, the group continued with their fighting exercises which, due to the weather, were somewhat shorter than before, the men preferring to sit in Peter's house talking and nibbling at the sweet breads and cakes prepared by Simone.

Slowly, as the winter was passing, Simone hesitantly gained confidence. At first she exchanged only infrequent, shy words with the men, but realising their teasing of her strange accent was only friendly banter, she gradually engaged in proper conversation and then quite readily swapped affable insults, often chiding them on their willingness to sit by the fire gossiping rather than applying themselves to more manly pursuits. Men though they were, she quickly established they were in her living room and could not make a mess or trample in with wet and muddy clothing without incurring her wrath. The men accepted her without question and soon they were all sitting at the table together with cups of wine, discussing what was to be done about freeing up the route to Caen when spring set in.

As gradually and subtly as Simone's self-assurance developed, so did her body. Still slim, she filled out the skin and bones, her face lost its gauntness and her hair grew long enough to be fashionably tied back. Her movements too were no longer cowed, and she flitted about with lightness and grace. The old man, being in charge of the group's purse, gave her money for food and essentials and went through her spending, reporting back to the others – out of her hearing – that she was scrupulously honest, was saving them money because they were not eating elsewhere in the town, and seemed to drive the hardest of hard bargains with the stall-holders in the market without upsetting them. But for the biting cold, it was a pleasant winter for them all.

15

As winter slowly eased and spring fought to assert itself, one afternoon, after the men had risen from their midday meal and dispersed to their tasks, there was a commotion in the main street as six armed men on horses clattered up, dismounted and went into the tavern. The people in the streets scurried away, fearing that armed men could not augur well, and those in the market who had not yet cleared their stalls for the day hurried to bundle up the last of their wares. Peter was in his house laughing with Simone over a dish she had invented which was far from her usual standard when the door burst open and the tavern keeper rushed in.

'Baron de Villiers wants to see you, now!' he gushed, breathlessly.

'What?' asked Peter, frowning and not understanding.

'Baron de Villiers with five of his men has come to town and is in my tavern demanding to see you immediately. He said he would cut off my ears if you did not show up.'

Peter laughed. 'Your ears are safe enough. Go back and tell him I am on my way.' The tavern keeper hastened back to his tavern.

'What do you think de Villiers wants?' asked Simone.

Peter shrugged his shoulders. 'We will see.'

'I am frightened. He is not known for his kindness and

understanding, so whatever it is, it's not going to be good for you.'

Peter shrugged once again, slipped off his chain mail which he had been wearing for that morning's fighting practice, replaced his shift and, unarmed apart from his dagger, strolled to the tavern, giving off the air of someone with not a care in the world and looking as though he was just a simple man.

He could not miss de Villiers, who was sitting alone at a table in the centre of the room swilling back a large cup of wine. His five men were at another table at the back of the room. De Villiers was as toad-like as he had been previously described to Peter. His stunted, bloated frame spread out over the chair in which he was sitting and the squashed face atop virtually no neck sported a large slobbering mouth and black beady eyes that darted constantly around the room as if looking for an insect he could snap up for a meal.

Peter walked up to him and smiled. 'I understand you wanted to see me, my lord.'

De Villiers' eyes darted to Peter's face, then darted away again as his slobbery mouth twisted into a snarl. 'So, this is the man who has been going around my lands taking money from my towns. What have you to say for yourself?'

'My lord, I have only tried my best to rid us all of the robbers and bandits who were making trade between towns and villages impossible. As for taking money, the towns have agreed to pay me to do this and continue to keep the countryside free.'

'Any money you have extracted is mine by rights. All these towns are under my protection and they pay their taxes to me.'

'With respect, my lord, payment was for services provided and I believe that while land, sometimes goods and passage over bridges and into towns may be subject to tax, services are not.'

'Wrong. I have it on authority that the services you say you have provided fall directly to be taxed.'

Peter smiled his most charming smile. 'I believe, my lord, you have been misinformed. No doubt the scribe has made a mistake. The phrasing of deeds and rights is often difficult and your scribe may well have misinterpreted what has been written in your charter.' The Toad's eyes alighted on Peter and narrowed, hardly believing that this upstart was questioning the word of a baron. Before de Villiers could reply, Peter continued, 'May I suggest that we both go over your charter to see whether what you have been told is correct? Obviously if it is, I will have no hesitation in paying you everything to which you are entitled.'

The baron's eyes continued to flick around the room. 'Not only do you question my word, you make pretence that you can read!'

'My lord, I do not for one moment question your word – merely the information which has been given to you. It cannot be your fault if you have been informed incorrectly. As to reading, with your help I am sure we can resolve what your charter says.'

This was too much for de Villiers. He straightened in his chair and looked around at his men. Just as he was about to bark out an order, the old man, William, Matthew, Tom and Pierre, fully armed with swords and axes, walked quietly into the room through the back door of the tavern and positioned themselves behind de Villiers' men. They did not draw their arms, but each had his hand across his body ready to grasp the hilt of a sword if needed. De Villiers was not slow to see he had been outmanoeuvred, so turned back to Peter with a malevolent smile.

'When you are in my lands, you are my servants, and if I say tax is due, you will pay. In one month from today I command you to come to my castle and give me half of all the money you have taken from my towns. If you do not, then I will brand you all outlaws with a reward on your heads and you will be hunted down like dogs.'

De Villiers waved a dismissive hand and Peter left – not by backing away, which was the respectful thing to do when leaving the presence of nobility, but by turning his back on the baron and walking normally to the door. Peter's men also left, via the back door. All of them, except Pierre, who was keeping a lookout in case de Villiers tried anything underhand, congregated back in Peter's house with sombre faces.

'We have a problem,' said the old man.

'Yes,' Peter replied, 'but let us wait until The Toad has left and Pierre is here with us. By the way, how did you know I was in the tavern?'

They all looked towards Simone, who was blushing deeply. 'I was fearful,' she said simply, turning away to attend to a pot on the stove which required no attention at all.

It was not long before Pierre arrived, reporting that de Villiers and his men had left the town after indulging themselves with the tavern keeper's best wine, for which they did not even offer to pay. Although the tavern keeper was glad that de Villiers did not tarry, he was mumbling about the cost of the wine which, in his view, was Peter's fault for causing the baron to come to town in the first place.

'Do not worry,' said the old man, 'I will pay him something. I know his profits on wine, so I will give him enough to cover the cost to him.'

Pierre settled himself down on the bench and Peter beckoned to Simone to pull up a stool and sit with them. There was a long silence, with no one wishing to say what they were all fearing.

Peter broke the silence. 'Well, old man, what is your assessment of the situation?'

The old man looked around the table at the troubled faces. 'Not good. As I see it, we have only two immediate choices: to pay what de Villiers wants, or to leave the area.' There was another silence. 'If we pay, then we have no assurance that such a man will be true to his word and let us continue to operate. Even if he does, he will demand more next time. If we leave, then we will be branded as outlaws and we will have to go far, far away to escape his area of influence, with no guarantee we can do the same as we did here, or that the baron in that place will not also demand payment from us.'

'Can't you just kill him?' asked Simone.

Pierre exploded. 'Kill a baron? Impossible! I do not doubt for one moment de Villiers is far from the most popular baron under the Duke of Normandy's governance and that he would not feature highly on Geoffrey's list of guests to a banquet, but these nobles stick together and I would rather be an enemy of de Villiers than have Geoffrey hunting me down.'

William, Matthew and Tom nodded. They all turned and looked at Peter, even the old man, who raised an eyebrow in expectation. Peter smiled to himself. The old man was thinking along the same lines.

'Well,' said Peter, 'Simone is right. If de Villiers is not around, then our troubles pass. Pierre is also right. If we kill him, the Duke of Normandy will not let it go by without retribution. However, your thoughts of getting rid of The Toad are along the lines of our usual fighting methods. For sure, if we, free men, were to shoot down any noble with our bows, then this would be viewed as unforgivable, an attempted insurrection at the very least. But what if de Villiers was challenged to an honourable battle – he and his knights against us, fighting with lances, swords and axes? What difference would that make, old man?'

'If The Toad accepted the challenge and we fought in the same way as they did,' said the old man, 'then whilst the nobles would not like it, it does fall within their code of honour as an honourable battle, evenly matched, and if we were successful we would suffer no retribution. The problem I see is whether The Toad would accept a challenge to do battle and, more importantly, what chance would we actually have against six or so experienced knights fighting on their terms? We must remember, our successes so far have been based on doing the unexpected. If we tried anything unusual, then that would give the nobles an excuse to say the battle was not honourable.'

They thought silently for a while. 'The Toad may look fat and slovenly,' said Pierre eventually, 'but he would not have become a baron if he couldn't fight. In my experience, those little fat men are often aggressive and strong, with unbelievable stamina. As to his knights, I exercised with them during my short time with de Villiers and assuming there have been no changes, they too can fight like demons.'

'How many knights does he have?' asked Peter.

'Five, six at the most,' replied Pierre.

'So it boils down to this. If we pay and stay, our future is uncertain. If we do not pay and leave, our future is bleak. If we fight de Villiers, it has to be by honourable challenge to battle, on his terms.' Nods all around. 'I am as certain as I can be that de Villiers will accept a challenge to battle. Do we think we can win?'

'Yes, we can,' replied William cautiously. 'The major problem we will have is the use of lances. We all have pikes, but have not really trained to use them on horseback, particularly against knights whose whole focus is to succeed in jousts at tourneys. Lance to lance, we will be doomed. We cannot go into this battle with lances.'

'What then?' asked Tom.

'We have to adapt our fighting methods to counter the lances, which will mean hard training for the next three weeks or so. Even then I cannot guarantee that we will all succeed and so we have to be prepared for casualties amongst us.'

'This is an important moment,' said Peter. 'We know the old man is holding sufficient money for each of us to return to England to rent a small piece of land and perhaps a humble dwelling which could be the start of a peaceful and fairly comfortable future. In the month we have, we could get back to England. Do we wish to take that opportunity, or do we fancy our chances against de Villiers?'

'No question for me,' spat Tom. 'We have worked too hard to give it all up now simply because of some greedy little baron. Besides which, we need a real challenge.'

They all agreed enthusiastically, except Simone, who looked down at the table with her shoulders slumped. No one noticed.

'So then,' said Peter, 'massive and sustained training, morning and afternoon for the next three weeks. We have to learn how to counter lances on horseback. William, you will have to take the lead on this and perhaps, old man, your jousting experience can assist us too.'

'Right,' said William. 'It is too late to start today, but at first light tomorrow I want you here fully armed with your horses and we can go outside the town to a suitable spot and start. Simone, would it be possible for you to make a cold midday meal and bring it out to us so we lose no time?'

'Of course,' replied Simone. She got up from her stool at the table and went to the cupboard, bringing out cups and a large jug of wine. 'Let us drink to your success.'

They toasted success and drank the jug of wine as they discussed the fighting areas requiring the most practice. When the wine was finished, they got up from the table with an air of expectation and purpose to leave and go back to their own beds.

'Before you go,' said Peter, 'not a word of what we are intending to anyone. I do not want the baron to know what we are up to and if we are far enough out of the town when we train, then no one will notice anything different.'

They all left and Peter slowly started gathering up the wine cups for Simone to wash. Simone stopped him and took his right hand, placing it firmly on her tiny left breast and at the same time putting her right hand behind his neck, pulling him down as she raised herself on tiptoe to kiss him feverishly and passionately on the lips. At first Peter was stiff and taken aback, but the fire in her kiss relaxed him as he slowly started to respond.

Simone broke away. 'At last! We cannot lose any more time. Come!' she said, pulling him by the hand towards the bedroom. 'Do not fight me. I have waited too long. Come on.'

Peter obediently allowed himself to be pulled into the bedroom and once there Simone pushed him onto the bed, kissed him with even more desire and started unfastening his clothes. All resistance evaporating, Peter helped her, and she quickly slipped out of her dress and lay down beside him, pressing her body into his.

Mindful of the instruction given to him by the old whore in Devonshire – it felt like a lifetime ago – Peter gently started to caress Simone's head and neck, but Simone needed no arousing. She was on fire, and with excited hands running over each other's bodies, they soon coupled, Simone urging every movement. Afterwards, spent, they lay holding each other gently.

'I should apologise,' said Simone, 'but I am glad, not sorry. I have tried to encourage you before, but you seemed immune. Never cold, but always a little distant.'

Peter grunted, almost too exhausted to speak. 'I did not think it was the right thing. You have been through too much and I wanted to let you have a real life, something you have not had since you were a child.'

'You have done that, and this is just perfect for me.'

Simone wriggled even closer to him as he wrapped his arms round her, as if to envelop her completely. After a while, she got up and went to the living room, returning with an oil lamp which she lit and put on the table beside the bed. She then went back into the living room and reappeared carrying two wine cups and a small jug of wine.

'I thought we drank all the wine earlier!'

'No. I always keep a spare of everything, just in case.'

'You planned tonight.'

'No, I did not. How could I have foreseen the coming of de Villiers and the change it is going to make to our lives?'

They drank the wine slowly, in silence, and when it was finished, Simone turned back to Peter and kissed him again. This time the old whore's instructions bore fruit and their bonding was slower, more measured and, eventually, brought them both to greater peaks of delight.

Up at first light the following morning, Peter went – fully armed – to the inn to retrieve his horse from the stable. Back at his house, he was greeted by the rest of the group. They set off out of the town to find a suitable field where William, who had been discussing tactics with the old man late into the night, gave them instruction on how to parry a lance with their swords on horseback.

'It is going to be difficult and completely about timing. Too soon, and the knight will be able to readjust his lance. Too late, and you are dead. At the right moment, lean forward in your saddle, bring your sword with as much force as you can muster across your body and hit the tip of the lance towards your shield, then angle the shield so that the lance slips harmlessly off it and away. You will not have time to strike your own blow against the knight, so do not try. Any attempt to do this will lose your concentration on the all-important blow to the end of the lance. Also, do not spur your horse into a gallop, as this will shorten the time you have to carry out the manoeuvre.'

Taking turns to charge on horseback, with a pike used as

a lance, while the others practised parrying with swords, they gradually began to master the technique, but not every time. Some struck too early, but more often they struck too late.

Simone dutifully arrived each noon with their meal and after they had eaten, she stayed to watch their practice. She had a sharp eye and suggested to William that some of the trouble could be that the swordsmen were first leaning forward in their saddle and then swinging their swords to strike the tip of the lance. If both were done in one fluid movement, then it would be far more unexpected and coordinating one movement would be easier than trying to manage two. After discussing it with the old man, they adopted this practice and immediately their success rate increased.

When the horses were tired, they fought each other on foot with sword and axe, thrusting, stabbing, slashing and bashing away for hours on end, building up speed, accuracy, strength and stamina.

At the end of each day they were all exhausted and returned to Peter's house to discuss things learned during the day, but immediately after eating they went back to their own billets to sleep. Tired though Peter was, it did not stop him and Simone exploring more of each other and satisfying their mutual and demanding desires.

As the weeks passed, Simone was not idle, for apart from her usual cooking, cleaning and watching them in their training, she took all their chain mail, cleaned, brushed and burnished each piece to a high lustre, then oiled it all thoroughly so that the chain mail moved freely on the body and did not inhibit any actions. The men's garments were also taken away, washed and repaired ready for the battle to come.

As far as the rest of the town was concerned, Peter's men were simply catching up on training which they could not do during the winter, and travellers and wagon trains continued to ply between towns and villages with minimal guards supplied and paid for by Peter's band.

They decided to take four easy days to travel to de Villiers' castle. During that time the horses would not be strained and the men could recover from their rigorous training, all to be sharp for the anticipated battle. Three days before they were scheduled to start, Peter asked the others to eat and stay in the town and not come to his house. No one was surprised. Simone's glowing countenance and the extra spring in her step had not gone unnoticed, nor had the concern which crossed her face when Peter was unusually bested in one of their training exercises. They smiled quietly to each other, not at all begrudging the loss of three good meals for Peter's time and happiness with Simone.

16

On the day of their leaving for de Villiers' castle, Peter arrived at the inn stable with saddlebags full of food for their journey. They saddled up and rode the horses quietly out of town towards their destiny.

The weather was fine and they made steady progress, neither hurrying nor dawdling. As the sun dipped below the horizon on the fourth night, they walked their horses into a wood just a few hours away from the castle. Unsaddling, they ate a cold evening meal, not in silence but in a sombre mood with a feeling of apprehension as to what the morrow would bring. All had been in battles before, but never one on which their fate depended so heavily. The old man and Pierre, being former knights, had faced knights with lances on horseback, so knew what was to come. The others could only imagine.

'So, old man,' said Peter grimly, 'tomorrow it will be. What do you think our chances are now?'

The old man took a deep breath. 'To be completely honest, it is not going to be easy. The thing that troubles me is that, while I am sure our training will mean that we have a high chance of avoiding being hit by lances on the first pass, after that . . .' He tailed off. 'The thing is, the knights are very experienced and they will not fall for the same trick a second time. They are well used to adjusting their lance and their

strike at the last moment to counter any unexpected movement. For the first charge, they will be confident of a lance
against a sword, but after that . . .' He did not finish his
sentence.

Peter smiled and leaned back against a tree in a completely
relaxed posture. 'But we have our secret weapon,' said Peter.
The rest frowned at him. 'Look, the knights will be on destriers
which, as we all know, are big and heavy. They will be at
full gallop when they engage with us and after missing the
first time, the knights will have to slow the destriers, turn,
readjust their lances and then bring their horses back to a
gallop before they can strike again. Destriers are just not
made to be manoeuvrable and will take a long time turning
in a big arc, whereas our little horses are agile, not going at
full gallop, and can turn on a silver mark. If, immediately
after the first strike, we turn quickly and bring our horses
up to full gallop, then we can be on the knights before they
can complete their turn. At the very worst, even if they have
turned, their destriers will not have steadied themselves to
gallop in a straight line and so the lance will be virtually
useless.'

They all thought about this. 'You are right,' said William.
'As a matter of course, as soon as the lance has struck, or
missed, the knight brings it up to the vertical ready to lower
again when his horse starts the second charge. There is every
chance that they will not have time to bring the lance down,
or if they do, they will not be able to position themselves
for a fatal blow. Yes. I think we have a chance there.'

The frowns turned to quiet smiles, lifting the sombre mood.
They decided on a lookout schedule for the night in case
any de Villiers men were about, then lay down to sleep.

At dawn the following morning, the group were up, saddled
and ready. 'Before we move off,' said Peter, 'string your bows
and fix them securely under your stirrup leathers well out

of the way so they will not interfere with your fighting, but in a position where they can be grabbed quickly in case of need. Luckily, the day is fine, so we will not have problems with rain on the bowstrings.'

Although not knowing what the 'case of need' might be, they obediently did as they were bid, mounted up and walked their horses towards the castle.

'When we get there, we will stop, with me in front, just out of crossbow range,' said Peter. 'We will wait, and if we have to stay there for any length of time without attracting attention, let us walk our horses slowly back and forth in a straight line, keeping the same distance from the castle walls. Finally, I do not want any of you looking fierce or efficient. Slump in your saddles and if anyone comes out of the castle, do not make eye contact, but look despondent, frightened if you can. Essentially, I want us all to look reluctant and unprepared.' They all grunted in acknowledgement.

On arriving at the castle, they took up their position outside crossbow range and after half an hour of waiting, slowly walked their horses up and down as Peter had directed. Eventually a soldier messenger rode his horse out of the open castle gates. Peter and his group stopped their walking and waited. The messenger approached and, looking them up and down with a sneer on his face, said, 'Baron de Villiers has charged me with accepting your taxes. He knows how much you have taken from the towns, so he will not be short-changed.'

Peter looked down at the ground, clearing his throat as if finding it difficult to speak, and replied without looking up, 'We have all the money with us, but I regret we do not think the baron has any right to it. We urge him to recon-sider.'

'The baron will not reconsider. Pay up, or face the conse-quences.'

Peter nudged his horse with his knee and it shuffled to

one side as he gave the impression that he was having diffi-culty controlling it. 'I am afraid, then, if the baron wants our money, he has to take it from us.' Looking briefly at the messenger, he took a deep breath as if steeling himself for something unpleasant. 'We challenge the baron to honourable battle.'

'What?' said the soldier, laughing and looking derisively at the group. 'You, fight the baron and knights in battle? Impossible! The baron does not fight with renegades, only with honourable men.'

'Oh well then, if the baron is frightened of us . . .' Peter left the sentence hanging. The messenger sneered. 'We are prepared to present ourselves in fair and honourable battle with the baron. If he refuses our challenge, then others will be the judge of whether the baron is frightened or not. Or perhaps he is without honour.'

'You tread on dangerous ground, renegade. I will tell the baron what you have said – word for word – and you will be sorry.'

The messenger wheeled his horse and galloped back through the open gates of the castle.

'What do you think?' asked Matthew.

'More than a good chance. If he comes out with his full army against us, then he knows he will lose honour, for we've invited fair battle. If he refuses to fight, then he risks being branded a coward. Evil and underhand though he undoubt-edly is, he could not take the chance that fellow nobles will speak behind their hands about a knight refusing the chal-lenge of a mere freeman, particularly as I hope the messenger will report back how ill-prepared and reluctant we appear. What do you think, old man?'

'Agreed. Unless he is actually frightened, he cannot possibly let this challenge go by.'

They continued to wait, the gates of the castle remaining open as if inviting them in. Eventually, de Villiers and five knights came through the castle gates. They rode towards Peter, stopping about a hundred yards away, fanning out in a straight line with space between them, ready for battle. Peter's men slowly strapped on their shields, loosed swords in scabbards and also formed a straight line immediately in front of the baron, walking their horses forward to stop seventy-five yards away.

'Old man, you have the sharpest eyes. Can you see any more knights on the battlements or at the gates?'

'No. I think we have the whole motley bunch before us.'

'Good. Stay slumped. Do not look eager. Move your horses about a bit as if you have difficulty controlling them.'

De Villiers' destriers stood rock still, sensing the battle to come and ready to be spurred forward. Peter's horses were a little skittish, but none on their backs took their eyes of the baron's men.

Eventually, de Villiers and his knights moved slowly forward. Peter's group stayed still, making their horses ready for the off. The knights slowly lowered their lances to the horizontal and the destriers surged ahead, gathering speed with every pace. Peter and his men drew their swords, readied their shields and urged their horses towards the thundering knights, not at a gallop, but slowly building up to a gentle canter.

This was the first time Peter had seen fully armed knights on their destriers riding at him in battle. In previous battles they had been a long way away with their attention on other knights, not on him. It was a terrifying sight of sheer power and intent and, but for his concentration on the formidable task before him, Peter could have been frightened. He fixed his eyes on de Villiers, who was charging directly towards him. His squat form seemed to mould into his destrier as his beady eyes glinted just above the rim of the shield hiding the upper part of his body. The lance was steady and with lightning speed de Villiers was upon Peter.

Peter's mind was numb and he completely shut out the noise of hoofs and the clatter of metal around him. He put all his effort and concentration into focusing on the end of the baron's lance speeding towards his chest. At precisely the right moment Peter lunged forward, bringing his sword across his body to hit the tip of the lance onto his angled shield, to send it sliding harmlessly away. While the lance blow was glancing, a white-hot pain shot up Peter's left shoulder with the force of the impact, and he wondered briefly how knights at jousts could withstand three or four such encounters.

Immediately the lance missed, Peter swung his horse about and the little fellow, eager to display his agility, spun around to spring into a full gallop within a few strides. De Villiers was hauling his horse around in a large circle with his lance vertical, ready to prepare for the next charge, but before he and his horse were in a position to do anything, Peter was nearly upon them. The Toad, realising that his lance would be no good, threw it to one side and brought his shield up to meet Peter's sword thrust, at the same time drawing his own sword.

Peter's horse spun again, heading back to engage the baron who, with his own destrier now at a slow pace, managed to turn to meet Peter head on. They clashed with sword and shield, horses shoulder to shoulder. De Villiers' destrier leaned against Peter's horse, as he had been trained to present a stable fighting platform for the baron, expecting Peter's horse to do the same. Peter's horse, though, was not so trained and, feeling the weight of the destrier against his shoulder, nimbly moved away. The destrier was not expecting this and lurched to one side. De Villiers was concentrating on his fighting, so was taken by surprise as his horse stumbled and momentarily half-lost his balance in the saddle, tipping towards Peter. Peter seized the opportunity and struck with all the weight of his sword and shield on the baron's side, knocking him off his horse to the ground.

The Toad was quickly on his feet and Peter moved his horse away to dismount and fight on foot. The Toad did not move, standing perfectly still and balanced with sword arm ready and his beady eyes peering just above his shield, waiting for Peter to come to him. His large kite-shaped shield covered all of his squat form from just below his eyes to his knees, leaving only his sword arm and a small part of his rotund body showing on either side. Peter advanced steadily and attacked. The baron easily deflected Peter's blows and parried with his own. Cutting and thrusting, Peter kept up a steady rhythm of aggression and warded off The Toad's attacks, though it was clear that neither one of them was overcoming the other. The Toad barely moved his feet any more than was necessary to counter Peter's thrusts and his eyes, which on their first meeting flicked back and forth, remained steady and glinting with expectancy. As the blows continued, Peter realised Matthew was right. Little fat men had far more strength and stamina than their appearance gave credit for, and this baron was using his brain as well as the power in his sword arm. He would not be defeated easily, if at all. Peter started to think too, but could see no way to strike a crippling blow. The baron knew all the moves and was very experienced in real combat, not just in training exercises.

Peter was beginning to feel weary and he contemplated using the same ruse on de Villiers as he had with Baron Gelling, pretending to tire more to lure The Toad into over-confidence. It was clear, however, that de Villiers was not to be taken in, for he was more intent on allowing Peter to attack and so conserving his own energy, waiting for an opening to strike the fatal blow rather than initiating any move of his own. That opening nearly came, for the steady glinting eyes flicked briefly to the top of Peter's right sword arm, then back again. Peter immediately disengaged and took a step back as if to ready himself for the next assault, realising The Toad had spotted a weakness which William had been trying to cure. Peter was inclined to move his shield to the left, across his chest, and so expose his right upper arm and shoulder. A well-directed blow there would render Peter defenceless. The baron had not struck and Peter assumed that he had not exposed enough of his upper arm, but de Villiers had identified the weakness and would bide his time until he was sure not to miss. So Peter must turn this weakness into his strength. The baron's near-stationary fighting position had meant that Peter's natural agility had not yet been called upon, so any lightning moves to one side or the other would surprise the baron.

Peter engaged once again with a little more ferocity and allowed his shield to expose a small part of his upper arm and shoulder, but not enough to invite a crippling blow. His following attack was even fiercer, exposing even more of his right shoulder. It was still not enough for the baron to be sure of a clean strike. Then, with a look of desperation in his eyes, Peter went at the baron again with as much aggression as he could muster, having no regard for the fact that his shield was not covering his right upper arm and shoulder. His weight, though, was evenly balanced on both feet.

The Toad's eyes briefly, almost imperceptibly, flicked to Peter's right shoulder as an advance signal, but as de Villiers' sword arced towards Peter's shoulder and his body moved forward to give maximum force to the thrust, so Peter sprang to his right and forward, bringing himself almost parallel to and nearly behind The Toad's shield. Too late, de Villiers realised that he had been outmanoeuvred, and before he could swing back Peter plunged his sword straight into those beady little eyes. Surprisingly, the baron did not drop to the ground at once. It was as if he had become rooted there and even with no eyes and a pierced brain, his body seemed to have a life of its own, maintaining a defiant upright stance. Slowly, very slowly, the knees bent and the baron crumpled, lifeless, to the grassy earth.

'And about time too,' said a voice over Peter's shoulder. 'Talk about making a meal of things! We thought you would never get it over with.'

Peter looked around to see his five comrades standing in a line, obviously having just watched him fight.

'Well, thanks for the help,' Peter retorted.

'We sorted out our opponents in quick time,' said William, 'but you wanted an honourable battle, so we couldn't help you.'

'More of that later. Quickly, get your bows and mount your horses. I want to be in through those open gates as soon as possible. Shoot anyone you see who might threaten us.'

Without waiting for a reply, Peter sheathed his sword, ran to his horse, pulled out his bow from its fastening under the stirrup leathers, mounted and urged his horse forward towards the castle gates while taking an arrow from his quiver and readying it for use. The others were but a few paces behind him.

The gates were still open and Peter's band rode directly in. Immediately in front of Peter at the other side of the castle courtyard a woman stood facing him, wearing a bright red headscarf and pointing feverishly to her right. Peter swung his horse to the left and let fly an arrow at a soldier on the castle wall who was about to fire his crossbow, hitting him square in the chest. Another soldier was making his crossbow ready and Matthew's second arrow tumbled him to the ground. Looking back at the woman in the red headscarf, Peter saw that she was now pointing behind him. He wheeled his horse around and saw, on the castle wall immediately above the open gates, a soldier who, from his dress, appeared to be the captain in charge or the master at arms.

He was straightening up, having picked up a loaded crossbow from the ground.

'Drop it or die!' shouted Peter.

The man hesitated, then continued to straighten up with the bow ready for use. Peter sighted along his arrow.

'Drop or die!'

Very slowly, the man let the bow fall, then dropped it to the ground.

'Good, now walk down those steps to the courtyard here. Make no sudden moves.'

The captain continued to look with defiance at Peter, but realising that he had only one choice if he was to keep his life, slowly walked down the steps and across to Peter's horse. There he stood still, waiting.

'Tell all your men to come into the courtyard now. Also tell them if anyone makes even the slightest hostile move, we will kill without hesitation.'

The captain said nothing and looked Peter squarely in the eyes. Peter glanced over his shoulder and saw a nodding of the red headscarf. All was well. He lowered his bow.

'We have command of this castle now, and command of you. Do as I say.'

The captain gave a deep sigh and called out to his men. About a dozen of them quickly appeared.

Peter directed them and the captain to one corner of the courtyard and told them to drop swords, axes, daggers and pikes to the ground. When this had been done, Peter spoke again to the captain.

'I understand there are six escorts of Elaine de Roche here. Where are they?'

'They were not interested in the baron's fight, so they're in their quarters,' replied the captain.

'You,' Peter said to the oldest-looking soldier, 'go and get them out here, unarmed, and also bring out all the castle staff – I mean everyone.'

The soldier scurried off and after a while the six escorts came out, followed reluctantly by the castle and household staff. Peter looked towards the red headscarf. It nodded once again.

'Baron de Villiers and his knights have been defeated in honourable battle and that means his castle and all his possessions are forfeit. We six here intend to take up residence in this castle.' Tom shot Peter a startled look. 'And you all have a free choice. You can either stay here and serve us, or you can leave now with your arms and possessions. If you want to leave, we will not harm or hinder you. We only want people here who wish to be with us and serve us.'

A murmur went around the courtyard, but before anyone else could say anything there came a shrill scream. 'How dare you! What are you doing here? My cousin will get to hear of this and you will all be hunted down!' Elaine de Roche ran out of the castle towards Peter, shaking her fist in the air. 'You have no right to be in this place. If the baron is dead, it is mine!'

'I do suggest you shut up and pay attention,' replied Peter. 'You may, or indeed may not, be a relative of the late Baron de Villiers, but what you are certainly not is the owner of this castle.'

Elaine de Roche raised her voice once again in a menacing scream of defiance and Peter pulled back his bowstring and loosed an arrow which shot between her open legs, pinning her dress to the ground. Startled into silence, she let her mouth fall open. Peter inserted a new arrow in his bowstring and disdainfully looked away from her towards the soldiers, escorts and house staff.

'You have had enough time to decide. What are you going to do?'

The captain cleared his throat. 'We are soldiers and will not find employment easily, so we are going to stay.'

Peter looked at Elaine's escorts. 'And what about you?'

'We are our lady's soldiers and must protect her,' came the voice of the leader.

'No,' said Peter. 'From this moment you are either with us or you leave. If you choose to stay, you will become a part of the troop here. There will be no division.'

Rather more quickly than Peter expected, all the escorts willingly agreed to stay as part of the castle's fighting force. I was right, thought Peter, there is no love lost between Lady de Roche and these men.

Peter turned to the household staff. 'And you?'

'We will stay,' replied a fierce-looking woman who no doubt was in charge.

'Excellent. First, I will look over the castle. Then in one hour I want to see the captain, the head of the house and the leader of the former de Roche escort in the great hall. Understood?' There was a nodding of heads. 'William here is in charge of all fighting and will organise training and discipline. No man will lose his rank unless it is proved that he is not fit to hold it. Come,' he said to Elaine, 'show me around the castle.'

She spat on the ground. 'I will have no part in this. Common men living in the castle is not allowed.'

'I am perfectly happy to go around by myself,' retorted Peter, 'but I was thinking you might wish to identify your own room so we do not blunder about there and, perhaps, plunder it. If you do not care, though . . .' Peter swung his horse around and walked it to the entrance of the castle. Dismounting, he noted that already the castle staff had assumed their role of service, for a groom was standing by to take the reins.

Elaine, having pulled her dress free of the pinning arrow, rushed breathlessly up behind him. 'I will come with you.'

Peter grunted and turned to the old man and Matthew. 'You two come with me. William, if you could start organising that rabble out there which calls itself a fighting force,

I would be grateful. Tom and Pierre, can you both explore all the outbuildings in the castle and see what there is that could be of use to us while we stay here. I'll see you in the hall in a couple of hours, or whenever you are ready.'

Peter, the old man and Matthew, with Elaine trailing behind, walked into the great hall of the castle, wrinkling their noses at the overpowering smell of neglect and decay. The rushes on the floor had not been changed in months, the shutters were pulled closed and in the little light from the doorway Peter could see that everything was dirty and dusty. Even the tables still had broken bits of food and wine stains scattered across them and there was a pile of broken benches heaped in one corner. They walked up the stairs to the upper floor. Every room they looked in was dirty and decrepit. Only Elaine's room showed any sign of homeliness. It was clean, though extremely sparsely furnished, with the shutters thrown open to give air and light.

'Which is The Toad's room?' Peter asked Elaine.

She pointed to a door at the end of the corridor. 'It is locked. He always locks it and takes the key. No one is ever allowed in, not even the servants.'

Peter walked up to a very stout wooden door and, turning the handle, confirmed that indeed it was locked. 'Well, I suppose we could go back and search his body for the key. There again, Matthew . . .' Peter smiled invitingly. Matthew hefted his axe and with three mighty, well-directed blows, hacked the lock from the door.

They walked in. The stench was overpowering. Elaine gasped and had to go back out for a while to regain her breath. Even hardened men like Matthew and the old man blanched. The shutters at the windows were fastened shut and had been like this for so long that the locks had rusted solid, taking a blow from Matthew's axe to free and open them on creaking, rusty hinges. Opening the shutters was a mistake. While the now open window leaked out some of the smell, the light coming in showed filth and grime beyond belief. The floor was cluttered with bits of old food, jostling for position between ancient, dirty reeds and layers of grime. The curtains of the bed were hanging in tatters, what was left of them held together by dirt. The covering on the bed could have been of any material and its colour had long since been eclipsed by filth. There was one ancient rickety cupboard holding clothes which, even to the naked eye, were a hotbed of lice and similar creatures, and an equally old chest of drawers, empty save for two daggers. By the side of the chest, propped up in a corner, was the biggest axe Peter had ever seen.

Gazing at it, Matthew said, 'I have yet to meet the man big enough and strong enough to wield that in battle. It would fair whack you out just lifting it.' They all grunted in agreement.

Looking around the room, Peter was surprised at how little furniture there was and indeed, there was no sign of any chest for the baron's money. True, it was rumoured he was poor, but even a poor noble had money. Where was it?

'Old man, look under the bed.' The old man grimaced and leaned down, trying not to kneel on the filthy floor or touch the bed.

'There is something under there. Do I have to actually get down on the floor?'

Peter nodded, and with a huge sigh the old man knelt on the floor, scrabbled under the bed and started pulling at something. 'My God, it is heavy! I can hardly move it. Matthew, come and give me a hand.'

With much puffing resentment, Matthew also knelt on the floor and with them both pulling hard there emerged a chest about two feet square and one foot deep. Unlike the rest of the room, this chest was not decrepit. Far from it. Made of the stoutest of wood, it was iron-bound with two formidable-looking locks.

'I think we will have to get the key for that one,' said the old man. 'Your axe is not going to touch it, Matthew.'

'Maybe not, but what about this one?' replied Matthew, pulling, with some effort, the giant's axe from the corner of the room, 'I think this might do the job.'

He slowly hefted the axe above his head and, carefully gauging the direction and distance, brought it down with a mighty whack on one of the locks of the chest. Two more blows, and the lock began to weaken. Another two, and it was open. The perspiration was rolling off Matthew's brow. The old man took over, but he did not have Matthew's strength and after six slow and difficult blows the lock still held fast. He handed the axe back to Matthew who, with deep concentration and determination, smashed the lock open.

'As you have done all the hard work', said Peter to Matthew, 'I think you should have the honour of opening it to see if all that effort was worth it.'

Matthew leaned down and opened the lid. No one said anything. The chest was full of coins, along with some gold brooches and small golden ornaments. Silver marks were in abundance. A real treasure trove.

Elaine was the first to break the silence. 'And that rotten, measly man fed us the poorest of food and denied everyone everything, saying that he had no money! If you had not killed him, I would kill him myself.'

'Well,' said Peter, 'it is not going to do him any good now and I am sure we can make use of it. Old man, you look after our money, so please take charge of the chest contents – and I suggest you take over this room.' The old man made to protest at the idea that he should be anywhere near the filth of the baron's old room, but Peter held up his hand, smiling. 'I know. The first priority is to get a team of house staff to strip everything out of the room and give it a thorough clean and wash down. I suggest we take the chest into another room until this one is clean and habitable, then the chest can be emptied and repaired.'

Together the four of them half-carried and half-dragged the chest into another room which had a lock on the door and Peter left the old man to secure the treasure as well as possible, while he went down to the main hall. There he found the captain of the soldiers, the head of the household staff and the escort leader all patiently waiting for him. Peter brushed crumbs of food and dirt off two benches, sat down on one and beckoned them to sit on the other.

'I take it none of you have been paid for a while.' They all nodded. 'By tomorrow, I want you to let me know how much in wages is owed to every man, woman and child in this castle, and the old man will pay them immediately. After that, everyone will be paid their due sum each week.' There was a startled silence. 'I am sure de Villiers kept records of some sort, so I will check what is owing and no one will lose out.' And no one will cheat us, he thought to himself. He continued out loud, 'It seems to me that the household is understaffed. I want you to engage more servants, enough to keep this place clean and tidy. Your first task, and I want a start today, is to strip out and clean the baron's room. One of us will be sleeping there and I want it sparkling with fresh reeds on the floor, to be changed regularly. The next task is this hall: the same, stripped out and cleaned from top to bottom. Tonight we will eat outside. I could not bear to have food in here at the moment. Which brings me on to the next thing. Food. Tell the cook we want good food, not the rubbish the baron has been serving up. The old man will give you the money. As I've said, the soldiers will train under William, helped by Matthew, Tom and Pierre. This training is important. William will not tolerate any slackers and if he believes anyone is not up to standard, that person will be dismissed. Finally, if you have any problems, questions or suggestions as to the running of the castle, do not hesitate. Speak to one of us. We might not agree, but we will listen. We all have to live here, so let us make it a place to enjoy. Any questions now?'

There were none, so they all left to carry out their appointed tasks.

'You will certainly get them on your side if you pay them what is owed them regularly each week. No one is paid like that.' Elaine was standing on the stairs, having overheard what Peter had been saying. 'You cannot buy me, though. I will be writing to my cousin the king and he will send his men to prise you out of here and have you executed for attacking a noble.'

Peter shrugged. 'As you will. In the meantime, I have not noticed a scribe here. I cannot believe for one moment that even someone as mean as de Villiers would not have a tame priest as a scribe. Where is he?'

Elaine pointed to the corner of the hall where there was a narrow corridor. Peter walked over, down the corridor to a door at the end. Opening it, he was confronted by a skinny little man in priest's clothing grasping the wooden cross hanging on a cord around his neck, cowering in a corner, too frightened even to have gone out in the courtyard with everyone else.

'I am called Peter. You need have no fear of me or the men with me. What we want from you is cooperation for the next few days. After that, you are free to go or stay as you will.' The priest nodded eagerly. 'Good. Then bring the scrolls of account out to me in the hall. I want to see who has been paid what, and the household expenses.'

Peter turned and walked out to sit on a bench in the hall to wait for the priest. He noticed with surprise that already the dirt, stale food and spilled wine had been cleaned off the tables and, while they still needed a good scrub, at least they were clean enough to lean on. The old man appeared, but before he could speak the priest arrived breathlessly, carrying a bunch of manuscripts. Peter motioned him to sit and the priest lost no time extracting one of the manuscripts and showing it to Peter.

'Here is the account of all the household expense. These others are wages and dues to the baron from his lands.'

Peter took the manuscript and, with the old man looking over his shoulder, briefly read down the list. The priest looked aghast that Peter and the old man could read and cowered even more, frightened that these two barbarians might find an error as a reason to kill him.

'As I suspected,' said Peter. 'Very little fresh produce has been bought and no spices. Even the wine is of the poorest quality. Old man, will you please go over all these with the priest and get him to explain what has and has not been paid, so we can start here with everything up to date. I have told all the staff and soldiers you'll pay them their back wages tomorrow and after that they will be paid weekly.'

Turning to the priest, he said, 'I understand there is no market in the castle any more.' The priest nodded vigorously. 'After the old man has finished with you tomorrow, I want you to go out to all the villages in the area and tell them the castle market is open again and there will be no fees, taxes or charge of any sort. I want as many people here as possible, buying, selling or exchanging their wares and goods. Tell them the castle is willing to buy fresh produce at the proper price.'

'But if you do not charge each stall or seller, how are you to get the money to pay for everyone here?' asked the priest.

'If we encourage trade, the peasants will soon see they can make money and so will produce more from their land. The more they produce, the more there is to tax each year. It will not be an immediate return for us, but in the long run we will have a much more stable income growth. We have other plans to open up trade between towns that are now effectively cut off by roving bandits and thieves. What you need to tell people is that they will be safe travelling to and from the castle and we in the castle will welcome them. Now go with the old man and explain your accounting.'

Peter got up and walked out to see what William and the others were doing.

It was after dark before they all got together again, sitting outside in the courtyard on clean benches eating from a clean table. The cook had hesitantly explained to them that the food that evening was the best she could provide with the poor ingredients in the kitchen, but she assured them it would be much better the following day after she had been able to buy fresh produce.

The six of them munched slowly through a thin stew containing gristly meat as they contemplated the change in their fortunes.

'Where is that little vixen – the one with the red head-scarf?' asked the old man.

Peter grinned. 'So you recognised her, then.'

'I thought it was a bit odd that Simone did not see us off when we left town, so I assume that you did not spend the evenings when we did not eat at your house in hot embrace, as we thought, but sent Simone off to the castle to spy out the land.' Peter nodded. 'And it was no coincidence that the gates were left open either. I guess she had a hand in that too.'

'Yes,' replied Peter. 'That was my biggest problem, convincing her to kill the guards at the gates so they could not be closed. She had not killed before and was very reluctant, though she did the job and was able to give me a signal as to where potential danger lay, as well as confirming when the danger was over. Very valuable.'

'Nice touch, the red headscarf. You could not miss her. Why is she not with us now?'

'She suggested she keep away from us and continue to

stay in the castle to find out what everyone is thinking and what they might do. The expansion in household staff has given her the opportunity of employment in the kitchens which, she says, is the best place to hear things – and she hopes the head cook will allow her to go out and buy fresh produce and spices. That way she can keep us fully informed of everything. Now then, tell me about your battles with the knights. You saw how I got on.'

They each related their individual fights. The knights had been expecting an easy victory and did not really take the battle seriously until it was too late and they were over-powered and killed one by one.

17

Summer ran into another winter, and spring was once again emerging. The mood in the castle had changed dramatically. No more the down-trodden, there was an air of lightness and contentment. The castle and its outbuildings were sparklingly clean, repaired and vibrant with life. Castle staff, happy to receive regular wages, had increased to a number capable of running each part smoothly and unobtrusively. The soldiers, at first a little resentful of the discipline and training introduced by William, melded into a fighting unit and realised that the replacement of their old, worn clothing, the addition of new equipment and their own increased skills benefited them all. They also came to understand that William's apparent bluff harshness masked a desire to ensure both their efficiency and their well-being.

The castle market got off to a hesitant start, with the locals unsure of the promised freedom from tariffs, but it soon blossomed and expanded. Peasants came from all the neighbouring villages to buy, sell or barter, and traders from nearby towns regularly attended when en route to the larger towns, even though town markets were more lucrative for them.

While Peter or the old man always stayed in the castle, the six made frequent visits to Courcy, Falaise and Le Plessis-Grimouff to collect their monthly dues, pay the employed guards and ensure that the routes between these towns were kept free of bandits. The time Peter and the old man spent together was not wasted, for they talked endlessly about all manner of things and shared views on matters and adventures about which Peter had read in manuscripts. The old man had lost none of his teacherly approach, for he questioned everything Peter said, getting him to explain or justify any comment, and swapped the conversation between English, Norman French, Latin and Greek to keep Peter on his toes. Peter could cope easily with the first three languages, but he had difficulty getting his mind and tongue around the Greek.

Once the soldiers in the castle were up to a reasonable standard, William took them into the countryside and cleared the area towards Caen of any potential thieves or renegades. To all intents and purposes, travel across the whole region was now safe. The peasants were able to sell their produce easily and for a good price. Traders were confident that they would not be robbed, or fleeced by a baron or town mayor, and there was much support for Peter and his band.

Simone continued to work in the kitchen, was soon entrusted with buying produce for the castle, and kept Peter appraised of everything that was going on. While she usually slept in her own room at the back of the kitchen, she paid regular visits to Peter's bed where they spent the night in each other's arms until she left before first light to attend to her duties in the kitchen.

Elaine, on the other hand, did not display any signs of happiness or contentment. After the initial evening meal, the group ate in the cleaned castle hall and Peter insisted she sat with them for every meal. At first she refused, but the kitchen staff, on Peter's instruction, would not give her any food, so with much ill grace she joined them in the hall, sitting alongside William on one of the benches. Once the castle staff had been brought up to a sufficient number to run the castle effectively, Peter put Elaine in charge on the basis that a woman of noble birth was best fitted to oversee and direct the smooth running of the household. She was initially inclined to refuse, but common sense showed her the wisdom of being in charge and it also gave her a purpose for each day, rather than being reduced to sitting in her room embroidering and festering over the perceived injustice of her position.

Elaine, a naturally good manager, carried out her new task with gusto and efficiency and none of the six men could complain that the food was not good or the services provided by the castle staff other than excellent. She did not, however, show any signs of relenting from her opposition to Peter's group and regularly interrupted discussion at mealtimes with snide comments about their 'illegal occupation'. Occasionally some responded with their own jibes, but Pierre was markedly reluctant to join in, often chiding his fellows for speaking to a noble in that way. Peter was careful that any discussions in front of Elaine ranged over the running of the castle and the general state of the safety of the countryside and did not give away any information about their methods or the loyalty that was becoming apparent in the troops and castle staff. Simone reported that while Elaine still exhibited an abrasive attitude and dismissive manner, this was gradually changing, because the staff, realising that in reality Peter was master of the castle, did not cower or bow down to her bullying, but smiled politely and encouraged her to be more complacent. Indeed, occasionally Elaine smiled quietly instead of screaming over a mix-up or transgression by the staff, who made light of and freely admitted their culpability and did their best to correct or make good any mistakes. Peter detected she was becoming more mellow, and gradually her interruptions at the table began to have a hint of constructive suggestion rather than dismissive aggression.

The priest, rather surprisingly, had returned to the castle

and was content just to administer the Good Word and leave the majority of the accounting to the old man. At tax-paying time the old man and the priest went to all the farms, villages and peasant holdings to collect what was due to the castle. The peasants and freemen, as always understating their holdings, possessions and money, were at first amazed that the old man never questioned or bullied them into producing more animals or goods to tax and if there was any doubt, he exercised that doubt in favour of the tax-payer. Word spread and soon the old man's generosity of spirit affected everyone to the extent that they felt bad about trying to cheat him and so declared their true worth. When the tax collection was over, the priest, equally dumbfounded by the old man's attitude of compassion, could not believe that they had collected slightly more tax than de Villiers had bullied out of the peasants the previous year.

Visitors at the castle were few. Minor knights holding land in small manors came one by one to the castle to see for themselves what was happening. Peter welcomed them warmly, ensured they had the best fare and comfortable accommodation, though he did not encourage anyone to stay for more than a night or two. It was difficult to judge the attitude of these knights. Although there was no obvious resentment, Peter realised that if it came to it they would not openly support someone who was not a true-bred noble. Peter hoped that the growing prosperity of the region would also benefit these minor knights, who would see the wisdom of leaving Peter and his group in peace.

One evening, as spring was taking hold and everyone's mood was buoyant in expectation of warmer days, Elaine seemed unusually animated during the meal and took on an air of importance, even power. When the meal was over, Pierre's curiosity got the better of him, although he maintained his usual courtesy towards her. 'My lady,' he said, 'what has made you so suddenly happy?'

Peter suppressed a scowl. He had rather hoped that ignoring the change in Elaine would force her to say something first.

Elaine dug into the pocket of her dress and produced a letter bearing what appeared to be an official seal. 'This,' she said, waving it about. 'I have written to my cousin, the king, and also to Geoffrey, Duke of Normandy, and told them that mere peasants have taken control of the castle. Now I have a reply. On behalf of Geoffrey the bishop is coming here, with his men, to confirm what I have been saying and you will be thrown out of here within the month. Here, read it if you like.' She tossed the letter onto the table. They gazed at it, but no one reached out to take it.

'I am sure you report truly,' said Peter, 'and so we must make preparations to ensure the bishop is treated with all the respect his office requires.'

'His men will lay siege to this castle and you will be defeated,' retorted Elaine.

'Perhaps. Let us see. In the meantime we would all appreciate it if you could instruct the kitchen staff to prepare for a grand meal when the bishop arrives and also arrange suitable accommodation for him, his staff and men.'

Elaine glowered, clearly not expecting this reaction. 'Are you not going to man the battlements to defend yourselves?'

'We will do what has to be done,' replied Peter, getting up and heading off to his room for the night.

Peter gauged that it would be a week at least before the bishop arrived, so all six men had a quiet conference to decide what to do. The bishop was unknown to any of them and who he might bring with him on this visit, apart from the usual entourage, was the subject of much debate. They all agreed it would be pointless showing any opposition and the old man was sure the object of the visit was a scouting exercise rather than any show of force. Although it was not unknown for bishops to command an army, it usually only happened when the full extent of the opposition was known – and Elaine could not have been certain of the number of local men who would actively support Peter's band if called upon to do so. Indeed, the very fact that all the towns and villages around the castle were pleased with the group's intervention in their affairs would be known to Geoffrey, so the old man believed it was unthinkable for such a careful man, whose planning over the years had secured his position, to risk any hostile action until he had all the information. So they prepared for a peaceful visit, remaining mindful that it might not end as such.

The great hall was doubly scrubbed and cleaned, and a new table placed in the middle ready for the feast. New benches also appeared and for the first time two large, impressive chairs were brought in, one set at each end of the table.

Simone reported back that staff and soldiers were apprehensive, but she had encouraged preparation of the best meal possible to put the bishop in a good mood and to impress his staff and troops with the well-run and efficient castle. The best wine was purchased, the bishop's room prepared, and then they all waited.

They did not have to wait long. Late one afternoon at the end of the week, the bishop arrived. He was accompanied by his staff – a priest and servants – and had twelve well-armed and disciplined soldiers to escort him. Peter was pleased that the old man's assessment had been right, although Elaine was clearly furious that a large army had not come to camp outside the castle and call on Peter to surrender.

The bishop was welcomed by Elaine, but before she could engage him in conversation he was politely taken off to his room to wash and prepare for the evening meal, led by one of the castle staff who had been well briefed by Peter to keep the bishop away from Elaine. At first Elaine was miffed, but she managed to hide her irritation, preparing to bide her time until the evening meal.

Peter took her aside. 'If I may suggest,' he said, 'before denouncing us all, let the bishop eat and tell us why he is here. Such a great man will take exception to discussing anything of substance over a meal, and will resent any woman, even one as noble as you, telling him anything before he asks.' Elaine bristled. Peter continued, 'You are far more experienced in affairs of state than I could possibly be and you will know what I say is correct. By biding your time you will impress more and your influence will be greater.'

Elaine looked at him and slowly nodded her head in acknowledgement of the wisdom of his words. Peter could have said nothing. His effort in spelling out the necessary courtesies so that she would not embarrass herself gave Elaine a pang of warmth towards him, but she quickly allowed resentment and resolve to stifle it.

Peter's band were early in the great hall for the evening meal, as servants bustled around serving cups of wine. Elaine, conscious she should not make a grand entrance, soon joined them and a little later the bishop and his priest arrived. William gestured to the bishop to sit in the fine chair at one end of the table and Peter took Elaine firmly by the elbow and propelled her towards the other great chair. At first she looked bemused, but Peter smiled as he sat down with the others, including the bishop's priest, on the benches along-side the table.

Immediately servants appeared with the first course and thereafter kept the food flowing so no one would feel deprived of anything. The bishop, a large man, though considerably slimmer than most bishops Peter had seen, engaged in polite conversation with Elaine and the others at the table, concentrating mainly on the political position at Geoffrey's court – about which few seated knew anything and upon which the bishop was all too happy to expound – and occasionally touching on trade, the seasons and the ever-important crops. He told them that Geoffrey's son Henry had returned from England and Geoffrey's wife Matilda was still seething from her failure to secure the English crown. The bishop hinted that she was encouraging Henry to gather forces to take to England to wrest from Stephen what she regarded as her rightful inheritance.

As the meal drew to an end the bishop, flushed with the good wine, turned to Peter. 'We hear that you, a foreigner, have usurped Baron de Villiers and installed yourself in this castle as ruler of the countryside around here. We hear you have even spread your rule to the towns.'

Peter turned to Elaine, giving her a penetrating look that instructed her to keep quiet, then shifted his gaze back to the bishop with his most friendly and charming smile. 'My lord bishop, it is undoubtedly true that I am not a native of Normandy, though far from usurping the late Baron de Villiers, we were lucky to defeat him in fair and honourable battle. I am sure you have heard tell of the sequence of events leading to the battle, so I need say no more.'

The bishop nodded, although his eyes narrowed. Peter continued calmly. 'It is also true that following our defeat of de Villiers we, as honourable victors, were entitled by rule of forfeit to all his possessions and lands, but we have not taken them. We have not filed a writ of possession with the king or with Geoffrey, Duke of Normandy, because the rightful heir to de Villiers' estate is my Lady Elaine de Roche and we six victors have but served her estate.'

There was an audible gasp from Elaine and Peter turned to her once again with that look on his face that meant, 'Keep silent!' She subsided in her chair and said nothing.

'Indeed,' he continued, 'you have seen how well my lady has overseen and directed the household from the food and service we hope you have enjoyed tonight. My role, and that of my comrades here, has been to bring order to the countryside around so the lands prosper and provide the necessary income for the castle. It is true that we have had to do this with some gusto, and it may well seem that we, not my lady, are in charge – but the reality is only the nobility can rule and my lady has had the good grace to allow us a free hand to do what we do best, while she does what she so clearly excels at.'

The bishop grunted, his lips pursed into a tight line. He looked down the table at Elaine, who had been stunned by Peter's words into keeping her silence and, far from meeting the bishop's gaze, was now looking dutifully down into her lap. Grunting again and apparently satisfied, the bishop finished his wine and got up to go to his room. 'I am not sure if Lady de Roche is de Villiers' true heir,' he said, 'and even if she is, she has estates of her own, so Geoffrey may well have other plans for this castle. I will report back to him and he will communicate his wishes in due course.' Saying nothing further, he left the great hall, followed by his priest.

When they were well out of earshot, Elaine exploded. 'What in the name of God was that all about? How dare you tell such lies and expect to get away with it! I will tell the bishop the truth in the morning.'

'Elaine,' replied Peter patiently, 'do think about what you are saying. We have not sent a writ of possession and therefore can quite truthfully say we are not claiming possession of the castle and its estates. Equally truthfully, you are de Villiers' cousin and being here when he died means that unless there is a direct relation, like a brother or son, as cousin and heir, or at the very least a potential heir, you can claim possession. I fully accept that we have not actually obeyed your commands or wishes, but then again, everything we have done has enhanced the castle and lands, even to the extent of opening up the countryside to allow free travel. It would, I suggest, be difficult for you to maintain you are in our power or have been kept prisoner when you run the household and have the benefit of our efforts. Sitting at the head of the table demonstrates your position, which would not have gone unnoticed by the bishop.'

'As you outmanoeuvred de Villiers, so you have outmanoeuvred me,' she exclaimed indignantly. 'I should not have sat at the head of the table! The tale you have spun is believable, but what now? If, as you say, I am in charge, you will all have to obey my commands, so if I tell you tomorrow, in front of the bishop, that you are to leave, you cannot resist. What is your answer to that?'

'Again I would ask you to consider what you are saying. If we were to leave, then I strongly suspect most, if not all, of your soldiers would leave with us. And then what of the minor knights who have been sniffing around over the last months looking for weakness and opportunity? Do you think for one moment that they would let you live quietly here when they detect rich pickings? Even if we do not want your soldiers with us, would they be strong enough to defend you against those knights? Act as you will, but do not act hastily. Make the bishop's time here enjoyable and memorable, and when he has gone we can talk about the future so all of us benefit.'

Elaine merely looked at him and with a huff rose from the table and went to her room.

'Do you think she will behave?' asked Peter of the rest.

There were some half-nods. 'It will be a close-run thing, but she is no fool and can see that if she makes a fuss now she could lose everything. Geoffrey would have no hesitation installing his own baron here and demanding a nice big payment for the privilege. What galls me, though,' the old man said, laughing, 'is having to be nice and defer to her for the next few days while the bishop is here.'

All except Pierre joined in the laughter.

'I think we should keep our soldiers largely out of sight

for the next few days,' said William. 'The bishop will know we have brought them up to a decent fighting force, but I do not want him to report back how good they have become in case Geoffrey feels threatened.'

With murmurs of agreement all around, they too went off to bed.

When Peter got to his room, Simone was already there, lying on the bed waiting for him. 'I thought you would still be in the kitchen clearing up,' he said.

'I made an excuse and got off early. It is fairly well known I have a man friend somewhere in the castle, but as yet no one has identified you. Anyway, from what I hear from the servants, it went off brilliantly. The bishop was well wined and dined and Elaine made no fuss about all of you being there. Only a part of what you said to the bishop was reported back to the kitchen, but I can guess the rest. We seem to be safe, for the moment at least.'

'Yes, if Elaine keeps quiet.'

'Oh, she will keep quiet. I have not told you before, but it has been suggested to her she ought to have a personal maidservant attending her rather than just any one of the servants who are around at the time. I haven't actually put myself forward, but I have made sure that when she needs or does anything important, I am on hand to carry out her wishes. As a result she has half-confided a few things to me, not least the fact that her animosity towards you is not as strong as she would have you believe. If she now thinks she is the real mistress of the castle, it will be easy to convince her to engage a personal lady-in-waiting, and if I am chosen, what better spy can you have?' She giggled and reached out to him, pulling him onto the bed.

The bishop stayed at the castle for only three days. During that time he and his men moved freely about, speaking to everyone. With Peter and the group the bishop was affable and appeared relaxed. He was somewhat vague about where he was going next, but showed no signs of disquiet of any sort. After the bishop's entourage had left the castle, Elaine, Peter and his group watched them disappear into the distance. Elaine returned to the castle to oversee the tasks for the day, while Peter and the rest moved towards the stables.

'That seemed to go off extremely well,' said Tom. 'The bishop looked very contented and not at all troubled about anything here.'

Peter and the old man exchanged looks. There was a silence, eventually broken by the old man. 'Too contented, perhaps. Maybe not troubled enough.'

Again there was a silence as they all thought about this. 'I think,' said Peter, 'it would be wise to accept that the bishop knows full well what has gone on here and that, in truth, we are in charge and running the castle. He and his men spent a lot of time roaming around and speaking to everyone, so it is highly unlikely someone did not tell him exactly what is going on.'

'I told the soldiers to watch their mouths around the bishop's guard,' said William, 'but soldiers are not known for keeping quiet, so I suspect that most things, if not everything, has been passed on. You are right. Before he left, the bishop surely knew Elaine was not fully mistress of this place, but he seems to have accepted it, for there was no sign from him that he was in any way concerned.'

'I am not surprised,' interjected Pierre. 'Geoffrey is a very smart man. Over more than eight years he carefully took Caen, Tourques, Lisieux, Falaise, Vier and more with carefully planned campaigns and he has surrounded himself with clever and loyal men. The bishop would not be a bishop to Geoffrey unless he had proved his loyalty and had the intelligence to act carefully. To me, his appearance confirmed this. He was not the fat, lazy, garrulous man bishops usually are. He was happy to walk around the castle grounds, even outside, without complaint and bishops rarely stir from their own chairs. Although he talked freely about the happenings at court and gave us snippets of scandal, it struck me that he chose his words carefully.'

'Yes,' said the old man. 'His priest spoke hardly at all during our meals, but spent a lot of time with our priest and we all know that man does not have the stiffest of backbones – so charged with having to tell all to a direct representative of the bishop, I can't but believe that he poured out his heart. There's no doubt in my mind the bishop is fully informed of everything, and he would have hoped that in not making a fuss here he would lead us to think all was well. What will happen after he reports back to Geoffrey, though, is something we have to consider.'

'Pierre,' asked Peter, 'you are a true Norman and have been here while Geoffrey has been establishing himself. What do you think he might do?'

Pierre thought carefully before replying. 'As has been said before, Geoffrey is cautious and a planner. He is still a relatively young man and he has been engaged in putting down three baronial rebellions over these last five years, so unless he feels his position is threatened, I cannot see him getting directly involved in any more fighting action unless provoked. Our small band, even with the support of the troops here and the local peasants, is far too insignificant to make anything except the smallest dent in Geoffrey's empire and he will know, as do we, that any attempt we might make to take over other castles would lead to Geoffrey fielding his full army and we would be overwhelmed. Nobles are always short of money, even if they seem to have plenty, and it is likely he will see an opportunity to sell the baronetcy of this castle to a wealthy knight, which would mean getting rid of Elaine or more likely marrying her off to a man of his choice. Not difficult, as she has her own lands as well, so would be a worthy catch. I think that Geoffrey is likely to invite Elaine to his court for a festivity where he can sound her out and also allow prospective husbands to look her over. If he forces her to take a husband, as is his right as the king's deputy, then she cannot refuse, although as we know she is a past master at delaying any decision like this.'

'There is one more matter we have to take into account,' said the old man. 'Geoffrey will soon know the full, not just the outline, details of our defeating six knights in fair combat, and he will be aware that we are running the castle and have rid the countryside of robbers and thieves. So he will realise that men like us are unlikely to be just meek servants of any new baron and somehow he has to get rid of us. He could easily command us to leave Normandy, but I do not believe he would see that as a complete solution. We could always pose a risk of some sort. I fear something else.'

Peter grunted. 'He could pay us off, but we are not threat enough for him to do that. I suspect he may well try to use the services of the local knights. If they could get rid of us somehow, this would please Geoffrey and, perhaps, one of those knights could have an eye on Elaine.'

'Would the knights band together with their men and attack us?' asked Matthew.

'In the short term, I doubt it. An attack would likely mean a siege and a siege army has to be fairly large and well prepared.' Peter paused and thought for a while. 'Let us prepare for the worst. First, until further notice none of us should leave the castle at all. Alone, or even with a band of men, we would give the knights the opportunity of attacking us and picking us off one by one. Second, we need information. William, can you select a few of your most trusted soldiers and ask them to go to each of the minor knights' manors and find out what they are doing and what the talk is. They can call into the manors on the way to the towns to collect the dues from the mayors and check on the wagon guards. It should not be difficult to pick up useful gossip.

Third, we must stock the castle with provisions and make sure these are replenished regularly to keep the freshest stuff available in case of a siege. Finally, our training should be stepped up and also basic training for the peasants we can call on to defend the castle. We do not want to make a fuss about this, so I suggest everyone is told we are training the peasants for their own good and in case Geoffrey calls on Elaine to provide men for his army. Everyone will understand that. Anything else?'

'Although it hurts me to say it, being an ex-farmer,' said Tom, 'we have to make preparations to lay waste to the land around here in case there is a siege. If there are no animals or crops, the besieging knights cannot feed their men.'

'Excellent. Take care of that, please, Tom. If there is nothing else, then we must get back to our daily chores.'

'There is just one more thing,' said Pierre hesitantly. 'I don't know why, but that bishop gave me the creeps. Perhaps it is because I am Norman and he is Norman, but I felt he was hiding something. Had he not been a bishop, I would have said it was something evil.' They all looked at Pierre, startled. 'I was sitting next to him, but did you not notice that he drank very little of the wine, and yet gave the impression he was relaxed by it? He took his cup to his lips often enough, but merely sipped it. Also his eyes narrowed whenever Peter was speaking, and his lips pursed to a thin line when he addressed Elaine. I would not trust him at all.'

The old man nodded his head slowly. 'Thank you, Pierre. I confess I did notice his eyes, but thought nothing of it at the time. I was too intent on suppressing my laughter at Peter's explanation of our role! We must be even more cautious and plan for the worst.'

With that they left the stables. The old man walked back to the great hall with Peter and before they reached it he said, 'You should become more friendly with Elaine. I think, deep down, she is on our side, but the nobility cannot see past their rank, so she would sacrifice us if she had to. The friendlier you are to her, the more chance there is of learning from her what is likely to happen and she may well give us early warning so we can take whatever action is appropriate.'

Peter laughed. 'I will try, but she is a strange one. Admittedly, she is not antagonistic towards us now, but that is a long way from confiding her inner secrets.'

As the days passed, the routine of the castle did not change and no one thought it strange Peter and his men did not go out into the countryside. Indeed, this was taken as showing confidence in the soldiers chosen to visit the towns, collect the monthly dues and inspect the travellers' guards. The heightened training with the inclusion of the peasants was also accepted without comment.

Peter gave greater encouragement to Elaine, even suggesting it was wrong for her not to have a personal maid-servant and asking if he should send for one from her own estates. She declined this offer, with more politeness than Peter anticipated, and they were all told at the evening meal that Elaine had selected a promising girl from the kitchens to train as a personal maidservant. No one asked who that girl might be, but Matthew could not prevent a sly smile escaping.

In her new post as trainee maidservant, Simone had fewer chances to slip into Peter's room at night, even though she was in closer proximity to him during the day, often carrying messages from Elaine. They occasionally met and talked in one of the rooms of the castle, with Simone confirming Elaine was beginning to confide in her – though little of what she said was of great relevance to the group's situation.

Late one night, as Peter had just fallen asleep, Simone crept into his bed and snuggled up.

'I thought you were at the beck and call of her ladyship,' Peter whispered in Simone's ear.

'She will not miss me tonight.'

He pulled her closer.

Passion spent, they were lying with their arms wrapped around each other when Simone murmured, 'You will have to bed her.'

'What?' said Peter, pulling away. 'Impossible!'

'Shush. Not so loud. It's not impossible and it has to be done. She thinks far more of you than she gives away. I've seen her looking at you when you were not aware. And you want to get into her confidence, so what better way than through her bed?'

'But I have no desire for her! I have you, and you are more than enough for me.'

'It is nice to think that, but we have to be realistic. We know sooner or later Geoffrey will be inviting her to his court, so if you are really close to her you have the opportunity of putting ideas into her head or, at the very least, finding out what she will truly do. It could save all our lives. Besides which, if I am to remain as her personal maidservant, then our times together will be very few and I would feel happier knowing where your affections are directed.'

Peter did not answer and it took him a long time to drift off to sleep. He understood the wisdom of Simone's words, but was far less certain about trying to turn the theory into reality.

In fact, he did not have too long to dwell on the subject, for mid-morning two days later Simone sought him out to say that Elaine had demanded Peter's presence in her room to talk about the future. Peter had anticipated before long Elaine would want to clarify her position and his own following the bishop's visit and the revelation, to her at least, that Peter was not disputing the fact that she was likely the rightful mistress of the castle.

Peter went slowly to Elaine's room, knocked on the door and went in. She was sitting on the long window seat staring out of the window. Peter closed the door quietly behind him and walked up to her. She did not turn her gaze away from the outside scenery.

'You wished to speak to me,' said Peter. 'Indeed, you demanded to see me?'

There was a long pause. Elaine did not move. She spoke without turning around. 'You said we should talk about the future for the benefit of both of us, and yet it has been weeks since the bishop left and you have said not one word. I cannot continue like this. I am the rightful heir to the castle and I can see no reason why I cannot confirm this to Geoffrey in a writ of possession and order my own affairs here, rather than having to obey you and your group. There is no other way.'

'Elaine. You are perfectly right. I should have spoken to you earlier. Indeed, we should all have explored the position we face, so that each one of us can benefit and not lose what we have together. I apologise. My mind has been taken up by other things and this was unforgivable.'

Surprised at Peter's conciliatory words, Elaine turned from the window and looked at him. 'So what is there to explore? I am of noble birth, the castle is rightfully mine, you are foreign peasants – free men at best – and you have no right here. The fact is, as you told the bishop, you have not sought a writ of possession. The time has passed for you to do this, as victor over de Villiers and by way of forfeit, so you are at my mercy.'

'That also is true, but you spoke about a future to benefit both of us. There is no benefit for my group to go and leave behind all we have fought for and worked so hard to achieve. Equally, I think you know there would be no benefit to you if we were to go.'

'How so? The castle and lands are mine. That is benefit enough, wouldn't you say?'

Peter smiled ruefully. 'Indeed, a great benefit. But how long would it last? Can we not be frank with each other? For my group to remain here, we need you, and for you to remain here, you need us.'

'How so?' she repeated.

Peter put on his most charming smile and sat on the seat next to her, an arm's length away. Elaine did not object. 'As I said before, it may well be you are the rightful heir to this castle, but it is not free from doubt and if Geoffrey, or indeed anyone else, wished to dispute your claim, then it would take years and cost a lot of money to appear before the king's court to get a definitive answer – which may not be in your favour. In the meantime, do you think it likely everyone will just sit around and wait to see what the king's court might decide?'

Elaine took her eyes off his, looked down into her lap and shrugged her shoulders.

Peter continued, 'Let us face reality together. With all the work we have both done and the changes we have both achieved, this castle – repaired, well run and vibrant – is a very valuable asset. Whoever is in charge commands a large swathe of the countryside with an influence over greater land, villages and towns because of the system put in place to keep open free and safe passage for travellers. Based on the taxes we raised just last year, it is likely this castle will become very prosperous. It is a prize worth taking – indeed, a jewel in the kingdom, I would suggest.' Peter thought he had gone a little too far in painting the picture he wanted in her mind, but still she said nothing.

'As I indicated to you when the bishop was staying, those minor knights around here would seize the first opportunity to take over this castle, so on your own you would be ever fearful. Even with your well-trained soldiers to defend the castle, with no one experienced enough to take charge of them, you could not depend on their fighting abilities or even their loyalty. Soldiers are rough men who need to be able to look up to a commander who is equally rough, and a lady of noble birth does not fit that category at all. Also, you must realise that you are mistress of two properties: your own estate inherited from your husband, and this castle. To my certain knowledge the king has been trying to tie you down to take a husband for your own lands. What do you think he will do when he finds out you have two estates when you file your writ of possession? You cannot avoid a royal decree of marriage forever without losing everything. Then there is Geoffrey, much closer to hand. He could quite legitimately sell off the baronetcy of this castle, evict you and simply defend in the royal court any challenge you might make about his right to do so. The sad fact is that your position is far more vulnerable than mine. The very worst the king, or Geoffrey, could do to me and the group is to banish us from Normandy and France, for we have not committed any crime and the fact the people around here are grateful for our keeping the countryside free of robbers would prevent Geoffrey using force against us.'

Peter knew he had gone too far this time. There was no doubt Geoffrey could easily say that a foreigner – from a country seeking to maintain Normandy as part of its kingdom – had unlawfully attempted to take possession of a valuable castle as a step towards England taking complete control of Normandy. However, this seemed to pass Elaine by. She continued to stare at her lap and as Peter was talking, her shoulders slumped slowly forward. She clearly accepted the truth in what he said and could see no obvious solution. She remained silent.

Peter allowed the silence to intensify, then he moved towards her, putting his left hand gently on her shoulder. She did not shake it off, nor did she tense up. 'There is no complete answer to anything I have said,' he added. 'But there are things we could consider.'

Elaine raised her eyes and looked at Peter. He detected a hint of tears. 'What can we consider?' she asked.

Peter gave a relaxed smile. 'The first is time. The longer everyone does nothing, the greater your chances of remaining here relatively unmolested. It would look bad for Geoffrey to sell the baronetcy and evict you if you could manage to remain here for two or so years. For Geoffrey to claim my group's right of forfeit unproven and your inheritance not legitimate, he has to act promptly, because with delay comes implied acceptance.' Elaine looked at him with a questioning frown. 'Accept what I say. I am, perhaps, a little more well read than you may think. I am not unaware of the laws and traditions of possession.' Her frown deepened, but her shoulders straightened. Peter moved closer and slid his hand to the back of her neck below her coiffured hair.

'The next thing we have to combat is your being summoned to Geoffrey's court. Once there, you could become pressured into doing things you would not want, or risk giving Geoffrey grounds to move against the castle. You know much better than I do what can happen at court.' She nodded slowly, accepting this point, and the movement of her head gave him the opportunity to begin lightly stroking the back of her neck – the words and instructions of the old whore in Devonshire firmly in the front of his mind. 'To begin with, I suggest you write a letter to Geoffrey, thanking him for sending the bishop here and saying you will be lodging a writ of possession soon to confirm your inheritance of the castle and its surrounding land. Such a letter will suggest to Geoffrey that a good time to ask you to his court would be when the writ of possession is received, so that you can both talk about it. If the writ is delayed, then it will not affect your claim, for the letter itself is notice of the claim.'

Elaine smiled slowly. 'I thought I was good at delaying things, but I see I have something to learn.' They both laughed quietly. 'And what will you be doing?' she asked.

'For the moment, nothing more than we are doing already. You will have noticed we are preparing the soldiers and some of the local peasants just in case Geoffrey tries a move against us. I think it is highly doubtful that he will do anything of the sort, but we must assume the worst. What I think we must both do is to ensure you are more involved in activities outside the running of the staff in the castle. You can accompany William and watch the training so that the soldiers and peasants become used to your taking an interest and being involved. William can coach you on some suggestions you might make which he can then follow. That will emphasise your authority here. What we can be certain of is that someone in this castle has allegiance to Geoffrey and will be reporting back to him, so your obvious involvement in things will emphasise your position here.'

Elaine smiled and moved towards him a little, as he continued to caress the back of her neck gently. 'I might begin to think you are trying to lull me into a sense of security and take advantage of me,' she said.

Peter leaned forward and with his right hand lifted her chin slightly and kissed her slowly on the lips. 'Now, how could I possibly take advantage of a noble, my better?'

She drew away from him. Her eyes looked a little glassy and she did not speak. Peter pulled her gently back towards him and kissed her again, this time with more warmth. At first she received the kiss passively, then slowly, very slowly, she returned it as his left hand slid around from the back of her neck to caress her cheek, eyes and forehead. She pulled away again, though this time not so far, and her breathing seemed laboured.

Peter continued his gentle caressing. 'To be frank, I do not believe we can really do nothing for another year or more to keep Geoffrey at bay for the two years needed. Geoffrey is far too experienced for that and even though he may well realise we do not pose any threat to him, there will be others in his court who will be reluctant to let pass the opportunity of this castle's rich pickings. It would be helpful if we knew more about what Geoffrey's court is thinking and urging. Do you have any friend or relation in Geoffrey's circle who could keep you appraised of things?'

Elaine smiled. 'I have relations everywhere and there is a young second cousin close to Geoffrey. She is rather beautiful and very personable, popular with everyone. She married one of Geoffrey's senior knights two years ago and I have heard she is one of Geoffrey's favourites. I am sure she would not betray Geoffrey – that would be a betrayal of her husband – but we have always got on well and I believe she would tell me things if I asked. I would, though, have to couch my letter very carefully.' Elaine wrinkled her brow, thinking of what she might write to get information without alerting her second cousin to the reason why such information was required.

'Perhaps we could write the letter together?' replied Peter, whose right hand was now gradually inching down from Elaine's face and neck towards her bosom. 'Indeed, the old man has more than a little experience in court politics and he too could be of help.'

'Perhaps, but later.' Elaine looked purposefully down at Peter's right hand, which was gently encircling her left breast, then back at Peter, putting her left hand behind his neck and drawing him towards her. With raised head, she kissed him firmly on the mouth – a kiss which encouraged him to go on.

Peter continued his gentle caressing, religiously following the instructions of the old whore in Devonshire, and while at first he felt nothing, Elaine's heightened passion was infectious and before long, without words, they rose from the window seat and moved to the bed.

It was well after noon when Peter left Elaine's room, somewhat numb at her wholehearted and enthusiastic acceptance of his advances. Indeed, when they finished, there was no recrimination or regret: an air of delight and contentment emanated from her. She would not let him go and encouraged him into more, eventually laughing happily when he left the room, posing naked on the bed as if to say she was still willing, but he was not up to it.

Peter met Simone as he was walking down the stairs to the hall, but Simone shook her head to indicate he should not speak to her as she made her way to Elaine's room. Peter took the hint and resolved to say nothing to anyone.

18

As the weeks turned into months, Elaine's confidence grew. She no longer offered only a bitter face and acerbic comments, but seemed to become a whole new person, enthusiastically throwing herself into every aspect of castle life. As Peter suggested, she took an interest in the soldiers' training with William's help, went out of her way to speak to all the stall-holders and merchants visiting the castle, and ensured that all the servants were working contentedly.

Together with the old man, Elaine and Peter constructed a carefully worded letter to Elaine's second cousin, which elicited several replies reciting the gossip at Geoffrey's court and generally detailing daily life.

Peter maintained his union with Elaine which, although unspoken, did not go unnoticed. The old man was particularly pleased, although Pierre seemed slightly resentful, but not in an aggressive or harmful way. It appeared that he could not quite come to terms with a foreign peasant sleeping with a Norman of noble birth.

Gradually, information came through about how the nobles were taking the occupation of the castle and the fact that Peter's group commanded such respect from the people in the area. Elaine's second cousin's letters indicated that Geoffrey's court was accepting the position, although the general view was that sooner or later Elaine would have to marry. Such talk as there was concerned who the lucky man might be. Traders were always a good source of gossip and from them there was no doubt the peasants and townpeople were happy, even though the minor knights were not so relaxed. Indeed, William's trusted soldiers reported back that the minor knights had been meeting together, and rumour suggested that the rich pickings at the castle had been discussed. It also became clear that the bishop, when leaving the castle, had visited each of the minor knights – something a bishop would never do unless there was a very good reason and confirming Pierre's impression that the bishop was not as open and friendly as he would have had them believe. The group felt the only reason for the bishop to do this concerned the castle, so they enlisted the help of a couple of the stall-holders to visit the manors of the minor knights in an attempt to find out more.

Once summer was well established, two significant things happened within days. The first was the arrival of a letter from Geoffrey, inviting Elaine to his court for a banquet. The second was some firm, disquieting news about the minor knights. The old man, Elaine and Peter composed a careful reply to Geoffrey, politely and regretfully declining his kind invitation on the grounds that the amount of work which Elaine was required to do to make the castle viable had left her tired and run down, and she feared that travelling so far would leave her in no fit state to actually attend the banquet. The letter concluded that she was determined to rest, so that the next time Geoffrey felt it appropriate to ask her, she would be well enough to go.

As for the minor knights, they were arming and preparing for battle. Peasants had been hastily recruited and trained and the information was that the knights were planning to band together to make a large army.

At the meal that night Elaine was not as buoyant as she

237

had been over the past months, clearly concerned over these two events. There was general, open discussion.

'It seems clear to me,' said the old man, 'that the letter from Geoffrey was not a coincidence. I would suggest that it was written to deplete our numbers here to give the minor knights a better chance at taking the castle. Had Elaine accepted the invitation, then she would have taken a guard of at least twelve men, as is befitting to her rank. I don't know how Geoffrey will take Elaine's refusal, or what he might do.'

'Nothing, I am sure,' said Pierre. 'Remember, I have been following Geoffrey's activities for some years and he prepares well, thinking of all the options. If he, or any of his personal guard or knights, were going to become directly involved, then he would not have sent that letter, because there would have been no need. The very weight of arms he could command to take this castle would mean we would surrender without a fight. No, I think the letter was an attempt to get an edge for the minor knights, no doubt urged on him by the bishop.'

'I can see sense in that,' said Peter. 'As Geoffrey knows Elaine is going to submit a writ of possession, it would be foolish of him to become involved in any direct action against the castle, because that would be seen as being hostile without cause. If the minor knights fail, then Geoffrey can distance himself from them. If they succeed, then he can quite rightly step in as an arbiter between them as to how the spoils should be divided. In fact, Elaine declining Geoffrey's invitation could work to our advantage, in that Geoffrey will know from his spies here Elaine is not too run down at all.' They all looked at Elaine whose appearance these days was one of vibrant youthfulness. 'And he will realise we have spotted the trap and he will distance himself, outwardly at least, from the minor knights.'

'So, all we have to concern ourselves with at the moment

is the army gathering around,' said the old man. 'William, what are our chances?'

'The soldiers here are trained and skilled as highly as I can possibly make them,' replied William. 'The peasants we have had here are acceptable and certainly would be enthusiastic against the minor knights – though I would not say the same if it was Geoffrey on the battlefield. The question I have is this: do we prepare for a siege or for open battle?'

'We have provisions enough for a long siege,' said Elaine, 'and Tom has prepared the farms to waste the crops and remove their animals so that any besieging army cannot easily feed itself. My concern is what Geoffrey will do if the minor knights just camp themselves outside and wait.'

'It all seems rather odd to me,' replied Peter. 'We are well into summer and it is not the time to attack a castle. Any knight will know that come the winter, a besieging army will lose men through sickness and desertion, even if they are reasonably fed. A siege should start in spring with the summer months ahead.'

'Perhaps the minor knights are going to use our tactics,' said Matthew. 'Challenge us to a noble and honourable battle outside the castle.'

Peter laughed. 'That would certainly be novel, but I do not think so. To do that, those knights would have to acknowledge we were also knights or nobles and I'm sure the bishop would have made it plain Geoffrey would not be well served if we were raised to the status of noble. Your thoughts, Pierre?'

'Norman knights are very arrogant and lay great stress on numbers. I think that they will appear with a great mass of men, believing we will be frightened into surrender. They will know how many men we have, even with the peasants, and as battle-hardened knights they will have no fear of pitting themselves against us. Although we defeated de Villiers and his knights, this will have little impact on the thoughts of these knights, because each one of them thinks they are better than every other knight. Their weakness lies in the fact that French knights do not take easily to being commanded. If there is a dominant baron, they obey without question. If there are two of equal nobility, barons or knights, each will strive to lead and so there is often a reluctance to follow. Geoffrey exploited this in one of his battles where he was greatly outnumbered but, correctly, banked on the lack of a single cohesive force following the orders of one baron.'

'Interesting,' said the old man. 'I too have heard of this Norman reluctance to submit to a single leader unless he's really dominant, though I am not sure how it will assist us here. We will have to wait and see and be ready to exploit any weaknesses.'

'Matthew,' asked Peter, 'how are the men coping with the Welsh bow?'

Matthew grimaced. 'We had a devil of a job to find any yew to make the bows and used elm and ash instead. These woods are good substitutes, but I have to say there was a marked reluctance on the part of the troops to learn how to use the bows. They still favour the crossbow, which does not require such strength to pull and set the bowstring and needs far less practice to be accurate. The position at the moment is that we are well equipped with Welsh bows and plenty of arrows. Every one of the troops can use them but – and this is a big but – few can pull the string back to the ear for full power and accuracy is not good at long range. If they have plenty of time, then they can nearly all hit a target at crossbow range. Only a few can get the full range potential with any accuracy. The real advantage is speed. At short range, even the slowest can get off at least four reasonably accurate arrows in the time it takes a crossbow to shoot two.'

'So you think the Welsh bow can be a great advantage

to us at short range and helpful at crossbow range, with an occasional well-aimed strike at the bow's full range?' said Peter.

'Yes. That sums it up.'

'Well then, I suggest Tom and the old man go out to the nearby farms and holdings tomorrow, pay the peasants the worth of their crops and houses, get them ready to take their animals away from here and prepare to lay waste to their land and houses so there is nothing any army can use. In order not to alert the minor knights to our preparations, it would be a good idea if the peasants do not actually destroy the crops and houses until after the knights' army has arrived. I think it would be a good thing to tell them also that when the battle is over, we will help them rebuild and make sure they have enough produce to get through the winter.'

Peter turned with a warm smile to Elaine. 'Can you double-check our own provisions, though I am sure you do not need to?' She nodded, and he went on. 'William and Pierre, we need to know the moment the minor knights are ready to set out, so can you seek out some reliable men or women who can move around the area of the knights' manor houses to get as much information as possible? Matthew, arrange for the best fighting peasants to come to the castle to live for the moment, for continued training with William, and step up the Welsh bow practice please. I do not know if the Welsh bow will be our saviour, but I would like to be prepared. Finally, I will tell the stall-holders and people tomorrow that the market in the castle is being suspended for a month in order to carry out some new building. I doubt if they will believe this, but I will say we are willing to pay them compensation for any losses they suffer. I do not want outsiders to see what preparations we are making – and William, can you double the guard on the gate to prevent any but those we trust coming in or going out? This should stop any messages getting out to Geoffrey, or more particularly the minor knights. Anything else?'

There was a long silence, broken by Elaine. 'I do not know if I will get another letter from my second cousin before any battle, so although I agree that Geoffrey will likely do nothing, it would be nice to know what is being said at his court. Otherwise, I cannot think of anything more.'

They all agreed and in sombre mood left the table for bed.

In less than two weeks everything was as ready as it could possibly be. Elaine was a tower of strength, going around the castle telling everyone that the minor knights were banding together to try to take over the castle and deprive them of their livelihoods. This brought a strengthening of resolve and all in the castle were determined to support Elaine and Peter's band in their efforts to stop the knights. News came the minor knights were on the move, and those in the castle made ready – fully armed but, as Peter directed, hidden behind the battlements so that no one approaching would see their preparations. The main gate was left open and, similar to the old man's tactics at the manor house, Peter had erected a few stalls outside with soldiers in peasant garb milling around to give the impression of an ordinary day.

The army came into view in the middle of the morning. There were six minor knights and their squires on horseback, each with six or so experienced, trained soldiers also on horseback, accompanied by twenty armed peasants on foot. In all it was a force of about one hundred and sixty against Peter's meagre band of his own group, twenty trained soldiers and forty half-trained peasants.

'Odds about right,' said the old man, peering over the battlements. Peter grunted, his eyes scanning the approaching army looking for weakness or advantage. One thing was obvious. Pierre was right. It seemed as if there was no universal agreement that one of the minor knights would be in complete charge. Each knight had his own men around him and those six groups were not deployed in such a way as to attack together or in waves, but were operating as individual units. One group was in front of and a little separate from the others, seeming to be more eager to get to the castle than the rest.

Peter came down quickly from the battlements and took hold of a peasant waiting for the order to attack. 'Drop your weapons, take off your battle shirt and walk quickly but easily out to the men outside and tell them to stay where they are until I shout. Quickly now!'

The peasant did as he was bid and Peter walked up to the open gates, staying out of sight of the approaching knights, to speak to the four men stationed there ready to close and bar the gates on his command. 'If I shout "Close!" then only half-close the gates and retreat immediately away from them. If I shout "Close fully!" then close and bar the gates completely. Do you understand?'

They nodded, and Peter went back up to the battlements.

'You have spotted what I have seen,' said the old man. 'Do you think it will work?'

'If Pierre is right, then it is a good chance for an early strike. Matthew, get your second-best archers ready on the battlements on each side of the main gate, ready to shoot down into the courtyard, and your best archers ready to shoot anyone outside charging the gates. Do not loose a single arrow until I command.' Matthew saw the point and hurried away to prepare.

The minor knight with his troops who was some way in front of the rest quickened his pace slightly towards the still-open gates. The soldiers in peasant attire outside took no notice and continued to pretend to buy or barter from the stalls. When the knight was a hundred or so yards away, he realised that with the gates still open he had a chance to get through before they could be closed, so he called out to his men and spurred his horse forward. Peter shouted down to the soldiers outside, who scurried into the castle. When the knight's force on horseback was twenty-five yards away, Peter shouted to the gate attendants, 'Close!' They pushed the gates half-closed and retreated.

The knight, not believing his luck, pushed his horse at full gallop through the half-open gates, followed by his squire and soldiers on horseback. At Peter's command, a withering hail of arrows hit them as they emerged into the courtyard, dropping every man. The peasants, lagging behind, did not see the devastation in the courtyard and also poured through the gate, each being easily picked off by arrows or hacked down by Peter's soldiers waiting on each side.

The other minor knights did not fail to see that their comrade had breached the castle gates, so, not wishing to be left behind, they all charged with squires and soldiers on horseback at full gallop. The lack of overall command meant that they all bunched together, getting in each other's way in a bid not to be last and miss the spoils.

'Ready to close fully!' shouted Peter to the guards on the gate. 'Matthew, all archers ready to loose over the battlements, but keep the men down until I say.'

Peter picked up a bow and watched the horde thundering towards him. When they were thirty yards away, he shouted, 'Close fully! Everyone help!' All the peasants close to the gates put their shoulders to the heavy wood to push them shut and bar them.

It was a close-run thing, but the minor knights realised the gates would be closed before they could reach them, so pulled their horses up short. The destriers, as always eager to obey but slow to perform, skidded to a halt with those behind knocking into those in front, creating mayhem a few short yards from the gates.

'Loose arrows now!' yelled Peter, and every man on the

battlements shot arrow after arrow into the melee. The confusion was so great and the horde packed so closely together that it turned into an advantage for the minor knights. Although the arrows could hardly miss, they struck the same target time after time, so that some knights, squires and soldiers had a dozen arrows sticking out of them or their horses, while others were totally unharmed in the press. Although William was screaming directions to his soldiers, they were so fired up with the sense of battle they did not comprehend what he was saying. Instead of being a complete massacre, many of the attackers got away. Only Matthew, Tom, the old man and Peter held their shots until targets became clear as the semi-vanquished rode away, and they managed to cut down three or four more.

The troops were jubilant. Not one of them had been even slightly injured and all around lay dead and dying attackers. William, however, immediately cut them down to size, saying, in no uncertain terms their failure to follow orders did not mean they were the victors, let alone safe, for there was still a formidable force outside. There was. Hardly any of the peasants had been injured and it appeared two of the knights were completely unscathed, with a number of soldiers still able to fight. Peter could not spot any squires still alive, however.

'First blood to us,' said Matthew, 'but they will be far more wary next time.'

'True,' replied Peter. 'Let them reorganise, and we will watch to see what they intend. I suspect nothing much today. Once again, no shooting unless I give the word.'

Indeed, nothing more happened that day. The army outside the castle moved away, tents were pitched and fires lit as they settled down for the night. Peter stood down half the garrison, telling them to take the bodies of the dead out of the castle and leave them there. While their colleagues kept a watchful eye, the designated soldiers stripped the bodies, inside and outside the castle, of anything of value. Peter told them that any plunder would be shared equally among the soldiers and fighting peasants. This was not so popular with the soldiers, but was certainly welcomed by the peasant army.

After going round the battlements and inspecting the castle, Peter returned to the hall at evening meal time. William, Matthew and Pierre stayed on the battlements keeping watch while Peter ate with Elaine, the old man and Tom.

'What will they do next?' asked Elaine.

'Obviously they will reorganise, and equally obviously they cannot give up, because that would be a loss of honour, particularly as I suspect Geoffrey's bishop put them up to it in the first place,' replied Peter. 'Once again, we have to wait.'

Oblivious of the others at the table, Elaine stretched forward and put a concerned hand over Peter's and sighed deeply.

The night passed peacefully, with each of the six taking turns to watch alongside a few soldiers. Everyone else slept, ready to leap into action should the army outside do anything. As the clear, bright, windless dawn broke, they all assembled on the battlements, but the attackers appeared to be in no hurry and it was not for some hours that there was any sign of movement from their camp. This time things were different. The two remaining knights advanced side by side, with their men evenly and properly distributed along the normal battle line. Their progress was slow, disciplined and deliberate. Whatever they intended, it was to be as a single unit not a disparate bunch of competing knights. The advance stopped just outside crossbow range and they waited, showing off their strength.

'Matthew,' asked Peter, 'do you think you can hit one of those knights – kill one if possible?'

'Yes. Only one?'

'One.'

Matthew took several arrows from his pouch and laid them on the top of the battlement, inspecting each one carefully. He made his selection and slowly drew back the Welsh bow. Peter's eyes were fixed on the two knights. He heard the twang of the bow as an arrow sped towards them, almost faster than the eye could follow, burying itself in the breast of one of the knights and knocking him backwards in his saddle. He would have fallen off completely, but the raised back of the saddle, designed to aid stability for the thrust of a lance, held him semi-upright for a moment. Before his lifeless body could slip to the ground, Peter heard the bow twang again and another arrow hit him, this time casting the knight to the earth. Immediately the other knight wheeled his horse around and shouted to the men around him as they retreated another hundred yards.

Peter looked at Matthew in amazement. 'I have done you a disservice. I knew you were good, but I did not realise you were that good. Remarkable. Two arrows!'

Matthew, quietly pleased with the praise, shrugged it off. 'An elevated position, no wind and as much time as I wanted made it easier,' he said.

'Right. William, please have all the horses saddled up and ready to move out as soon as possible. Select your most convincing-looking soldiers – any who have chain mail would be best – and put them on mounts to look, as closely as they can, like knights, or at least like experienced fighting men. We also need Elaine's standard to carry with us. Everyone else, get ready to go out of the castle in full battle formation.'

There was much scurrying in preparation as the horses were saddled and brought out into the courtyard, the soldiers and peasants forming up around them. Peter kept his eye on the army outside. It had regrouped and was, once again, standing in line, this time well out of Welsh bow range.

'Open the gates and let us go out to meet them!' shouted Peter.

There was a loud cheer from the men as the gates opened and the castle army moved out, with Peter at the head of the column, his group close behind, followed by everyone else marching purposefully. The heavy wooden gates closed behind them. Once clear of the castle, they formed up in line of battle with those on horses in the middle, foot soldiers and peasants spaced equally on each side and the archers, in one group, to the right ready to break away further to the flank to give the best continuous cover without hitting their own men. The whole little army stopped a hundred yards from their antagonists and waited as Elaine's standard, carried by one of the mounted soldiers, drooped limply in the sun-drenched air.

After a short time during which both sides eyed each other and tried to gauge their opponents' strength, Peter moved his horse backwards, then alongside the soldier carrying the standard.

'Let me have the standard, please, and everyone else, stay where you are.'

He took the standard and, holding it high, walked his horse slowly forward towards the waiting foe. He was quietly amused and pleased at the resolve of the archers, when he saw out of the corner of his eye the bowmen taking arrows from their bags and laying the arrows on their bows ready to fit to the string.

When Peter was about fifty yards from the opposing army, the one remaining knight took his own standard from the standard bearer and held it high, walking his horse towards Peter. They stopped a horse length away from each other. Peter saw that the surviving knight facing him, Sir Stephan, was the only one of the knights who had visited the castle to whom he had warmed.

'I take it you have come to surrender,' Sir Stephan said.

Peter gave his warm, engaging smile. 'I do not think you believe that.'

Sir Stephan smiled grimly. 'You are vastly outnumbered and out in the open here, you have no chance. Your mounted men, who I know are not knights, have no lances, so how do you think you can possibly survive our first charge?'

'Sir Stephan, let us be practical. The whole purpose of your being here is to take the castle, To do that, first, your men have to defeat us on the battlefield here, second, in order for you to benefit you have to survive, and third, you will have to take a still defended castle. Now, while it is true that those of us on horseback do not have lances, you will know that just six of us defeated de Villiers' knights with their lances, so we have nothing to fear in that respect. Also, our men are all well trained, whereas the majority of your men are conscripted peasants who have had only the rudiments of training. In fact, were I to wager on whether you would take the castle, then my money would not be on your army.'

Sir Stephan said nothing, although his eyes betrayed a half-acceptance of what Peter had said.

'We will not surrender and will fight to the end,' continued Peter. 'We have done and sacrificed too much to give up what has been achieved. I understand that you will not surrender to me, and for you not to engage in battle now would lose you honour. But . . .' Peter let the word linger. 'There is a third way. If we both agree that our forces are relatively evenly matched and the outcome for either of us is uncertain, then it would be no shame for us to agree a truce.'

There was a long silence whilst Sir Stephan considered. Eventually he said, 'I have lost five of my knight friends as well as trained soldiers and peasants, so am I to walk away from here with nothing? You ask too much.'

Peter shook his head. 'I suggested we should be practical. Although you would leave here with nothing except your life and your army, you are in a position to benefit considerably. As you say, you have lost five knight friends, which means there are five manor houses and lands without a master. What is to stop you taking over these manor houses and lands, putting your own men in to run them and profiting greatly? I would suggest nothing. Furthermore, if you agree a truce with my lady Elaine de Roche, and if you both agree to support each other as allies, then you will also benefit from my lady's influence at the king's court, as well as from my lady's soldiers and guards keeping the countryside open and free of bandits, robbers and thieves. This surely would please Geoffrey, Duke of Normandy, for he will realise that such an alliance with you, who have sworn allegiance to him, will ensure the complete loyalty of the castle and its inhabitants.'

Sir Stephan gave a wry smile while he considered what Peter had offered and the options open to him. 'I confess I was not averse to your being in the castle with Lady Elaine notionally in charge, because it has brought prosperity to the countryside. Others, though, have not been of a like mind and I fear that sooner or later Geoffrey will want to stamp his mark more firmly on the lands around here. If I appear to be tied to you, how will my position be then?'

'Your fealty is unquestionably to Geoffrey. Lady Elaine will do nothing to suggest that is not so. Indeed, she would do herself great harm if she even hinted otherwise. If it is made plain our alliance is for the better service of Geoffrey, no ill will befall you even if Geoffrey decides to replace Lady Elaine. Come, let us both go to the castle to draw up a deed between you and my lady, or, if you feel threatened, then I will have a tent brought out and it can be done here.'

'I do not feel threatened and although you are not of noble blood, I have no reason to believe that you would take advantage of me being in the castle. However, others might view it differently and it would look more like surrender if I went to the castle, abandoning my troops here. I see force in your suggestions and I am prepared to sign a document of truce and support, but I think it best to have a tent brought out here to show an equality of bargaining.'

Peter laughed. 'Absolutely right. May I suggest you go back to your men and stand them down? I will do the same with my men and get a tent, a scribe and my lady out here so we can all agree the wording before seals are affixed. Agreed?'

'Agreed.'

They both wheeled their horses about and cantered back to their respective lines. Peter gave a brief breakdown of the potential agreement and William returned to the castle to fetch the scribe and Elaine, along with a suitable tent for the negotiations. The men were stood down and sat about on the grass looking relaxed and unconcerned, but with Pierre, Matthew and Tom keeping a very watchful eye on the opposition.

The truce discussions and agreement for mutual cooperation under the auspices of King Louis VII and Geoffrey, Duke of Normandy, dragged on for most of the afternoon. Sir Stephan was well educated and cautious, weighing each word in the document for any hidden meaning or detrimental effect. The old man guided Elaine, although she showed a sharpness of understanding which augured well for the future. At last all was agreed, seals pressed into the document, and a signed copy made for Sir Stephan to take with him. As the evening light started to fade, both armies left the field of near-battle. The danger was over.

19

The moment they were back in the castle, Peter, his group and Elaine thanked all the men for their efforts. Elaine announced that extra food and wine would be available for everyone that evening. William, cautious as ever, took a number of his senior soldiers aside and instructed them not to drink, but to take it in turns to watch out just in case Sir Stephan returned. He promised them that the following night they would be able to make up for missing out that evening.

In the great hall, Peter took Elaine and the old man aside. 'I think it is very important that you immediately write a letter to your second cousin in Geoffrey's court to let her know what has happened here. Geoffrey will hear about it soon enough, but I would like the first news to come from you, suitably worded. Are you strong enough to work on it now?'

'Of course!' retorted Elaine. 'I am a noble and what has happened today does not make me weak.'

So together, over several hours, pausing to take only the smallest snack from the food being enjoyed by everyone else, they carefully composed the letter.

My dearest cousin,

Whilst I am in the deepest shock, made worse by my current run-down condition, I feel I must write to you without delay to put your mind at rest, for I am sure you have heard of the dreadful events which have taken place here today.

Without giving me any warning, six of the minor knights with an army of over one hundred and sixty men took up arms against me. By sheer luck my gallant little force managed to defend my honour and the castle. My mind is reeling with the closeness of it.

I was fortunate in that Sir Stephan, a knight who has visited me here and for whose honour and fealty to Geoffrey I have the highest regard, called off the assault at the last moment and generously agreed to a truce with full cooperation between us, so that Geoffrey and the king can be served to the full. I am for the moment safe.

I cannot bring myself to think what Geoffrey is going to say when he hears that his knights have, without cause or provocation, taken up arms against a cousin of our dear king, and I will be writing to Geoffrey as soon as I am well enough to set out dispassionately the evil events of today. For the moment my thoughts are in turmoil, my body weak, I am utterly exhausted and I cannot wait to go to my bed, where I hope sleep will numb the shock of it all.

Your affectionate cousin and friend,
Elaine.

'I'm not sure about saying we had no warning, and I have not mentioned that five of the six knights were killed,' said Elaine doubtfully.

'You are saying in your letter the knights did not give you warning, not that *we* had no warning, and Geoffrey will know soon enough who was killed and who was not,' replied the old man. 'In a few weeks you can write to Geoffrey in more detail, though still saying you are not strong enough to venture out of the castle. What we are after now is time, to reassure Geoffrey that his role in all this is not suspected and that you are his loyal servant. With the pact you have signed with Sir Stephan, there is no immediate excuse for Geoffrey to interfere in what is happening here and he is essentially thrown back onto finding out precisely what happened today before thinking again about getting you a husband.'

Pleased with their efforts with the letter, Elaine summoned a dispatch rider to set out at first light to deliver it to her second cousin, knowing that the shock she would feel about the attack on Elaine would mean that she would tell her husband, who could not keep the letter's contents from Geoffrey. When all was done, they went wearily to bed.

The castle reverted to normality within a few days as the stall-holders and traders returned. There was a noticeable lightness of step on the part of all the castle inhabitants, buoyed up by the knowledge of what they had been through and achieved together.

Peter, on the other hand, was far from easy in his mind and eventually the old man took him to one side. 'What is troubling you? We are in no danger now. Even if Geoffrey dislikes what has been done here and is furious that his, or his bishop's, plan has been thwarted, he will do nothing for the moment, for he has no grounds to challenge us. Even if he does not believe Elaine is too poorly to travel, he could not possibly do anything about it. She is after all the king's cousin and, even if a distant one, sufficiently close to royalty to demand circumspection.'

There was a long silence. The easy smile which so readily graced Peter's lips was absent as he frowned, trying to put his misgivings into words. 'What troubles me,' he said eventually, 'is the next step. I fully accept all you say, but we both know that sooner or later Elaine will not, as a single woman, be able to hold onto this castle and her own lands. Leaving aside the money we found in the chest, with all the lands she has she is a wealthy woman and there are too many poor, or at least relatively poor, barons about to let her alone. With wealth comes influence and an influential woman, whether distant cousin to the king or not, will not be tolerated. Pressure will be put on Geoffrey and what I have not yet worked out is how we can prevent this.'

The old man went to a cupboard in the hall and drew from it a jug of wine and two cups. He put them on the table and pushed Peter into the chair at the head, pouring two generous portions of the best wine. 'Drink and relax.'

Peter took a deep draught and put his cup back on the table, still with the frown wrinkling his forehead. The old man filled the cup again and raised his own cup in toast. Peter took a small swallow.

'Break the problem down into its parts.' The old man raised his hand to prevent Peter's retort that he had already been trying to do this. 'The two dominant factors are a husband for Elaine and the totality of Elaine's land holdings.' Peter nodded. 'You are thinking of a solution along the lines of avoiding the first and keeping the second.' Peter gave another small nod. 'Well, what about sacrificing one for the good of the other?' Peter looked at him uncomprehendingly. 'I feel you are too close to the problem – too close to Elaine, perhaps. We both know you cannot be her husband, and I suspect you do not want to be.' Peter nodded and chuckled at the same time. 'Then why don't *we* find her a husband and present this potential husband to Geoffrey, saying that Elaine would take the man and agree to give up her inherited lands to Geoffrey, or the king if he gets involved, provided she and her husband can stay here as rightful inheritors from de Villiers?'

'Marvellous, but who can we find as a suitable husband? What chances are there of her accepting someone we have chosen? And, just as importantly, will she willingly give up her inherited lands?'

'Knowing Elaine as I do, particularly recently now she is completely out of her shell and well in charge of what she wants, she has to select the potential husband herself – but that is not to say that we should not choose who she selects!'

The frown left Peter's face as he laughed. 'So let us discuss the potential choices.'

'Oh no. I can see your mind whirring already. I'm sure you had the answer before you spoke. I will leave you to your thoughts.' With that, the old man rose and went out of the hall leaving Peter sitting in the chair, staring at the table, wine cup in hand.

A few moments later Elaine came in with an armful of clean bedclothes. Since the battle with the minor knights she had lost all semblance of superiority and from time to time willingly helped the servants, as well as discussing castle affairs with them.

'I don't believe it. Drinking in the middle of the afternoon! What ails you?'

Her voice broke into Peter's thoughts and he looked up at her with a half-smile. 'Unusual, I grant you, but some difficult decisions have to be made and I was taking courage from the grape.'

'What decisions?'

'Come and sit down. Do you want your chair?'

She shook her head and, putting the clean bedlinen on the table, sat down where the old man had been, waiting for Peter to tell her what was going through his mind.

'I think we have to be realistic,' Peter started. 'We are all secure here for the moment, but we both know it will not last. We also both realise that our relationship cannot continue. I am not of noble blood and anyway I doubt I would be a suitable suitor, bearing in mind your direct lineage to the king.' Elaine said nothing, but looked at him soberly. He smiled. 'It seems to me if we are all to stay here, we must have someone of real rank in charge of the men. You are, of course, in overall command, but to the outside world you command peasants, not men with rank and position.'

Elaine became very wary. 'How do you think this can be changed?' she asked, narrowing her eyes, ready to dash any hopes Peter might have of forcing her into anything. She leaned forward, picking up the old man's half-full cup of wine and sipping it slowly, her eyes never leaving Peter's face.

Peter went on. 'We actually have a knight in the castle, though he does not admit it.' Elaine looked at him questioningly. 'Pierre,' Peter said simply. She gasped.

'It is obvious Pierre is a little different,' she said. 'His manners and demeanour point to a certain gentleness, but what possible reason could he have, as a knight, for hiding his position and taking orders from you?'

Peter told Elaine of Pierre's turn of bad fortune and the unwarranted slur on his name which led to him being banished. 'The point is, although Pierre was banished, he did not have his knighthood taken away, because only the king can do that, not an aggrieved baron whose daughter embellished the truth. He is so ashamed of the whole incident, and indeed of his unwittingly being in the position of opposing Geoffrey, that he refuses to acknowledge his rank and so happily fits in with our little group. I believe you get on with Pierre, so do you not think it would be a good idea to convince him to acknowledge his knighthood? It would solve your problem. You would have a man of position under your command.'

'You are right,' replied Elaine, somewhat more readily than Peter expected. Perhaps she looked on Pierre rather more favourably than he had thought possible. 'But, as you say, it is the rest of the world which has to accept his rank and if he suddenly declares it now, there will be suspicion, certainly, and probably some objections.'

'True, but if we do things slowly and carefully we can make it look as though Pierre's position here as knight is an advantage to everyone else – Geoffrey, for example.'

Elaine said nothing, but gave Peter a sidelong glance, indicating that he had to make good on this statement. Peter took a deep breath. 'First of all, you have to write to Geoffrey soon, telling him directly about the minor knights trying to take over the castle. While that letter has to show your indignation and describe fairly accurately what happened, it can be slanted towards indicating Pierre's strength and determination in a time of crisis. All I have to do is to convince Pierre to reclaim his knighthood, or rather to lay himself at Geoffrey's mercy, as a knight eager to support the Duke whilst in your employ.'

She laughed. 'I think you will have the greater difficulty convincing Pierre than I'll have composing a suitable letter!'

Although the old man appeared to have abandoned to Peter the task of finding Elaine a husband, after consultation with William, Matthew and Tom, he was enlisted to speak to Pierre about reclaiming his position as a knight and being the commander of the castle forces. Neither Peter nor the old man said anything to Pierre about being a potential husband to Elaine, and Pierre's initial hesitancy about the remainder of the plan was, surprisingly to Peter, short lived and he embraced it with enthusiasm. Elaine too played her part as she and Pierre spent periods together going around the castle to check and instruct, spending particular time with the soldiers who cheerfully accepted Pierre's elevated status, helped by William, who readily deferred to Pierre. For the evening meals, Pierre sat on Elaine's immediate right, the senior position.

After a few weeks Elaine sent another letter to her cousin

at Geoffrey's court, giving more detail of the defence of the castle and setting the stage for Pierre's elevation, even referring to him as 'Sir Pierre'. She emphasised that the pact with Sir Stephan strengthened the bond with Geoffrey and that her men were ready and willing to serve Geoffrey when called upon. Her cousin's reply was somewhat swifter and longer than anticipated, surprisingly giving information of Geoffrey's plan to visit the royal court towards the end of August. Elaine, Peter, Pierre and the old man read the letter through several times and they all agreed that while it was written in Elaine's cousin's hand, there were all the signs of third-party input.

'My overall impression,' said the old man eventually, 'is that this letter is encouraging. Perhaps "Sir Pierre's" presence here is actually offering a solution to Geoffrey. He has been suppressing a number of rebellious barons these last few years and he may well have more on his plate distributing favours and administering the lands of the defeated barons than he would wish. Elaine being settled here with Pierre, as well as the support and encouragement of Sir Stephan, who is well known to be fiercely loyal to Geoffrey, means that he doesn't have to be troubled by finding you a husband for the moment and need not listen to those in his court who will urge preference and reward in the shape of this castle.' There were slow nods all around. 'I do not think it will be so for ever, though,' the old man continued. 'This castle and its lands are too rich a picking.'

'Yes,' said Peter slowly. 'Pierre should go to Geoffrey's court as soon as possible to see for himself what Geoffrey's reaction really is. I do not think it is coincidence that Elaine's cousin mentioned Geoffrey will be at the royal court at the end of August.'

'Into the lion's den?' asked Pierre. They looked at him. 'Oh well, sooner or later I will have to do it, so why not now? I don't know, though, if I will be able to report back faithfully – assuming, that is, I am allowed to leave. Geoffrey is well known for his charm and joviality, but his grasp of power and lands indicates a strong, selfish character and he will likely not actually reveal his true intentions. It is important he at least allows me to swear fealty to him.'

'Agreed,' said the old man. 'A letter back to your cousin is needed, Elaine, giving advance warning of Pierre's arrival at Geoffrey's court for the purpose of swearing fealty, so that Geoffrey will be ready. Should Geoffrey not immediately accept Pierre's fealty, then we will know we are going to be in trouble rather sooner than we might like. It is nearly August, Pierre, and you must set out within the next week to be sure that Geoffrey will be there when you arrive.'

Elaine immediately wrote a letter to her cousin informing her of Pierre's intention to arrive at court shortly, and sent it off by messenger that afternoon. A second letter was composed to Geoffrey, introducing Pierre and commending him to Geoffrey's service. This letter Pierre would carry. Then Pierre himself was made ready. His shield was emblazoned with Elaine's crest, a shift in Elaine's colours was hastily made for him, and his accompanying six soldiers and other staff were presented with new clothes, their armour and arms all burnished to the highest shine in order to make the best impression.

The first week in August arrived and Pierre departed with his troop. 'Very impressive sight, I must say,' grunted William as Pierre left the castle. 'No one could doubt Pierre's position, though whether Geoffrey will agree . . .' He left the words hanging.

It was only just over two weeks before Pierre returned, but the days dragged slowly for those left in the castle without news. Even people outside the group knew of the importance of Pierre's mission and none could be other than apprehensive. Elaine seemed to be the worst. She no longer sought Peter's favours and returned to her moody snappishness, eating sparingly and morosely with the others each evening. Tom tried to make light of it all, but even his banter failed to lift the mood. So it was very much 'heart in mouth' for everyone when Pierre rode slowly in through the castle gates one day, dismounted and walked into the hall. Taking off his helmet, he smiled broadly, lighting up his handsome face.

'Sir Pierre of Castle Gronin greets you well!' he said, bursting into laughter. There was an audible puff of breath as the tension left each one of those who had been left behind.

Pierre related that he was greeted with enthusiasm by Geoffrey who, surprisingly encouraged by the bishop, immediately accepted his oath of fealty and impressed on him the importance of the alliances that Sir Stephan, Elaine and others had formed to support him. When the rather touchy subject was raised of Pierre's involvement on the wrong side with a baron who refused to surrender, Geoffrey merely shrugged it off, dismissing the event as simply unfortunate and in no way affecting the present. 'A knight is always a knight,' Geoffrey had said and he showed Pierre a list of loyal barons and knights, on which Pierre's name already featured, and which Geoffrey was going to present to King Louis over the following weeks when he was at the royal court.

'Henry was very much in attendance at Geoffrey's court,' continued Pierre, 'and he is as charming as his father. He questioned me in a light-hearted way about us all here at the castle, but I got the strong impression that he was gauging our true loyalty and strength. He seemed particularly keen to find out why five Englishmen had left England, asking me if there had been a fall-out with King Stephen. I told him as little as possible, but, old man, if you want to regain favour with the nobles you could do worse than go to see Henry.'

The old man grunted, but did not reply.

20

Pierre's successful return from Geoffrey's court raised the spirits of everyone and he was easily and readily accepted as the commander of the army, sharing with William the training and responsibility for the soldiers' welfare. Elaine regained her liveliness and the whole castle fell into an orderly, happy and peaceful routine. It did not last.

In the second week of September a messenger arrived with a letter from Elaine's cousin. Returning from the royal council, Geoffrey had been stricken with a fever from which he did not recover. Geoffrey's son Henry was invested as Duke of Normandy, Anjou, Tour and Maine. While such investiture was to be expected on Geoffrey's death, it threw up uncertainty, for no one knew whether Henry would honour all his father's allegiances or seek his own.

The old man took Peter aside. 'We are very much in the unknown now. Henry will have his own favourites and some of Geoffrey's men at court will be eased out. Although Geoffrey gave every impression he was content with us here, the fact that Henry questioned Pierre about us leads me to believe we may well be close to the top of his list for changes.'

Peter nodded slowly. 'Indeed. We have, perhaps, been too lucky for too long and although I do like it here, I've been thinking for a while that we should move on.' He looked the old man in the eye. 'How is our money situation?'

'Good. On the basis the de Villiers coin and valuables we found locked away in the chest under his bed plus the taxes collected from the peasants this year are divided seven ways – that is, between us six and Elaine – as well as the marks we have been paid by the various mayors, divided six ways, we each have enough to buy or build a small manor house with sufficient land to support us in a modest way. If we cut Elaine out, then we will each have more, of course, but I guess you would not do that.' Peter shook his head. He had no wish to cheat Elaine. 'I have already divided the money into seven portions just in case we have to leave here in a hurry.'

Peter laughed. 'Old man, you really do look ahead! We must all thank you. I think, though, before we actually make serious plans to leave, we ought to consider one more throw of the dice to see if our luck still holds. It is something which very much affects you, so you will have the final word.'

The old man was silent, waiting for Peter to continue. 'What we know is that Matilda is very much still aggrieved at Stephen cheating her of her inheritance and from what Pierre has said she has been encouraging, if not actually urging, Henry to do something about it. The fact that Henry was knighted by his great uncle, David, King of Scotland, shows he is not immune to the possibility of taking on Stephen, though perhaps he might wait until Eustace, Stephen's only son, inherits. Let us assume that sooner or later Henry will invade England: would it not be to his great advantage to know there are Englishmen willing to support him? Most of Matilda's allies in England have died, and while I am sure Henry has curried favour with many nobles during his stay in England, he may not actually have sworn allegiance from them.'

'I do not disagree with anything you have said,' the old man put in, 'but how does this affect me so much?'

'You have already fought against Stephen, so your loyalty

to Matilda has been shown and it would be readily believed if you offered such loyalty to Henry. Tell me, did Matilda actually know it was you and not William de Cahaignes who took Stephen prisoner?'

'It is possible. I really do not know, though if she hears my name she should recognise that I was one of the knights released by the church to aid her campaign.'

'There we have it: the key. If you agree to go to Henry's court, seek out Matilda and discover whether she recognises your former loyalty, then you can offer allegiance to Henry. Bearing in mind that while Stephen is still alive you will have little chance of settling down in England unmolested, with Henry's grace we can all live here and be ready to join him in any invasion plans he might have.'

The old man turned away from Peter and walked slowly to and fro, head down, thinking. This was unusual. The old man's mind worked as fast as Peter's, so it was clear that the idea troubled him. Peter remained silent, watching.

'I understand your reasoning,' the old man said eventually, 'but I have been evading detection for so long now, I have difficulty deciding whether I could actually identify myself to any noble. We have to consider all Henry's options. It is not impossible to believe he might wish to ingratiate himself with Stephen for the moment – lead Stephen into a false sense of security, perhaps, by demonstrating he is content with his dominions and happy to let Stephen rule England. If this is so, then Henry could take me prisoner and send me back to Stephen. If that happened, then all here are in danger, for Henry could quite legitimately maintain that you have been harbouring a criminal and this would give him the excuse to take the castle and return you all to England as traitors.'

'But if you seek out Matilda first, as she still hates Stephen for taking her inheritance then she would not willingly do anything which would put you, one of her supporters, in danger – so if Henry is minded not to accept your oath of fealty, I am sure Matilda would warn you.'

The old man nodded slowly. 'We can certainly trust Matilda's hatred of Stephen, so I think you are right.' He smiled. 'We have to take the chance and I will go, though I think it would be helpful if you came with me. She is bound to ask about what has been happening here and she must know that, in effect, you have been in real charge. With us both there, it will demonstrate that we are hiding nothing and being faithful to her and Henry.'

Peter agreed and they made plans for their journey.

The following week the old man and Peter set out on their way to Henry's court, planning to see Matilda first. They travelled well armed but alone, carrying spare clean clothing in anticipation of the audience.

In the middle of the second day they saw a small group of six men riding slowly towards them. Their appearance from a distance indicated a disciplined band with shields stowed on saddles and no sign of hostility. Peter and the old man cautiously loosened their swords and surreptitiously made their shields ready for instant donning should it be necessary. Whilst they had no fear of regular soldiers who would be bound to a knight or baron and so allied to Henry, it was wise to be prepared. As they approached, Peter became aware of a similar band on his right and one on the old man's left. Turning around, he saw another band of six well-armed soldiers cantering up behind.

'We are surrounded. I do not feel good about this,' said the old man. 'Friendly forces would not approach from all sides. Too many for us to fight, and now they are too close for us to out-ride.'

With no other choices open, Peter and the old man stopped their horses and waited for the four bands to reach and form a circle around them.

'Good afternoon,' Peter said, looking towards the leader who had unslung his shield and brought it around to his front, displaying the emblem of Geoffrey's bishop. 'Can we assist you?'

The leader laughed. 'Indeed you can. My lord bishop invites you to meet him.'

'An invitation, it seems to me, not to be turned down.'

The leader laughed again. 'How right you are.'

'Then we are delighted to accept the invitation. We were going to Henry's court anyway and your added protection in such a wild countryside as this is welcomed.'

The leader laughed even more loudly, but moved to one side, and with his band surrounding Peter and the old man, they set off at a brisk pace.

It soon became apparent that the direction in which they were headed was not towards Henry, but further south. Neither the old man nor Peter said anything, but they exchanged glances, acknowledging wherever they were destined was unlikely to bode well for them. As evening approached they came to a small village. Some of the men went into the village, returning later with wine and bread, whilst the others dismounted and prepared themselves for the evening meal and sleep. Before the food was served, the leader approached Peter and the old man to tell them they had to surrender their weapons. Severely outnumbered as they were, it was pointless refusing or making a fuss, so they both obediently handed over swords, daggers, bows and shields. The leader made a rudimentary search of their saddlebags and, finding nothing to interest him, left the two alone to eat the food they had brought with them. Within earshot of and surrounded by the soldiers, neither spoke and when the sparse meal was finished they settled down to sleep.

Up with the sun the following morning, the troop mounted and made their way through the village, where they encountered a number of traders going out in the opposite direction.

By the middle of the afternoon Peter saw they were approaching a large manor. It was not fortified with a surrounding wall, but was well built with what appeared to be thick stone walls for the lower floor, atop which was a sturdy wooden second floor supporting a substantial pitched wooden roof. The windows on the lower floor were just thin slits and those on the upper floor were fitted with heavy shutters. The door to the house was large and heavy, wooden with metal inserts to aid its strength. It was not a castle, but was eminently defendable.

As they approached, the door of the manor was opened by a soldier and Peter and the old man were hustled off their horses and propelled through the door into an imposing hallway, down a corridor stretching the length of the manor to a corner room at the end, where they were pushed in and the thick wooden door slammed behind them. The room was bare. No furniture, mattress or utensil could be seen in the light filtering through the two slit windows.

'Not very encouraging,' said the old man.

Peter grunted. 'On the basis it is indeed the bishop's men who brought us here, and given the obvious lack of hospitality, do you have any thoughts on how we could have upset him so?'

The old man shook his head. 'I think we have to make ourselves as comfortable as possible and just wait. Someone will tell us eventually.'

They settled down on the floor and without evening meal or interruption slept fitfully through the night. Come midmorning, the door opened and two soldiers looked in, checked that Peter and the old man were sitting on the floor away from the door where they could do no harm, then walked in with two wooden bowls and wooden spoons, which they placed on the floor before backing out.

'Being a bit cautious, were they not?' asked Peter rhetorically.

They moved towards the bowls, which proved to contain a thick and very palatable soup. They ate eagerly. The day passed slowly and they mostly concentrated on their own thoughts, speaking little. It was readily agreed they could do nothing and plan nothing until they had information on why they were there and a better idea of the number of people in the manor and its layout. The view from the window slits was of countryside and they assumed the stables, and perhaps quarters for the soldiers, were at the back of the manor. Just before sunset the soldiers returned to go through the same routine, taking away the empty bowls and replacing them with full ones. Before they slammed the door shut, one kicked a wooden bucket into the room.

'Ah,' said the old man, 'good timing! I was just beginning to burst.' He picked up the bucket, put it in a corner of the room and relieved himself with a mighty sigh.

The next morning's soup arrived, carried by the same soldiers in the same cautious way, but this time they lingered outside the open door somewhat longer, seemingly expecting Peter or the old man to complain or ask questions. As the two prisoners remained silent, the door was slammed shut.

At midday a faint noise of horses came through one window slit. Looking out, they saw the bishop, his priest and six armed men ride up to the manor. The bishop and priest dismounted and disappeared, no doubt through the front door, while the solders took the horses around towards the back of the manor.

'Some answers,' Peter said. 'We have been left in ignorance because the bishop has been away. The stables are indeed at the back of the manor and he has at least thirty-two armed men under his command. The twenty-four who took us, the six we have just seen and the two who bob in and out of our cell. Leaving aside that heavy bolted door, the odds seem somewhat stacked against us.'

The old man smiled. 'Let us see.'

The bishop was in no hurry to confront the two, for it was not until the next morning they were taken out of the room by the two soldiers, marched back along the corridor and up the stairs to a substantial, airy corner room, with windows wide open, where the bishop was sitting in a large throne-like chair to the side of a big oak table bearing the remains of the bishop's first meal of the day. The two soldiers stood behind Peter and the old man while the bishop looked at them, his eyes hard and his mouth twisted between a sneer and a cruel smile. Neither of the two said anything.

Eventually the bishop broke the silence. 'I hope you are enjoying my hospitality.'

'I confess the beds are a little hard,' replied Peter, 'though the soup is good, if somewhat lacking in variety.'

'As smart as ever,' the bishop retorted. 'But perhaps not smart for much longer.' There was a long pause. 'Would you like me to tell you why you are here?'

'Whatever pleases you, my lord bishop,' replied Peter.

'Well, it does please me. You as common men killing those minor knights did not go down too well with Henry. Geoffrey was slightly more relaxed about it, though it troubled him to have such a strongly defended castle in your hands and not directly under his control, so the appearance of your Sir Pierre swearing allegiance to Geoffrey put his mind at rest. When Henry succeeded Geoffrey, things were different. He blamed me for putting the idea of taking the castle into the minds of the minor knights, but even more he blamed me for urging Geoffrey to acknowledge Pierre as a knight, so putting the castle out of Henry's gift. The result was that I was banished from his court, no longer to be the senior bishop, and in all likelihood my own life expectancy is not great. For all his affable exterior, Henry does not tolerate what he perceives as disloyalty.'

'My lord bishop, we're both perplexed to hear of your very unfortunate and unwarranted treatment, but surely Henry can understand that men need to defend themselves and that even the best-planned battle can go wrong? When we see him, we can emphasise and confirm our own and the castle's loyalty to him.'

The bishop sneered. 'You will be seeing no one. At the moment your Sir Pierre has sworn fealty to Geoffrey, but he has not done so to Henry, so if this does not happen, Henry would have the castle back in his gift. I thought Pierre would be setting out to Henry's court to swear such fealty, but instead of intercepting him, my men caught you two, who were no doubt going to speak to Henry. When you both disappear, Pierre will have to go himself to Henry and if I am the author of Pierre's misfortune, then I will be back in favour.' He paused as a genuine smile replaced the sneer. 'As a bonus, I have the two who were responsible for my, as you put it, unfortunate and unwarranted treatment, and as everyone knows you two are the driving force behind Elaine de Roche's apparent successes, without you the castle poses no threat.'

The old man spoke for the first time. Seemingly bemused by the turn of events, he took a few tentative paces towards the bishop before stopping as the soldier behind him leaped forward. 'My lord bishop.' He paused as if gathering his thoughts. 'I can assure you no one at the castle would be happy to know you are not in favour with Henry. While you were graciously with us, we were so pleased you took such interest in what Elaine de Roche had achieved and I am sure the action of the minor knights was inevitable anyway. We can understand their jealousy. It was perhaps our fault we did not do more to make greater friends with them. That you should be blamed for their action is quite wrong, and in truth Geoffrey had no choice but to acknowledge Pierre as a knight, for that is what he is. We were expecting an audience with Matilda, whom I was privileged to support when she was in England, and when she sees us we can explain precisely what happened and emphasise both our own and your loyalty to Henry.'

The bishop sneered once again. 'You really do not understand Henry. He listens to fine words and gives every impression of agreement and acceptance, but deep down he believes in action, in results. Nothing short of the castle handed to him on a plate will satisfy him.' Turning to the soldiers, he commanded, 'Take them away.'

Peter and the old man were pulled roughly out of the room and taken back to their cell.

'What did you see out of the windows?' Peter asked.

'Was it that obvious?'

'Only to me. A bemused old man spouting nonsense you are not!'

The old man smiled. 'You were right. The stables are at the back of the manor, as is a wooden building large enough to house all the soldiers. Undoubtedly there will be some soldiers in the manor day and night, with the usual staff, but the odds are better while we are in the manor.'

'Better they might be when we get out of this room, but how do you plan to do that?'

The old man's smile broadened. He leaned down, unfastening the bindings of his right trouser leg, and there, strapped to his calf, was a knife. Peter had never seen such a weapon. The knife was twelve inches in length but seemed only as thick as a piece of heavy parchment. The handle was the same thickness as the sharp, pointed blade. 'This is an Italian knife made of the finest metal. It is not strong enough to parry a sword blade, nor even perhaps another dagger, but it will cut surely and deeply. The only difficulty in using it is the thin handle, which does not give the best of grips, but if I wrap a piece of cloth securely around the handle it will make a formidable weapon.' The old man unfastened the binding of his left trouser leg and wrapped it around the knife handle. When he had finished, he cut in half the binding from his right trouser leg, the knife blade slicing through the cloth as if it were a blade of grass, and used each half to replace both leg bindings. 'No one will notice the difference,' he said.

He handed Peter the knife and set out his plan. 'I would expect our two soldier guards to return before the day is out – if not to take us to our death, then to bring food. You are by far the most nimble, so I'll cause a small distraction to give you time to spring up off the floor and use the knife on the guards. Once they are dead, we can take their arms and make our way to the front door, dispatching anyone in our way. Once out, then I'm afraid we will have to run. I cannot see a way of making it around to the back of the manor and taking our horses with all those soldiers so close. It will not be too long before we are either spotted or missed, but the soldiers will be unlikely to chase us on foot, so we will have extra time while they saddle up. If we make for the wood over there, then we have a chance of either evading them or at least being able to fight on our own terms – although in truth vastly outnumbered.'

Peter nodded. 'I would imagine not all of the soldiers would saddle up and chase us to begin with. If it is half a dozen or so, then we have a chance.'

'One thing you must promise me,' said the old man. 'You are a natural runner, so you must go at your top speed and do not worry about me. I could never keep up with you, and while you cannot out-run a horse, you are able to cover a greater distance than they would ever imagine, so you have the best chance to get away. You can make your way back to the castle and bring our men back here to rescue or avenge me. Do you agree?'

'I agree this far. If we both make it to that wood, then we stick together and fight it out. If they are quicker to chase than we think and we do not get to the wood, then I will leave you.'

'Good. So we can do no more than wait.'

The day once again passed slowly as the two men waited for the guards to appear, but the delay was not without its compensations. The fact no one appeared too soon gave comfort that they were not going to be put to death immediately and the usual early evening meal would be given to them.

As sunset approached, with ears straining to hear the sound of the door bolt being pulled back, the old man moved towards the bucket in the corner of the room and Peter readied himself to spring to his feet. Right on cue, the door swung open. The old man made as if he was relieving himself.

'Oi, you, get back on the floor!' shouted one of the soldiers. The old man turned around and in doing so kicked the bucket over, allowing the contents to spill out onto the floor. The guards stared at the mess streaming across the flagstones towards them. Peter leaped to his feet, knife in hand, and expertly sliced through one soldier's throat and then buried the knife in the second soldier's chest while the first soldier gurgled blood and air as he slumped to the ground. The old man was close on Peter's heels and pulled the swords from the dead soldiers, handing one to Peter as he retrieved the old man's knife from the chest of the second guard. They both pulled the guards into the room, shutting and bolting the door. Pausing outside, they looked along the corridor. There was no one in sight and it seemed that no one had heard the dying breaths of the soldiers.

Peter and the old man walked quickly but silently along the long corridor, opened the front door and went out. They quietly closed the door behind them.

'I suggest we walk rather than run,' said the old man. 'We have got this far without arousing attention, and running will alert anyone looking out of the windows. If we just walk, we may go completely unnoticed.'

They both walked steadily towards the woods. They were almost half way when there was a shout from an upstairs window. The bishop was leaning out, screaming for his guards.

'Walking over!' exclaimed the old man, and they sprinted for the trees. To begin with, the old man showed a surprising turn of pace.

Their good luck then seemed to desert them. Either the bishop's men kept a number of their horses saddled, or some could ride bareback, for around the side of the manor appeared four horsemen, followed by a number of others straggling behind.

'We are not going to make it!' gasped the old man. 'Go!'

Peter grasped the old man's arm and propelled him faster towards the trees. 'We still have a chance. Don't worry, if they get too close I will leave you.'

The old man had not enough breath to answer as the trees loomed larger and the soldiers closed the gap. Looking over his shoulder, Peter saw that indeed they would not make it to the wood.

He was about to let go of the old man and sprint off ahead when the familiar twang of an arrow drew his attention, first to the wood – where no one was to be seen – and then to the fast-approaching soldiers, who were suddenly less one in number, then two less, then three, and finally none were left riding in the first group.

Wheezing and gasping, the old man made it to the wood alongside Peter as more arrows miraculously appeared from nowhere, striking the straggling group of soldiers, some of whom fell from their horses. The remainder wheeled around and rode rapidly back to the manor.

'Nice piece of running, that,' said a voice to Peter's right.

Matthew came out from behind a tree, beaming a smile. He was followed by William and Tom.

'What in the devil's name are you doing here?' demanded Peter, who was not at all out of breath, even though he had run over three hundred yards, practically carrying the old man for part of the distance.

'Explanations later,' replied William shortly. 'We had best get out of here. If the whole herd of the bishop's men come after us, we may be in trouble.'

William ushered them deeper into the wood, where six horses were tethered.

'I am afraid,' said William, 'these horses are blown. Although we each had two horses, we have ridden them hard – too hard. They are in no fit state to out-run any bishop's men giving chase, but if we take it easily, we ought to be able to put sufficient distance between us and the manor to make it difficult for them to find us, particularly as the sun's nearly set and it will be dark soon.'

William was right. The horses had already given their all and the group could do no more than set a fast walking pace. Even then, from time to time the exhausted horses stumbled in the dim light cast by the first vestiges of a new moon. They plodded on uncertainly for a few hours and then, with no sign of being chased, just after midnight they stopped to rest, more for the sake of the horses than anything else.

'I am afraid we have no food,' said William. 'We left in rather a hurry.'

Peter laughed. 'Worry not. We are just grateful to have you here. So tell me, how did you know what had happened to us?'

William sat on the ground and made himself comfortable while Matthew and Tom secured the horses so they could graze and rest.

'You may remember when you were leaving the village

where you stayed overnight with the bishop's men, you met a few merchants leaving in the other direction.' Peter nodded. 'One of those merchants was a man we paid compensation to when we closed the castle market before the minor knights' attack. He was grateful and recognised both of you and realised that without arms and surrounded by the bishop's men, you were not travelling with them of your own free will. He made haste, indeed incredible haste, to the castle to let us know. The day before he arrived, Elaine received a carefully worded letter from her cousin – who seems to have fitted easily into Henry's court – indicating that things have changed there and the bishop was out of favour. Elaine was like a whirlwind. She immediately realised you were in trouble and although we needed no urging, she had us on our horses with a spare mount each in no time and away to rescue you. Luckily the merchant was well travelled and knew where the bishop's manor was located, so with his directions – which turned out to be remarkably accurate – we made all haste to get there. We had only just arrived when you two came walking out of the front door!'

'We were lucky indeed that you arrived when you did,' said the old man. 'What we have to think about now is what the bishop is going to do next. It seems to me we would be exceptionally unfortunate if his men found us now, but having told us preventing Pierre from giving his personal allegiance to Henry is the key to his plan to ingratiate himself into Henry's favour, he cannot just do nothing. We must get back to the castle as soon as possible and get Pierre safely to Henry.' The old man looked at the six horses which, even in the dim light, gave no encouragement. They were too tired even to graze. 'I fear Peter could run there quicker than those horses, which need at least a week to recover their strength.'

'One man taking it in turn to ride each of the six could get there in a reasonable time,' said Peter, 'but that would leave the rest of us on foot and be far too risky. We have no choice but to press on at first light with what we have. If we cut across towards a trading route, we might come across some merchants and borrow their horses.'

Nothing more could be added, so they settled down to sleep, each taking it in turns to watch out for the bishop's men.

All the next morning they rode as steadily as the condition of the horses would allow and as the sun passed its zenith they spotted a merchant's wagon train in the distance making its way towards them. As the merchants came closer, they were surprised to see five saddled but riderless horses attached in line to one of the wagons. They were even more surprised to recognise the woman sitting on one of the wagons, looking every bit as if she belonged there.

'Simone!' exclaimed Peter when they got within speaking distance. 'What are you doing here?'

The wagon train drew to a halt and Simone jumped down. 'Come, dismount and have something to eat, and I will tell all.'

Needing no urging, the five men got off their weary horses and gathered around Simone's wagon as she handed out food and poured cups of wine for them all.

'We cannot tarry here too long,' said Peter. 'We must get back to the castle and warn Pierre he is in danger.'

Simone put a hand on Peter's arm. 'What you must *not* do is go back to the castle,' she said. 'Eat and I will explain.' They all looked at her expectantly.

'Elaine has turned out to be much sharper than any of us realised. After William, Matthew and Tom had left, she questioned the merchant very closely and then spent a long time re-reading the letter from her cousin and talking to Pierre. For some reason she then confided in me, asking for my opinion and then including me in her conversations with

Pierre. She concluded that as it was well known the bishop was an intelligent, scheming man, the fact that he had bothered to take you must mean that he had a plan to do some ill towards the castle, and the only way to deflect this would be for Pierre to immediately set out to Henry's court to swear allegiance and tell him the bishop was up to no good. She also reasoned that if the bishop's men had taken you they could also take Pierre, so she immediately sent a letter to Sir Stephan, pointing out that neither he nor Pierre had yet given formal allegiance to Henry and it would be in everyone's interest if they went to Henry's court together to do this. It would demonstrate to Henry the solidarity to his cause of this part of the country. Furthermore, with Pierre and Sir Stephan together with their men, the bishop would not dare attack them. So you see,' she smiled, 'there is no reason to hurry back to warn Pierre, for he already knows.'

'You are right,' said Peter, 'we have underestimated Elaine. But why are you here?'

'We reasoned – and it may have been my idea – that the bishop would not give up easily, so when William, Matthew and Tom had sprung you from the bishop's grasp there was every chance his men would be lying in wait for you to return to the castle. Elaine went further and said that it must be assumed that until Pierre and Sir Stephan had been fully accepted as loyal servants of Henry, the scheming bishop could still find a way to set Henry against you. You therefore had to be warned to stay away. It did not take a military genius to work out that for William, Matthew and Tom to get to the bishop's manor would need continuous fast riding day and night, and the horses would be exhausted by the time they got there, so we had to send out fresh animals for you. Also, it was expected that neither you nor the old man would be armed, so I have brought shields, good swords and daggers for you both. With the possibility of the bishop's men being close, it would have been foolish to deplete the castle's soldiers. So I am here protected by an innocent merchant wagon train. We thought you would be looking for merchants to exchange horses.'

Peter grunted, realising the risk she had taken. Merchants were fairly safe now, but not completely so. Without armed guards there was always the possibility of bandit attack. Simone slipped her arm though Peter's and walked him away from the others.

'I have more to tell,' she said quietly. 'Elaine does not want you back. Henry is still very much an unknown. She believes he will accept Pierre's and Sir Stephan's fealty, but to ensure a more long-lasting safety she has written a personal letter to Henry saying that she freely gives him the estates she inherited by marriage. In doing so she demonstrates her loyalty and expresses her resolve to keep the castle and her men freely at Henry's disposal. She has also written that you five are no longer in her service. Elaine has asked me to tell you that doing this was far from her heart, but she feels your long-term safety demanded this split, at least until Henry accepts that neither she nor you are any danger or challenge to him. She hopes that one day you can come back and live in peace.'

Peter was at first stunned, but slowly he realised the wisdom in Elaine's actions. He and his group were, after all, mere commoners – and nobles knew what moves to make to maintain their position. He returned to the others and gave them the news. Only the old man, who had greater experience than any of them of how the nobility functioned, seemed unconcerned, saying he was surprised Elaine had not dispensed with their services earlier.

In theatrical style, Simone sweetened the bitter pill. 'Here,' she said, pointing to six bundles which had been hidden from view by the covering on the wagon, 'is your money. Pierre refused to take his share, as he felt so badly about your being forced to leave. You can go from here with money enough for your future, wherever that might be.'

'Are you not coming with us?' asked Peter.

'No,' replied Simone in a level voice. 'It grieves me more than it did Elaine, but I have to recognise reality.' She looked at Peter. 'I would be a burden to you. Perhaps not now, but the future holds so much for you and I would not fit in with it. Being Elaine's personal maidservant is more than I could ever have wished a few years ago, and I am more than content.'

Her words stuck Peter a surprisingly harsh blow. His immediate thought was to dissuade her, but a steady look from the old man brought him to his senses. Having no means of obtaining allegiance to Henry and being now an enemy of the bishop, his future was far from certain. Simone was right. With an effort, he turned his cheerless thoughts into a charming smile and said to her, 'Sad though I am, I have to go along with your wishes, but with your help we have been lucky to make a good deal of money, so at least you must take your share.'

'Absolutely not! What would I do with all that money? I would spend my life avoiding avaricious peasants sniffing around. I have made enough for myself, for my needs, and I can make more when necessary. I have no desire for grandeur. I am happy doing what I am doing, and who knows? I might meet a quiet, respectable lad willing to take me on!' She laughed.

There was nothing more which could be said or done, so they finished their meal, chatting quietly. Then Peter and the old man collected the shields and daggers that Simone had brought, exchanging the poor-quality swords they had taken from the bishop's men. Before the five men mounted the fresh horses to leave, Peter took Simone to one side and embraced her gently, whispering words of thanks and encouragement. She hugged him in return but said nothing for words would break her resolve. With grateful farewells they rode off and bade farewell to Simone as the wagon train continued on its way.

'Where to now?' asked Tom.

'I think back to England,' said Peter. 'We can at least use our money to rent some land to work and each of us can build a small manor, or just one manor where we can all live. It will give us a stable base while we see what develops. I realise, old man, that you cannot put down any roots yet, so I hope you will live with me until the troubles with Stephen blow over.'

'I doubt my troubles in England will blow over in the near future,' replied the old man, 'though I am happy to live with you, or all of you – but I must always be ready to take flight.'

'I am not so sure about working the land,' said Tom, scowling. 'The last time I tried that, I got caught up with that shrew of a woman. Indeed, if I am anywhere in her vicinity I have no doubt she will search me out.'

They all laughed. 'I am sure,' responded Peter, 'that if we can repel bandits and a Norman army, we will have no problems protecting you from your woman.'

'Ha. You don't know her. I would face a thousand Norman armies rather than five minutes with that crone!'

They all laughed again and urged their fresh horses towards the Norman coast.

21

In case the bishop's men were following, they spent the night in a small copse away from any road or habitation, but the next evening, spying a large monastery, they decided to have a relatively comfortable night and, hopefully, a reasonably good meal. The old man spoke to the monk who welcomed them, giving him twice the normal sum for board and lodging for the night. The monk, believing they were knights, or at least senior figures in the heraldry, was singularly surprised to receive such a sum, for often knights demanded shelter and food and offered little or nothing in return. They were shown to a spotlessly clean room with well-filled fresh straw mattresses on the floor and told that a bell would indicate the start of the evening meal.

At the sound of the bell they all trooped down to the large dining hall, which was filling up with monks sitting at sparse wooden tables on wooden benches. The monk who had admitted them to the monastery beckoned them to the high table, which was equally sparse, though it had plain chairs round it rather than benches, and where the abbot was sitting alongside an elderly man whose bearing, if not his dress, indicated nobility. As they sat down, Peter could not take his eyes off this man. He was wearing ordinary, unremarkable clothes under his hauberk chain mail, but on top was a long white surcoat of linen with a red cross marked on it, stretching from top to bottom and from side to side. The man returned Peter's gaze without embarrassment or concern.

'May I introduce you to Sir Richard de Menzies,' said the abbot, 'who has graced us with his presence tonight.' He waved his hand in introduction, but did not ask any of them their names, nor did he explain who Sir Richard was.

Before anything more than cursory greetings could be exchanged, with Sir Richard merely nodding in their direction, the first course of soup was served with freshly baked bread. This was followed by a rich meat stew, all accompanied by good-quality wine. Between mouthfuls, the abbot kept up a dialogue about the monastery, its workings and good works, although he invited neither comment nor reply. The five were happy to listen and enjoy the food. When the meal was over, Sir Richard spoke for the first time.

'So we have before us hunted men.'

All five were silent and Peter smiled thinly, putting his head to one side as if to invite an explanation for the comment.

'Do you deny it?'

Taking a deep breath, Peter replied, 'It is true, sir, we seem to have fallen out of favour with the bishop and it may well be that his men are on the lookout for us, but I am not aware of being, as you say, hunted.'

Sir Richard frowned deeply and looked puzzled. 'The bishop?'

'Indeed, yes. As we understand it, Geoffrey's former bishop has been slighted and he believes we may be the cause of his falling out of favour with Henry.'

Sir Richard laughed heartily. 'I can assure you, it was not the bishop to whom I was referring, but Henry himself.'

At this Peter frowned, and he heard an intake of breath from the others. Had Pierre and Sir Stephan failed in their quest, or had something else gone wrong? Quickly calculating, Peter realised there had been insufficient time for Pierre to reach Henry's court and then for Sir Richard to come from the court to the monastery. No, it was something else.

'Forgive me, sir. I know of no slight we could possibly have inflicted on Henry and I can assure you we are not aware of being hunted men. Indeed, if we were, it would have been foolish for us to have sought shelter here – a monastery loyal to and under the protection of Henry.'

Sir Richard continued to smile. 'The word is that the bishop is building forces around him to challenge Henry, or at least to defend himself against Henry, and it is said that two of you were seen, fully armed, in the midst of the bishop's men and three more of you were spied riding furiously towards the bishop's manor, giving every indication you were all joining his army. Is any of that not true?'

It was Peter's turn to smile. 'I can certainly vouch for the large number of well-armed men the bishop had around him.'

'Had?'

Peter's smile deepened and he told his tale of being captured, the reason for that capture, and their escape, concluding with the information that Sir Pierre and Sir Stephan should now be with Henry giving their oath of fealty and an explanation of why the group had left Elaine's employ. 'So you see how we assumed it was the bishop's men who were keen to find us, not Henry.'

Sir Richard looked hard at Peter and surveyed the others. 'I believe you, but as there is only your word for this, you are in grave trouble.'

'Surely the bishop will eventually confirm our story. In his own words, he is trying to get back into favour with Henry, so he would have no reason to support a tale he was building his forces against Henry.'

'That might have been the case, but I can assure you it

is highly unlikely the bishop can confirm anything. Henry is not a man to wait and see. He has already sent a well-armed force against the bishop and if, as you say, the bishop's men are depleted by half a dozen or so, then Henry's success is assured. Unless he flees, it might be that the bishop will be captured and taken back to Henry, but I strongly suspect he will fall in battle. So, as I say, you are in grave trouble.'

Silence fell as the group contemplated their almost impossible position. To have the hand of the bishop closing on them was one thing. To try to outmanoeuvre the long arm of Henry was something else. Nowhere in Normandy was safe. All Channel ports would be watched and it would take many days of very uncertain travel for them to cross the border out of Normandy and get far enough away not to run into a knight or baron sympathising with Henry's cause.

'I understand Henry is an honourable and reasonable man. I am sure, if we were to give ourselves up to him and explain precisely what happened, he would understand,' said Peter rather wistfully.

'I think you know you are deceiving yourself,' responded Sir Richard. 'Henry believes the bishop was plotting against him and so is having him eliminated. The last thing Henry wants to know is that the bishop's intentions were to regain good grace, not to offer aggression, for that would show a lack of judgement by Henry.'

Sir Richard let the silence deepen. Even the garrulous abbot was still.

'There may be a way out.'

Sir Richard's words hung in the air. He took a sip from his wine cup and settled himself back in his chair.

'Following the disastrous Second Crusade against the Infidel,' he began, 'King Louis VII felt humiliated and while still full of religious fervour, he has been unable to shake off the belief that it was his personal failure to acknowledge the absolute supremacy of God which prevented success.

The pope is keen to mount a Third Crusade, but has been hampered by Louis' belief. We, the Templars, know the reason for our failure was that we relied too much on the hysterical and persuasive preaching of the fanatical Abbot of Clairvaux, Bernard, whose very mantra was that doing the will of God was enough to guarantee success, rather than realising discipline, leadership and battle order were the only way to defeat the Infidel.

'The pope has tasked me with the duty of going to the various rulers of the Christian world to convince them to learn from the failure and to persuade them that a well-ordered, properly disciplined army is necessary if we are to succeed. I have spent many weeks with Louis and on my way back to England called in on Henry to encourage his support for the pope's wishes. Henry was sympathetic, but non-committal in his charming way. While I was in Henry's court, I learned that he had banished the bishop, the bishop held much ill will, and that Henry was determined to put down any possible resistance, actual or perceived. Henry also alluded to a band of men under the protection of Elaine de Roche, about whom he was less than comfortable. As I was leaving, I heard the tale of five men joining the bishop, giving Henry the excuse to denounce those men as well. By now he will know that these five men were not actually with the bishop, but he will have no reason to change his mind.'

Sir Richard stopped and surveyed the group. Peter was thinking furiously. He knew of the Templars as servants of the pope and assumed that the white surcoat with the red cross had been recently adopted to mark them out as such.

'Informative,' said Peter, 'but it does not identify a way out of our predicament. If anything, it demonstrates a lack of any hope.'

'I have been travelling for many months now with just a small escort of two men, and I have not been molested, nor has any man sought to challenge me because I am a Templar on the pope's business and I have the pope's complete protection. Anyone who touches me touches the pope. If you were to become Templars, you would be immune from Henry.'

'But we are not knights,' said Peter. 'I believe only knights can become Templars. Anyone less than a knight would merely be in the service of the Templars and not immune.'

'Partly true. One of you is a knight.' Sir Richard looked keenly at the old man, who returned his gaze unwaveringly. 'If that one was to become a Templar, then I would give my protection to you all and write a personal letter to Henry explaining exactly what happened to you. He would accept my word and would not need to tell anyone else, but could simply withdraw his interest in hunting you down. You would all be safe.'

There was another long silence. None of the group wished to say anything to the old man, far less encourage him to do something he would not want. The silence was eventually broken by Sir Richard, who addressed the old man directly.

'I know well of your past deeds and accomplishments, for when we first met I was impressed with your demeanour and soft words. I perceive you hold no great loathing for the Infidel as we Christians are supposed to have. You are perhaps too well read, too well educated. I suspect you are able to read, if not speak and write, the Infidel tongue and have gained much knowledge of their ways, perhaps even some sympathy for them.'

Again there was a silence. 'Some,' replied the old man at last. 'I do not see them as enemies. Their beliefs are not so different from ours. I can understand the reason for us to protect the Holy Land and be able to worship at the font of our religion, but I do have difficulty believing this can be achieved by force of arms rather than through discussion and accommodation with those you call the Infidel.'

'Your thoughts are not alien to many in the Templar

movement, but are somewhat in a minority with the rest of the Christian world. I urge you to join us, not for your fighting prowess, which is well known, but for your knowledge of letters and accounts. We are in sore need of someone who can properly oversee the organisation of our manuscripts and accounts. I cannot guarantee that you will not be called upon to fight. Indeed, I can say in honesty it is a possibility you will be so called, but it may not be for years.'

The old man said nothing, but looked at his comrades in turn as if weighing up the problem facing them all. Peter knew the old man's thoughts were rapid and wondered why he did not reply instantly. He had no need to put on a show of composing himself.

'Why don't you think it over during the night and give me an answer some time tomorrow?' Sir Richard said after a while. 'I can promise you, if you all wish to leave here this evening, no one will stop you. Your horses are in the stable ready for you. The abbot will be duty bound to tell Henry you were here, but I think he will probably send an old monk on foot with the news.'

The abbot smiled thinly and nodded. With nothing more to be said, the five left the table and went to their allotted room, where in silence they prepared for bed, each occupied with his own thoughts.

Eventually the old man spoke. 'It seems to me we do not have any choice but to accept Sir Richard's offer. We cannot remain here in Normandy and as we have incurred Henry's wrath I would not put it past him to tell Stephen that all of you have been associated with me, which means we will not be safe in England. Unless we can make it to another country far way from the influence of those two, none of us has much of a future.'

'But Henry does not know who you really are,' said William. 'Indeed, none of us does.'

The old man gave a rueful smile, which took on an

expression of hopelessness in the flickering light of the oil lamps. 'Do not underestimate Henry. He will have made enquiries and the mere fact that I "have no name" would alert him. Sir Richard knew me straight away and I only met him once. Indeed, Sir Richard's paramount mission is to get as many nobles as possible to accept the pope's demand for another crusade, and as the Templars are servants of the pope I expect he would believe it his duty to tell Henry who I am, for that would mean Henry owes Sir Richard a favour. So, we cannot depend on ill news not reaching Stephen.'

Peter broke the silence which followed. 'You have already given us so much. Surely you cannot sacrifice the rest of your life doing something you do not want to do without us putting up a fight! If we were to leave here at first light, we could keep away from any habitation and make our way to Italy, perhaps, where, I believe, the weather is balmy and the people friendly. If you were to tell Sir Richard that we wish to have the chance to escape, but if we fail, then you will take up his offer, this might be a fall-back position – for you at least.'

All four slowly nodded agreement, with Matthew emphasising the point. 'We have all acted as one and each must support the other. I cannot agree to you joining a band of men, of whom we know very little, simply to save us. I am willing to take my chance.' There was a deep grunt of approval from Tom and William.

'No, no,' replied the old man. 'It is not like that at all. I know much about the Templars, and while I might not agree wholeheartedly with their goals, they are a well-disciplined and respected body and I would have no difficulty fitting in with them, particularly if, as Sir Richard suggested, my main task is to look after the manuscripts and accounts. I am still not old enough to sit around all day and do nothing and I have neither the knowledge nor any real desire to be a landowner farmer, so perhaps Sir Richard's offer is a blessing. You must not feel I am sacrificing myself. Rather, it is a new venture for me, leaving you four to go back to England and do what you will there.'

'But Sir Richard said you sympathised with the Infidel,' said Peter. 'What would your position be if that came to the notice of the pope, or you were asked to take up arms against the Infidel?'

'If I am asked to fight, I will fight with all my skills and endeavour,' replied the old man, smiling. 'While I think that Infidel beliefs are not really too far from Christian beliefs – save in one respect which I would have difficulty accepting – this does not mean I will waver in overthrowing them if that is what the pope wants. Christian fights Christian, so what is the difference?'

'May I ask, what is the one respect you would have difficulty accepting?' Peter wanted to know.

The old man laughed. 'It is simple. The Infidel does not believe in drinking wine, or indeed any form of alcohol, and as you know, I rather enjoy a cup or two of wine.'

At this they all laughed and the mood lightened.

'Tomorrow morning I will see Sir Richard and tell him of my decision and make sure he writes a suitable letter to Henry. Indeed, I will suggest that my first task as a budding Templar should be to draft the letter for him. I am sure he will agree. This means we can all go back to England and when we get there you can go your separate ways safe in the knowledge you will not be hunted.'

They all nodded slowly, in one way depressed their group would be broken, but at the same time feeling a weight being lifted from them.

'There is one final thing,' said the old man. 'To become a Templar, a knight is obliged to give to the Templars all his worldly goods and thereafter to hold no possessions other than those given to him by the Templars. I would hate to

291

think that the gold, silver and marks I have which came from all our efforts should go to the Templars, who are rich enough anyway. So at this moment, I donate to all of you in equal shares my portion of our funds – with one proviso. When I leave the Templars as a really old man and I call on you, you will let me stay for a while and partake of a little of your good wine.'

There was much cross talking about how stupid the old man was to even think any one of them would not give him shelter and the very best of wine, irrespective of the money he was going to give them, which they didn't want anyway, as it was his. The old man then pulled his hoard from his saddlebag and, despite their protests, divided it equally among them.

The following morning, the old man and Sir Richard had a long discussion. The old man agreed to become a Templar on the strict and absolute understanding that the Templars would protect the other four until the old man was fully initiated into the movement. Sir Richard said the old man could draft an appropriate letter to Henry explaining the truth of what had happened, and while he was doing this, Sir Richard wrote his own letter, to be given to Peter, granting to the group the Templars' protection. When everything was finished, Sir Richard, his two original companions and the group of five set out towards the coast, leaving the abbot to get the all-important letter to Henry by the swiftest means.

It took a month of gentle riding before they arrived in Calais late in the afternoon. After taking their horses to the stable, they walked slowly back towards the entrance of their chosen inn.

'And so we meet again!' A voice boomed out behind them. Turning, Peter saw the bishop in full fighting attire with a cruel leer on his face and sword drawn. 'God has indeed answered my prayers and you will not get away this time,' continued the bishop, his face screwed up into a malevolent scowl.

Peter was conscious of movement around him and, looking about, he saw a dozen of the bishop's men surrounding them, all with drawn swords ready for the fight to come.

'Templar, move away with your men!' the bishop snarled. 'I have no quarrel with you.'

Sir Richard gave the bishop a steely glare. 'These men are under my protection, which means the protection of the pope. I suggest you move away and leave us alone.'

'Never! I have suffered too much because of these scoundrels and they are going to pay. Because of them I was forced to leave my manor and flee from Henry's wrath.'

With that, the bishop and his men moved forward. Peter's group drew their shields firmly onto their arms and unsheathed their swords, moving into a tight circle, back to back and shoulder to shoulder, ready for the attack.

What the bishop lacked in skill he more than made up for in determined frenzy, attacking Peter with a whirlwind of blows which took all Peter's strength and speed to ward off. The group were initially hampered by the fact that they were in a tight circle, preventing the footwork to aid their fighting, so they merely defended the blows which rained upon them until their attackers began to tire and let their guard slip a little. Slowly, the steady, disciplined skills of the group created openings for well-directed thrusts or cuts and the bishop's men started to fall, dead or incapacitated.

The bishop, though, driven by a fanatical hatred, did not tire. While Peter could block the flashing blade, he was unable to mount an attack of his own until the falling of the bishop's men gave the group room to move out of the tight circle and engage with some space between them. Now able to manoeuvre, Peter's light, quick footwork allowed him to dodge some of the bishop's blows and get into a rhythm of his own, but the sheer energy of the bishop gave him first blood as his sword, glancing off Peter's shield, struck Peter in the left shoulder, causing the involuntary movement of his shield arm away from his body. Seeing the opening and foaming at the mouth, with a scream of victory the bishop hurled himself at Peter with such force that, had they collided, Peter would have been knocked to the ground. However, a lightning-quick step to his right at the last moment was too fast for the bishop to counter, giving Peter the opportunity to plunge his sword into the bishop's side, cutting deep and fatally. The bishop continued to scream until he hit the ground in a twitching heap.

Peter spun round, ready to help his comrades with the remaining bishop's men, but those still on their feet lost heart once the bishop fell, and surrendered. Out of the dozen, six were left standing and each had a wound of some sort.

'You seem to attract trouble!' said Sir Richard, catching his breath. 'Will we have to fight our way across England?'

'I hope not,' replied Peter. 'Look on the bright side. We have dispensed with the bishop and so Henry will be very grateful to you, and that will aid your mission to recruit him for the next crusade.'

Sir Richard grunted. 'I fear Tom has suffered a severe blow.'

Peter had not noticed that Tom was down and immediately rushed to his side to join William, who was already kneeling there. Tom had indeed taken a serious thrust which had penetrated his hauberk, deep into his side, and a small trickle of blood was escaping from lips compressed with pain. William exchanged a glance with Peter, indicating that there was nothing anyone could do. This did not stop Peter giving words of comfort and encouragement to Tom, who smiled grateful thanks, gasping slowly, 'At least I will not have to avoid that shrew of a woman. I do not think I could settle to quieter ways.' His breathing became more laboured and he closed his eyes, gathering strength for his last words. 'My money. Divide it between you and have a few cups with it for me.'

Peter felt the deepest sadness. They had all come through so much together and it had never crossed his mind that they would not all return safely to England. Now there were just four of them and soon, with the old man joining the Templars, there would be three – the soldiers of Baron de Cours. Sir Richard went to the inn to ensure that they had places there for the night, while William and Peter made arrangements for a simple funeral the following day. Then they tended each other's wounds, none of which were serious. Despite their victory over superior numbers, they did not feel jolly that night. Sir Richard and his men understood the loss of a close comrade, so the meal was eaten in virtual silence and they retired to bed early.

The following morning Sir Richard wrote a letter to Henry informing him of the bishop's demise and engaged a reliable courier to get the letter safely to its destination. The old man sought out a boat for the Channel crossing, learning that the bishop had already engaged two boats for himself and his men to go to England – where, the old man suspected, the bishop thought he would be free from Henry's wrath. The bishop had already paid a deposit for the boats, so the old man was able to negotiate a keen deal for them to cross the Channel when the winter seas allowed. After this was done they all went to the local church where a short prayer, led by a priest, was said over Tom's coffin and he was buried in the churchyard.

22

Two weeks after their arrival in England following an uneventful crossing that had been delayed until January by the dreadful weather, Peter, William and Matthew bade a final farewell to the old man, who struck off towards London with Sir Richard and his two companions to prepare to become a Templar. Depleted in number and also in conviviality, the three made their way slowly back to Devonshire, stopping each evening at an inn or staying in the open as the mood took them and the winter weather permitted. Peter intended to visit Baron de Cours before going to his village to see his parents. There were no particular plans for what they might do after that. The other two were simply content to follow Peter's wishes.

Halfway through a mild February, riding through the area of Devonshire protected by Baron de Cours, the horses suddenly became skittish.

'What is wrong with them?' grumbled Matthew.

'I think they can smell something in the air which is upsetting them,' replied Peter. 'I do not know why, but I feel we should proceed cautiously. Animals do seem to have a sense which we do not.'

William nodded and they all dropped their pace, spreading out and looking carefully around.

Spying a large wood on a hill at the edge of the baron's

personal estate, Peter directed them to enter it. Dismounting, they tethered their horses and walked slowly through the wood towards the other side. Before they reached the edge of the wood they noticed a large number of trees had recently been felled and then heard the not-unfamiliar sound of a large band of men.

'Spread out wide and keep crouched so as not to attract attention,' muttered Peter as he carefully picked his way forward, making as little noise as possible.

When they reached the edge of the wood, they saw spread below them an army of something approaching a hundred men surrounding the castle of Baron de Cours. The castle was clearly under siege.

Peter beckoned to the others. 'What in the world is happening here? De Cours is not a man to make enemies willingly and I cannot believe he has upset Stephen. William, over there is a big tent with a standard flying from it. Whose standard is that?'

William screwed up his eyes to stare at the standard fluttering in the gentle breeze. 'I have no idea. I have never seen it before. What I can say is that it is not Stephen, or indeed anyone acting on behalf of Stephen, for they would have the royal standard flying as well.' He looked again and shook his head. 'No, it is a mystery to me. If the old man was here, I am sure he could tell us.'

Peter surveyed the area and gathered from the way the tents, cooking fires and men were situated that this army had been there for some weeks and seemed content to remain. There was evidence of minor damage to the castle wall, caused, no doubt, by a recently constructed trebuchet, whose arm was being winched down ready to accept a large rock to be propelled against the castle wall.

William snorted. 'It will take years for that little thing to make any appreciable breach in the walls of a de Cours building. They will have no fear of that inside the castle.'

He looked around again. 'What is of more concern is over there.' He pointed towards a very large siege tower still being built. 'If they complete that and can wheel it close enough to the walls, it is large enough to hold twenty or thirty bowmen who can quite easily cut down the de Cours men on the top of the wall and allow the remainder of this attacking army to scale the walls with the ladders they are also making. I've never seen such a large siege tower. Whoever is in charge has planned well.'

'How many and in what state do you think the de Cours men are?' asked Peter.

'Knowing the baron, I cannot believe he let his army dwindle too much in numbers since we left, so I would guess there are at least twenty well-armed and disciplined men, with perhaps another ten or so loyal peasants he has managed to take in. An army the size of the one mounting the siege could not have sneaked up, so de Cours must have had some early warning of its approach.' William pondered for a moment. 'As you know, there is a good fresh-water well in the castle, always enough food to last for at least six months, and unless things have really changed, the morale of the soldiers will be high. They can last out well into next winter and I cannot see the besieging army staying around that long.'

'In other words,' said Peter, 'the key is the siege tower. When that is completed, there is a good chance the castle can be stormed.'

'Right. I am certain the baron has seen the construction of the siege tower. It is within sight of the castle. So I would expect him to make shelters on top of the walls for his men to hide behind when the barrage of arrows comes from the tower. But – and it is a very big but – if his men are sheltering, they will not be returning arrows and the moment they expose themselves to repel those climbing up ladders, they will be sitting targets.'

'Yes,' said Matthew slowly. 'And I do not suppose the commander of this army will be too bothered about a few of his own men scaling the wall being hit by his archers' arrows. He is obviously determined, mounting a siege so early in the year when winter has yet to depart. I'm afraid it looks bleak.'

Peter beckoned them away and they walked back to their horses, making sure they were at the furthest point away from the siege army as possible.

'Facts,' said Peter when they were settled. 'Three of us fighting cannot make any difference here, even if we could get into the castle. The castle can hold out for a long time, but when the siege tower is constructed it is unlikely that de Cours will be able to hold off troops scaling up ladders against the wall. I would guess it will take a week before the siege tower is ready.'

The other two nodded in agreement.

'So, any ideas?'

'The siege tower is the key,' replied Matthew. 'No siege tower, no successful assault. We have to destroy it, though they may well build another one in time.'

'Agreed,' replied Peter. 'If we are successful in destroying this siege tower, we can be assured they will guard the building of another one to prevent us repeating the exercise. However, destroying the siege tower will gain time, I reckon about a month. This will give us the opportunity of, perhaps, getting reinforcements from sympathetic nearby barons. Are we willing to give it a go?'

'Of course!' retorted William. 'Whatever de Cours might have done since we left, we cannot stand by and watch him destroyed. We, indeed the local peasants, all owe him too much. How do you think we can destroy the tower?'

'Fire,' replied Peter. 'That is the only way and it is not going to be easy. The tower is built of new wet wood, made wetter by the winter rains, and so it will not burn easily, but once we get it going it will be difficult to put out because the sap from the newly felled trees will feed the fire. We need oil, tallow and straw. There is a monastery close by and I was friendly with one of the monks there. Unless de Cours has upset them, I think I can get tallow from the monks, perhaps some oil. At first light tomorrow I will go off to the monastery, whilst you two go to any nearby farms which have not been razed to the ground by the siege army and gather as much dry hay and straw as possible. Obviously, if you find tallow or oil, bring that as well. Money no object.'

The following morning they set about their allotted tasks. Peter had no difficulty gaining entry into the monastery and was pleased his old friend, who was equally delighted to see him, was still there. Peter, with his saddlebag of money hoisted over his shoulder, briefly explained the problem and what he was after.

'I would really like to spend time with you hearing about your adventures, but I can understand the urgency of your mission, so my curiosity will have to wait for another day,' said the old monk, smiling. 'I am afraid I cannot authorise letting you have either oil, which is in precious supply, or tallow. Only the abbot can do this, and I will immediately go and ask him.'

It seemed an age before the monk returned. 'The abbot is very reluctant to become involved in secular problems,' he said. 'Particularly this one, for I'm afraid Baron de Cours has given grave insult and Baron Walter Fitz Nichols is within his rights to demand deliverance on the bargain he has made. The abbot does not want to be seen as interfering with the honour of the nobility, but he is not without sympathy and commands me to bring you to him. I'm afraid it is completely up to you to persuade the abbot. It is out of my hands.'

The monk took Peter to the abbot's chamber, a sparse

cell adorned only by a narrow bed, a table and two stools. The abbot was sitting at the table writing laboriously on a crumpled piece of parchment. Peter stood at the door waiting to be invited in. The abbot looked up and motioned Peter to the other stool, where he sat in silence. At last the abbot looked deeply into Peter's eyes and said, 'You have a strange request, young man. As I am sure you have been told, it is not the place of a monastery to take sides in local differences and I have great reluctance to listen to your wishes, but I have been persuaded to hear what you have to say.'

Peter nodded gravely in acknowledgement of what the abbot had said. 'My lord abbot,' he said in Latin, 'I come here in all humility to crave your assistance to save life, and indeed to protect a great benefactor of this monastery and all the peoples around.'

The abbot could not keep the surprise from his face. Not only had this young man had the courtesy to wait outside his cell before being bidden to enter, but he had also addressed him in Latin, apparently having as good a grip on that dead language as the abbot himself.

Peter went on. 'I do not know what insult has been perceived by Baron Walter Fitz Nichols, but I do know Baron Robert de Cours, who is a kind and gentle man ruling his lands with compassion and generosity. Indeed, he has shown such consideration to me, I am bound to do my utmost to prevent what surely will be his slaying. I therefore come to you with a fervent plea that you will in some small measure help me in what I need.'

Peter slowly produced his most charming smile. The abbot continued to look at him with some sympathy in his eyes, but no sign of agreement in his face.

'I am told you are the shepherd boy who joined the baron's army to save your father from conscription. Is that right?' Peter nodded. 'Then it is best that you do not know what insult has been perpetrated on Baron Walter Fitz Nichols.

What you must know and understand is that I cannot take sides in this. My only master is God and this monastery has not been the subject of patronage from any single noble. It is true,' he smiled wanly, 'Baron de Cours has been very generous towards, us but that generosity does not buy fealty, merely acknowledgement of our service to God and the people.'

Peter felt things were slipping away from him. He nodded again. 'I fully understand that, and I would not dream of compromising this monastery in any way. The service of God is paramount, even though this might mean putting service to the people second. I am simply here to purchase from you as much oil and tallow as you can spare. You do not know why I want these things and I will not tell you – other than to say that I bear no malice or ill will towards your flock. I have here all my worldly wealth, which I will willingly donate to this monastery if you could see fit to accommodate my modest requirements.' Peter unslung the saddlebag from his shoulder and opened it up for the abbot to see.

The abbot looked long and hard at the contents, realising that a great sum was being offered. Taking a deep breath, he spoke at last. 'Young man, I am tempted by your generosity, but luckily God has given me the power to resist temptation.' He smiled. 'God has also been benevolent enough to give me the ability to see honesty and true endeavour, and I believe you have both. I am torn and I have found in such circumstances prayer is a great guide, but I suspect there is little time for prayer.' He paused, looking down at the manuscript he had been annotating when Peter had come into the room. 'I suppose it is not completely impossible that you might want large quantities of oil and tallow to use for peaceful means, trade perhaps. At this moment I do not know with any certainty, so what I suggest is that you leave me to pray for guidance while you seek out

Brother Benedict and buy from him, at a fair price, as much oil and tallow as he will let you have. Do not urge him to give you more than he offers.'

'Thank you, my lord abbot. I am truly grateful.'

'There is nothing to be grateful for. I am merely allowing a little money to be made by selling oil and tallow. Go.'

With that the abbot bowed his head as if in prayer, so Peter got up from the stool and left quietly.

He had no trouble finding Brother Benedict, who was short, dumpy and full of bounce. Peter wondered how such a man could adapt himself to monastery life, but had little time to ponder as Brother Benedict opened his store.

'Take what you want before the abbot finishes his commune with God,' he said. 'I will charge you the market price.'

'But I cannot take all your oil and tallow!' responded Peter. 'You must have enough for your own needs.'

'Leave us something then. We can get by. After all, being the servants of God we must suffer deprivations gladly.' He laughed and bounded towards two large jugs of oil and heaved them out, along with a box brimming with tallow. 'This should be enough for what you want – that is, if I knew what you wanted it for . . .' He gave a broad wink and helped Peter take the precious oil and tallow to his horse, both of them having difficulty securing such a load safely on the animal. Peter paid the price Benedict asked and when he tried to add a few more coins, the monk waved them away. 'A fair price is a fair price,' he said, bouncing back into the monastery.

It was well after nightfall before Peter and his burdened horse rejoined his companions in the wood.

'I though you had got into some trouble,' said Matthew.

'Not at all. I have so much oil and tallow I had to ride especially carefully so as not to break the jars or indeed rub the flanks of my horse raw! I think we should sleep now and prepare ourselves at first light tomorrow for the attack on the siege tower. We'll do it tomorrow night.'

After a good night's sleep, the three spread the straw and hay on the ground, rubbed tallow over it and then made up tight bundles which they could easily carry. Come the clear and almost moonless nightfall, full of February chill, they crept to the edge of the wood and watched the besieging camp until it had settled down for the night, leaving a few guards or sentries watching the castle. None were placed at the rear of the army, for they did not expect approach from that direction.

Having given time for everyone to go to sleep, the three men, carefully carrying the bundles of tallow-soaked straw and hay with the two jars of oil, slowly crept into the camp towards the near-complete siege tower. They arrived there without challenge or disturbance. Pausing at the bottom of the tower long enough to ensure they were undetected, Peter climbed thirty feet up a ladder to the top platform with two bundles of straw and a jar of oil, while the other two made it to the lower platform, about fifteen feet from the ground. William and Matthew stayed to one side of the lower platform, allowing Peter to pour his jar of oil over the wooden planks and down the inside of each upright post. The oil seeped into the wood and through the gaps to drip down onto the lower platform. When Peter signalled he had finished, he started to spread the tallow-soaked straw on the floor as the other two repeated the same oil-pouring and straw-spreading routine on the lower platform. It took little time and when all was finished, Peter clambered halfway down from the top platform to give his empty oil jar to Matthew. Armed with both empty jars, Matthew went back to the bottom of the tower and then very quietly made his way towards the two sentries overlooking the castle gate, carefully placing each oil jar on the ground without a sound.

With a hand clamped over their mouth and throat expertly slit, each guard slipped silently to the ground and into the afterlife.

Matthew made his way back to the tower and signalled to the other two that his task had been completed. Peter and William struck flints, coaxing dry straw into embers then smouldering fire as the tallow burned. Climbing quickly down, they made their way out of the camp and stopped to watch the results of their handiwork.

The top platform was too high for them to see anything, though there was a faint steady glow from the bottom platform. It seemed that an age passed with no appreciable change, the light coming from the lower platform appearing no brighter than a good oil lamp. Peter was just beginning to doubt success when the glow was obliterated by wisps of smoke, just discernible in the night-time dimness. Then the fire erupted. Flames shot upwards from the lower platform, which seemed to encourage the burning on the upper platform, for immediately it responded with red-hot sparks flying into the air.

'Sparks mean the timber's burning,' said Peter. 'It is time to get back into the wood and well out of sight.'

They made their way cautiously back to the cover of the trees. From there they could see that the siege tower was engulfed in flames and in the light thrown by the huge fire they saw figures dashing around looking for a means to douse the conflagration. It was too great a task, however, for even if large quantities of water had been to hand, the fire had taken too much of a hold and there was no means of getting even to the lower platform without being burned alive.

'Very satisfactory,' chuckled William.

They stayed at the edge of the wood watching as the tower burned to the ground. From the movement of various troops around the stricken guards and the general shaking of fists towards the castle, it appeared that the ruse to make the besieging army believe the attack came from the castle had worked.

Before first light and after tidying up the area where they had been, the three left the wood on horseback to put a few miles between them and the attacking army, just in case the commander was suspicious and ordered a search.

Allowing two days to pass, Peter, William and Matthew then carefully made their way back to the wood and to their camp observation point. New timber had been cut from the wood and preparations were being made to build another siege tower. The old one was a blackened mess, hardly even a skeleton, giving silent tribute to their earlier night's work. They lay there for some hours, watching and gaining quiet satisfaction.

'We have a month before the new one will be ready,' Matthew eventually said. 'So what is next?'

For a while, Peter said nothing. He seemed more focused on the large tent of Baron Walter Fitz Nichols than on the work being done on the timbers for the new tower.

'Now that is strange.' Peter seemed almost to be talking to himself. 'Over the last hour or so two messengers have arrived, one at a mighty gallop, and one has left. Is it possible Fitz Nichols is getting reinforcements?'

'For what purpose?' replied William. 'An army twice the size would gain them nothing until they have a siege tower built. If Baron de Cours is not frightened by one hundred men camping outside his castle, then I cannot see that having another fifty, or even another hundred there will make him quake.'

'Agreed,' responded Peter, 'but something is going on. I suggest one of us stays here overnight to watch what is developing. If all else fails, we can waylay one of the messengers and see what missive he is carrying.'

*　　*　　*

The following morning brought more mystery: two messengers at first light and the construction of the siege tower halted. It seemed as though the men were collecting things together. By midday it was clear that whatever the intention of the army below them, it was not to mount an attack, or even to prepare for battle ahead. The afternoon heralded the arrival of oxen and wagons from the very edge of the camp into its centre and the soldiers began packing the wagons with possessions. The last to be packed was Fitz Nichols' tent, and when that was secured in the wagon, Fitz Nichols himself mounted his horse and called his men around him as they made their way away from the castle, eastwards, with the servants and foot soldiers strung out behind.

'What could possibly have made them leave?' asked Matthew. 'Surely the loss of the tower was not enough to call off the siege.'

'No idea,' responded Peter. 'It must be very important for them to start out at this time of day rather than waiting for first light tomorrow. I suggest we follow them at a safe distance to see if they are truly leaving the area, or if they are developing a cunning ruse.'

For a week the three trailed the retreating army which was making great haste away, stopping at night only for the briefest of spells. The sergeants were constantly harrying the foot soldiers and servants to keep up, and whatever their destination, Fitz Nichols was in a hurry to get there.

Satisfied that the besieging army had abandoned its earlier quest, Peter turned William and Matthew around and they rode steadily back towards the castle. When they eventually arrived there, the gate was still closed and the guards remained on high alert.

'Who are you and what do you want?' shouted a voice from the battlements.

'Guthrie?' William shouted back, recognising the voice of

the challenger. 'Open this damned gate and be quick about it!'

A head appeared over the battlements. 'My God, it is William! Open the gate!'

There was much scrabbling behind the gate before it slowly opened to allow the three to enter. As soon as they were through, it was shut and barred once more. They rode up to the entrance of the great hall and grooms came forward to take their horses while one of the familiar elderly servants appeared in the doorway.

'Please tell the baron that William Decar is here and would crave a little of the baron's time.'

Without a word the servant scuttled off, returning almost before the three had dismounted, beckoning them in. The baron and baroness were sitting in their usual chairs before a blazing hearth, but Peter was aghast at the change in the baron. He looked old and frail, a shadow of the man Peter had known.

'My lord, we are able to tell you that there is every sign Fitz Nichols is leaving the area, travelling east with his whole army,' said William, bowing slightly.

'And how do you know this?' replied de Cours.

'We have been watching and saw them packing up, then we followed them for a week. They are making great haste somewhere,' William responded.

Peter was inwardly amused that back in the de Cours castle, William automatically took the lead and the baron equally easily expected him to do so.

De Cours thought for a moment. 'The fire. Did you have anything to do with that?'

William smiled. 'We saw an opportunity and took it.'

For the first time the baron looked at Peter and Matthew, clearly recognising them both.

'Well then, I owe you a debt of gratitude. Whether the destruction of the siege tower was the reason Fitz Nichols left or not, that tower was a worry to us. You must all spend your time here as my guests. I will have rooms prepared.'

'No – please, my lord, we are all quite happy to stay with the troops in their accommodation,' replied William, almost in horror that he would have to live in the castle.

'We will not hear of it,' the baroness replied quietly with a soft, engaging smile. 'You are not employees here, but guests, so must be treated as such. If it became known we were lacking in hospitality, we could not live it down! Rooms will be prepared and fresh clothes brought to you with hot water.' Her smile widened. 'You all look as though you have been sleeping under bushes for months and we cannot have that. Go and refresh yourselves before the evening meal is served. I expect you down here on time, clean, shaved and in good spirits, for we want to hear all your news and adventures.'

At a loss for words, William was led away by a servant, followed by Matthew and Peter, and they were each given a spacious, clean room with a fresh-looking bed.

Peter was particularly glad of the opportunity to bathe and change into clean clothes. He felt like a different person and when they assembled in the hall for the evening meal he was amused to see how William's bearing had changed. Having acted like a humble servant when he first arrived in the hall, he was now displaying the relaxed manner usual to him when amongst his own. Matthew was somewhat more reserved, but took strength in the presence of his two companions.

Except for the baroness, who was already seated at the table, the great hall was empty. Realising the siege was over, Sir John and the other knights had left the castle to return to their own loved ones. The baroness beckoned them to sit. A cup of wine was served as the baron entered. Peter tried not to look at him too closely, though he was unable to miss the absence of the firm stride and noble bearing.

The baroness saw Peter's expression. 'My husband has not been well,' she said, 'but he is gaining strength daily and will soon be back to his old self.'

The baron grunted and waved his hand dismissively, as if to indicate any minor ailment he might have had was but a trifle and he was as fit as ever. All three, however, realised that if the baron was gaining strength daily now, he must have been all but dead a week ago.

The meal passed well, with very good food and wine. Encouraged by de Cours and his wife, they gave a potted version of their adventures since leaving the castle. At first William took up the tale, but very shortly he looked towards Peter to continue. Peter chose his words carefully, trying to convey the spirit of their travels but not give too much detail, for he did not know what the future might bring and the less people knew about what they had actually done, the better.

'So our little shepherd speaks French, I see,' said the baroness at the end of the meal. Peter had not consciously realised that from the moment they had first arrived William had addressed the baron in French, and so it was only natural that they had all continued speaking in that language.

He smiled. 'A while in Normandy requires a certain understanding of the language, my lady, if one is to achieve anything.'

'Unless my ears have developed an ailment of which I have not been aware until now, I would say "a certain understanding" is an understatement! Your fluency is remarkable and if I did not know to the contrary, I would have said you were brought up in the language.' She gave Peter a deep, quizzical look and while the baron noticed nothing, it was clear that the baroness had confirmed to herself something she had suspected for a long time. 'And might it just be that of the group of six who appear to have done quite well for yourselves, it was the little shepherd boy who was the leader?'

The look on William's and Matthew's faces confirmed this, even though Peter brushed it aside with his charming smile. 'My lady, we were a close group, each with our own talents, and so there was equal contribution rather than a single leader.'

She returned his smile. 'I am sure. Now, although the baron is healing well, we cannot keep him up too late, so I will take him to our bedchamber. Please continue here as long as you wish. There is plenty of wine and more cheese if you want.'

With that she gracefully rose from the table and helped the baron out of the hall. In silence they watched them leave, exchanging glances of sadness and apprehension at the baron's condition. This, though, was not the place to talk about it, so they kept their own counsel, finishing the wine and then going to bed.

Unusually, the sun was well up behind a cloud-filled sky before Peter rose from the comfortable bed. He washed and donned his clean clothes, noting his dirty garments had been taken from the room, and went down to the hall where the baroness was sitting at the table finishing her morning meal.

'Your comrades are already up and about, no doubt talking to our soldiers to get the up-to-date gossip,' said the baroness. 'That is good, because I wanted to have a quiet word with you alone. Have something to eat first and I will come back and join you in a few minutes.'

She rose, leaving the hall as Peter started to eat. As he was finishing, she returned. 'Come,' she said, 'let us go for a walk outside. It is not raining, so it is a beautiful day.'

Peter thought the reason for the walk was not to admire the day, but more to ensure what she was going to say to him was not overheard by others. Sure enough, with cloaks wrapped around them, they walked slowly through the castle courtyard, out of the now-open gate and well away from anyone who might overhear. The baroness slipped her arm though Peter's and started to speak.

'Your friends will soon find out what I am about to tell you, but I would like you to hear it all from me first so there is no misunderstanding.' She paused as if marshalling her thoughts. 'First, Robert. Some months ago he was taken gravely ill. No one knew what had befallen him and he lay for days unconscious and barely breathing. I really thought he was going to die and in desperation I allowed a village woman to tend him, for she said she had been given the power and knowledge to cure many ailments. I understand this woman is known to the peasants.' Peter nodded, knowing the woman in question, who seemed to have the most detailed knowledge of all the herbs and plants growing in the area and often produced a potion which cured, or at least aided a cure. 'This woman tended Robert for weeks, never leaving his side, and slowly he recovered. She is still in the castle making Robert's food and he is gaining strength quite remarkably. Oh, I know you think he looks like a finished old man, but he is not. If you had seen him but a few weeks ago, you would believe it a miracle.'

They continued walking in silence. There was nothing Peter could say, although he could not believe the baron would recover to become again the man he was when Peter had left the castle years earlier.

'So,' continued the baroness at last, 'that is one of our problems which is being solved, but not, alas, our main trouble.' She paused again to steel herself before saying more. Peter could feel the tension in her body as she tightened her grip on his arm.

'You will remember our daughter, Amelia.' This was a statement rather than a question. 'She has always been a wilful child with a mind of her own. Robert has encouraged her and bowed to her wishes, for we never had a son. After birthing Amelia I was injured inside and could not

312

have any more children. This was a blow to both of us and it seemed as though Robert poured all his affection into Amelia. Well, it is she who is the cause of our latest and most serious problem.' She paused again.

'Some months ago, before Robert took ill, King Stephen stayed with us for a few nights as he was passing on his way to another battle. He still seems to spend all his time chasing around England bringing nobles to heel. Stephen was very taken with Amelia. She can be most charming and she deployed all those charms on him. The upshot was that Stephen felt she was worthy of marriage to a favoured noble. I was not at all disappointed, for Amelia is well within marrying age and has shown no sign of wanting a union with anyone who has visited us. With Stephen as her champion, she would be matched with someone close to the king, which would be good for all of us. However, unknown to me, Robert agreed with Stephen that this man should be Walter Fitz Nichols, and foolishly Robert pledged Amelia's hand in marriage without bothering to inform me or Amelia! So the king went away to tell Fitz Nichols of this arrangement and when Fitz Nichols sent a letter to Amelia outlining his plans for their marriage, Amelia flew into the most impossible of rages, flatly refusing to marry him or anyone else we "chose" for her. No amount of persuasion would change her mind and she swore to kill herself rather than submit to any man in marriage unless she selected him. We were at a loss, not made any easier by Amelia writing to Fitz Nichols herself, refusing to marry him. We do not know what that letter said, but before long Fitz Nichols was here with his army demanding Robert should hand over Amelia. Robert was not well and could not think of a way of placating Fitz Nichols – and as Amelia had locked herself away, refusing even to see him, Fitz Nichols stormed out and laid siege to the castle, saying his honour was besmirched and he would see us all damned.'

313

'But surely, seeing Fitz Nichols' army outside the castle, Amelia must have reconsidered?' Peter said.

'Indeed, yes. She realised what was going to happen and reluctantly changed her mind – simply to save us. However, after seeing Fitz Nichols and hearing what he had to say, Robert would not let her sacrifice herself to such a man and he vowed to resist. He said he could petition Stephen, but that was impossible while Fitz Nichols was besieging us. Now, though, he thinks he has time, but I am not at all sure. He is still too ill to travel and I do not believe he has the strength yet to marshal all his diplomatic skills.'

She let go of Peter's arm as if, now unburdened, she did not need his physical support. She walked away from him and then said suddenly, spinning around to face him, 'I need your help. We need your help. What can you do?' She looked at him pleadingly. Peter opened his mouth to speak, but anticipating what he would say, the baroness waved him to silence.

'I know the position is impossible and I know you are not a knight, but when you were with us you demonstrated great skill and understanding of things – and the rather abbreviated story of your exploits you told us last night reinforces my view that you can think of something.' She smiled a tight smile. 'During the siege I prayed deeply for a saviour, and then you appeared. That must be an omen. We do not know why Fitz Nichols left, but the more I think about it, the more I believe that if his siege tower had not been destroyed, he would have finished us before he moved off. Whoever called him away could have waited a few days to allow the castle to be stormed, but perhaps not a month or so while the siege tower was rebuilt. So you see, although you did not know what result your actions would bring, instinctively by destroying the siege tower you did the right thing. We need some of that instinct now.'

Peter frowned, not knowing how he could solve the

problem, or what possible plan could be suggested which would be of any assistance. He remained silent, thinking how much he missed the old man.

'Can I discuss this with my colleagues?' he asked.

'Of course. Speak to anyone you like. We will also all discuss it at our evening meal. Perhaps with us talking it over, a plan will evolve. Amelia has been so ashamed of the trouble she has put us in that she has not ventured out of her room for weeks, but I think I can convince her to join us tonight and even she might have something in her wilful mind which will be of use.'

Peter shook his head, resigned to the impossible task. They both turned and walked back into the castle. The baroness went into the hall and Peter made his way to the soldiers' billets, where he came across William and Matthew in conversation with a group of soldiers, laughing and joking, obviously swapping soldier anecdotes. Peter beckoned them outside and quickly discovered they already knew the reason for Fitz Nichols' attack on the castle. Peter outlined the problem the baroness had given them and they talked over possible solutions, none of which came anywhere near an answer.

At the evening meal Amelia sat next to her mother. Peter was amazed how beautiful she had grown – a real woman with dignity and composure. She was polite and thoughtful to all three, treating them as nobles, not the common men they were. During the meal the baroness brought up the topic of Fitz Nichols. De Cours was uncomfortable that they were seeking a solution in public when he should have been in charge and taking control of things himself, but was silenced by a withering look from his wife when he stated as much.

At the end of the meal nothing had been decided and the baroness directly and pointedly asked Peter for his thoughts. Peter took a deep breath. 'First of all,' he said, 'I know nothing of this Fitz Nichols. Who is he and why does he appear to be so close to Stephen?'

'He is from Ireland,' said de Cours. 'He came here with his army and offered his services to Stephen. The Irish are like the Welsh. They fight like demons and were so successful under Stephen's banner that Stephen has taken Fitz Nichols to his bosom and regards him as a man to be rewarded. I have known of Fitz Nichols for some time, but only met him when he came here. Even before he opened his mouth I did not like him. He has an air of evil about him and I do not doubt for one moment he is cruel. The idea of giving my Amelia to him was unthinkable. His actions and manner after we spoke confirmed my view.'

'Right,' said Peter. 'If Fitz Nichols is under Stephen's protection then he, although Irish, would have to conduct himself in the ways of the court and abide by the honour of English nobility.' They all nodded. 'That being the case, then he is within his rights to say his honour has been besmirched by Amelia not abiding by the promise of her father.' They all nodded again. 'In fact, and please forgive me, the person who has really caused the offence is Robert de Cours, for it is you, baron, who have in effect broken your pledge. Fathers are supposed to control their daughters.' Peter expected a snort or some reaction from Amelia, but she sat silently, looking down at her hands.

The baron nodded slowly. 'What you say is right. I am the one who is truly guilty.'

'That being the case,' continued Peter, 'the obvious solution would be for you to challenge Fitz Nichols to single combat. If Fitz Nichols won, then his honour would be restored and your pledge of Amelia nullified. If you won, he could not claim Amelia, assuming that he actually lived. The problem, and again forgive me, baron, is that you are not yet fit enough to fight anyone.'

'And I take it you have a solution to that?' said the baroness.

'Not really. Is it possible for the baron to put up a champion to fight on his behalf? I have in mind Sir John.'

'No,' replied the baron. 'Short of Sir John insulting Fitz Nichols enough for a single combat challenge, that would not be possible.'

A sly smile crossed the baroness's face, not missed by any of them.

'I have a feeling,' said the baron, 'that I am not going to like what I hear.'

The baroness laughed. 'The issue is that Amelia has been promised to Fitz Nichols and the one who has denied the marriage by changing his mind is Robert. What if another could prevent such a marriage?'

'Who? How?' they all seemed to say together.

'What if Amelia was to marry someone else now, this week? Fitz Nichols would have to dispose of that person in single combat before he could do anything else, for no other way would be honourable. So, my dear, we marry you off.' There was a long silence. 'To Peter!'

Matthew choked on the sip of wine he was taking and Peter nearly exploded. Surprisingly, Amelia said nothing and kept her gaze down on her lap.

Peter managed to form a reply. 'Leaving aside the fact that I am not a noble and that marriage, even to such a spirited beauty as your daughter, is not actually on my horizon at the moment, there is the big question of whether Fitz Nichols would actually challenge me and – the biggest concern – whether I could beat him.'

'You would challenge him,' replied the baroness. 'After the marriage you would find out that Fitz Nichols had designs on your wife, so you could make the challenge. As to your abilities to win, I have not the slightest doubt.'

'Well, I do! William, tell them.'

William burst out laughing. 'I think this time our bite has

been too big. Although tying you down with a wife is not such a bad idea . . . it would keep us all out of trouble for a while.'

'Not what I wanted to hear!' retorted Peter. 'The basic idea is remarkable, but perhaps the sacrifice – for Amelia – is too great. There is another way. I am sure you know that before I left here Amelia and I had a private conversation.' No one said anything. Peter looked at the baroness and she nodded slowly. 'Yes, I knew little would pass you by and if you knew, then I guess others in the castle would have found out somehow. Well then, we could put it about that we were, without the baron knowing, secretly betrothed before I left and now I am back to claim Amelia. There has to be a formal betrothal, before a priest would be best, with a plan that we should be married early next year. That would give time for us to prepare and I could send the challenge to Fitz Nichols along the lines you suggested. Once I have won the combat,' Peter paused, offering up a silent prayer for success in that arena, 'the betrothal can be broken off with no harm to anyone.'

'But will you win?' asked Amelia, almost beseechingly. Peter was not sure if she was concerned over his well-being or her own and her family's future.

'Yes he will,' said William. 'We have time to train and hone his skills and the fact he is not a noble with a history of jousting will make Fitz Nichols over-confident and we can use that to our advantage.'

They talked things over for an hour or so, but nothing could be added, so they retired to bed – the baron and his family with light steps, glad to have a plan of action, Peter full of foreboding. William was probably right. Too big a bite had been taken.

23

The following morning was a bustle of activity. The baroness made arrangements to send for a priest to get him to draw up the formal betrothal and prepare a short service to confirm the promised marriage between Amelia and Peter.

William was like a whirlwind. He had taken charge of the soldiers at the castle and got them on the training ground, saying that Fitz Nichols could return at any time and they all had to be at their fighting best. He also sent the groom off to buy a horse – not a destrier, but a smaller, more nimble horse similar to the ones Peter had equipped them with when they first left the castle. He took Peter's chain mail away to the blacksmith to repair the rent caused by the bishop's sword, to strengthen where necessary and then polish and oil. Early in the afternoon he spent a long time with de Cours, then sent several men out with a letter written by the baron to knights living in the area.

Peter and Matthew joined the soldiers on the training ground, going though the basic movements of fighting to improve their skills and sharpen their reactions.

In the evening Peter ate with the baron, baroness and Amelia. Both William and Matthew moved back into the soldiers' billets, saying that they were needed there for morale-boosting reasons. Peter also tried to move out, but the baroness was adamant he should stay. Being betrothed, she reasoned, it would look ill if he was not accepting their hospitality.

Within two days the betrothal manuscript had been drawn up, signed and witnessed, then a short church service took place in which Amelia and Peter pledged themselves to each other. The baron felt they should wait a month before Peter wrote to Fitz Nichols, not only to give them a little more time, but also to allow the news of the official betrothal to seep out. The more people who knew about it, he said, the more likely it was that Fitz Nichols would need to accept Peter's challenge. Peter also suggested his letter to Fitz Nichols should be written in Latin. It was unlikely an Irish knight would be too familiar with that language and he would need a priest to translate it. This would mean that Fitz Nichols could not simply shrug off the content, because a priest would know of the challenge as well, and he would then have to explain to his peers why he was not accepting it.

In the following days and weeks, William tutored Peter rigorously and closely. Peter practised fighting with a lance on horseback, swordplay and axe-wielding. William forced Peter to practise far beyond the stage of tiredness and into exhaustion, and each evening Peter ate his meal and then went immediately to bed, needing every second of sleep to get his strength back.

Late one afternoon Sir John arrived and paused for a while, watching Peter practising jousting on horseback, time and time again lancing at a dummy strung on a frame. Sir John spoke a few words to William and then disappeared into the hall to give his regards to de Cours.

That evening, at Sir John's suggestion, William and Matthew joined everyone in the great hall for the meal. No sooner had they started eating than Sir John addressed them, clearly and with some authority. 'We knights have been finding out as much as we can about Fitz Nichols. He is currently in the north assisting Stephen to quell a dissident baron and the reason why Fitz Nichols left his siege here was because of Stephen's urgent summons.'

William had often dismissed Sir John as a bit of a dolt with little imagination and no real thinking power, but Peter appraised him anew. If it was important enough, Sir John could be focused and whatever de Cours said in his letter to him had given Sir John the necessary impetus to concentrate his mind on this issue.

'Fitz Nichols has received Peter's letter,' continued Sir John, 'and is seething. He intends to reply, accepting the challenge, as soon as his work is done in the north. Our information is that Stephen has been triumphant against the dissident baron, so we should expect a letter any day now.' He paused, looking at them all in turn. 'On the subject of Stephen, he is not pleased at all. He feels that his marriage-broking has been cast aside and even if Peter was to defeat Fitz Nichols, I fear Stephen will somehow take it out on us here. Stephen is strong on loyalty and he, no doubt fuelled by Fitz Nichols' anger, believes there has been great disloyalty shown by Baron de Cours.' Sir John paused to let this sink in. The lightness of mood the family had felt over the past few weeks disappeared at a stroke. Amelia looked as though she was going to cry.

'We must take things one at a time,' said de Cours, showing the strength of character he had possessed before his illness. 'Fitz Nichols is the primary target. When he has been disposed of, we can turn our efforts to placating Stephen. We all know he can be swayed and our fealty to him will still count.'

'I'm afraid,' said Sir John, 'that satisfying Stephen will be very much something for you, baron. None of us can do anything. Now to Fitz Nichols as a man. He is a fierce fighter, and skilled. He will not be defeated easily, but there again I guess you knew that anyway.' William nodded. 'So far as we can find out, he has no particular weakness in his fighting abilities and he very much favours the mace, which he can wield with deadly accuracy and great force.' At this William grunted. 'He shows no mercy and, as we suspected, is well known for his cruelty. He does not forgive or forget a slight, but is not known to lose his temper.'

'How about his abilities with the lance and sword?' asked William.

'He is not the best jouster, nothing like as good as me, but then again, who is? But from what I have seen this afternoon, even if he is only average, he is going to stick Peter like a pig on a spit with no trouble at all.'

A long silence followed this revelation, all the more telling because of Sir John's expertise with the lance.

'I suspected we were not going to be good enough in that area,' said William. Then he added, smiling, 'But we do have a trick up our sleeve. What about his swordplay?'

'Very good, but not exceptional. He is fast and accurate without too much finesse, we are told, but we have to be cautious as none of us has seen him fight. I would give Peter an even chance with the sword, but what about the mace?'

'Hopeless,' replied Peter. 'It is not a weapon for me. I don't know if it is lack of strength or what, but I have never been comfortable with it. If Fitz Nichols uses the mace, I will have to be defensive with sword and shield until he tires, then take what advantage I can.'

'Assuming he tires!' retorted Sir John, not softening the information or giving any encouragement.

'Peter!' Amelia burst out. 'It does not look good. Is there no other way?'

'I'm afraid the die has been cast. Even if we get Fitz Nichols' letter tomorrow, it will be some weeks before combat will take place and with the help of Sir John, I can sharpen my skills more.'

They continued going through the information given by

Sir John, but no one could think of anything helpful to say
or do as the meal was eaten.

The following day Sir John and William had a long discussion over Peter's shield and William took it away to the
blacksmith for modification.

'We have decided,' said William, 'that if you are to defend
the mace with shield and sword, your shield should be
strengthened. It must not be too heavy, but the plate has to
be thicker around your left arm area, or his mace will surely
break your arm. Also, let's abandon the lance practice and
go back to the way we met the de Villiers' charge. Sir John
will use his lance and you can practise tipping it aside at
the last moment with your sword. Speaking of which, I have
a new sword for you. I convinced de Cours that you should
have the best, and he has given you his own sword.'

William went into the armoury and picked up de Cours'
sword to give to Peter. Peter hefted it and found that it was
well balanced, a little longer than the sword he had been
given by Simone, and of the finest metal, sharp and strong.

'Use this from now on to get the feel of it. After the
jousting practice Sir John will be taking you though the paces
of defending a mace. I know you can do it anyway, but his
way of fighting will be different from mine and you can
gain extra experience.'

So the days continued. Peter practised endlessly and honed
his skills, aided and encouraged by Sir John, who seemed
pleased, almost honoured, to be helping Peter. Perhaps,
thought Peter, he is wise enough to realise that if I lose
things will be black here.

The Fitz Nichols letter came. It was short and to the
point. The challenge was accepted and arrangements for
the fight were being made. It was to be held at Salisbury at
the end of September. Later information revealed that

Stephen would witness the combat and that he expected de Cours and his family to be there as well.

Although Peter was confident in himself, he well knew that he was about to face his greatest challenge. This time no tricks would be possible. The fight would have to be strictly along the lines accepted by the honour system and his demise was a very clear, even high, possibility. He wrote a thoughtful letter to the old man in London, addressing it to the Knights Templar, thanking him for everything he had done, explaining how and why the battle with Fitz Nichols was so necessary and expressing his disappointment that it was possible he would not be around to offer the old man the hospitality he had promised in the future. Peter felt a good deal better after he had dispatched this letter to London, but he did pause to wonder why it was so important to him to say goodbye to the old man while he had not even thought about visiting his own family.

Before the last week in September, de Cours with his entourage arrived at the appointed place in Salisbury, setting up tents to await the arrival of Stephen and Fitz Nichols. As the baron explained, it would not do for Stephen get there first and have to wait for them. After two days Stephen and his court arrived, pitching marquees well away from de Cours. Marshals went about arranging the jousting field and directing the building of a dais on which the noble spectators would sit. De Cours made his greeting and supplication to Stephen, as was the custom, with Stephen graciously accepting and not showing any hint of animosity. Peter too carried out his duties by calling on Fitz Nichols to confirm that the single-handed combat would take place and offering him the choice of weapons. As Sir John predicted, these were to be lance, mace and sword.

Peter wandered, as if aimless, out onto the field where the fight would take place. His demeanour showed despondence, but that was affected for the benefit of Fitz Nichols. Being September, winter was not yet showing its hand, but during the days before there had been some heavy rain and the ground was wet and a little sticky. Clouds were scudding across the sky and Peter reasoned they would get more rain before the fight. Indeed, this was so. The night before the combat was to take place, the heavens opened and rain thudded down onto the tents and the ground. It was too wet for any movement in the camps other than what was strictly necessary as people huddled under shelter eating a cold evening meal.

Early on the morning of the day which would determine Peter's fate, he walked out onto the area set aside for combat. The stewards had chosen well. Although the ground was soft from the rain, it was not waterlogged. However, Peter thought, the turf was yielding enough to give his lighter, more agile horse some advantage, albeit small.

William helped Peter to dress ready for the task ahead. The chain mail was bright and well oiled, each link checked for strength. The baron's sword had been honed and polished and Peter's shield strengthened. He carried a long lance in his hand ready for the joust. De Cours had insisted that his emblem should be painted on Peter's shield and that Peter should wear a surcoat in the baron's colours. He was, after all, fighting for the honour of de Cours, who should not be seen to be shy in acknowledging Peter's position of being betrothed to Amelia and soon to join the family.

Clothed, armed, mounted and in every way looking like the knight he was not, Peter rode into the arena. There he was joined by the imposing figure of Fitz Nichols. Slightly shorter than Peter, he was much broader and seemed to ooze strength and confidence. When they approached the seated nobles on the dais to present themselves to Stephen, as was the custom, Peter was taken aback to see the old man and Sir Richard, both with the red cross surcoat, seated alongside the king. The old man looked at Peter with a level stare, neither encouraging nor discouraging. No time to wonder. Peter had other things to worry about. He briefly looked to his right, where the de Cours family was sitting, and after lowering his lance to Stephen in the time-honoured way he rode across to Amelia to do the same. She smiled encouragingly, although Peter detected more worry in that smile than warmth.

The marshals called the riders to be ready and they cantered off to opposite ends of the marked-out jousting area to await the signal to start. There was no fanfare of trumpets as marked a royal joust, simply a silence as everyone waited for the marshal's banner to drop.

Peter watched the marshal carefully. As he began to drop the banner, Peter immediately spurred his horse forward into a gallop. Fitz Nichols was taken by surprise that Peter was so eager and was even more astonished at the quickness with which Peter's little horse gathered speed towards him. Realising that the gap between them was rapidly diminishing, he urged his own horse to a gallop and in doing so his lance wavered from the horizontal. Experience took over, however, and in a few strides Fitz Nichols was properly set for the first clash. Then came another surprise. When Peter was just a few strides away, he threw his lance to the ground, drew his sword and quick as lightning leaned forward to strike his sword tip against the end of Fitz Nichols' lance, knocking it aside to pass harmlessly away from Peter's body. As in the fight in Normandy against de Villiers, Peter spun his horse around to charge back to Fitz Nichols before the knight could steady himself and bring his lance down for a new pass.

Realising the uselessness of his lance because Peter was too close, Fitz Nichols dropped it and, snatching his mace from the horn of his saddle, closed with Peter, swinging a mighty blow which Peter caught squarely on his shield.

Adopting the tactic practised with Sir John, although it was not apparent to the onlookers, Peter did not use his sword with any real intent to harm his opponent, but concentrated on fending off the mighty blows from Fitz Nichols' mace.

As before in Normandy with de Villiers' horse, Fitz Nichols' destrier had been trained to lean into the opposing horse to present a stable platform for its rider, but Peter's horse would have none of it. As soon as it felt the weight of the destrier, it skipped to one side. Peter was anticipating this but Fitz Nichols was not, and time after time his blows were missing or falling more lightly than he intended, not helped by the fact that the wet ground made it more difficult for his heavier horse to follow. However, although Peter's little horse was helping and his shield had been strengthened, the shield soon became battered and was fast losing its shape. His left shoulder and arm were becoming numb and he realised he could not continue in the same vein for very much longer.

After a particularly fierce attack from Fitz Nichols, as Peter's horse moved off he encouraged it further away, then charged back at full speed, slipping low under the swinging mace, below his own saddle, and lashed his sword at Fitz Nichols' horse, cutting below the stirrup at the girth straps securing the saddle. The sword bit into the horse's side and almost completely severed the saddle straps. Fitz Nichols looked down and realised that his saddle was not secure enough for him to stay mounted. He immediately pulled his horse away and dismounted, standing with shield up and mace at his side, waiting for Peter to ride him down.

Peter walked his horse up to Fitz Nichols and then, just over a mace blow away, slowly started to dismount. Fitz Nichols, seeing his chance, jumped forward and swung his mace hard at Peter's side. Peter was ready. He had anticipated someone who was cruel and mean would take unfair advantage if presented with it, and although he seemed to be dismounting slowly, he was in fact holding his position ready to be able to kick his horse into action at the last moment. The agile animal responded and Fitz Nichols' mace found air. There was an intake of breath from the spectators. Disabling a horse in single combat was just about acceptable, but when the mounted combatant did not take advantage of a dismounted opponent and got off his horse to continue the fight on foot, this was viewed as highly honourable. What was definitely not acceptable was for the dismounted combatant to strike the other when he was dismounting and unable to defend himself. Sympathies were moving towards Peter. Fitz Nichols realised his mistake and his eyes darkened as he allowed Peter to dismount and prepare himself.

The next five minutes must have been boring for the spectators, for although Fitz Nichols swung blow after blow with his mace, few made contact as Peter skipped lightly to one side or the other. The slightly soggy ground helped the lighter Peter. Again experience came to the forefront. Fitz Nichols, realising that his mace was not going to win the fight after all, stepped back, threw it to one side and drew his sword. Peter breathed more easily, feeling that at last they were evenly matched.

The clash of swords was in earnest. Fitz Nichols was good, fast and stronger than Peter. His cuts and thrusts were not random, but carefully crafted to tease out any weakness Peter might have. Peter too was looking for an opening, but none presented itself. So then, he must use his mind as well as his sword. Peter moved forward into a steady pattern, then moved back. Again he went forward with the same pattern, then back. For a third time he followed the same pattern, except that instead of aiming for Fitz Nichols' body, he dropped his sword low at the last minute, cutting the inside of Fitz Nichols' lower right leg, drawing blood. Not a wound to worry Fitz Nichols, but at least it was first blood to Peter.

Stepping back as if to gather himself, Peter said, just loud enough for Fitz Nichols to hear, 'Typical Irish, attacking a man from the back then sticking his foot out too far.'

Fitz Nichols' face darkened as his lips compressed into a cruel, thin line. His eyes did not blaze up into a fever of anger, but they bored into Peter. He came forward once again in a measured and determined way. Peter stood his ground this time, blocking and deflecting all blows without proffering any of his own. Swords and shields were ringing. 'Come on, you can do better than that!' said Peter, laughing as a particularly vicious thrust was set aside. Fitz Nichols redoubled his efforts and Peter eventually had to give ground, stepping back out of harm's way. 'Better, but still not good enough.' Fitz Nichols said nothing, his eyes narrowing and his cheeks flushing, if not with anger then at least with resentment.

During the next encounter both traded blow for blow without either man gaining advantage. This time Fitz Nichols stepped back. Peter wondered if he detected some tiredness. After all, what with the mace and the sword, Fitz Nichols had landed twenty or thirty blows to Peter's one. 'Come on!' said Peter as he bounded forward, attacking with apparent frenzy but in reality not putting any force into his thrusts while making Fitz Nichols work hard to defend and counter with swordwork of his own. This time Fitz Nichols was clearly breathing more heavily as they broke away.

Peter's breath was also a little short and he exaggerated it by wheezing slightly, staying on his heels, not on his toes, and dropping his shield slightly as if tiredness was overcoming the adrenalin. Fitz Nichols moved forward with purpose, sensing an opportunity. Peter defended, offering few strikes of his own, and was the first to step back to break off the clash. He wheezed a little more strongly. Once more Fitz Nichols came on, not in a great hurry as Peter had hoped, but with deliberate step and even more deliberate and calculated thrusts. Peter stood his ground, delaying each block of Fitz Nichols' sword until the last minute to give the impression of tiredness. Still Fitz Nichols' blows were measured, nothing was hurried or wasted.

Dropping his sword arm even more, Peter gave Fitz Nichols a chink of opportunity. The knight gave a mighty lunge, which Peter took deftly and squarely on his shield, pushing Fitz Nichols' sword down. At the same time Peter leaped with all his agility to his left, striking a mighty blow with the flat of his sword at the top of Fitz Nichols' shield. The blow was so fierce it tipped the top of Fitz Nichols' shield towards him, allowing Peter's sword to slide upwards towards Fitz Nichols' head. Fitz Nichols instantly realised what was happening and dipped his head forward so that Peter's sword blade would not hit him in the face. He was not quite quick enough, though, for the sword smashed into Fitz Nichols' helmet, cutting into the metal and knocking the helmet completely off the knight's head.

Peter swung round, expecting Fitz Nichols to close immediately, but his opponent was flat-footed, his eyes glazed. Peter realised that although the cut to the head was not fatal or even apparently wounding, either that or the helmet being knocked off and digging into the back of Fitz Nichols' neck had stunned the man. Peter moved in quickly and steadily, not letting this advantage change his style, but attacking skilfully. Dazed though Fitz Nichols obviously was, his resolve and experience shone through and he fought back, keeping his sword and shield close together so as not to offer any bodily target, waiting for his head to clear. Peter took another swipe towards the lower part of Fitz Nichols' left leg. Fitz Nichols smacked his sword down to knock Peter's sword aside, but Peter did not continue with the blow. Leaping to his right this time, he brought his sword up, over the left edge of Fitz Nichols' shield, and drove the blade into Fitz Nichols' throat, severing artery and windpipe.

Fitz Nichols did not fall immediately. His eyes locked on Peter's, not in surprise but in resignation, as the breath rasped and gurgled out of his throat. He slowly sank to his knees, his shield digging into the soft ground and making a tripod to support his body. Peter was suddenly at a loss. What was the honourable thing to do in such circumstances? Should he dispatch Fitz Nichols with a quick thrust, or let him die slowly? Undecided, he stood watching as the hand of death closed and Fitz Nichols toppled to his right in a heap.

Peter turned from the corpse and walked towards the noble spectators, stopping before Stephen and dropping to one knee. He bowed his head in supplication and waited.

'A very commendable performance, young man,' said Stephen. 'Indeed, impressive.'

Peter raised his head and looked at the king. 'What is to happen to me now?' he asked.

Stephen smiled a lopsided smile. 'We shall see.' With that he waved Peter away.

Peter rose and walked slowly back to his tent as exhaustion bore down upon him, making every step a challenge. When he got there, he threw his shield to one side, dropped his sword and took off his helmet, moving to sit on a stool with his head in his hands, too tired to move or think.

He did not know how long he stayed like that. He was jerked from his trance by the voice of the old man. 'You still carry your luck, I see.'

Peter looked up. 'Yes, it would seem so.'

'But also you used your skills to your best advantage. There is no shame in that.' There was a long silence. Peter had nothing he wanted to say. 'You goaded him, did you not?'

Peter nodded. 'Did anyone else realise?'

'No, I do not think so. I know your way of fighting and could see a change in Fitz Nichols, so I guessed you said something to him. So what are you going to do now?'

Peter used all his resolve to straighten up on the stool. He took a deep breath. 'I do not rightly know. I suppose it is up to the king, who, I understand, is not happy that his match-making did not go according to plan. It will be even worse when he finds out it was all a scheme to get rid of Fitz Nichols, a man for whom he had high regard.'

'I should not worry too much about Fitz Nichols' demise. Sooner or later the king would have seen through him. Fitz Nichols' men are more important to Stephen.'

Peter smiled. 'Then perhaps this gives me my opportunity. Fitz Nichols' men are leaderless, so I think my next venture would be to go to them and take charge.'

The old man laughed. 'You are incorrigible!'

'Did you get any feeling about what is going to happen to de Cours when you spoke with the king?'

'Sir Richard did most of the speaking, mostly explaining who you were and what you had done in Normandy. I merely filled in when Stephen wanted to know more about your character. I have to say that dismounting as you did served you well. The king appreciated it.'

'Thank you for coming. I did not expect it.'

'To be honest, it was Sir Richard who insisted. He was impressed with you in Normandy and wanted to see how you could handle yourself in honourable combat. I was reluctant because I felt you would be unable to use your natural talents to influence things and might be overcome by the rigours of the strict rules of single combat. I am glad I was wrong.'

'How are things with you?'

'As you can see,' the old man said, pointing to the red cross on his surcoat, 'I am now a Templar and I have been using my time getting to know their ways and trying to organise accounts and things. It is a big task, but I am enjoying it. But more of that later perhaps. You need to rest.'

The old man leaned forward, squeezed Peter's shoulder, turned and left. Peter watched him walk away through the tent doorway. He continued looking out at nothing in particular, letting his mind wander. Suddenly his eyes focused on Amelia and Baron de Cours, who were outside the king's tent. Amelia was kneeling before Stephen, who stood with his hand on her head. It was too far away for Peter to hear what the king said, or even to judge what was going on between them. Amelia got to her feet, curtseyed, and she and the baron walked away, back towards their own tents. Peter shrugged his shoulders in resignation. He would no doubt find out in time. The movement made him realise how much his body was suffering from the battering by Fitz Nichols. He rose unsteadily to his feet, painfully struggled out of his surcoat and chain mail and lay down on his mattress, falling into instant slumber.

No one disturbed him and it was not until the sun was setting and the smell of freshly cooked meat wafted into his tent that he awoke. He was refreshed, his mind alert, though his body ached. He quickly washed his hands and face and went towards de Cours' tent where the baron, baroness, Amelia, Sir Richard, the old man, William and Sir John were sitting outside at a long wooden table, talking as they waited for the meal to be ready.

'Awake at last,' said William. 'How are you feeling?'

'Well, if a little sore.'

'Good,' said de Cours. 'Come, sit down. You have done us a great favour and we will be forever in your debt.'

Peter sat down at the table opposite the baron.

'We have been talking about the future,' de Cours continued. 'I have had an audience with Stephen and he is inclined to forgive our thwarting his marriage plans, and even being the cause of his losing Fitz Nichols, but the price is heavy.' The baron looked down at the table as though the weight of the world was upon his shoulders. Taking a deep breath he continued. 'I have to contribute to his treasure chest in an amount that I have difficulty finding. It will mean our coffers will be empty for a year or more to pay a half now and the balance in three months. Also, he wants me to contribute fighting men to his cause, under his banner. This will be at least Sir John, his squire and a dozen or so good fighters, which will leave our castle very vulnerable.' He let out a deep sigh.

Peter frowned, picking up the baron's black mood. 'I really do not know what can be done in the long term, but I feel the first thing is to get things back to as normal as possible and tell the world the betrothal is off. I will renounce it straight away.'

'It takes two to renounce a betrothal if honour is not to be offended,' said Amelia.

'Sorry, you are absolutely right. Together we must renounce it.'

'But I am not going to!' retorted Amelia. 'We have a formal betrothal, witnessed and blessed by God, and I am going to hold you to it.'

Peter was dumbfounded. He looked at everyone around the table. Their faces were impassive. Only Amelia showed emotion – an expression of determination and resolve.

'But we agreed.'

'No. I did not agree. You agreed amongst yourselves, but I said nothing. When we met before you went to Normandy, I said I would wait for you and I have. We have a binding betrothal.'

Peter could not believe his ears. He looked around for some support, but got none. 'If I say no, there is nothing you can do about it. I have no lands to forfeit or title to be taken away. I am a common man and will remain a common man.'

'No you will not,' replied Amelia with a defiant smile on

her face. 'Stephen has stipulated you must marry me. The only way he can keep his honour after he arranged my marriage with Fitz Nichols is if we do marry.'

Peter put his elbows on the table and lowered his face into his hands as a wave of despair engulfed him. His luck had at last run out. It was not as though there was anything wrong with Amelia; she was beautiful, accomplished, from one of the best families, and would make an admirable wife. It was just that Peter did not feel he was ready for marriage and certainly not marriage into nobility, where his own position would always be inferior.

He raised his head and looked at the old man, who returned his gaze in the same way as he used to when he was Peter's teacher, encouraging thought and solution. The despair lifted as Peter weighed up the alternatives and he looked at the baron, baroness and Amelia in turn.

'Perhaps our problems can be turned into an opportunity. Although I am sure Amelia will not agree, I think it would be a grave mistake if we were to marry immediately, for that would mean the baron having to find money he does not have for the wedding ceremony he would want to give his only and beloved daughter. Also, my being a part of the family will be a drain on resources, so I would ask you all to consider this.

'Fitz Nichols' men are without a leader and it is likely a number will return to Ireland rather than go under the direct banner of Stephen. Some may be persuaded to stay if we could offer them an alternative which would give them greater reward. I propose Sir Richard goes to Stephen and suggests that I be allowed to approach Fitz Nichols' soldiers and offer twenty of them fighting employment under my command but Stephen's banner. You, baron, will contribute a few men too. I am thinking of Sir John, his squire and four men. We will fully equip this fighting force and pay them, taking the burden off Stephen.'

'But that would mean about thirty men for Stephen – hardly the large numbers he wants to ensure his position is maintained,' said de Cours.

'True if we are talking about a normal fighting force. I have in mind that every man will be well armed, taught to use the Welsh bow and will be mounted on light, manoeuvrable horses. Remember, half of Stephen's problem is that he has to chase across the country from one minor skirmish to another and if he had a fast-moving band of loyal men who could get to and quell impending unrest he would be well served.'

Sir Richard laughed long and hard. 'Priceless! And sufficiently outrageous to appeal to Stephen.'

'But contribution to Stephen's treasure chest will mean I will not have the money to equip thirty men with horses, far less pay them,' said the baron.

Peter smiled. 'I have more than enough money and will have sufficient left over to allow you to pay Stephen the full treasure chest contribution immediately. I suggest Sir Richard tells Stephen he will be paid everything at once if he accepts our proposal, which should encourage him to agree.'

Slow nodding and smiling faces all around, except Amelia. 'So, what about our marriage? Are you trying to get out of it?'

'Certainly not. It will have to be postponed until I get back but think of the advantages: not only will your father have funds to maintain the castle and staff, with only a small depletion in his fighting men, but I will be under the direct command of Stephen and if I can carry out his orders faithfully there is an opportunity for me to advance myself, perhaps return more than just a lowly peasant.'

Amelia did not look convinced but the enthusiasm from her parents suppressed any further argument from her.

'I guess Matthew and I will not be retiring to take up farming just yet as you will need someone to train the Fitz

Nichols men,' snorted William. His smile broadened. 'In fact, it should prove to be a good adventure for us.'

Two months passed in frenetic activity. Sir Richard had no difficulty convincing the king that Peter's intended band would be of benefit and Peter was surprised a large number of Fitz Nichols' men were eager to join him. The successful combat against Fitz Nichols obviously convinced the men that Peter would make a good leader. William and Matthew helped Peter choose the twenty best and most suitable fighters, who eagerly went to the de Cours castle to train. Sir John fell into the spirit of things and gladly helped William and Matthew put the former Fitz Nichols men through their paces. Equipping the men with good quality arms took a little time but the most difficult task was finding the right horses and in the end there had to be a few compromises with some mounted on hunters rather than the nimble horses Peter favoured.

Conscious he would have to return to Stephen before his little army was fully trained, Peter made it clear that training was to occupy every moment of spare time. There were no complaints as each man took pride in his position. Amelia made arrangements for every man to receive a shift with the de Cours emblem and the new kite-shaped shields also bore the de Cours crest. Eventually everything was ready and the band prepared to leave the baron's castle.

The last meal at the castle the night before their departure was almost a celebration. The baron was overwhelmed by both William and Matthew giving him their money for safe keeping, or to use as de Cours felt fit and, while still not fully recovered from his illness, he had regained much of his strength and all of his noble bearing. The baroness was delighted with the change in him and Amelia seemed to accept what was going to happen.

At the end of the meal they retired to their rooms and,

as Peter was checking his equipment for the following day, the door opened and Amelia came quietly in. Before Peter could protest she walked up to him and put both arms around his neck, burying her head in his chest.

'Do not say anything; just listen,' she whispered. 'I love you deeply and I can face your not loving me. Go safely on your new adventure. I will wait for you to return and if you truly believe we should not marry then, I will release you from our betrothal.'

Peter put his arms around her shoulders and held her to him, recognising she was a remarkable woman. She pulled him tighter and raised her right leg over his thigh, pressing herself into him. Peter felt an almost magical warmth spreading up from his thigh to envelop him in calmness and contentment. They stayed holding each other for a few moments longer before Amelia gently moved away, pulled his head down and kissed him warmly on the lips. Peter could not but return the kiss. She smiled, disengaged herself, and walked out of his room, leaving Peter in a trance. He shook his head to clear it and slowly removed his clothes before getting into bed. Sleep did not come easily as his mind ceaselessly wandered between what the future might bring and the immediate past of Amelia in his arms.

The following morning the little army gathered in the courtyard with Peter at its head. The baron and baroness were there to see them off and Amelia was standing at the gate waiting for them to pass. Peter gave the signal and, with William and Matthew immediately behind him, followed by Sir John, his squire and the remaining band, they rode out of the castle. As Peter passed Amelia he leant down, touched her arm and said quietly, 'I will be back.'